DAUGHTER OF THE DROWNED EMPIRE

FRANKIE DIANE MALLIS

SEVEN QUEENS PRESS

ISBN 978-1-957014-00-5 (Ebook)

ISBN 978-1-957014-01-2 (Paperback)

ISBN 978-1-957014-02-9 (Hardback)

For Atiya, who was the first to believe in the magic, and who never stopped believing, even when the magic was extremely slow to reveal itself.

MAP OF LUMERIA

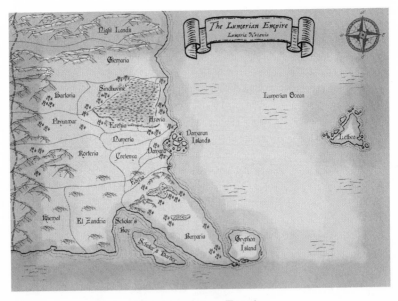

The Lumerian Empire

MAP OF BAMARIA

The Map of Bamaria

THE FIRST SCROLL:
VORAKH

CHAPTER ONE

THE TIMEKEEPERS SHOUTED the hour as indigo bloomed across the darkening sky. Behind me, the sun sank into the crashing waves of the ocean. The bells clanged louder, and my feet pounded against the waterway. I was late. I turned a corner as sweat beaded the nape of my neck. The fortress was so Godsdamned big.

My arms pumped at my sides as I ran faster; the water rushed beneath my feet. I had to reach Cresthaven's entrance before the bells stopped, but I was still nowhere near it. There was at least another quarter mile of fortress and waterway. Above me, the ashvan horses began their descent, already wrapping up their hourly patrol. Luminescent blue light glimmered from their hooves against the night, illuminating their jewel-toned bodies. Their lights vanished into the night sky, and only starlight remained.

Shit. The bells would stop at any second.

My sandals, laced up to my knees, were definitely not meant for running. Then again, neither was I, a lady of Ka Batavia.

The glass floor curved around a stone corner, and the bells stopped just as someone shouted my name.

Shit, shit! I was definitely in trouble.

"Lady Lyriana." One of my father's sentries. "Your grace? Are you there?"

I rounded another corner, sliding on the glass of the waterway. Stupid slippery glass waterways and over-sized fortresses.

Running into the torchlight, I found my father, the High Lord of Bamaria, standing impatiently before the front doors. His black robes blew in the summer breeze, and the golden Laurel of the Arkasva sat atop his head. He gave me one look. *The* look. *The I was definitely in trouble look.* Luckily, not the kind of trouble he would take the time to yell at me for. Not yet anyway. We had a public appearance to make.

I reached the promenade, completely out of breath. Several sentries watched me from the corners of their eyes, curiosity and judgment in their expressions. My cheeks heated as I rushed to the end of the line and tried to calm down. Servants and guards always talked, sharing gossip about their charges. But *it* had just happened. Had word spread already? Did they know the reason I was late? Or why I had lingered so long at the pools?

My eldest sister, Meera, rolled her eyes at me but didn't look upset—which was good. Even though today was *my* birthday, tonight was to be the most important night of *her* life, so attention on me had been somewhat minimized—to say the least.

Meera's light brown hair was styled in perfect waves down her back. A golden diadem swept across her forehead, positioned partially like a crown, the ends threaded into her locks. Fitting, since tonight she'd come into her title, Heir Apparent, next in line to rule as Arkasva. She would be practically a queen—except for the fact that Bamaria was part of the Lumerian Empire and bowed before the Emperor. Still, it was never a good idea to piss off an almost-queen, especially when she was your eldest sister.

Morgana, our middle sister—eternally angry at the world —scowled beneath sleek black eyebrows pointed down in disapproval. I stuck out my tongue and took my place at the back of the line beside our cousin, Jules. She shook her head at me, eyes sparkling with mischief.

"Your hair, Lyr," she chided, slender arms reaching to rearrange my long waves. A flick of her hand readjusted and centered my diadem. Jules was the only member of our party not wearing one. She was our cousin and of noble blood, but unlike me and my sisters, she was not in direct line to the Seat of the Arkasva. "Shall I assume your disarray came from your rush to get here or…other activities?" A sly smile lit up her face.

"Running," I said pointedly.

"Of course." She nodded sagely, her expression making it clear she did not believe me. One more sweep of her fingers through my hair, pushing the loose waves over my shoulder, and she nodded. "Now, you look perfect."

"As do you," I said with a grin. It was a big night for Jules as well.

We began our procession down the main waterway.

She took my arm in hers. "Well?" she asked. "I need details. What happened?"

Morgana twisted her neck to peer over her shoulder. "Please. We already know you kissed him."

"Morgs!" I snapped. "Shut up."

"Did you?" Jules asked. "Kiss him?" she whispered.

Soturi, camouflaged to blend into the landscape, began to emerge—our ever-present escorts and guards—replacing the sentries at the fortress's entrance. Three fell in step with my father. Meera as Heir Apparent had two guards, while Morgana, Jules, and I each had one following in our shadows. Mine was a surly soturion named Markan who'd watched over me since I could stand. His muscles flexed as he walked beside me, his golden armor clinking in tune to the slaps of his sandals against the waterway's glass.

I caught Jules's eye and nodded.

She squealed. "You and Tristan! I'm so happy for you."

"Shh!" I clamped my hand over her mouth. Markan was too close, and he didn't need to know any details about what we'd done—or that it had been the reason I'd been late. Nor was he entitled to know that I'd sat by the edge of the pool long after Tristan had gone, replaying the whole interaction in my head again and again.

Tristan's scent, mint and the salted air of the ocean, still tickled my nose. My skin tingled with excitement, remembering the feel of his touch. His warmth. The way he'd tightened his grip on me, his fingers pressing into my back as we'd kissed and kissed, our bodies pressing closer, and hands exploring until I was dizzy from it. I'd kissed a number of boys before, but this...this was far more than a kiss. And Tristan wasn't just some boy. He was the future lord of his Ka and already a master mage. The most eligible, and attractive, bachelor amongst the Bamarian nobility.

Our party reached the outer wall of the fortress and our personal seraphim port. A dozen of the giant birds, covered in cloudy white feathers with wings of pure gold, lay in waiting, their topaz blue carriages strapped to their backs. We split into three of the jewel-encrusted carriages. Jules, Morgana, and I piled into the last one with our three escorts.

Soturion Markan sealed the doors and retreated behind the partition with the other escorts. The floor shifted beneath us as our seraphim stood. She flapped her wings, rattling the windows as we took flight.

Once we were soaring, Jules sighed happily. "I'm so glad this happened on your birthday, Lyr."

"Yes, it's wonderful she formed an alliance between Ka Batavia and Ka Grey to be sealed in marriage," Morgana said dryly.

"I'm seventeen," I said, startled. "No one is getting married." Not yet. There weren't even talks of Meera finding a match, and she'd be the country's High Lady within years.

Morgana narrowed her eyebrows. "Lyr, get your head out of your scrolls. Tristan's twenty. Which is young." She held up her hands. "But not for Ka Grey. They're so Godsdamned old fashioned, Lyr. If he kissed you, then the proposal we've all suspected for years is coming."

"No, it's not. That's ridiculous," I said.

Morgana scoffed. "Lady Romula doesn't let *Lord Tristan Grey* piss unless it makes her more money or furthers her position in Bamaria."

"Ew, Morgs." Jules tapped a finger against her chin. "Though fair point."

I frowned. "But Lady Romula is already Master of Finance. What higher position could she possibly want?"

"Grandmother of the groom to Lady Lyriana Batavia, Heir to the Arkasva, High Lord of Bamaria, third in line from the Seat," Jules said slyly. "As soon as your father passes the Laurel to Meera, you'll be second from the Seat, Lyr. It'll be tempting for her."

I shrugged, glancing out the window. The beaches and countryside had already given way to the city of Urtavia and the Temple of Dawn, an ancient building designed in the shape of the Valalumir—the seven-pointed star. But the effect was only visible from above. Our ancestors desired everything to be aesthetically pleasing from the sky, spending so much of their day flying on the backs of seraphim.

We landed at the entrance to the red ray of the temple, the private door used only by my Ka. My father and his guard, along with Meera and Jules, both wearing the ceremonial white robes, were to enter the temple first—since all three had important roles to play.

Jules turned to yell back at me and Morgana. "See you after! And Lyr, I hope you're not planning to spend all night with Tristan, because my magic and I have big plans for us! You too, Morgs!"

Morgana rolled her eyes as I grinned stupidly. Jules and I had been concocting all sorts of mischief for the night. Months of planning had gone into it. Elaborate spells, and jokes to play on all the guards at Cresthaven. And sneaking out to the city.

"No sleep!" I yelled back.

"None!" Jules threw her hand over her mouth and blew a kiss. "Love you!"

I threw one back and waved her inside. A sharp gust of wind blew my hair over my eyes and tangled it in my diadem. The wind was caused by the flapping wings of another seraphim bird landing. The descending topaz carriage was adorned with a giant flag boasting the sigil of Ka Grey: silver seraphim wings beneath a full silver moon. The carriage doors opened, and four mages exited followed by Tristan, looking breathtakingly handsome in a new blue tunic and bright silver belt. His stave was tucked into a silver scabbard hanging elegantly from his hip. My stomach tightened at the sight of him. His hand rested on his belt, the hand which had run down my back, over my hips, and across my breasts just an hour ago.

"Four escorts?" Morgana sneered. "I'm second to the Seat, and I only came with one."

"Stop," I said. "Lady Romula has always been...a bit extra. Tristan's different."

"Right. And I'm the Empress of Lumeria." Morgana shook her head disdainfully and with her single soturion escort retreated into the Temple of Dawn.

Tristan ran his hand through his floppy brown hair—hair that I now knew was as soft as it looked. He strode toward me with the unapologetic confidence of a lord who would one day rule his Ka. A lord who would one day take a highly coveted seat on the Bamarian Council.

I took his hand and led him forward. Before any of our escorts could catch up, I settled us into a dark corner of the temple's outer alcove, my back pressed against the cool stone. I licked my lips, slid my hands around his waist and pulled him close. One more kiss—one more moment just for me and my birthday before we had to put on our masks and present ourselves as pure, chaste nobility. His tongue slid against mine and for a moment, it was pure bliss. Until the shuffled footsteps of our escorts made themselves known and we sprung apart laughing.

Everyone who was anyone was inside. Nobles from ancient Kavim gathered in the aisles, admiring each other's dresses and jewelry while gossiping. Beyond the inane chatter, anticipation hung in the air. Today there was an Heir Apparent in the Revelation Ceremony.

We gathered in my family's pew in the red ray, closest to the raised circular dais of Auriel's Chamber. On the lower stage, the soon-to-be mages and soturi sat cross-legged. Ropes glowed blue, sizzling with magic, creating a barrier between ceremony participants and those who'd come to watch. Just past the rope was the Seat of the Arkasva, my father's golden throne.

With all the initiates in place, Arkmage Kolaya rose onto the dais, standing beneath the eternal flame. She was ancient, with dark brown skin and white hair that fell in twisted braids to the floor. As she began the opening prayers, chanting in High Lumerian, Tristan took my hand, his finger rubbing small circles into my palm. I angled toward him, and our knees bumped together. Grinning, Tristan leaned over, pulling my hair back to plant a kiss on my neck.

I shivered.

"For Gods' sakes, Lyr. Everyone is looking at you," Morgana hissed.

Peering over my shoulder, I found Aunt Arianna offering an understanding but stern look of disapproval. We were in public, at a state affair. A holy one at that. Every other teen in the back rows of the pews were doing Gods knew what with each other, but I couldn't. I had a role to play. Lady Lyriana Batavia, Heir to the Arkasva, High Lord of Bamaria. A paragon of virtue; pure, proper, and polite at all times. My relationship with Tristan would be endlessly scrutinized. As noble heirs to the heads of our Kavim, it was a matter of state, a political alliance. I could sense it now, the penetrating gazes of the nobility, their speculations.

Was Ka Batavia going to ally with Ka Grey?

The question was almost enough to slow down my desire for him. Almost. I rested my hand on the wooden bench beside Tristan, my fingers inching towards his so we could touch unseen. I moved my knees from his—only an inch.

I glanced back at Aunt Arianna, and she nodded in approval as she wrapped an arm around her daughter, my other cousin, Naria. In two years, we'd both be wearing white and participating in the Revelation Ceremony together.

Naria had never gotten along with me or my sisters. She wasn't like us in personality, temperament, or looks. All Batavia women had brown or red hair. Naria was blonde. Blonde like her father, my uncle Tarek, had been. He'd died a traitor.

"When in the heavenly realms the Gods and Goddesses dwelled," chanted Kolaya, "Canturiel created a light so beautiful and valiant it shone day and night. The Valalumir, he named it. Every color of the rainbow could be seen inside, brighter than anything Heaven could hide. It never burned those who touched, nor blinded those who stared. Such was its beauty the sun felt less fair, for this light was brighter, kinder. The stars and moon felt their beauty wane." The eternal flame over her head burned through every color of the rainbow, casting new tones onto the white-clad initiates all patiently waiting beneath.

Tristan took my hand, his fingers running slowly up and down the length of my palm, and instantly I was lost in the endless brown of his eyes.

The Scrolls of the Valya floated out of their honeycomb homes in the walls to be read by every Lumerian. Well, every Lumerian who was actually paying attention. Several rows away in the green ray, Lady Romula watched her grandson and me with disapproval. Sighing, I released Tristan's hand, unrolled the scroll in my lap, and sat straighter. Just a few more hours, and we'd be without an audience.

At last, the chanting ended. The soft scraping sounds of the Valya being rerolled whistled throughout all seven rays of the temple, and soon the scrolls were flying in every direction, returning to their homes in the walls.

The Red Watcher of the Light and the Violet Watcher of the Light, veiled head to toe in their colors, joined Arkmage Kolaya on the upper dais for the ceremony.

Kolaya began calling the names of the nineteen-year-old mages and soturi-to-be. Tristan's large silver signet ring pressed against my skin. Despite my earlier words, I suddenly couldn't stop imagining our official engagement... being bound to Tristan for life...sharing his bed. When that happened, he'd offer me jewelry with the sigil of his Ka, and I'd give him something with mine. My stomach twisted.

"Jules is next." Aunt Arianna tapped my shoulder. I turned to smile at her but found Naria watching Tristan with an open, hungry expression in her eyes. She'd tried to kiss him at the summer solstice the previous year. He'd rejected her, but she clearly still wanted him. I glared until she realized she'd been caught and suddenly became busy with a sapphire jewel on her gown.

"Lady Julianna Batavia," Kolaya's deep voice vibrated.

Hushing sounds drifted through the temple. Feet scraped against the floor in their search for stillness. Several people coughed, their wooden seats creaking as they leaned forward.

"Your Aunt Gianna, *Ha Ka Mokan*, would be so proud," Arianna said quietly.

Automatically, Morgana and I repeated the words for the deceased, "Her soul freed."

Jules stood, looking like a goddess in her white robe, and stepped onto the stage. The eternal flame flared and crackled, glowing pure white before it hissed. As Jules approached, the flame paused on red. Batavia red. Our color. A sign of good luck. It lit her wavy brown hair in a fiery red glow. My heart raced with excitement for her.

"Lady Julianna," Arkmage Kolaya said, "what path do you choose?"

"Mage." A glowing smile spread across Jules's face, and my heart burst with pride. Her eyes found mine. She winked, and removed her white robes, revealing a violet, floor-sweeping gown. We'd spent weeks shopping in Urtavia for it, driving the dressmakers farther than Lethea with our demands until we'd found the perfect one.

The Watcher bowed her head, putting the white robes aside, and Jules held out her right hand. Kolaya's ceremonial dagger reflected light as she slashed the skin above Jules's wrist. Right slashes were for mages, left for soturi. Blood beaded on her skin. Jules pursed her lips together, but ever the perfect noble, she didn't flinch. She glided to the Violet Watcher's table, extending her arm. Her blood dripped into the ceremonial bowl of water. The small splash echoed through the temple.

"My oath begins here," she said.

The Violet Watcher opened her trunk and produced a stave for Jules, a beautiful twisting of gold and silver wood from the sacred sun and moon trees. Arkmage Kolaya cupped her hands above Jules. Sparks pulsed until a golden sphere of light crowned. With a thrust of the arkmage's hands, the golden light illuminated Jules's body, descending to the floor where it vanished, along with the Birth Bind that had contained her power—until now.

I could barely breathe as I waited for her to raise her stave, her name magically burned into it. Now she would show off her first essence of magic. Her mother, Aunt Gianna, had been a highly respected, powerful mage, like all women of Ka Batavia, so anticipation was high throughout the temple.

But Jules dropped her stave. It hit the dais with an awkward clang.

My throat tightened, my face heating. Embarrassment came first. Red hot humiliation for Jules. I was mortified and ashamed. That wasn't supposed to happen. No one dropped their stave, not when they were experiencing the most powerful moment of their life. This was an utter disgrace on Jules and our Ka.

It wasn't until her stave rolled off the floor of the Chamber through the initiates sitting on the lower level and landed on the temple floor that the shame disintegrated and fear took hold of me.

Something was wrong.

Morgana grabbed my hand. "No," she said, her voice a strangled whisper.

Jules's eyes widened into an expression full of terror. Her lips parted.

"Why isn't she picking it up?" I demanded. It wasn't proper to leave a stave on the floor.

"No, no, no!" Morgana's whisper had gone silent, but I could still sense her forming the words as her grip tightened. Her nails pierced my skin until I cried out. She'd drawn blood.

"Morgs!" I tried to wrench my hand away, but she only shushed me and held tighter as Jules screamed from the stage, a blood curdling, animalistic sound.

Tristan whispered something harsh and unintelligible in my ear. But I couldn't think, I couldn't hear—because his highness the Imperator had stood up.

Fear and dread washed over me. His seat was already front row, but he walked forward, standing just outside the magically protected borders of the ceremony. The Imperator stopped behind my father. He stood casually, sweeping back his cloak, black and bordered in gold. But there was nothing casual in his face. He was a predator, as dangerous as the wolf on his sigil. The powerful magic coursing through his body swirled in a dark aura around him.

Morgana shook, inching closer to me, still clutching my bleeding hand. Tristan sat forward, cocking his head to the side. Since he'd been a boy, that had always been his tell that he was angry. He no longer touched me. His lips, which had been so soft when we'd kissed, formed a harsh frown, and he turned toward his grandmother, and then the Imperator, offering a signal I didn't understand. A black cloud settled over my heart. His aura pulsed with darkness, with vengeance, and with hatred.

Jules screamed louder, and I stood. I had to reach her, to protect her. She was my cousin, my sister...my best friend. But Morgana grabbed my waist with an unnatural violence. My back smacked against the wooden pew, shooting daggers of pain up my spine. Fresh tears formed.

Arianna's fingernails pierced my shoulder from behind, pinning me down. "Still, Lyr," she said sharply. "Be still."

Jules's cries shattered through me as my tears fell. She was thrashing at the air, clawing at some invisible opponent, making sounds that were more monstrous than human. I'd never seen her look like this. Something was so very wrong, and it was scaring her. We had to help her, go to her. But I was trapped, pinned by my aunt's nails.

Tristan stood along with the rest of the temple. The Imperator took another step toward Auriel's Chamber, his black eyes on my cousin. He strode in front of my father, breaking through the ceremonial ropes. I'd never seen them crossed before. I didn't think it could be done. But the Imperator was no ordinary Lumerian. He was the only man in Bamaria who outranked my father; he was the Emperor's own blood.

"No," the word rushed from my lips.

"Shut up, Lyr," Morgana hissed. "Shut up!" She turned to me so slowly I couldn't tell if she'd halted her movements or if my mind was slowing down the event. "Don't move," she mouthed.

My whole body trembled, my vision blurring, throat tightening.

"Why?" I croaked, knowing in my heart what was wrong, but not ready to admit it. "What's wrong with her?" My voice was desperate, weak, the voice of a terrified child.

Morgana's dark eyebrows were drawn together, her chest heaving. "Vorakh," she hissed.

My head swam as black spots obscured my vision, and confirmed what I knew.

Vorakh. Taboo magic. Forbidden.

The Senate and Emperor had forbidden the vorakh centuries ago, marking the magic as taboo. There were three powers named, all uncontrollable, dangerous, and volatile. First was traveling, the ability to vanish and reappear in a new location. The second, mind-reading. The third, visions, the ability to see into the future. Anyone found in possession of them was immediately bound and arrested. They sometimes developed in mages a few years after revealing their magic. But the most powerful mages revealed their abilities immediately. Tristan's family, Ka Grey, specialized in hunting vorakh, in bringing those that escaped the Revelation Ceremony to his Highness, the Imperator for justice.

The Imperator stepped onto the stage. Initiates scattered quickly, scurrying out of his way. Behind him was his lackey warlord, the repugnant man known as the Bastardmaker. He was said to have fathered half of the Soturi of Ka Kormac—by force. His hand was already on the hilt of his sword.

"Lady Julianna Batavia." The Imperator's voice echoed like a death march drum.

"Stop them!" I cried.

Arianna leaned forward, her voice like a knife in my ear. "You'll damn us all, Lyr, if you don't shut up. Control yourself now. You must control what they see. Especially him."

My vision went in and out of focus, and my breath caught. The temple walls felt like they were closing in on me, the ceiling ready to cave in. I felt certain I was going to die and the temple was going to fall and crush me. I couldn't actually be seeing what I saw—Jules having a vorakh, the Imperator and Bastardmaker approaching her....

"Lady Julianna Batavia, by order of the Senate and Emperor Theotis, High Lord of Lumeria Nutavia, you are hereby under arrest for the possession of vorakh, in the first order, the power of visions."

The room roared, drowning out my screams. Every member of the nobility was calling for her arrest, for her blood, when just minutes ago the hypocrites had watched her with awe and respect. Even the Watchers stepped back, their veiled faces cast down.

The Imperator's eyes flicked to the Bastardmaker. "Seize her!"

I searched for my father, trying to get his attention. He was Arkasva Batavia, High Lord of Bamaria. How could he allow this to happen? How could he allow his niece to be taken?

He sat in the Seat of power. He was still as a statue, his expression full of neutral indifference. I wanted to run and jump on him, claw at his skin until he did something, rip the golden wreath from his head and shove it down his throat until he remembered he wore the Laurel of the Arkasva. He had power. Why wasn't he saving Jules?

The Bastardmaker moved swiftly, his meaty hands closing around Jules's wrists as he tugged her over his shoulder. Jules screamed harder when his arm clamped over her legs as he hauled her over to a spidery looking mage from Ka Kormac.

"Bind her," snarled the Imperator.

The mage lifted his stave. Black shadows uncoiled into long ropes around her, glowing red before settling into a glittering black. Jules slumped forward, silent, eyes rolling back before the Bastardmaker dragged her outside. The temple doors closed with an ominous slap, the sound thudding across the walls of the seven rays. They'd gone out through the red entrance—a door meant to be private and reserved for use only by my Ka, my family. Jules was gone, already out of reach, and we remained behind, trapped in the temple.

"She'll be kept in the Shadow Stronghold and bound until transport to Lethea can be arranged," announced the Imperator.

"Lethea?" I struggled for air that would not come. One did not come back from Lethea. Jules didn't deserve to go there —she wasn't a criminal. She was a nineteen-year-old girl with her whole life ahead of her. My cousin. My best friend. The kindest, sweetest, funniest person I knew. She couldn't go there. We couldn't allow it.

I tried to stand, thrashing against my aunt who kept me still. I tried to hit Morgana, to get her to move, to stop this, to save Jules. But Morgana slumped down in her seat, her arms wrapped around herself, her face white against her black hair.

My aunt's arms relaxed their restraint, just as Tristan took hold of me, his cheek pressed to mine.

"Lyr." Tristan's voice was firm, and his arms were everywhere, suffocating me, pulling me against his body. His touch was as intimate as before, but this time, he was imprisoning me. "Lyr, you have to stop. Calm down."

I pushed him away. Was he farther than Lethea? I would not calm down. The Bastardmaker had taken Jules! The Bastardmaker! Everyone knew it wasn't safe to be alone with him. She was in danger.

Tristan's eyes darkened. His mouth was tight. "Lyr, I'm sorry. I...I cared about Jules—a lot. But...." His fingers pressed into my arms.

"Cared?" I asked. Why was he using the past tense?

"She has a vorakh," Tristan said. There was a note of finality in his voice. "She's not who we thought she was. You must let her go. She has to die in Lethea."

I snapped my arms back, but Tristan's hold on me was too tight. Sweat dripped down the back of my neck. I was too hot and too cold. I was about to scream in his face. Jules adored Tristan, had grown up beside him, and this was how he repaid her?

"Thank the Gods for Ka Grey," Naria crooned. "Your family has kept Bamaria safe from vorakh for years. It's lucky Jules was exposed so easily."

I could feel the contents of my stomach churning and rising. Just like that, Naria had turned on our cousin, her own blood, her own Ka. Aunt Arianna remained calm as ever; only a small storm of emotion in her eyes gave her away.

My father stood, stepping forward, limping on his right leg. He'd been attacked by a mob after he became Arkasva, and the injury had only worsened over the years due to a spell one of the mages had threaded into the attack. His laurel slid forward, shadowing his eyes. He quickly readjusted it, centering the golden wreath on his head.

Shouts sounded from all over but were silenced by a look from my father, High Lord of Bamaria, along with a show of power from his warlord, hand on the hilt of his sword. No emotion appeared on my father's face as he waved to the unsettled crowd in an unspoken command for them to take their seats and remain calm. We did not grieve vorakh. We destroyed it.

"Continue." He lifted his hand in dismissal, his fingers moving carelessly in a practiced flourish. Waves of calm seemed to emanate from my father, unnatural, forceful.

Arkmage Kolaya's eyes were wide as she rushed back to the center of the Chamber. In silence, the High Lord of Bamaria limped back to the Seat, the steps of his uneven gait echoing.

I was awake in a nightmare. The Revelation Ceremony went on, like Jules's arrest had never happened, like I'd imagined it. Arianna continued holding me down, ensuring my silence.

I watched the ceremony with blurred vision, a sick feeling rising in my stomach. I couldn't stop picturing Jules standing outside the temple, blowing kisses, so happy and excited for tonight, for her chance to finally use magic.

Tristan took my hand and assured me that what had happened was for the best. My skin crawled from his touch, but I didn't pull away, not even when he told me Jules was dangerous and what had been done to her was to ensure my own safety as much as everyone else's. Nor did I push him away when he continued saying that mages who had the vorakh of visions went mad, and their minds deteriorated into violence that led to murderous rages. Nor when he told me he knew it hurt in the moment, but this was to protect me, it would be all right. I remained frozen, numb. I let him continue to touch me with every poisonous word.

"Lady Meera Batavia, Heir Apparent to the Arkasva, High Lord of Bamaria."

I sucked in my breath as Meera stepped onto the Chamber, removing her robes. Her blood dripped, her blessing commenced, and her stave was produced. The sun and moon wood gleamed under burnt embers, revealing her name carved into the stave. Meera's eyes dipped down. I followed her gaze to where Jules's stave had been left behind. Untouched.

Gold pulsed overhead, expanding, washing Meera's body in light. The diadem she wore over her forehead, a simple, small golden circle that marked her station, shined like a beacon. Meera's mouth opened, a perfect mirror image of Jules's face when her visions had come.

Morgana's fingers clamped around my arm, but I was already shaking.

By the Gods, please!

Meera's expression took on a stilted, awkward look. One eyebrow lifted oddly. Every breath she took and every lift of her arm was jerky and unnatural. She took a step forward, uneven with her weight, and lifted her stave. Wild blue sparks shot forth, a simple, basic show of magic—not impressive for an Heir. Under normal circumstances, it would have been an embarrassment. In that moment, it was a relief. Meera returned to her seat with those same jerky, odd movements.

The Imperator inched toward the stage again, one leather sandal resting on the Chamber's lower floor, the eternal flame crackling into a riot of color. Suspicion curtained in the slight lift of his lips. I could feel it, his pointer finger slowly tapping his cheek, his wolfish eyes focused and alert. But Meera had no vorakh. And though the Imperator was nephew to the Emperor, even he dared not arrest an Heir Apparent without ample proof.

The ceremony ended, and Markan appeared at my side, dismissing Tristan by wishing him a good night. Markan never spoke. Something was happening. There was a flash of blue stone glowing beside his ear—a vadati stone. He was receiving orders. Were they to get rid of Tristan so we could rescue Jules? The Bastardmaker couldn't have gone far. My heart leapt.

Tristan looked disappointed. "I thought we could...spend more time together, and if you need any comfort...." There was an almost flirtatious tone in his voice, as if tonight had been normal, as if there was anything for me to celebrate.

"Sorry," I said. "I forgot about our private gathering for Meera tonight. To celebrate her coming into her title. You know she hates a big fuss." The lie came out of nowhere, as did the strength in my voice. "I'll send word to you tomorrow. Good night, Tristan." I held out my hand for him to kiss.

His mouth felt disgusting and wet against my skin. My fingers twitched. Were these really the same lips I'd craved at the start of the night? The ones I'd pulled against my own in a dark alcove outside?

A moment later I was hidden in the back halls of the red ray with Markan, I rubbed my hand against my dress, wiping the feel of Tristan's kiss away.

We turned a corner, ending up right where the Bastardmaker had taken Jules.

"Markan, are we going to find Jules?" The words came out rough; my throat still felt dry.

"We're flying to Cresthaven, your grace. Your father ordered you and your sisters' immediate return."

"No." My stomach twisted. "What about Jules?" I eyed his vadati stone, now white and clear.

"I protect you, your grace. Not cursed vorakh," he said, voice gruff.

"Vorakh! Jules is my cousin and your lady, you gryphon-shit bastard! You're going to help me get her back now! Or you'll answer to your Arkasva with your life."

"Forgive me, your grace. I am answering to my Arkasva."

I turned and ran, my arms pumping at my sides as fast as I could make them. Markan's sandals slapped against the ground behind me. I ripped off my diadem and flung it back at him, but Markan was on me in seconds, grabbing me from behind and scooping me over his shoulders. I yelled and punched his back, squirming to escape, but he was nothing but thick, corded muscle, his body as strong as a stone wall. He walked outside to our waiting seraphim; the carriage doors were already open.

I couldn't let him take me away from here, away from Jules. If I could escape, I could run. I could find her.

"Markan! Stop! I order you to release me! Now!"

"Your father ordered me first." Markan pulled a golden cloth from a belt pocket.

"No!" I kicked, struggling against him. "We have to get Jules. Markan!"

But Markan was done talking. He covered my mouth and nose with the cloth. The scent overpowered me.

"No, no, stop—" My world went black.

I came to, my vision groggy and head pounding. I was in the Seating Room, where the Council met and made state decisions. Ropes fabricated of pure light secured my wrists to my chair. Dizzily, I turned and found Meera and Morgana tied up beside me.

Morgana was staring straight ahead; her body erect with tension. Meera watched me carefully. Her usually perfect hair was unkempt, her expression wild.

My father entered, limping toward his Seat. His energy was off. His aura was dark and swirling. He pointed his stave at the small side table. A dagger appeared on the smooth surface.

"Father," I asked, gripping my chair. "What's going on? Where's Jules?"

He grabbed the dagger's hilt, pointing his stave at it until the blade shined black as onyx glittering with silver sparks. The dagger hummed low as he sheathed his stave. The ropes around my wrists vanished, reappearing around my waist. My father approached; the blade pointed right over my heart.

"Hold out your wrists. All three of you will swear to me now."

"Swear what?" I asked. "Father! Stop! You're scaring me."

"Do as he says, Lyr," Meera said. There was an underlying command behind her words, a new force in her aura I hadn't felt before, like glass shattering, rain pouring.

"I don't understand. What am I swearing?" I sobbed.

"Meera is a vorakh," my father said. "Like Jules." His voice broke on her name.

I swayed in my seat, my hands grasping hold of the edges of the chair.

"The Seat of the Arkasva is within the magic boundaries protecting the ceremony," he said, voice low. "With Jules…it was too late. I had to make a choice. I chose Meera, I took control of her body, used my own magic to hide hers. If anyone finds out she's a vorakh, finds out I interfered in the Revelation Ceremony, we're dead. Dead as Ka Azria."

"Ka Azria?" I asked, feeling sick to my stomach. "I-I don't understand."

His eyes jumped between us. "You know what happened to them. But do you know why everyone in Ka Azria was killed?"

Ka Azria. They were a scary story, a campfire tale used to terrify noble children. Ka Azria had been powerful, rich, and beloved in Elyria, a neighboring country in the Lumerian Empire. Then one day, they were all killed—by order of the Emperor. I wracked my brain, realizing I'd only ever known they'd been executed. It had been before I was born. I'd never once thought to ask why the Emperor had ordered their deaths. Having grown up with the story, I'd never questioned it. Never asked why. Never needed to. A chill ran down my spine as my stomach twisted. Just like that, I knew.

My father confirmed it. "An Heir of Ka Azria was vorakh. They thought they could keep her condition secret, keep her safe. But they made a grave error. Too many knew, too many were sworn to silence in their fortress. They were betrayed. We will not make their mistakes. No one else will know. No more of the Ka, no one in our household, not even a single escort in our service. The stakes are too high. We four keep this secret. We four die by this secret. Swear it. Your arms. Now!"

Tears streamed down my face as I turned up my left wrist, revealing pale, sensitive skin that had never seen a scratch or blemish. The skin of a noble. I held my arm steady with my hand, as it shook with fear of the coming pain, fear of everything. My father slashed my wrist, striking fast and violent, a snake claiming its prey.

"Now say it," he commanded. "Swear it."

"*Ani dhara me sha el lyrotz,*" I said, voice trembling. An old magic lived in those words. One that would hold me. One that would punish me if I ever proved untrue.

I give you my oath in blood.

I closed my eyes as the magic sank into my wrist, the cut bleeding out onto my dress. Every drop felt like a death sentence. It was a trade. By swearing to this, by moving forward, I was forsaking Jules. I would never see her again. And in exchange, I got to keep my sister.

We four keep this secret.

I staunched the wound and closed my eyes.

We four die by this secret.

THE SECOND SCROLL:

THE BLACK SERAPHIM

CHAPTER TWO

(TWO YEARS LATER)

Meera's ashen hair was wild, flying in every direction across her face. A single hazel eye peeked out. She lunged with a hiss; her jagged nails spiked like claws. I cried out as she reached my wrist, the pain burning. There were two scars there now, two blood oaths concealed beneath a tattoo.

One year ago, Morgana had turned nineteen and participated in her Revelation Ceremony. That night had also been unkind.

"Meera. Meera! Wake up. Stop it, it's me. It's Lyr." I wrestled her to the floor, aiming to fall on a pile of pillows. My legs pinned hers down. Her hips bucked, throwing me off. I flew backwards and landed hard on my back. Before I could scramble away, she pounced on me, imbued with a frightening strength. The visions came with their own power, giving her the force of a soturion.

She scratched her nails down my back, drawing blood, and I cursed, less from the pain and more at myself for neglecting to file them for her. She hadn't been like this her first year of vorakh. It had been rough, but she'd still taken basic care of herself. In the last few months, something had changed. Her episodes lasted longer, they were more violent, and she was barely sleeping or bathing. Lately, she'd only been presentable in public thanks to me. I'd taken over her grooming and styling. But I'd been so distracted worrying over my pending Revelation Ceremony, I'd forgotten her nails needed a trim.

Sucking in a breath, I used what remained of my strength to roll her onto her back, straddling her waist and pinning down her hands before she could hit me. She was thin and frail in appearance, but her visions came with a warrior's strength I could barely match.

She thrashed beneath me, and blood spurted from her nose as a scream ripped through her. A bright light shined around her aura, blinding, and a feeling like glass shattering and exploding into a thousand sharpened shards blew back at me. Her eyelids fluttered, revealing white, as she smashed her skull on the floor.

"By the Gods!" I grabbed her head before she could hurt herself further. "Meera? Meera!"

Her eyes closed, and she stilled, seemingly asleep. A minute passed before she woke, her eyes pale and empty, staring right through me like I wasn't there. At last, when her eyes focused, tears welled, rolling down her cheeks.

I sat back on my knees, quelling a violent shudder in my chest. The sense of relief that came when her visions ended weighed down on me each time. "You're all right?"

Meera drew in her bony knees. Her tears mixed with the blood from her nose. I smoothed her hair back and drew her blanket up. She clutched it, pulling it over her shoulders, shivering. The coldness in her aura struck out, reaching for me, until I froze and burned with its strength. I retrieved a second blanket and rubbed my arms for warmth. The day was hot enough to melt the makeup off my face, but visions left her and anyone nearby as cold as ice.

Quickly, before she noticed, I hunched over her desk and jotted down the length, symptoms, and intensity of the vision on a scrap of parchment I always kept on me. I eyed the previous log times. It wasn't her longest vision, which was a relief. But it was her most intense. Her nose had never bled this much before. Maybe I needed to rethink the tea I'd been making her. It had improved her symptoms for a time, but now....

"Lyr? What are you...?"

I rolled up the parchment and tucked it inside my cuff. Shaped into the golden feathers of the seraphim bird, the bracelet held Meera's secrets and never left my bicep.

"Do you want to talk about it?" I opened her wardrobe in search of socks.

She shook her head.

Her closet was nearly empty. I reminded myself to do another wash of her clothing that weekend. The morning after we'd sworn, Father had removed all the upstairs staff. Only the soturi, instructed to remain on the first level, and our cooks stayed. We had to do our own laundry, cleaning, baths, hair—an unheard-of list of chores for ladies of our station. To compensate, appear normal, and be sure we always remained above suspicion, I'd become an expert in everything. Sewing, haircutting, dressing, cleaning—I did it all, and I did it perfectly. I had to. One misstep, one bad hairstyle, one ill-fitting dress, and we could have the whole country gossiping and looking for answers to questions we couldn't afford to be asked.

I dug through towels and pajamas before finding a woolly pair hiding in a corner. A quick sniff confirmed the socks were clean. I slipped them over her feet before dampening a towel at the sink basin and gently mopping up the blood on her arms and face.

Meera inhaled, trying to sit up. "Lyr, I'm...I'm sorry." She flinched as the towel hit a fresh cut and hissed through clenched teeth.

I tossed the towel into an overflowing hamper then pulled the blankets over her shoulders. "It's not your fault."

"I know, but...." She stared with wide eyes. "Lyr, did I hurt you?" Her voice sounded so small, like a child's. It made me feel like I was the eldest sister.

Automatically I turned, shielding my bleeding arm from sight, and shook my head. I'd have to cover that with a bracelet. I'd created a collection of body jewelry to cover all manner of cuts and bruises. "No. No, you didn't. I'm fine. How are you feeling? Do you want anything? Water? Tea?" I rummaged in a drawer and found a batch of moon oil I'd brewed. I'd discovered the recipe in an ancient scroll when researching treatment for visions. It eased the pain after episodes and miraculously didn't require magic to make— otherwise I'd never have been able to do it. I held the oil up for her, wondering if I should add some to the tonic I had her taking each night, but she shook her head.

"No, not yet. Lyr, I...." Her eyes focused, and for a moment I thought she was about to tell me what she'd seen, to share her visions with me the way she used to.

But the door burst open, and Morgana spilled into the room. Her aura—darkness and shadow, thunder and lightning —swirled together with Meera's energy. Morgana's black hair was as unruly as Meera's, and her skin looked nearly white. The black thrumming, pounding storm of Morgana's aura pulsed as it had since her Revelation Ceremony when she'd revealed her own vorakh: mind reading. When Meera had visions, Morgana had no choice but to feel and experience them, too, doubling her suffering.

My fingers went to my wrist, tracing the two raised scars, the blood oaths. One for Meera's vorakh. One for Morgana's.

"Morgs." Meera reached for Morgana, passing right over me. "It was horrible. I saw—"

"I know," Morgana said. "I know. I saw it, too."

I sat back, biting my lip, as my older sisters comforted each other, hugging and speaking in hushed whispers— sharing a secret I was not privy to. I knew they didn't want to burden me further. I knew they wanted to protect me. But I was the one who pulled Meera back from her visions, not Morgana. I was the one washing her clothing, trimming her nails, brushing her hair, and overseeing her daily care as she weakened. I brewed her tea and tonics, made her moon oil, and tracked her episodes while Morgana lay in bed with the pounding headaches she'd had since that night.

I knew her own vorakh was debilitating; having every nearby person's thoughts shouting in her mind drove her mad. But still. I was the one who flew constantly to Scholar's Harbor, reading every scroll I could find on vorakh powers, praying to discover answers, to learn some piece of information to help. I'd even convinced the Scholars to allow me access to the restricted scrolls of the Great Library, traveling miles underground to read their sacred texts. I spent my days in the pyramids, buried beneath ancient scrolls written thousands of years ago in Lumeria Matavia that could only be viewed under glass. I became fluent in translating High Lumerian to read the old writings. I spent nights in the Museion, speaking to philosophers and inventors, trying to find more than just some tonics and oils to slow down the effects.

Instead of having fun as a young noble lady who had the right and gold to afford every delight of Bamarian culture and society, I was washing my sisters' laundry while my boyfriend and friends danced and drank and laughed at parties.

My sisters could not protect me from the hardships. I was tired of them pretending they were doing so by keeping Meera's visions from me.

"How do you feel?" Morgana brushed Meera's hair behind her ears. "No, I know, it's all right. What? No. No. Meer, stop. None of that matters. It will be all right. It will." On and on went the one-sided conversation as Morgana read Meera's mind, answering her questions before she could ask them out loud, comforting her in ways she needed but couldn't express.

Meera used to confide in me. But since Morgana developed her vorakh a year ago, I was always on the outside. Though if I were being honest, I'd felt disconnected since Jules died. We'd been such a tight foursome, always together, always laughing and scheming...now...I was lost.

"Meera, no," Morgana said. "No. We're happy to take care of you."

My hands balled into fists. *We?*

Morgana's head snapped toward me, her nostrils flaring.

You're not the victim, Lyr! I could almost hear Morgana, as if I were the mind-reader.

Morgana sneered. "Close enough. You missed a dirty word at the end." She took Meera's hand. "No, Meer. Don't you think that. No. Lyr's fine. She's just being dramatic."

Swallowing a growl, I chucked the bloodied towels into Meera's overflowing hamper—feeling another twinge of guilt and anger. I should have emptied it for her. But it was my birthday. Auriel's Feast Day. The day of my Revelation Ceremony.

I reached for another towel on the floor, but it flew up into the air on its own before I could grasp it. The towel floated, and landed softly in the hamper. Meera's closet opened, and another blanket on a shelf too high for me to reach unfolded itself and flew to cover my sisters.

Fine. Just fine. If Morgana was going to be flying around towels and blankets, and Meera didn't want to talk to me, then clearly, I was no longer needed.

"I'm going to the Feast Day Festival," I announced. I had to get away from my sisters. Away from everything.

"Markan will be thrilled. He hates festivals, and all forms of enjoyment," Morgana said, smoothly tucking her stave into her belt.

I looked away, trying to clear my mind, but Morgana caught on.

"You are bringing him, aren't you?" she asked.

No! I want to be left alone. As soon as anyone spotted my father's guard, they'd know there was an Heir amongst them. I didn't need or want the extra attention; I'd have enough of it tonight. I just wanted to breathe. To feel normal. Maybe even to celebrate my birthday a little. I was sick of being fearful of every step I took. And I was definitely not letting Markan come. I'd never forgive him for drugging me and keeping me from going after Jules. I didn't care if he'd been acting on my father's orders or not.

"Lyr, Father said not to go today," Morgana said.

I snorted. "Father says not to go every day."

Morgana sighed. "Today is different. Everyone's still focused on the attack. Tensions are high—"

When aren't they? "The border incident was a week ago. But today—today's my birthday. In case you forgot—"

"Of course, we didn't forget." Morgana rolled her dark eyes and returned to comforting Meera. Her face softened, and I knew she felt bad for snapping at me. In truth, she and Meera had surprised me at breakfast with gifts and helped the cook prepare all my favorite foods. Morgana had even made my bed—well, she'd tried.

"If you insist on going without an escort like a stubborn idiot—well, it's true—at least ride in a litter." Her eyebrows narrowed, and a smirk spread across her lips. "Never mind."

"Never mind what?" I glared. "Damn it, Morgana. Stop reading my mind!"

"You should have said you were going with Tristan. We all know that Lord Tristan Grey wouldn't deign to walk the streets like a commoner." Morgana snorted. "And of course, he'll have his own legion of escorts. Just try not to start any riots before tonight."

I slammed the door and retreated down the hall to my room to tend to my wounds and add some carefully curated cuffs to conceal my latest cuts and bruises. I styled my hair into large, long waves to cover my scratched-up back, slipped on a dress, and sent word to Tristan to meet me.

When it was time, I pulled on a black hooded cloak and rushed through the long winding halls of Cresthaven down the grand staircase into the Great Hall. It was already midday, and the sun shining through the stained-glass windows cast a thousand colors onto the white and gold marble floor. Intricately painted columns lined the Great Hall depicting the portraits and deeds of my ancestors, the Arkasvim who'd ruled for a thousand years.

I was just about to escape when I found Aunt Arianna. She wore an ocean blue gown that wrapped around one shoulder. The material was held together by golden seraphim wings, custom made in the style of our sigil.

"Lyriana, happy birthday." Arianna pulled me into a hug, her arms tightening around my back before her deft fingers swept my hood away. A half smile crossed her lips. "Sneaking off?"

I steadied myself. "Of course not."

She plucked at a fold of my cloak. "It feels like standing on the sun to be outside. And unless I'm mistaken on the newest fashion trends this summer, I'd say you were attempting to hide." Her forefinger wrapped around a lock of my hair. In the sunlight it shined a bright, fiery red. She smiled and let my hair fall in a loose wave over my shoulder.

I readjusted the hood, causing the rest of my long hair to spill out. Inside or at night, its appearance barely garnered notice, but under the sun, my hair acted like a beacon, calling everyone's attention to me. The color was like its own aura, announcing my presence.

"Darling, I know you resist the escorts, but they really do keep you safe. For me? Take at least one? It's dangerous out there." Arianna's hands ran through my freed hair, her eyes thoughtful. "I'd swear I was a youth again looking at my sister. You do look so like Marianna, *Ha Ka Mokan*."

"Her soul freed," I said in a whisper.

I'd heard this a thousand times. Like my mother, I had fiery red hair, but only in the sun. Without it, my hair was a deep brown, almost as dark as Morgana's. Beneath the sun, it was as red as a Batavia. I'd seen portraits of Arianna at my age. Her hair had also been bright red, and though she always told me I looked like my mother, I thought I looked almost identical to her as a girl.

Arianna inhaled; her expression steely. "Are you nervous?"

"No."

"Liar." She chuckled. "I told your grandmother, her soul freed, the same thing. Worry not. Naria is also a wreck. I don't think the poor child slept a wink last night."

"*Ha Ka Mokan*," I uttered quickly for my grandmother, then shrugged over Naria's nerves. I loved Aunt Arianna, but I didn't give one shit about how my cousin felt.

The doors to Cresthaven opened, flooding the Great Hall in light.

Soturion Euston and Soturion Rhodes, ever present at their post, stepped back to reveal His Highness, Imperator Avery Kormac, High Lord of Korteria, and his warlord, Arkturion Waryn Kormac—the Bastardmaker.

My breath caught, and my chest tightened; a feeling like a rope twisting too tightly around my belly put me off balance. Instantly, I was back in the temple two years before: the eternal flame hissing, its light flickering through a hundred different colors; the Imperator stepping onto Auriel's Chamber, ordering Jules's arrest; the Bastardmaker taking her away; Jules lying helplessly over his shoulder, his dirty hands on her body; her screams ringing in my ears.

A wave of water threatened to drag me beneath the surface and drown me before I blinked and saw I still stood in the Great Hall. The ceiling dipped…then righted itself. I sucked in a breath.

"Your highness, Imperator Kormac." Arianna lowered her chin in respect.

His black eyes flicked to me, and with only a tiny stumble, I repeated the gesture.

He stepped forward, his black robes swirling behind his leather sandals. The borders of his robes were threaded with gold. Across his chest, his silver armor had been fashioned to look like a wolf's pelt with the sigil of Ka Kormac—a snarling wolf—in the center.

The Bastardmaker stepped forward. His red arkturion cloak rustled around his waist where it had been skirted in pleats. The excess was draped over his shoulder beneath a wolf's pelt hanging from his back. The wolf's head was still attached with its mouth forever open, fangs exposed. The carcass stared lifelessly at the ceiling, jiggling grotesquely with every step the Bastardmaker took.

"Lady Arianna." Imperator Kormac kissed my aunt's hand, then turned and bowed to me. "Lady Lyriana Batavia, Heir to the Arkasva, High Lord of Bamaria. Your grace."

"Your highness," I managed. I felt myself shrinking from his attention but stood tall. I couldn't let him intimidate me. Not in my own country, not in my own home. He was not Ka Batavia, even if the golden borders on his robes gave him jurisdiction here.

"Special birthday wishes are in order," he said. "I've heard it's either very lucky to be born on Auriel's Feast Day, or most unfortunate. I hope it is the former for you." He paused, looking me up and down. "Your grace, you will not mind my saying that you have really blossomed into a young woman." His hands undulated in the air, tracing the lines of my curves.

I stepped back in disgust and swore I heard the Bastardmaker whisper, "Asherah."

Arianna remained composed as ever, smiling politely at the intruders. Had she not noticed the insult? Or was she simply keeping the peace? I debated glaring in response—a debate I squashed quickly. I knew what day it was, what was at stake. I forced a smile, thinking of the old saying, *Never wake a sleeping wolf.* Two wolves from the hills of Korteria stood before me now, both very much awake.

"Arkasva Batavia awaits you in the Seating Room," my aunt said. "I'll join momentarily."

Imperator Kormac bowed, and his chin-length blonde hair fell over his face as the Bastardmaker moved forward, his watery eyes lingering too long on me.

Once the sound of their footsteps faded, I reeled on Arianna. "What are they doing here? Since when is Ka Kormac invited to sit in the private Council meetings of Bamaria?"

"Keep your voice down," my aunt hissed, her blue eyes moving back and forth to be sure we were alone. She placed her hands on my shoulders, walking me backward behind a column. "Of course, they'd never be invited to the Council. They're here for a safety meeting. With recent events, the Senate wished to revisit our plans for border protection protocol when the university's in session. The Emperor himself signed off on it."

My stomach twisted. Of course, he had; the Imperator was the Emperor's nephew. "But we're in Bamaria. It's a Bamarian issue."

She shook her head. "Students are arriving today from every southern country in the Empire, and while they are enrolled in the University of Bamaria, their protection needs extend beyond the Soturi of Ka Batavia. As long as we keep our doors open for students across the Empire, the issue is bigger than us. And as Master of Education, I could hardly refuse a Senate-requested meeting about student safety."

"We're not allowing more soturi from Ka Kormac inside Bamaria, are we?" In recent years, they'd been granted permission to guard the university and Urtavia, the city surrounding it. No other country tolerated foreign soturi to be armed within their borders. But ever since my father had come into power, we'd had to endure it. All my life, I'd watched with increasing dread as Ka Kormac's presence grew in numbers; year after year, more of their soldiers arrived, all under the guise of student safety.

"I must attend the meeting to find out," she said. "With the recent attack, Lumerians are nervous sending their children here. Your father must appear strong enough to protect them."

"He must appear strong enough? Who thinks him weak?" I bit my lip.

Arianna's nostrils flared in frustration. We both knew the truth: many thought him weak. Riots and protests had broken out when he became Arkasva seventeen years earlier. It had been the country's greatest scandal—the first man ever to rule Bamaria, the first male Arkasva Batavia. Never before had the country been ruled by a High Lord. Traditionally, the line had always passed to the next woman in the Batavia bloodline, from mother to daughter, or sister. Power did not pass from wife to husband. But Meera was only four when my mother died, too young. Tradition would have had the Seat of the Arkasva pass to Aunt Arianna, but my mother's will had named my father as Heir Apparent.

Despite his best efforts to quell the unrest and defeat the rumors of will tampering and a coup at my mother's deathbed, he'd been unsuccessful. During his first public appearance, protests turned into a mob of frenzied Bamarians out for his blood. He'd doubled the soturi's efforts to police

Urtavia against riots. But his limp reminded everyone of what had happened. The claims of illegitimacy had never left him, even after he named Meera as Heir Apparent and agreed to abdicate to her once she finished her schooling.

"Our borders haven't been attacked in years," Arianna said. "Bamaria is strong. We defeated the monster. The people know this, but they need reminding. We must control what they see."

I swallowed. *Control what they see.* It was the lesson Arianna had forced me to learn when Jules was taken, and what I'd done every day since. I'd become the most perfect Heir to the Arkasva. Always dressed in the latest fashions, paying attention in temple, earning perfect grades and saying the right thing at the right time. I told witty jokes, performed the most fluid water dances, and never appeared with even a pin out of place. If Meera was shy and frail, I was bold and strong. If Morgana drank too much and slept around, I was the pure, virtuous lady by strong and handsome Lord Tristan's side. I strangled rumors, covered missteps, and danced day and night to keep everyone's eyes on me and not my sisters. I couldn't lose anyone else I loved.

I tried to consider the perception of what was happening now with our borders. An increased presence of soturi might make people feel safe after an attack—*if* the soturi were from Ka Batavia. But when we relied on soturi from another country, loyal to a foreign Ka and Arkasva, didn't that make us look weak?

Arianna smoothed my cloak. "Be careful out there today." She squeezed my shoulder. "Meera and Morgana aren't joining you?" Something in her tone hinted at far more than her question—a sneaking suspicion.

"I'm meeting Tristan, and they have other plans." My skin itched, my blood oath scars suddenly irritated. I wrapped my hand around my wrist even though I knew she couldn't see the marks. A week after my arm had stopped burning, I'd gone with Meera and Morgana into Urtavia for a tattoo. In case anyone realized the skin there was permanently mutilated, I could blame it on the tattoo artist. Meera had gotten a sun, Morgana the phases of the moon. I'd chosen the Valalumir and inked the sigil of Ka Batavia inside the seven-pointed star. When Morgana's vorakh had appeared the following year along with a twin blood oath to scar my skin, I'd added smaller stars on either side, extending from my elbow to wrist.

Arianna nodded, offering me a quick, tight hug. "I'll see you tonight, my dear."

The doors flew open as she waved, heading down the hall, and I felt that familiar twinge of guilt twist. I'd wanted to tell her about Meera and Morgana so many times to bring her into our circle and seek her comfort and advice.

The tattoos felt inflamed beneath my hand, irritated, almost feverish. The blood oath sensed my desire to break my promise, warning me of the consequences if I should speak. Father's words about Ka Azria that first night rushed through my mind.

They made a very grave error. Too many knew.

Arianna should've been told, she should've been sworn in. But every time the oath was sworn, its power weakened. *We four keep this secret. We four die by this secret.*

I walked quickly past Euston and Rhodes, still as statues guarding Cresthaven's doors, and denied my escort as I headed down the waterway. Soturion Markan frowned and walked forward from beneath the shade of a tree where he stood guard. Again I denied him, offering an obscene gesture. He stood back, technically unable to refuse my dismissal, or so I liked to think…we both knew I was only trading my personal escort for Tristan's. Otherwise, Markan would have gone to my father to intervene or followed me anyway. Fucking bastard. Himself to Moriel.

With the sun at its peak, the waterway was full of glittering blue ocean waves running beneath the clear glass. I watched the stream rushing past, trying to keep up with its flow until I reached the seraphim port.

Tristan stood waiting, handsome as ever in a teal blue tunic with a silver sash low on his hips. His sandals laced up his calves, the black leather glistening with silver thread.

"There's my birthday girl. I was about to storm the fortress to find you." His lips were on mine instantly, his hands running up and down my back, tangling in my hair. I froze, and my lips stilled. A second later, I kissed him back. I'd had a delayed response to his touch every day for the last two years.

"Sorry I was late," I said.

"No escort today?" Tristan took in my cloak, black and what he would have considered poor-quality material, along with my bare forehead. No golden diadem in place. He shook his head. "Lyr, you are an Heir to the Arkasva. It's not a bad thing to act like it."

"It is when the Arkasva forbids his Heirs from entering the city."

"Forbids without an escort," he countered. "Just bring one, then there's no need to hide. Come on, I can practically hear Soturion Markan pouting." He made his own pouty face. "You're making his job obsolete."

"It's easier this way," I said. "I don't have to worry about any extra attention."

Tristan pulled me closer. "Why do you care so much? Lyr, you're perfect. In every way. You put too much pressure on yourself."

I swallowed. Tristan knew me too well, knew how much I performed for the public, acted for their approval. He said I had a face I wore when I was Lady Lyriana and one I wore when I was just Lyr. I always worried he'd begin to understand my true motivation and my underlying fears behind my masks—that Ka Azria's fate could be mine, that my sisters would end up like Jules, and that, above all, he'd be the one to turn us in.

"Are Galen and Haleika at the festival?" I asked, changing the subject.

Haleika was Tristan's cousin and a good friend of mine, along with Galen, a member of Ka Scholar. We'd been in school together since we were all five and Tristan was eight.

Tristan nodded. "They went hours ago." He spoke low, his voice full of intrigue. "They are spending quite a bit of time together lately."

"Really?" I said in mock surprise. "Well, that is…just the most surprising thing ever."

Everyone knew they liked each other but were too afraid to admit it, and it was just the sort of mindless gossip I needed to distract me from my sisters.

Tristan laughed. "I bet you three kisses that Haleika caves first and tells him how she feels. Five kisses that it happens this month."

I frowned. "You think very highly of your kisses."

He playfully swatted my arm then pulled me close to plant a kiss on my cheek. "Maybe I should bet you something bigger?" he asked, voice low. His hands ran down my sides, gripping my hips, pulling me flush against him.

"You also think very highly of your—"

"Shhh!" he said, kissing me. "Anyway, I didn't say where those kisses would be."

I forced myself to relax under his flirtation and deepened the kiss.

He pulled back and laughed, his gaze falling behind me. "Where are Meera and Morgana?" His brown eyes passed down the waterway to Cresthaven. The fortress's gold and blue tiles glistening beneath the sun had the appearance of waves rising from the ocean. "Surely they're not going to miss it." There was an air of disapproval in his voice. Lately, he'd been noting how infrequently they appeared on the social scene.

Why couldn't we continue talking about Haleika and Galen? Flirting and kissing? I was so tired. For what felt like the hundredth time that day, I lied for them. They were fine. Just going later. Working hard on some birthday surprise for me. Nothing to worry about. Tristan held me close, as if I were the dearest thing in the world to him. And yet...if he discovered Meera's secret, or Morgana's, I knew he'd turn us in. I knew he'd believe he had to. Tristan was a loyal Lumerian, and a fierce vorakh hunter.

I squeezed his hand. "The seraphim's ready. Let's go."

Tristan nodded and waved to the two mages who formed his personal escort.

The great white bird with wings of pure gold feathers lay flat on the ground before us. The blue carriage strapped to her back, adorned with mosaic tiles, glittered in the sun. I climbed aboard after Tristan; his escorts followed and closed the door.

The floor shifted beneath my feet as the seraphim rose, causing wind to swirl through the windows. As the bird's giant wings flapped, her golden feathers gleamed with sunlight. A tilt of the carriage, and we were off. Just as the seraphim began to soar, Tristan closed the windows and the partitions, giving us privacy from the escorts. Again, he asked about my sisters. Was Meera feeling well? She'd looked rather frail the other day at dinner.

I couldn't take it anymore. Part of me wanted to cry. To tell Tristan everything. For him to hug me and hold me and tell me it would be all right. I wished for him to know the truth and still believe I was perfect and worthy of his love. I wished for him to say my sisters were also worthy of protection and kindness. I wanted him to soothe the scratches on my skin and kiss away the cuts of Meera's nails, the bruises that purpled my back. I was tired of bandaging my own wounds. Sick of icing my bruises in secret after I'd taken care of everyone else. Exhausted from determining which dresses and jewels hid and concealed our scars and always making sure I was in the dark or partially clothed when Tristan and I were intimate. I wanted to tell him my secret and for him to promise he'd protect me. But I couldn't. We were on opposite sides of a deadly wall.

With Tristan I always had two options. Lie to him. Or distract. Today, I chose distraction—needing it for myself as well.

I crawled onto his lap, my lips on his. I was stiff at first as usual, as the memory of Tristan telling me that Jules had to die bubbled to the surface. It always held me back, kept me from completing our relationship physically, though we came close. I willed my lips to soften over his.

"Hey," he said, eyes darting to the partition concealing his escorts. "Are you all right?"

I bit his lower lip. "Why are you still talking?"

His breath quickened, and his hips lifted, pressing against me. This wasn't the quick flirtatious touch we'd had outside. Warmth filled his aura, wrapping like a cocoon of lust and sensuality around me.

I closed my eyes as he pulled back my cloak, his mouth seeking my neck, tongue hot against my skin, arms holding me even closer, hips rocking against mine, and I pretended that he did understand, and that everything was all right. I pretended that he didn't just know me but understood me, the real me, and that everything was perfect between us—and it was, as long as he kept touching me. As long as I kept my eyes shut.

CHAPTER THREE

AS THE SERAPHIM landed, Tristan's escorts pulled back the partition, heading straight for the litter station. I rearranged my dress, smoothed back my hair, and pulled my hood up once more. Tristan coughed, readjusting his tunic and belt.

Urtavia, the biggest city in Bamaria, was overflowing with people. The sun combined with the population left the air blisteringly hot compared to the fields and waterways outside Cresthaven. My hooded cloak only made it worse, and I cursed myself for having such a recognizable appearance. The air was thick with the scent and taste of spices. Lumerians from all over were speaking in multiple languages, as singers and musicians appeared, loudly announcing the celebration of Auriel's Feast Day. Energy swirled over the streets, auras mixing and pulsing together, creating one expansive, chaotic flow that consumed the city.

Our seraphim settled at the port, flapping her wings slowly, offering me a gust of cool air until a port attendant floated a water bowl before her beak, and her wings stilled as she drank.

I caressed the gold encircling my arm, the place where I kept Meera's secrets. It was a perfect match for the seraphim's golden feathers. Tristan eyed it adoringly, the corner of his mouth lifting. He thought it was cute how I never took it off. A matching cuff was on my other arm, just over my newest wound, and an anklet concealed an unfortunate bruise.

He led me forward, his fingers entwined with mine as his escort returned with a litter adorned with gauzy white curtains that had been embroidered with silver moons. Of course. Ka Grey had to have silver everything in honor of their sigil. Tristan's grandmother, Lady Romula Grey, never left her villa without silver dangling from her ears, fingers, arms, and any other place she could accessorize. The escorts returned and nodded at Tristan before standing back to make way for our ride.

Four mages stood beneath the litter, their eyes turned up in concentration as it hovered above their shoulders. The lead mage called out, and in unison, the rest dropped their gazes and stepped aside, allowing the litter to float to the ground for me and Tristan to enter.

We slid inside onto opposite benches filled with lush velvet pillows boasting silver embroidery. Tristan looked pleased. He started to draw the curtain shut, but I insisted on keeping it open. Shut curtains invited others to look inside and see who sat within. Open curtains forced onlookers to avert their eyes. And in any case, I'd come to see the festival. If I'd wanted to stare at curtains all day, I'd have stayed in my room.

We moved slowly, floating over the heads of the other guests in attendance. Lumerians from every corner of the Empire filled the streets. Couples sat outside restaurants, wine and fruit trays floating to their tables. The city was always full of bazaars and small shops, but vendors were ever present today, having set up tents and stalls full of tables to show off their wares and spells.

The people in the streets wore a bright clash of colors, all representative of their own countries and Kavim. The Lumerians hailing from Elyria wore orange, the color of Ka Elys, the tribe that replaced Ka Azria. Lumerians who'd sworn to Ka Elys but still lived in Bamaria wore purple. My eyes jumped to the Korterians moving through the crowd; the brutes wore Ka Kormac's silver wolf on their tunics and pins of snarling wolf heads.

A troupe of dancers came next, full of girls from Ka Daquataine performing the traditional Lumerian water dance. Their hips rolled sinuously to the beating drums, their undulations perfectly in sync. Four girls stood outside the dance floor holding blue satin ribbons for each dancer to jump and step over. Additional ribbons were tied around each girl's ankles, symbolizing the Lumerian Ocean.

The dance performed over Urtavia's main waterway, full of blue streams, gave the girls the illusion of dancing on water. I knew a few magic spells completed the effect. One girl in the center caught my attention, her movements precise and fluid. Even the other girls seemed to be watching her for cues, as if they depended on her alone to keep the beat. I wondered why she wasn't in the front row. She seemed to be the unofficial troupe leader. The dance ended and another began.

My gaze wandered beyond the performance. The streets appeared unusually empty of soturi.

Tristan leaned closer to me as I scanned. "None of those girls can move their hips like you." He took my palm in his, slowly bringing it to his lips before sliding his hand around my waist. "You're a far better dancer."

As if I were jealous and needed reassurance from him. They were impressive, but I knew I was better. I rolled my eyes. "Studying under Bamaria's top dance instructors will do that." I loved water dancing, both watching and performing it. But I was more focused on picking out the soturi silently watching over the city. I recognized several from Ka Batavia wearing golden armor with thick shoulder plates sharpened into seraphim feathers that curled over their biceps. Their green cloaks, infused with Lumerian magic to camouflage and blend in with their surroundings, were hooded over their heads, even in the heat. The long material wrapped in pleats around their waist was held together by a leather belt with seven hanging straps, each one decorated with seven golden Valalumir stars sharp enough to slice off an arm or leg in battle.

But after scanning the rest of the street, I couldn't find any more soturi. The numbers just didn't add up. A day like today should have at least doubled the guard, especially after the attack on the border.

"Why aren't there more soturi on patrol?" I asked.

"Because of the akadim attack?" Tristan traced lazy circles over my hip and nuzzled his face against my neck, his breath hot on my already heated skin. "That was a week ago. What are you worried about? You're safe, and if it comes to it, you know I'll protect you." His hands rose up my torso, his fingers tickling the underside of my breasts.

I shook him off. "I know it was a week ago. But with the festival, our guard should be in full force. Riots could happen at any moment with these numbers."

Tristan pressed a kiss to my shoulder and sat back. "You probably just can't see them, Lyr. You're not supposed to." He shrugged. "They're trained to be unseen."

"I can always spot a soturion." Knowing them and growing up in Cresthaven with the constant intention of sneaking out as a young girl had left me highly skilled in that arena. I used to have contests with Meera, Morgana, and Jules to see who could sneak the farthest away from Cresthaven before getting caught. I always won.

The crowd outside erupted into applause as the drums hit a crescendo and the dancers finished their performance. Tristan signaled to his escorts standing outside. The litter lurched, and we began floating forward. Quickly, I pulled several gold coins from my pouch and slipped them to an escort. He ran it over to the dancers and returned before Tristan noticed.

More shops and vendors appeared on the streets, and we floated past a troupe of acrobats and a greasy looking mage who'd trained an old seraphim to do tricks. I turned away in disgust. We used the seraphims for travel, but they were also part of the sigil of Ka Batavia. They were meant to be honored and respected, not turned into circus performers. The show ended, and the crowd dispersed, revealing Turion Brenna Corra, Master of Peace on my father's Council. Brenna was one of the esteemed, earning at the young age of thirty the rank of turion, a general of the soturi. She was even rumored to be in line for arkturion one day. With the low number of soturi standing guard in the streets, I was relieved to see her. She was worth five soldiers.

Brenna shifted, and the steel starfire swords strapped to her back caught the sunlight. Instantly, the swords' color turned from silver to red flames. It was the same effect the sun had on my hair. As she shifted again into the shade of a red store awning, the swords released their flames, returning to silver.

Bamaria's timekeeper rang the warning bells for noon. Glimmers of onyx, moonstone, and topaz shined in the sky as our ashvan horses flew into the air, circling Bamaria as they did every hour to search for threats. The guards marched to their new posts, and Brenna stepped away from the awning.

That was when I saw them. The city was filled with soturi, just not our own. Instead of women and men in golden seraphim armor, everywhere I looked I found only brutish looking male soturi, all wearing silver armor and the sigil of Ka Kormac—a snarling wolf. These men were loyal to the Imperator and the Bastardmaker, hailing from the cruel hills of Korteria. I didn't know them, so I hadn't seen through their camouflage.

Leather sandals marched on the streets. The Soturi of Ka Kormac did not even try to blend in or hide; they blatantly showed themselves off to my people. Meanwhile the guard was changing, and every single soturion was a member of their soturi—not ours. A young soldier from Ka Kormac just reporting for duty stood beneath the sun, and his starfire sword, slightly thicker than any carried by Bamarian soturi, turned to flame. His eyes focused on me, staring right into the litter, and I glared back. I'd known they were present in Urtavia, but seeing just how many there were made my heart race. This wasn't just a case of extra forces on the street after an attack or because of the festival. This wasn't even about student safety, as Aunt Arianna wanted me to believe.

Ka Kormac, the soturi loyal to the Imperator, the man who had ended my cousin's life and threatened everything I held dear, was occupying our city.

CHAPTER FOUR

SHOUTS SOUNDED AROUND us, aimed at the soturi marching through the streets. I wasn't the only one dismayed at seeing the wolves. It was custom for foreign soturi to disarm in another country unless they were part of a personal guard. Their starfire swords and gleaming Valalumir stars hanging from their belts highlighted their wolf sigils, alerting everyone within the vicinity to their presence. The chaotic, light, quick energy of the festival-goers exploded into dark, hot, barely tempered rage.

"Go home!" came a shout.

"Back to Korteria, wolf-shit," sounded another.

This spurred others on, and soon insults against Ka Kormac ricocheted through the streets. But just as quickly as they began, the tide turned. Against me.

"Fuck Harren Batavia! He let them in!" the shout rose above the others with an unsettling force. My father's name had been cursed and informally presented without his title.

I stiffened as Tristan shifted to my side of the litter, placing his arm protectively around me as the shouts continued.

"We never had an akadim attack before him!"

"He can't rule Bamaria, so he's got Kormac doing it for him!"

"The fool can't keep akadim away! He'll get us all killed!"

And there it was. The reason my father hadn't wanted me in the city today. The recent attack was on everyone's mind, stirring up tensions and fear. An akadim, a monstrous beast of the old world, had nearly breached our borders.

A new wave of shouts, curses, and cries of terror sounded. And then an akadim appeared, coming down the street. My heart jumped. But it wasn't real. A mage had used some crude magic to assemble the monster's nearly fifteen-foot-long body. It was a mix of a Lumerian man and something ancient, evil. Its eyes were red, its mouth full of fangs. Its razor-sharp nails were the size of my arm.

Several soturi from Ka Batavia stepped out, their eyes full of scorn as the akadim floated past. The soldiers were retired, all discharged from service due to battle wounds. One was missing an eye; another's arm had been ripped off. Akadim were said to hold the strength of five soturi, making killing them the most difficult task to complete. Most who fought the beasts didn't live to tell the tale. Those who did were often disfigured, barely escaping with their limbs and souls intact. The unluckiest escaped with invisible scars, ones only they knew existed. Akadim had a way of preying on their victims—a way that often meant death was the most desirable outcome.

"*Shekar arkasva!*" A mage waved a flag with what appeared to be the sigil of Ka Batavia, but the colors were wrong. Instead of golden seraphim wings beneath a silver moon, the seraphim's wings were painted black.

I pulled on Tristan's arm. "Look at the sigil on that man's flag," I said.

Tristan was staring with great concentration at his feet. He couldn't stand the sight of blood or mutilation but looked up at my request, squinting.

"Shekar arkasva!" the man called again.

"Shekar arkasva?" Tristan asked, pulling the curtain forward. He looked a little green, catching sight of the disfigured soturi. There was a soturion outside our litter in the purple of Ka Elys, the Bamarian branch. Both his legs were missing, along with an eye. He walked on legs made of sun and moon tress, protruding out from his tunic and spelled to move and bend at the knee. "What does that mean?"

"It's High Lumerian," I said. "False arkasva." I had a bad feeling. High Lumerian wasn't spoken by commoners.

"False arkasva?" Tristan frowned.

The phrase sounded familiar, but I couldn't pinpoint why. "Does it mean anything to you?"

"Nothing good. We should return to Cresthaven." Tristan was already leaning out of the litter, signaling to his escort.

I stayed his hand. My father had been driven out of the streets when I could barely walk. I refused to let them push me out now. These were my streets, laid down by my ancestors. "No! We're going forward. We'll be past all of this soon. I know you don't like the sight of—"

"I can handle wounded soturi! It's just...it's dangerous out there."

I shook my head. "The shouts will die down. They're only excited because the guard changed. Look. Ka Kormac's soturi are already camouflaged. The people will forget—go back to being more interested in shopping." As if proving my point, a group of girls a few years from their Revelation Ceremonies swarmed a tent full of gowns.

"Lyr," Tristan said, "be reasonable. There's a foul mood in the air, one aimed at your father, which means it's aimed at you. We must return you home to be safe."

I poked my head out of the litter, careful to keep my black hood up. The darkness of the mood outside was like a smothering kiss, swallowing my breath. I pushed past it. "Forward, I command you."

Tristan's escort nodded and signaled. Our litter lurched as the mages marched on, their magic tethering us to them. Tristan sat back, no longer touching me.

"Why, Lyr?" Tristan asked. "Why of all days do you have to be so reckless?" He cocked his head to the side. His aura pulsed, fiery with anger, making the litter unbearably hot. He hated when I overruled his orders to his escort. Though he'd be lord of his Ka one day and was three years older, I'd always outrank him.

Bristling, I pushed back against him.

"Because I am not done. I had it in mind to buy a new necklace for my birthday." Because I'd be wearing it during the Revelation Ceremony, I was planning to buy the biggest, most eye-catching one I could find. Perhaps my jewelry choice would distract everyone in the temple while Father controlled my body. Beyond that, I simply refused to return home early and admit defeat, admit that Morgana and Father were right. I'd been playing the role of lady perfectly for two years. But I was sensing that time was coming to an end; some new energy was burning inside of me. I wanted to be reckless, wanted to stretch my own will.

Tristan frowned, his nostrils flaring. His anger and concern warred with his desire to make me happy on my birthday. At last, his face softened. The force of his aura receded. "Promise me, if it gets any more dangerous, we'll leave at once. I hate to say this, but public opinion of your father isn't great now. It's just not the day to be caught in the passion of the mob." He took my hand again, his fingers entwined with mine, warm, familiar. "I love you. And we're about to…." He sighed and shook his head. "If anything happened to you…."

"I know," I said quickly.

He'd trailed off before he could say engaged. We both knew our engagement was coming once I revealed my magic, but it still felt too heavy to say aloud.

"And I promise," I said, "if it becomes too dangerous, we'll go." Though I had every intention of being the one to decide if and when the situation was severe enough.

Tristan tried to be discreet, but he leaned out of the litter once more, ordering the escort to move away from the protesters, before he drew the curtains in. I let him win that one.

Within minutes, the shouting died down, and I breathed a sigh of relief.

Soon we found ourselves surrounded by a small bazaar of tents selling goods meant for wealthier patrons. Our litter was lowered to the ground, and we climbed out. I shook my head at the ease with which Tristan moved. He believed being amongst the wealthy made him safe. I knew better. Father had almost been killed by the wealthy—by my own uncle. And because of his betrayal, Aunt Arianna had been arrested. She'd suffered in prison for days before they realized she hadn't been aware of or involved in her husband's rebellion.

I scanned the tents, perusing several tables full of jewelry. Delicate necklaces with charms of golden seraphim birds and Valalumirs were the year's trend. Too dainty for me. I had big features: full lips, a strong nose, and a wide collarbone. I needed something large and dramatic for it to even be seen on me. There was one seller in particular who specialized in those pieces.

I pulled my hand from Tristan's, planting a kiss on the corner of his mouth. "Are you going to buy me anything for my birthday?"

"What do you want?" he asked, his eyes flicking toward my hand.

I swallowed, knowing his mind was on an engagement ring. Would he buy it now? Had he bought it already? Or was it an heirloom of Ka Grey from their vaults?

"Surprise me," I said. "I'm going to pay a visit to Ramia."

Tristan nodded but only after he made me agree to keep an escort at my side and meet him in thirty minutes. We turned in opposite directions.

"Your grace? My Lady Lyriana has come alone? Come, your grace, come here!" Ramia poked her head out of the silk curtains billowing over the flaps of her tent. "NO!" she snapped, yelling at a vendor across the street who was striding toward me. He seemed to have gotten wind of who I was and thus how much was in my purse. "She won't buy from you," she hissed. A caress of power sparked around her, shimmering and slippery but full of strength.

"Stupid librarian," he muttered.

I waved off Tristan's escort, signaling him to wait outside the tent for me.

Ramia pulled me inside, brushing her own fiery red hair behind her shoulders. "Idiot." Her voice was heavily accented. "Just because I'm librarian doesn't mean I can't have side hustle." She tied the tent flaps shut and winked at me. "Plus, it is known I make far better jewelry than anyone else."

I grinned.

Ramia worked with the Scholars, caring for and maintaining the Great Library in the pyramids of Scholar's Harbor. Her job kept her confined to one of the smaller pyramids, in the section that dealt with Afeyan scrolls.

Because Morgana had once asked, I knew Ramia was nearly fifty. But she had an ageless quality to her, appearing barely a few years older than me, a side effect of being half-Afeyan.

"Happy birthday, your grace."

Frankincense burned in every corner of the tent, making my eyes water as I relaxed onto a floor cushion. Beside it sat a silver tray of tea and a slice of honeyed cake.

"I made for you," she said.

"Thank you." I blew on the tea, inhaling the sweet scents of cinnamon and cardamom before I took a sip. "How did you know I was coming?"

"A gamble. I'm surprised you did come. An Heir to Arkasva Batavia out loose in the wild streets of the city," she said with a smirk. The noises of the festival, the music, the voices, and the bustle of bodies outside seemed to swell in response to this. "Your father isn't more strict since the attack? Catch." She tossed a small silver bracelet into my lap.

I shrugged and picked up the bracelet. "He is."

Ramia laughed, a mischievous glint in her eyes. "But you come anyway. Good. I have something special for you and would have to make personal delivery if you not come. Not that!" she added, pointing to the silver bracelet in my hand. The chain had been threaded through with black silk, holding some mixture of herbs that should have never been blended. It smelled horrid.

"What in Lumeria?" I asked.

"It's latest rage," Ramia said. "Magic bracelets to get rid of akadim. I sell a hundred this morning alone."

"This won't protect against akadim. Magic has no effect on them."

"I know this." Ramia smirked. "Lumerians buy stupid things when scared. Every vendor has them. At least mine are pretty."

I tossed the chain onto a small table, rubbing my hand on my cloak to rid myself of the scent.

Ramia removed a key from the gold and silver bangles adorning her arm. She pulled back a curtain and unlocked a box.

I knew whatever was inside would be a prized piece. Jewelry to adorn me tonight and draw everyone's attention away from...hopefully nothing—by the Gods. But also, something pretty. Something that was just for me. Something I could claim for myself on my birthday, the way I used to with Jules. *Birthday jewelry*, we'd called it. Every year on both of our birthdays we'd go shopping for the perfect pieces. Now many of Jules's old items helped hide Meera's secrets on my body.

My mouth fell open as Ramia revealed the jewels nestled within the folds of a black velvet cloth. It was the biggest necklace I'd ever seen. It would cover me from collarbone to shoulders, dripping down the tops of my breasts. It was more than a necklace, it was armor. No one would be talking about anything else tonight. The entire piece was composed of golden Valalumirs. In the center of each star was a tiny diamond that glittered and flickered with red flames as the sun shined through the curtains. These weren't ordinary diamonds. They had been made with starfire.

I gasped as the starfire came to life, and Ramia grinned so wide, I thought her face would snap. It was so intricate and large. I hadn't even known starfire could be worked into diamonds. We were able to mine the raw material, but we couldn't forge anything with it. For that, we needed the Afeya, immortals from Lumeria Matavia who'd survived the Drowning. They alone had the skill and knowledge to forge starfire, but, as far as I knew, they could only make it into weapons.

"Ramia, how…how did you make this?"

"I only half-Afeyan," she said curtly. "I cannot work starfire."

"But…then how?"

"Simple. I didn't make your necklace. I find it."

"No! You…."

Ramia nodded, her eyes twinkling.

Part of Ramia's job in the library was to clean up and sort artifacts found in the Lumerian Ocean. Ancient items from Lumeria Matavia, the motherland we'd lost a thousand years ago, continued to emerge from fishing expeditions. Some items were useful, restored and distributed through the

Empire, like vadati stones and starfire. But many had lost their magic or were broken beyond repair. Those items were placed in the Museion on Scholar's Harbor for visitors to see and admire. This necklace was meant to be behind glass, not for sale in a street tent.

I should have reported her. But...it was so beautiful, and it seemed like the perfect thing to wear at the Revelation Ceremony. Ramia had called it my necklace, and on some level—though I couldn't explain it—she was right. This necklace had been forged as a distraction. Forged for me.

Though I could feel it was ancient, it appeared pristine, almost new. She had to have really cleaned it up after it'd sat a thousand years on the bottom of the ocean.

"Have you been to ancient artifacts exhibit recently?" Ramia asked, her voice low. "I know you haven't. Because if you go—you'd know already we have five pieces just like this on display. What we do with another?"

"Make a profit, clearly," I said, voice dry.

Her lips curved seductively. "Something like that."

I shook my head, still uneasy. Ramia swooped behind me, pulling my hair over my shoulder, and fastened the clasp behind my neck.

The metal warmed against my skin as the necklace molded itself around me, fitting perfectly against every curve and angle of my body. It really felt as if it had been made for me, as if it were already mine and had been worn a hundred times.

Ramia shoved a mirror in my hands, and I had to admit, the result was breathtaking. I looked beautiful, stunning, and I felt strong, powerful even. My large features were in perfect proportion, and the shade of gold was just right for my skintone. I was glowing. Right or wrong, I knew there was no way I'd leave without it.

"It fits you perfectly." Ramia pulled back a flap of the tent, and sunlight burst through the curtains, lighting my hair and the necklace with red flames. We were a perfect match. For a second, I felt dizzy, seeing a vision of a golden beach with waves crashing on the shore and a sun setting into a reddened sky. I held up a hand, my fingers unfamiliar, mine but not mine—they were longer, darker. Ramia closed the curtains, and the vision faded.

"The Valalumirs are in the ancient style—like your tattoo."

I stared down. She was right. The seven-pointed star had many variations and appearances. I'd chosen the oldest version for my arm—a perfect match to the necklace. Now I had a necklace to match the stars of my tattoo, just as my golden-winged cuff matched the sigil inked inside.

"You look just like Goddess Asherah," she said. "Fierce and powerful. Mighty soturion."

I laughed outright at this. "Trust me, I'm no soturion."

Ramia threw her hands up. "Mage! Soturion! Who care? You look like Goddess."

She meant it as a compliment. And maybe it still was for the Afeya. But lately the name Asherah had come to mean "whore" in Bamaria. All thanks to the presence of Ka Kormac.

Ramia narrowed her eyes. "Or maybe you look like Heir Apparent?"

"Ramia!"

She laughed. "I know, I know, you the youngest daughter. Rule goes to Lady Meera. But some...some would prefer you."

I swallowed hard. Was this true? I was too afraid to ask. I wasn't sure I'd like the answer, whatever it was. Either Bamarians preferred me to Meera because they liked me better or because they suspected something was off about Meera. I couldn't entertain the thought. I had to get through this night first. And this sale.

Taking a deep breath, I asked, "How much?"

Ramia shook with laughter, her bracelets jingling. "Your grace, even if you combine your purse with Lord Tristan's inheritance, you never afford this necklace." Before I could protest, she said, "Priceless artifact from Lumeria Matavia. Forged before Drowning. No one can afford. Besides, selling artifact illegal, and I have no plan to spend the night in Shadow Stronghold." Ramia shuddered. "So either it go behind glass, sit useless for eternity. Or...." She winked mischievously. "It is worn tonight by beautiful Heir to the Arkasva, High Lord of Bamaria."

"For?" I asked carefully. She wasn't going to make me empty my purse, but I knew better than to assume this was a true gift. Ramia was, after all, half-Afeyan, and the immortal creatures were infamous for the deals and bargains they brokered.

She grinned. "One day maybe you grant me favor I need?"

"A deal?" I asked, heart jumping. Deals with the Afeya were dangerous. But Ramia only laughed in response.

"I only half-Afeyan. No deal. Just favor. One day."

I swallowed hard, stomach tensing.

Minutes later, I was outside, the necklace wrapped securely within the skirts of my gown, heavy on my waist. My black hood was up, concealing my hair. Tristan's escort walked silently behind me as I wound through the tents and vendors.

"...And she is not allowed to see. Those are the rules for you and me. Vorakh! Vorakh! They all must drown!" A children's song rose above the din of the crowd.

I turned abruptly and slid through an opening between two tents before the children dancing in a circle could complete their stupid song. I'd sung it as a kid, too, but now it haunted me. Tristan's escort followed quickly behind, pulling me back before I crashed into a small vendor's table. The vendor stood before his tent, smiling hopefully beneath a black mustache that curled at the ends. He gestured to a wide selection of golden sigil pins.

"You are unmarked, my lady. Come buy a pin to complement your beauty. Show all of Lumeria where your loyalties lie."

I gave a tight smile. He didn't recognize me and had no idea he should have addressed me as "your grace."

Out of politeness, and because I'd nearly destroyed all his merchandise, I scanned the pins. The majority showed the sigil for Ka Batavia—golden seraphim wings in flight beneath a silver moon. I found a few with the sigil for Ka Grey—silver wings beneath the moon. There were also some pins for Ka Scholar—a white scroll crossing a golden pyramid—and the sigil for Ka Elys—an ashvan horse racing across the sun. I picked through them until, to my disgust, I came across several snarling wolves. Ka Kormac. A Bamarian seller should only have had pins for Bamarian Kavim, not foreign tribes. Not ones occupying our city.

"They are enchanted, my lady, all to hum the song of their Ka."

I wasn't impressed. What good was a singing pin? In any case, I would not purchase from a vendor who sold sigils of Ka Kormac. I pushed one away in disgust. "Are these pins all really loyal to Ka Batavia?" I asked, scanning the crowd for Tristan. It was almost time to meet him.

"I have more," the vendor said quickly, lowering his voice. "Perhaps you seek something…else?" He vanished into his tent and reappeared excitedly with a small black box that he placed on the table. He peeled back a velvet cover, gesturing for me to select one. I fished inside and removed a tiny golden pin, far smaller than the others for sale.

"You like?" he asked.

It was too tiny for anyone to notice, and the craftsmanship was shoddy. I was about to return the pin, but its sigil caught my eye. It was recognizably the sigil of Ka Batavia, but the seraphim's feathers had been painted black. It was the same image I'd seen on the man who yelled, *"Shekar arkasva."* False arkasva.

"I do not recognize this one," I said. "Which Ka does it belong to?"

"Ka Batavia," he said jovially.

"No. The sigil of Ka Batavia has golden wings. These are black."

The vendor's cheeks reddened, and he grabbed the pin from my hand, dunking it into the box and replacing the velvet cloth. "My mistake, my lady. I'll have it destroyed immediately."

"Pins?" Tristan's arms wrapped around me from behind. He stuck his face over my shoulder, glancing with disinterest at the display. "I thought you wanted real jewelry."

The vendor now seemed to realize whom he stood before. Lord Tristan Grey with his silver-threaded clothing, oversized sigil ring, handsome face, and personal escort, was easy to spot. It was well known whom he courted, who was about to become his betrothed. The vendor started to shake as his eyes took in my features shadowed beneath my hood. I could see his mind reeling, recognizing the insult he'd committed in using the wrong address for me. He roughly shoved the box beneath his table. Something in his aura retreated like he was sucking everything back into himself, his cheeks and nose turned red.

"Let's return to the litter." Tristan's fingers entwined with mine, leading me away. The vendor was sweating profusely, his eyes darting around as he produced boxes for his merchandise.

Our escort stood back as the mages lowered the litter to the ground. Tristan pulled back the curtains to allow me inside first, all the while teasing about the beautiful jewelry he'd bought for me. He leaned back on the velvet pillows, and his fingers slid up the length of my arm. He pushed back my cloak and grazed the sensitive skin behind my elbow, his hand only pausing for a second over my golden cuff tightened around my upper arm. My muscles went taut.

Tristan barely noticed. Clearly spending money had improved his mood.

I pushed his hand away from the cuff—away from Meera's secrets—and placed it on my leg with a knowing look.

But the litter came to an abrupt stop, and our noses bumped. I slid off his lap.

Tristan poked his head outside. "What happened?"

"My lord," said his escort. "There seems to be a situation."

My heart stopped. A *situation*. That was the word they always used, the code word in Ka Grey. For vorakh.

My stomach twisted as I drew back the curtains. Mages wearing the silver sigils of Ka Grey wings and moons on their tunics emerged from the shadows. I should have spotted them; known they were there. From the knowing look on Tristan's face, I realized he'd been fully aware. That was why he'd let me win and stay out—his own backup had been rampant in the city.

"Tristan," I said, grabbing his arm.

He quickly kissed my cheek before he positioned himself at the door of our litter. "Wait here, you'll be safe with my escort."

"Tristan," I said again, voice trembling as I fought back tears.

"I'll be fine," he said, mistaking my worry for his safety.

He leapt from the litter to the ground, drawing his stave from his silver scabbard.

In a flash, he was racing through the crowd, his mages appearing in formation behind him. The vorakh in question, the *situation*, was one of the dancers we'd seen earlier from Ka Daquataine—the one who'd been so fluid, so free with her movements, I'd thought she was the lead dancer. Now, she was standing still, her eyes widening in fear. An edge of cold breezed through the curtains and wrapped around me until I was shivering. I knew that cold. The cold of visions. The girl's face was a perfect mirror of Meera's. Her fellow dancers surrounded her, their stances protective, but wary. They hadn't been watching her earlier for dance cues; they'd been watching to see if she'd have a vision.

But as Tristan fought his way through the crowd and the other mages appeared, staves drawn, the dancers backed away. There was no saving her. Just as there had been no saving Jules.

The girl thrashed and screamed, her eyes turning feral. Tristan slowed, widening his stance, as he pointed his stave at her throat. My body went numb. I was frozen with the chill eking off the force of the vorakh, the fear I felt, the cowardice, and the weight of the mask I wore every day.

Everything in my body shouted at me to move. To help her. To save her. To jump on Tristan's back and stop him from what he was about to do. I wanted to shout at her friends to defend her, tell them they were cowards. But how could I when I was no better? I couldn't save her. I'd stood back when it had happened to me. And I'd stand back now, no matter how sick I felt. If I didn't, I might damn my sisters.

Tristan moved like a mountain cat, smooth and quick. Lethal. He was already one of the most accomplished mages in Bamaria.

"I am Lord Tristan Grey." The fierceness of his conviction, the fire of his anger, and the rage and hatred he held against those with vorakh—especially those with visions—burst from him. He could not control his temper, not when it came to this. Those who remained in the crowd slowly backed away, offering a wide berth between him and his prey. "You have been accused of possessing vorakh in the first order, the power of visions. I will bind you and hand you over to the Soturi of Ka Batavia, where you will be arrested and sentenced by his Highness, the Imperator."

The girl screamed harder, her entire body convulsing. The crowd was shrieking in support of Tristan, condemning her.

"Vorakh! Vorakh! They all must drown!"

He stalked forward and thrust out his stave. She ran at him, her fingers pulled back into claws, swiping at Tristan. But he was faster. Stronger. Black shadows unfurled from the tip of his stave, coiling and uncoiling, until they snapped like snakes around her body, glowing a violent, bloody red, before settling into glittering black. The girl's scream stopped as the binding took hold, her arms trapped by her side. Her power was no longer hers to touch. Her mouth remained open in horror, eyes widened, as she slumped forward, eyes rolling back. The girl fell into Tristan's arms. He hoisted her over his shoulder, her body limp, and carried her over to some nameless soturion of Ka Batavia. He took her with ease, tossing her over his golden-armored shoulder like she was nothing more than a sack of rice. Then the soturion was off, and Tristan stood in the crowd receiving applause while tears streamed down my cheeks. I slumped back in my seat in the litter, every inch of my body shaking.

CHAPTER FIVE

"GODS, LYR!" TRISTAN climbed back into the litter.

I hastily wiped the tears from my cheek, panic swelling inside of me. Tristan had taken that girl down so easily, without a second thought. Like she hadn't mattered.

Jules hadn't mattered...not after everyone saw what she was. It had been the same.

"Lyr?" He crouched in front of me, taking my hands in his. "It's all right now. It's over."

I swallowed, nodding. Right. It was all right. It was over. Tristan had been the hero, not the villain, in that scene. I couldn't be crying for that girl, just as I hadn't been allowed to cry for Jules. I had to be Lady Lyriana again. My chest heaved as I drew up the words I needed to say, tasting the bile of them on my lips.

"I was worried for you," I said in a hushed whisper. There was still too much emotion inside of me to use the full force of my voice. "She was so violent." I thought of Meera. Of the map of cuts and bruises that wounded my entire body. Of the scratches down my back from today alone due to the unnatural strength that came with her vorakh.

"Lyr, I'm all right," he said, cupping my chin. "I was never in danger."

"I know, but...." I trailed off. Tristan's physical well-being had never been in doubt, not with his skill and strength. But emotionally, vorakh affected Tristan as much as they did me. Just for different reasons. "I hate when these things draw up bad memories for you." When he was a small boy, his life had been destroyed by vorakh. He'd seen something no one should at any age. From then, his Ka had made hunting vorakh their pride, along with silver.

His eyebrows drew together in concern, his eyes shining as he leaned forward and kissed my right cheek, then the left, before his lips found mine, tasting of the salt of my tears.

I learned long ago that as much as I'd been bred a noble and Heir, raised in a court of charmers and liars, I couldn't always wear a mask clever enough to disguise my feelings. As much as I hardened my heart, there was a part of me that couldn't lock away my emotions. And when my heart threatened to reveal the traitor I was, I knew the only way to hide a lie was to reveal a truth. It was true that Tristan was affected by this, and as much as what had just happened made me sick and want to throw myself out of this litter, I did care for him. Deeply.

Our kiss deepened, and I slid off the bench onto his lap where he still crouched on the floor. "I love you," I breathed.

"I love you." He braced himself, one hand holding onto the bench, the other snaking around my waist, and kissed me with a fierceness I'd rarely felt. I'd seen how powerful he was as a mage. I knew what he did, what his family stood for. But I'd never witnessed it in action or felt the ferocity running through him right after, a ferocity that ran through the part of his body very much at attention between his legs.

Vorakh hunting, the arrests...they left him in a heightened state. Excited. I'd known this, but I'd never been with him so close after one. I was going to be sick. But if I pulled away now—after I'd initiated so much physical contact, after I'd expressed how much I cared....

I sucked in a shaky breath and pressed against him, closing my eyes, willing my sadness and fear and anxiety and disgust to transform into something else entirely. My hips rocked against his. Gods, he was so hard. I bit my lower lip, and ground against him as I forced an escaped sob to sound like a moan. Tristan inhaled sharply.

The litter turned a sharp corner, and he fell forward, pressing me into the bench.

"Sorry," he said, pulling away from me, sweating, face red.

He gave me a small smile then helped me back onto the bench, sitting beside me. "I'm starving," he said, readjusting his belt. "Want to find a restaurant and grab a late lunch?"

"Famished," I said, fixing my hair and cloak. I was beyond grateful for the shift in both conversation and activity.

Tristan stuck his head through the curtains, ordering the mages to carry us toward a place we frequented.

I closed my eyes as he did so, exhaling slowly.

After lunch, we met up with Haleika and Galen, who were, as predicted, flirting and teasing each other so badly I was ready to shout, *Just kiss already!* Seeing them had been nice, until Tristan began recounting to them the story of the dancer he'd arrested. Every word out of his mouth—the venom he had for her, the way he described the madness he claimed was in her eyes—made me feel sicker and sicker.

I quickly made an excuse about needing to shop so we could leave them just to get Tristan to be quiet. We headed back into the pop-up bazaars.

We'd only been back in the litter for a few minutes when we came to another abrupt stop. Tristan looked out to investigate, and my stomach lurched. *Please don't tell me there is another innocent person with a vorakh he'll have to bind and arrest.*

"We're looking for a way to maneuver around the crowd," the lead escort called.

I drew back my curtains. Hundreds of Lumerians were pressing against each other, pushing and pulling, all trying to reach the center of a circle that had formed within.

Shouts and curses vibrated through the yells and screams as sparks of magic exploded from drawn staves. Five Ka Kormac soturi in silver armor had dragged a young soturion into the center, drawing him into a fight.

He wasn't much older than me, perhaps Tristan's age. His armor was simple, black leather over metal, and his green soturion cloak was ragged, full of rips and stains. Not from any of the Kavim in Bamaria. Not Korteria either.

"Where's our guard? Why aren't the soturi stopping this?" A growl rose in my throat.

"The soturi are *doing* this," Tristan said.

"They can't. Fighting is banned in the streets."

"Tell them that." Tristan's voice was filled with sarcasm.

"Themselves to Moriel," I cursed. Ka Kormac's soturi were on duty, but the brutes weren't doing their job—as usual they were the very ones creating chaos.

You must control what they see. We were strong, and we had to appear so to remind everyone of the power of Ka Batavia.

Fire was burning inside of me, a raging desire to set things right. I couldn't help Jules. I couldn't help that girl, not without risking everything. But this? This I could do something about.

I pulled back the curtain. "Down."

Tristan's eyes widened. "What! No, Lyr, I was kidding. You can't go out there! Are you farther than Lethea?"

"I'm not crazy. I need to do this. We can't have fighting like this. Not today."

"But how are you going to stop it?" He grasped his bench as the litter tilted and we touched the ground. "Lyr, think!

There's a mob and no soturion from Ka Batavia in sight."

"There's me," I yelled as the shouts grew louder.

Tristan shook his head, hand already around the hilt of his stave. "I can't protect you against this many people."

"I can protect myself."

"Lyr, you're not a soturion."

"I am the daughter of two arkasvim, the High Lord and High Lady of Bamaria."

"And people aren't happy with their High Lord, which makes them unhappy with you. Lyr, stop. You've proven your point." His face was filled with anguish. "I won't let you go."

"You can't stop me." I exited the litter, signaling for Tristan's escort to accompany me forward. "Make a path."

The escort nodded, stave already drawn, and much to the annoyance of the crowd before me, they were forced to step aside, parting the way. Tristan's grandmother didn't trust soturi, so she only relied on the most skilled mages for protection. I was grateful for that then.

"Lyr!" Tristan yelled, leaping from the litter behind me.

I quickened my pace and headed down my makeshift aisle, reaching the center. Shock at a girl simply pushing her way to the front of the fight caused some of the crowd to still and watch me. My throat hitched from the attention.

I found the young man, still surrounded, dodging hits and kicks as his attackers grunted and closed in around him. He fell to the ground, his face smashing against the waterway.

"Stop! Release him at once."

"Under whose orders, girl?" snickered the soturion watching me.

"Under mine. You stand in the streets of Urtavia, Bamaria, ruled by Arkasva Batavia. Ka Kormac has no authority here. Now cease and let him go. I command you."

The crowd laughed at my demand. The soturi were amused enough to stop attacking. As he jumped to his feet, the young man's eyes landed on me. They were a bright, brilliant green, and for a second my chest tightened, my heart skipping. I knew those eyes, that exact shade of green. I'd dreamt of them for years.

Time stopped, I was dancing under the stars, staring into those eyes.

Rhyan. Rhyan was here.

His eyes flashed with recognition, running up and down my body before settling on my face. One dark eyebrow lowered, his lips quirking into a smile. "Hello, lover."

I froze, my heart pounding.

"Go home, girl," shouted the soturion. "Asherah." He gestured crudely between his legs.

"You brute!" I took a deep breath before I lost my nerve and pulled back my hood. My hair spilled across my shoulders in long, wild waves. Deep brown a moment ago, the strands now lit up beneath the sun into an unmistakably bright, fiery red. Batavia red.

The crowd went silent, and the soturi stilled. Several Lumerians standing close to me backed away, their heads hanging low, before they sank and prostrated to their knees.

"I am Lady Lyriana Batavia, Heir to the Arkasva, High Lord of Bamaria. And you will release him at once."

CHAPTER SIX

MY ORDER TO the soturi left them stunned, and while their mouths dropped and eyebrows scrunched together, my mind raced over what I was seeing.

What in Lumeria was Rhyan doing here? Or, rather, what was his Grace, Lord Rhyan Hart, Heir Apparent, doing here?

Lord Rhyan was from the North, the opposite end of the Lumerian Empire. His father was not only Arkavsa Hart, High Lord of Glemaria, he was Imperator to the North—the twin in power, and cruelty, to Imperator Kormac.

Ka Kormac was the most brutish and violent of the Kavim in the south. Imperator Kormac, the source of my nightmares, ran his country with an iron fist, a fist he'd extended to my country and to Jules. But the horrors I'd heard of Korteria, Ka Kormac's country, were nothing compared to the whispered cruelties committed on the snowy mountains of Glemaria, where Rhyan hailed from.

Students at their Soturion Academy were frequently killed in training or injured to the point of forced withdrawal. A year ago, rumors spread that Rhyan had killed a fellow classmate with his bare hands during a tournament in honor of the birthday of his father, the Imperator.

Twice, Lord Rhyan had visited Cresthaven, accompanying Imperator Hart on official state business. First, for a summer when I was seven, and then again for a month just before I'd turned sixteen. That first summer, he'd mostly stalked around the fortress looking too beautiful for his own good and bored out of his mind. He ignored every attempt made by me and my sisters to be friendly, scowling with derision whenever we said hello or sat down to dinner.

It seemed every other day his father was growling for him to come to some state meeting or scolding him for one of the many fights he'd started. I could feel the snowstorm of the Imperator's rage from the other end of Cresthaven. The first time, I'd been scared his father would blow Cresthaven down until Jules assured me auras didn't have that kind of power.

But when Rhyan had come to visit the second time, nineteen and a novice soturion, I'd been mesmerized by his eyes, so bright, so green, like glittering emeralds. He'd been cold then, too, snide and full of vitriol. But that visit had coincided with the summer solstice celebration, and we'd ended up sharing a dance beneath the stars. With his arms tight around me, his fingers threaded through mine, our palms pressed together, he'd seemed different. Sweet. Almost vulnerable. When the dance was over, we'd disappeared into the forest, hand in hand. I leaned back against a sun tree, and there, he'd kissed me, slowly, with such surprising sweetness. The icy exterior he'd projected had completely melted away as he held me like I was precious, so gentle in that stolen moment. He had been my first kiss.

Rhyan looked almost the same as before—a little older, a little rougher, his jaw more squared and in need of a clean shave. But there was one marked difference in his appearance. A red, angry-looking scar crossed through his left eyebrow and eye.

"*Shekar arkasva!* Daughter of a usurper!" The shout came from deep within the crowd, pulling me from Rhyan's gaze.

Cheers answered in support, screaming like a rising wave through the mob.

The wolfish soturi smirked harsh, toothy grins. They understood crowds as well as I did, and it was obvious what had happened. Neither Ka Kormac nor Ka Batavia were popular in Bamaria at the moment. But in the battle of who was least popular at that exact second, I had lost the crowd to the bastards of Ka Kormac. With one snarl in my direction, they resumed their fight. The path Tristan's escorts made began to falter. One second, Tristan stood right behind me; in the next, dozens of people surged around us.

"Lyr!" Tristan pushed through the crowd, fighting his way back to me, his remaining escort fast on his heels, staves drawn. "LYR!"

But within seconds I couldn't see him. I could barely breathe as the mob drew closer, stinking of unwashed bodies. Sweat mixed with the putrid herbs from the anti-akadim bracelets, a thick scent that filled my senses and coated my skin.

I threw out my arms in defense, but they were brushed aside. A mass of bodies descended on me, pushing me back and to the ground. An elderly man fell on top of me, his arm crushing my chest. I gasped, choking for breath, pounding on him to get off. But someone else toppled on him, pinning down my arms. Panic rose, my breath shortening, and a twisting, shredding feeling cut its way from my heart to my stomach. I was being crushed, everything caving in. I couldn't breathe....

And then...the pressure released. The bodies were flung off me. I gulped at the sudden onset of air, and breath filled my lungs. Tristan stood there, one hand reaching for me, the other wrapped around his stave, holding the crowd back. A man charged at us, and with one flick of Tristan's wrist, he flew backwards, crashing into the mob behind him. Tristan pulled me to his side, and his stave released a white light that domed over us. A protective wall of silver glittered beyond it. His escort behind us also pointed their staves, reinforcing Tristan's dome with extra shields of protection.

I squeezed Tristan's hand, my fingers gripping tighter than they ever had before, and stood.

"Lyr!" Tristan's voice was a strangled whisper. He pulled back, his eyes scanning me for injury, lips pursed in concentration as he held the protection spell around us. "By the Gods, Lyr. I could have lost you. Are you hurt?"

"No, I'm not. Just surprised," I said, willing my voice to sound even and calm. Automatically, I twisted from his hold, so used to hiding my injuries from Meera. My knee buckled, but I shook it off, determined to look strong. Part of me was ready to run back into the litter and home to Cresthaven, but hearing the fight continue made my blood boil. I'd come this far, and now that I'd seen it was Rhyan out there, I wasn't leaving without him.

It was five against one, but as I looked closer, I saw Rhyan wasn't defending himself. He was on the offense. He knocked two wolves to the ground and was circling a third. These were anointed soturi, trained to be the toughest warriors in Lumeria, skilled and strong enough to kill akadim. And they were being taken down by Rhyan, half their age.

With a swift spin, Rhyan knocked the soturion before him unconscious. The two remaining soturi's faces were red. The closer one grabbed Rhyan's arms from behind, turning him to face me. His eyes locked with mine.

My heart pounded, and I stepped forward. "I said, release him. You're unlawfully holding his grace, Lord Rhyan Hart, Heir Apparent to the Arkasva, High Lord of Glemaria, Imperator to the North."

Tristan stiffened beside me. I could practically feel his eyes wandering over Rhyan's disheveled appearance and finding him lacking as a lord and Heir. "Shit...Lord Rhyan? Lyr, he's dangerous."

"He's not," I seethed. "I know him."

"So do I," Tristan said darkly.

Rhyan bowed formally, with an elegance seen only in those groomed to be High Lord. "Lady Lyriana Batavia, Heir to the...." He stood, waving his hand with a flourish of dismissal. "Well, we all know who you are, your grace. I had hoped to see you! Though I wasn't expecting to in the streets. And while we're discussing titles, I must inform you of the error you've made with mine." He wriggled his nose. "It's just Rhyan now."

"You stupid girl," shouted the soturion.

My hands fisted. "I believe you've mispronounced your grace."

The soturion sneered. "This gryphon-shit here is forsworn, *your grace*. You know the law. Forsworns must be punished upon crossing the borders of the Lumerian Empire— especially this one. We're giving him justice."

"You are a watchdog, not a judge! And you're on my land now, where I am Heir. Only the Council of Bamaria can give him justice."

"Watchdog!" The soturion growled, tightening his grip. His gaze moved past me, and I knew what he was planning. But I was faster.

Before he could appeal to the crowd, I shouted, "Any forsworn that enters these lands may first seek sanctuary with Arkasva Batavia. Clemency may be granted, especially on such a holy day as Auriel's Feast Day! As Heir, it's my duty to bring him before my High Lord. Bamarians still have a great sense of justice, and I will uphold it." I lowered my voice. "You have no jurisdiction here. Now, unless you want to be considered forsworn yourself and reported to your arkturion, you will release him to me."

"Lyr, no!" Tristan yelled behind me.

I walked forward, leaving behind the protection of Tristan's magic, took Rhyan's hand, and pulled him to me.

His soturion captor was too surprised to hold onto Rhyan with any real effort. That was the problem with these wolves, they always underestimated Bamarians. And women.

"Seriously? What are you—" Rhyan started.

"Suit yourself, your grace!" called out the soturion. "This here shit killed his mother."

Rhyan stiffened, becoming a deadweight that I had to literally tug forward. He twisted around and spat at the soturion. "I'll kill you next," he snarled.

The crowd was closing in on me again, but I was faster this time. Tristan's escort created an opening for me to pull Rhyan through, into the dome of light. My hand still tight around his, we emerged back into safety. It was like stepping into fresh air—air tinged with Tristan's fury. His anger spilled out from his aura and threaded itself into the shield.

"Lyr," Tristan hissed. "This is a bad idea. He's forsworn."

"He's an Heir," I snapped. But I was starting to doubt my choice.

"Pardon me," said Rhyan. He spoke with a light northern lilt I hadn't heard in years. "But while I was an Heir to the Arkasva and Imperator and so on, I'm not now, and cannot be addressed as such. I am forsworn, as Lord, um—sorry...." Rhyan paused, scrunching up his face at Tristan. At last, his gaze fell upon Tristan's ring, and he smirked. "Ah, of course. Dripping in silver, I see. I am as *Lord Grey* says I am. A forsworn bastard, at your service." He bowed deeply, the movement gracefully at odds with his words and appearance.

I glared. "Whatever you are, you're coming with me. End of discussion." I took Tristan's hand. "You too, Lord Grey." I dragged both of them back to the litter.

We drew the curtains, sitting tensely and separately, our eyes moving back and forth between each other. Outside, the crowd still shouted, but their calls sounded distant, blurred by the protection Tristan's escort continued to shine around us. Tristan released his spell on the dome, but he still held his stave, pointing it at Rhyan, the tip aimed at his throat.

"You understand if I don't trust you," he said.

Rhyan smiled. "Hold your toys as long as you like, Lord Grey."

Tristan glared but turned his attention on me, holding his stave steady like a knife. Rhyan rolled his eyes at the protective stance, but now Tristan's anger was focused on me.

"Well, Lyr, in case you were wondering, your plan to not draw attention to yourself worked brilliantly. You might as well have forgotten the cloak and worn your diadem instead. Next time bring Soturion Markan and the Arkasva's entire personal guard. Maybe hold a flag and walk behind a string of musicians. I'll hire someone to release fireworks spelling your name."

"Enough, I get it." I sank back against the pillows.

Rhyan shifted in his seat, his knees angled toward me. "Oh, that was you being discreet?" He lifted one eyebrow—the one without the scar. "I must ask you for tips on how to do so in the future—seeing as how I'm a depraved criminal on the run from the law and Emperor and all. Now, personally, I thought it would be best not to shout your name and title to the crowd you were trying to hide from, but what do I know? Please, enlighten me."

"I wouldn't speak if I were you." Tristan cocked his head, shifting closer to me. "We just saved your life." He lifted his stave to Rhyan's neck, suggesting he could end it as well.

"Saved me? From what? Those Kormac pups?" Rhyan grimaced and leaned back, coolly pushing Tristan's stave aside. "I don't love things pointed at my neck, if you don't mind."

"I do mind."

Rhyan smirked. "I assure you, your threat is just as strong from here...unless your magic only spans a few small inches?"

Tristan glowered but pulled his hand back, his grip tightening around the stave.

"Anyway," Rhyan continued, as if we were old friends having a casual conversation, "maybe you couldn't see from behind your fancy curtains, but I had it under control."

Tristan scoffed. "And those pups had you on your back."

I sat forward. "There were five of them on you."

Rhyan rolled his eyes, a look of derision spreading across his face. "Typical mage ignorance—no offense. But five on one is standard for a soturion. I trained with tougher opponents before I could shave."

"Tougher than the one you killed in your father's tournament?" Tristan asked.

"Tougher than you imagine yourself in your dreams," Rhyan said, his voice low, his aura pulsing, warmer than I'd expected of someone who'd been so cold. "You truly shouldn't have bothered. I could have taken them all down if I wanted. But unlike you," he slowly pushed Tristan's stave, which had wandered back toward his neck, aside, "I was actually trying to be discreet. A few more minutes, and they would have tired of me."

"And with your little plan to wait them out," said Tristan, "you drew a mob."

"Well," Rhyan said with a shrug, "I can't say every plan I have has worked out for me. Obviously, since I'm forsworn and all." His right eye narrowed while the left with the scar remained still. The scar was still red. I wondered if it was a recent injury. As if he noticed me inspecting it, he mussed the curls on his head and pulled his hair forward, obscuring the uppermost part of the mark. So, he was embarrassed by it. Odd—most soturi showed off their battle wounds.

"Was it also your bad planning that caused what happened with your mother?" Tristan asked.

With a snarl, Rhyan leapt from his seat, arm swinging, before he caught himself and sat back. A blast of heat from his aura pushed me flat against my seat.

Tristan was on his feet instantly, a burst of red shooting from his stave and pinning Rhyan against the wall. "I have half a mind to toss you from this litter and call out to Ka Kormac."

"But you won't," Rhyan said through gritted teeth. "Because she wishes me here."

"You're very confident for someone on the run from their own Ka and country. Remember that right now, your life is in my hands."

Rhyan folded his arms across his chest. "You barely made it two feet without needing your escort, Lord Grey."

Tristan seethed. "I just took down a vorakh."

I stiffened in my seat. Rhyan stilled, too. His eyes darkened, watching Tristan carefully. "I saw. Very brave of you to unhand the little girl."

"You've never seen a vorakh kill, have you?" Tristan snarled. "You've never seen it tear someone apart limb by limb. Seen the violence and madness that erupts like a storm."

I dug my fingers into my hip. I'd seen it, felt it that morning with Meera. My back still ached where she'd drawn blood. My arms stung all over.

"You have no idea what I've seen," Rhyan said. "Enough to make your family's little vorakh-hunting operation the joke that it is."

"Enough!" I shouted, feeling sick. "This isn't a 'who's the toughest lord' contest!"

"Apologies," Rhyan said, his gaze now on me. "I was trained a nobleman, let me find my manners. Your grace, it is truly such a joy to see you again." He leaned forward, his expression suddenly serious, one eyebrow lifted and the edges of his mouth quirked, almost into a smile. "Do you want me to use your full title?"

"I think we've established who I am," I said dryly. I'd made it clear to all of Urtavia.

A ghost of a smile passed Rhyan's lips as his green eyes went back to me. "What has it been now since I've seen the youngest Batavia...ten years?"

"Three!" I said, my voice higher than I'd meant it to be.

Rhyan scratched his chin, his gaze roving down my body. "But you were a child."

I glared. "On your first visit! But last time I was nearly sixteen. Why else then did you call me...." I trailed off, my cheeks heating.

"Call you what?" Rhyan asked slyly, one eyebrow lifted again.

"Partner," I stammered, too embarrassed to call him out and infinitely too aware of Tristan's gaze on me. "You called me partner."

"Is that what you heard?" he asked.

My chest heaved. "Isn't that what you said?" I challenged, my breath hitching.

He gazed intently at me with emerald eyes as though he was reconciling his memory with my current appearance. He smiled, the corner of his mouth lifting. Was he remembering me? Remembering the dance? He had to remember unless... had he confused me with someone else?

I bit my lip, staring back at him, my insides at war. I wanted him to say *lover* again, wanted proof he remembered me—remembered our kiss. But I just as desperately needed him to say *partner*.

"Partner," he said with a grin. "Because we were dance partners. That one night."

"R-Right," I said. I was back at the summer solstice again. Rhyan's hand on my hip, his lips brushing against mine, tasting me, moaning into my mouth as the kiss deepened and I'd pulled him closer.

Sitting across from me now, he wore black leather boots to his knees—knees that stretched into far more muscular thighs than I'd recalled. Across his black armor was the usual blade strap, a thicker issue than my Ka's. It covered his sigil—silver gryphon wings. His green soturion cloak was full of rips and stains, proving he'd been living roughly. His boots, far too hot for a southern summer, were also proof of that—he couldn't even afford sandals. His golden-brown curls needed a wash and trim, falling over his forehead too long to be soturion regulation. Dark stubble covered his cheeks and chin like he hadn't shaved in days. Up close, he looked even older, the lines of his face too hard for a man of twenty-two. That and the scar were the main changes. But even with these changes…by the Gods, he was beautiful.

He lifted his uninjured eyebrow. His green eyes were on me with such intensity, the way they'd been that night, I sucked in a breath. My stomach tightened, and warmth spread across my limbs. He *had* called me lover.

Liar.

"What happened to your face?" Tristan asked bluntly.

Rhyan blinked, his eyes taking on a grayish hue as he dropped his gaze from me. "That," he said, "is a long story. You'll have to tell me the story of one of your scars as well."

Tristan lifted his eyebrows in curiosity. With both so dramatically raised, I wondered if it was purposeful. Rhyan seemed unable to move his left eyebrow.

"Can you see out of your left eye?" Tristan asked.

Rhyan coughed and moved his gaze to Tristan, then back to me as if proving he had perfect vision. "I can see just fine. The injury is, alas, cosmetic."

"Alas," Tristan said, his voice lilting with a northern accent.

I nudged him in the ribs.

"He's a murderer," Tristan whispered in my ear, gripping my arm. Rhyan's eyes narrowed to where Tristan touched me. "He killed his mother, that's why he's forsworn."

My chest heaved as I worried I'd made a grave error—after all, I didn't actually know Rhyan. We'd just danced together. Once. And kissed. Once. But I was too stubborn to go back on my decision. Worst-case scenario, Tristan was fast with his stave, and four escorts were outside the litter, ready to come to our aid with one call.

"So, you two?" Rhyan asked, glaring pointedly at my hand. "Where's the ring?"

"We're not betrothed," I said.

"Yet," Tristan said fiercely.

"Why not? It's been—what? Three years?" Rhyan asked innocently.

"Two," I said. Three years ago, I'd been kissing Rhyan.

Rhyan's eyebrow narrowed. "What's the hesitation? Worried she's far too smart and beautiful to say yes?"

"I am saying yes," I snapped.

Rhyan sat back, his expression coy. "That was quite a forceful 'yes.' Lord Grey, you should be concerned; if they have to protest this loudly, something's brewing."

"We're waiting for her Revelation Ceremony, brute. Not that it's any of your business."

"State business is everyone's business," Rhyan drawled. "But since we're on the topic, what path will you be choosing tonight, your grace?"

"Mage," Tristan answered.

"Oh," Rhyan said. "I didn't realize you were in the ceremony tonight, my lord. I thought you were my age."

"*She's* choosing mage." Tristan's neck reddened.

"I believe my partner can answer for herself," Rhyan said.

"I'm choosing mage," I said through gritted teeth.

"Like your fiancé," Rhyan said. "Sorry—almost fiancé. Are you sure you don't want to be a soturion?"

"Lyr is destined for more than punching people in the face and doing push-ups."

"You're right," Rhyan said brightly. "That sums up exactly what soturi do, Lord Grey. Maybe if I hadn't been punched in the face so many times, I might have remembered your name when I saw you." He rolled his eyes again and turned his gaze out the window, his cold demeanor settling on him like a piece of armor.

The litter slowed to a stop. We'd reached the borders of Urtavia and climbed out into the seraphim port. My seraphim stooped down, allowing us into her blue-jeweled carriage.

Tristan hesitated as we entered. He seemed to be under the impression that Rhyan, a forsworn, should sit behind the partition with his escort, as if he were some sort of prisoner. But was he? He was forsworn...and I, third in line to rule Bamaria, had ordered him to come with me to Cresthaven. But he was also an Heir to the High Lord and Imperator—or had been. And he still had a right to sanctuary according to Bamarian law, especially today, even if...even if the rumors were true. Rhyan had been rude, and cold, and aloof on his visits, except when we danced. But was he capable of murder? I closed the partition decisively behind the escorts, and the three of us sat in uncomfortable silence, Tristan's stave pointed the whole time.

The hour was called upon our arrival. All through the sky, the shimmering jewel-toned manes of ashvan horses sparkled as they flew in circles over Bamaria. A shadow loomed over us as we entered the walls of Cresthaven.

The Ready walked briskly down the waterway to greet us, his red arkturion cloak flying out behind him. Golden armor in the tradition of Ka Batavia covered his torso. The shoulders were shaped into sharpened seraphim feathers that glittered in the sun, making it difficult to look at him. A stern face topped with thick black hair, shorn short, stared down.

Arkturion Aemon Melvik was warlord in Bamaria and had a reputation as the deadliest warrior in Lumeria. Everyone called him "the Ready" since he'd single-handedly stopped the rebellion against my father in the streets all those years ago. He added an air of severity to my father's rule. But right then, that air was directed at me. With a sharp slap of his fists against his armor, he ordered me to step forward.

"Arkturion Aemon," I said, trying to gauge how much trouble I was in. I'd snuck out to the city without an escort when I'd been forbidden, and in the midst of this, I'd accepted a priceless stolen Lumerian artifact for my personal collection, publicly rebuked the soldiers of a foreign soturi, been tackled by a mob...and I had brought home a forsworn from the other end of the Empire who was possibly guilty of murder.

Aemon's dark eyebrows knit together, and he frowned, revealing the deadly expression he wore as the Ready. Black swirling mist, deep and endless as the night, snaked out from his aura, pulsing with little sparks. When he was the Ready, he was a God of death, and his aura flared strong enough to let everyone know. Like it did right now.

I was in huge trouble.

"Myself to Moriel," he snarled. "You snuck out. Today. What were you thinking?"

"I-I just...." I stammered as his eyes swept over my disheveled cloak. It had torn when I'd fallen, and my dress carried quite a few odd stains. Auriel's bane! I tried to slide my pouch between the folds of the gown, praying to all the Gods he wouldn't notice. "Ka Kormac is causing chaos in Urtavia, doing whatever they please," I countered.

His hand rested casually on the hilt of his starfire sword, blazing in the sun against his red cloak. "And what would you know of it?"

"Plenty. They're fighting in the streets instead of patrolling. They attacked Lord Rhyan Hart, Heir Apparent to the Arkasva, High Lord of Glemaria, Imperator to the North."

"Honestly," Rhyan said, "I appreciate what you're trying to do here, *partner*, but the title—it's a mouthful. And outdated."

His eyes met mine. I glared in return.

"Soturion Rhyan is forsworn," Aemon snapped. "Of course, they attacked him."

"My fault, Arkturion." Rhyan stepped forward, bowing low. The grace in his movements was so at odds with his torn clothing. "I should have hidden better."

Tristan looked horrified. "Arkturion, you knew a forsworn was within our borders?"

"Of course, I knew. He's been here under my protection for a week."

A week! A week he'd been staying on the grounds of Cresthaven? How had I not known?

"And, of course, Ka Kormac was stirring up trouble— that's what they do," Aemon continued. "Soturion Rhyan is here to request sanctuary at tonight's Revelation Ceremony." He paused, looking thoughtful and more Aemon-like again. "Go. You need to clean yourself up. Word's out now, but you should be safe within these walls. Stay hidden until nightfall." Aemon's eyes fell back on me, his expression full of accusation. He reached into his pouch and produced a small gold coin with his likeness on it. "Better to shift your accommodations for now. Give this at the guesthouse door."

"Yes, Arkturion Aemon." Rhyan accepted the coin and bowed again. "I thank you for your hospitality." He turned back to me, taking my hand and kissing my wrist with a slow, sensual press of his mouth. My skin tingled beneath his touch. The sensation nearly shocked me. For once, there was no feeling of disgust, no wanting to pull away, no needing to talk myself into his touch, like I did with Tristan. His hand fell from mine, but his gaze remained on me. "Absolute

pleasure to see you again, your grace. Oh, and Lord Grey."
He offered a salute.

"Lord *Tristan* Grey," Tristan snapped.

Rhyan nodded, an overly serious expression on his face.
"Of the most noble and fierce vorakh-hunting Ka!" He pulled
the hood of his soturion cloak over his head and within a few
steps off the waterway, vanished into the trees, camouflaged
by his cloak's magic.

Tristan's hands balled into fists, but he resheathed his
stave.

Aemon removed a vadati from his belt and brought it to his
lips. "Eathan." Smoke swirled within the clear moonstone,
glowing blue. "She's home."

Lord Eathan Ezara, my father's first cousin, served on the
Council as Master of the Horse, my father's Second. Shit. If
Aemon was communicating with Eathan about me, my
absence had been noted. There would definitely be
consequences later tonight.

"Good. I'll alert the others," Eathan's voice spoke through
the stone. The blue light faded, and the vadati returned a
cloudy white. Carefully, Aemon returned the stone to his belt
pocket. Only a few dozen sets of vadati had survived the
Drowning, and the Council kept a strict registry of them,
assigning them to only the most powerful in the twelve ruling
Kavim. I self-consciously felt the pouch holding my necklace
from Ramia. If the Council knew where she'd found it before
giving it to me, we'd both be held responsible.

"Can you manage to avoid further trouble before your
Revelation Ceremony, your grace?"

My stomach hollowed. I'd almost managed to forget it was
in just a few hours.

"Lord Tristan," said Aemon, "I hear you apprehended a
criminal. Thank you for your assistance."

Tristan nodded politely.

Aemon bowed and walked off, leaving a still-annoyed Tristan alone with me.

I pulled Tristan into a hug, my lips finding his. He broke the kiss first, sighing and wrapping his arms around me.

"I'm sorry," I said, suddenly worried I'd screwed everything up. What had been wrong with me today? I had been reckless. First with the necklace, then crying when Tristan had bound the girl with vorakh, and then with Rhyan —Myself to Moriel. I knew damn well what was at stake and what role I had to play. "Tristan, I don't know what came over me. I'm so sorry."

He shook his head. "It's all right, Lyr. You're under a lot of pressure."

I bit my lip, watching his eyes. "You haven't changed your mind about...."

He kissed me again. "Never." His face softened, the anger leaving him.

The moment between us weighed unbelievably heavily. Today was maybe our last day together of not being engaged. I didn't know how soon he'd propose, but I was pretty sure his grandmother would be ready for contracts and negotiations come morning. Unless...unless I revealed a vorakh. Then he might be coming to bind me himself. I eyed the scabbard at his hip, imagining him unsheathing the stave, pointing it at me.

I walked alone back to Cresthaven, making a rude gesture at Markan in the spot I knew he was hiding in the bushes. Doing my best to shield myself from the sentries' curious stares, I crossed the Great Hall and raced up the stairs. Morgana was still in Meera's room, reclining on her bed, a glass of wine in her hand, a half empty decanter on the nightstand. A roll of moonleaves hung from her mouth. She pulled it from her lips, emitting slow puffs of smoke, and reached for the open window to tap off the excess ash.

Meera was furiously painting a mural on her wall, which for the past two years had been a messy rainbow of color. She held her paintbrush in one hand and her stave in the other. It was her way of forcing the images out of her mind. Many of the scenes had been painted on top of each other, leaving her wall full of multi-colored textures.

Morgana lifted her glass to acknowledge me without looking. She'd *heard* me but remained focused on Meera's painting. It took her a minute, but as she glanced in my direction, her mouth opened. She put out her moonleaves on a shard of moonstone on Meera's nightstand.

"What in Auriel's Bane! They were? Wait…what? Fuck. Bastard arrested another." She sifted through my thoughts, attempting to learn the details of my adventure. High from the moonleaves, it took her a few moments. No medicine eased the pain of her mind reading. Her only hope was dulling her senses, a remedy that left her mostly wasted and drunk when she was conscious. At last she shook her head, black eyebrows narrowed with understanding. A lot had happened since I'd seen her. She set her wineglass on the nightstand.

Meera's stave froze from accenting the finishing touches she was painting on a girl's hair—a girl with bright red hair. She glanced at me over her shoulder. "What happened? Who arrested who? And please speak out loud." She sounded exasperated. "I'm too tired for one-way conversations."

I couldn't answer. I was too focused on the girl in the painting. "Is that…?"

"You?" Morgana bit her lip. "We think so."

I followed the scene that depicted me walking through a darkened forest. An akadim appeared, three times my size in every way, its features sharp and grotesque. Its wide mouth swallowed the sun and then opened to release the moon. Meera had painted my arms sprouting black feathers. In the next image, I was no longer human but a seraphim flying beneath the moon. A seraphim with black feathers.

"A black seraphim?" I felt hollow. "I saw that image twice today. First on a flag and then on the pins of that vendor. He tried to tell me it was the sigil of Ka Batavia." It had seemed like an honest mistake at the time, but...three black-winged seraphim in one day?

Meera paled. "But our seraphim are gold. What...what does that mean?"

"I don't know—Morgs?"

Morgana shook her head. "I've never seen that before. There's no such thing as black seraphim."

I fought through the twisting nerves in my gut. "I think it's important. The first person I saw with it was shouting '*shekar arkasva.*' "

"False arkasva," Morgana said, reading my mind for the translation. She frowned. "I'll listen for anyone thinking that phrase." She pulled out her stave, lighting a fresh roll of moonleaves before taking a puff.

I returned my attention to the black seraphim on the wall, further unnerved as I glanced at the broad brushstrokes that turned me into a black seraphim. In the next panel, I was in flames. The final image was of me again. Meera had captured my exact likeness—my hazel eyes, heart-shaped face, strong nose, and bright red hair. A black hole stood in place of my mouth, like I was screaming.

I stepped back into the doorway as the air rushed from my chest. The expression she'd painted on me was identical to the one Meera wore during her first vision. The same face Jules had made. I exhaled sharply, my stomach sinking.

"Lyr?" Morgana's voice was gentle. "We don't know that it means anything. The black seraphim or Meera's vision."

"They never mean anything," Meera said sadly, black paint on her cheeks.

"I know it doesn't mean anything," I snapped. "There's no such thing as black seraphim!" I slammed her door and stormed to my room, watching the sun sink down and wishing I was just a normal girl celebrating my Revelation Ceremony and birthday. But Jules was gone, and nothing was okay, and I was either about to be engaged to a man I could never trust or lose everything I'd fought to protect. We'd kept our secrets for two years because I bore the weight. I carried the burden and carried my sisters along. But if the pattern continued...Ka Batavia would become the new scary story used to terrify noble children.

Meera and Jules had visions. The first order of vorakh. Morgana could read minds, the second order. Logic demanded I be the third, that I manifest traveling. Logic also demanded that everything ended for us tonight. My father had concealed two expressions of vorakh right under the Imperator's feral nose. We'd never pull it off a third time. We couldn't be that lucky.

I slipped on my white robes, fixed my hair, centered my diadem over my forehead, the gold weighing down on me, and waited alone in my room for the sound of bells that would signal it was time to meet my fate.

CHAPTER SEVEN

I SAT ON the floor at the center of the Temple of Dawn beside my fellow initiates—every nineteen-year-old of the southern half of the Empire without magic. Tristan's cousin Haleika had propped herself next to me, along with Galen. They kept looking at each other and turning away before the other noticed. It was sort of cute—the kind of thing another version of me would have delighted in and gossiped about all night.

But all I could think about was Jules, sitting in this very spot two years before. She'd been so excited, so hopeful.... My stomach twisted.

I caught Naria's eye on the opposite side of Auriel's Chamber. My cousin turned her nose up and returned her attention to the young man beside her, a blonde soturion-to-be with the same black, soulless eyes as Imperator Kormac; he was the Imperator's eldest son and Heir Apparent, Lord Viktor Kormac, great-nephew of the Emperor.

He turned his gaze on me. It was filled with an unexpected boldness, not in league with the level of deference and respect shown to an Heir to the Arkasva. Viktor, Lord and Heir to the Arkasva, in his own right outranked me, but not in my own country. He was one of the few here possessing the rare privilege of wearing a diadem, dark silver and shaped like wolf claws across his forehead. I glared until I realized Imperator Kormac sat in the pew right behind him. Panic rose in my chest.

The eternal flames crackled, flashing shades of green, blue, purple, and white again, as Arkmage Kolaya stepped onto the dais, her white robes trailing behind her. Her golden belt with seven straps of cloth holding Valalumir stars in every color swayed as she settled into place, pressing her hands together and chanting the invocation. Scrolls of the Valya hovered in their honeycombed shelves of the temple walls and floated through the seven rays until every Lumerian in attendance was seated and in possession of the text.

I readjusted my robes and shifted, unable to get comfortable. I hadn't eaten dinner; I was too nervous. But now my stomach was rebelling, roiling with hunger.

I twisted to peer at my family's pews where Meera was still and pale in her seat. Morgana looked stiff next to her, unnaturally so. She'd had three glasses of wine at dinner and carried a silver flask full of fermented moon tea inside her belt. But her black eyebrows were tensed, her face contorted with pain. Her diadem had already shifted off center. She swayed in her seat as a middle-aged mage cast her eyes down on her in disapproval. I'd seen the judgmental looks before, the snide comments of how hard it must be to live as we did in Cresthaven, wealthy Heirs to the Arkasva. What a pity that the Lady Morgana was drinking it all away.

The stories hurt. But it was better they saw her as a drunk than a vorakh.

Kolaya's chants, the annual retelling of the story of the God Auriel stealing the Valalumir from Heaven and falling to Earth for the love of Goddess Asherah, came to an end. The Valya scrolls rolled up, floating back into the walls. My father limped onto the stage, the Laurel of the Arkasva glowing golden atop his dark hair.

"Citizens of Bamaria, my fellow Lumerians and guests, tonight on the auspicious and forgiving evening of Auriel's Feast Day, we welcome a lost soul to our midst," he said solemnly.

A set of doors burst open from the temple's green ray. Two golden-armored soturi of Ka Batavia hauled Rhyan forward like a prisoner. He still wore his ruined cloak and uniform, but he looked clean and freshly shaven. His mess of curls had been shampooed and somewhat tamed. The soldiers reached the center of the Chamber, walking through one of the thin aisles between initiates, and lifted Rhyan on stage, forcing him to his knees before everyone.

Tristan's expression tensed from his seat. Mages and soturi stirred in every corner of the temple, their whispers quickly building into murmurs that echoed off the walls.

"He should be dragged to the border," came a whisper from behind me.

I turned and glared at the girl from Ka Elys. "You disagree with the decisions of your Arkasva?"

Cowering, she whispered, "No," and stared down at her hands. I turned back to my father.

"It's been years since a request like this was made." My father's voice rose above the noise, but the murmurs continued.

Kolaya stepped forward, slamming her stave down. Unlike the staves carried by mages, hers was six feet tall and held a clear quartz crystal at the top. Blinding white light sparked, spreading through the entire building.

The temple silenced under her spell. She nodded to my father, tapped her stave again to retrieve the light and stolen sound, and stepped back.

"Surely," my father continued, "your memories are not so short as to forget the courtesies of Bamaria. A forsworn may seek sanctuary with us on Auriel's Feast Day." He turned toward Rhyan. "Please, my friend, tell us where you come from."

Rhyan bowed his head. "I have come from Glemaria, ruled by His Highness, Imperator Devon Hart." He spoke slowly, his northern lilt formal with the affect of a noble.

My father smiled. "We welcome you, Lord Rhyan Hart, Heir Apparent to the Arkasva, High Lord of Glemaria, Imperator to the North."

The whispers now seemed more excited by scandal. Here was an exiled lord of the north! An Heir Apparent, no less. What was he doing in the south? He'd killed another student in a tournament. He'd killed his mother. He was unhinged, dangerous, wild. And guilty. A murderer. Why else had he traveled so far for sanctuary?

"I thank you, your grace. But I am just Rhyan now," he said humbly. "An apprentice soturion. Nothing more."

"Soturion Rhyan," my father said, "are you prepared to swear your loyalty and services to Ka Batavia in exchange for shelter and forgiveness?"

There was a loud hush across the room as Rhyan rose to his feet. "No."

The whispers turned to shouts of anger and more calls for his demise. Rhyan had the right to seek shelter here, but only if he could prove his worth and swear his oath to Ka Batavia. To be relieved of his status as a forsworn in Glemaria, he had to become a Bamarian and be sworn to Ka Batavia.

The Ready rose, his hand on the hilt of his sword. The audience hushed as he approached the Chamber, his red arkturion cloak sweeping elegantly behind him. He shared a quick look with my father then nodded to Rhyan, urging him to continue.

"Arkasva Batavia," Rhyan said, "I come begging for shelter and a chance to finish my studies. In exchange, I offer you my sword and loyalty. I wish to be a soturion of Ka

Batavia in all but name, so I may one day return home to seek justice in Glemaria."

The anger in the room was palpable. Even with the unrest stirring beneath my father's rule, the respect shown to the arkasva was sacred. Yet with the Ready on the stage slowly turning in a circle and staring down every set of rows of the seven rays, the room remained hushed.

"Good people of Bamaria, do you not know we are all in Soturion Rhyan's debt?" My father stepped forward, letting his words linger. "Last week, an akadim nearly reached the Bamarian border. We thank the Gods no one was hurt, for the akadim was slaughtered on sight, killed by a highly skilled soturion." He limped to Rhyan's other side, his hand on his shoulder, turning them in a full circle. "And the soturion who slew the beast," my father said, his voice louder, "the soturion who slew it alone, saving countless Bamarian lives, stands here beside me."

Rhyan had killed an akadim.

My mouth fell open. I thought of the many soturi who'd failed, wandering the streets of Urtavia missing arms and legs and with their faces permanently scarred from claws. Most did not live to tell the tale. The beasts didn't simply kill their prey. They sucked out their souls to feast on and drank their blood. The hellions even mated with victims—and not always in that order. The lucky ones were left for dead. The unlucky were forsaken and became akadim themselves.

For Rhyan to have killed one...any arkasva would have welcomed him with open arms, no matter his reputation. But instead of being impressed with Rhyan's strength, there was even more anger in the temple.

"Where were our soturi?" came a shout.

"Why didn't we stop the threat?" came another.

The questions fired off rapidly. Why had this been left to a forsworn boy? Where was the Ready? Why had our warlord neglected to scout this menace? Was our school even safe? If

Ka Kormac was here to protect us from such threats, why had they not stepped in?

Kolaya stepped forward again, her stave lifted.

"SILENCE! By order of the Senate and Emperor Theotis." The Imperator approached the Chamber, his black and gold robes trailing behind him like a looming shadow. The temple hushed before Kolaya could cast another silencer, and all eyes turned to the Imperator.

"Arkturion Aemon, you swear this forsworn killed the akadim?" The Imperator lifted an eyebrow in disbelief.

Aemon's eyes narrowed. "I saw him following the kill. I bear witness."

Imperator Kormac shook his head. "But you did not see him slay the beast yourself?"

"Had I been present, he would not have slain the akadim. I would have." Aemon's voice darkened, as did his expression. He was no longer Aemon, Arkturion and Warlord of Bamaria. He was the Ready, the deadliest warrior in the Lumerian Empire, the God of Death. His power pulsed, inking the temple in shadows. Then, just as quickly, the darkness lifted.

Imperator Kormac's lips quirked. "The question remains of how an akadim was allowed to breach the borders of Bamaria when none of the Soturi of Ka Batavia were present."

None of the Soturi of Ka Kormac had been present, either!

"A full investigation is unfolding, as you know," my father said pointedly.

"Yes, well, as lucky as he was to slay an akadim by himself," the Imperator said, his voice full of skepticism, "no lost soul may be accepted by a new Ka in whatever way you're allowing admittance without being spoken for by someone of his home Ka and country." The Imperator glared at Rhyan. "You're on the wrong side of the Empire, boy. I'm afraid we don't have many northerners here."

"I vouch for him." A soturion sitting in the green ray stood suddenly, walking into the aisle for all to see. He had light brown hair that curled like Rhyan's, only his held specks of gray. "I am Soturion Sean of Ka Drona in Bamaria. But I was born into Ka Hart. I am first cousin to Imperator Devon Hart. Does that satisfy you?" He spoke with a heavy northern accent.

The Imperator gave a curt nod. "You recently married and relocated to Bamaria?"

Soturion Sean pressed his lips together. "Yes, your highness."

"How convenient," drawled the Imperator. "Felicitations."

"And if it pleases his highness," my father said, "Soturion Rhyan submitted to the Bound Five, further proving his strength and willingness to submit to our rule. As you can see," he gestured to Rhyan, "he survived remarkably unscathed."

This led to several hushed gasps. A Bound Five was used as punishment in soturion training. The warrior's hands were bound behind their backs while five soturi attacked them. Death was a real possibility. If they fell, they were not mourned, only deemed unfit to fight.

Suddenly, Rhyan's cavalier attitude at facing five soturi in the streets made sense. He'd already killed an akadim and faced down five soturi with his hands tied behind his back.

I wasn't sure if Rhyan was a murderer or not. But I knew without a doubt he was a dangerous enemy to have.

The Imperator laughed. "Killed an akadim, survived a Bound Five, and not a single mark?" His eyes ran up and down Rhyan's body. "I would have liked to see this myself. I'm surprised a show of such importance was done in secret."

"I do believe," Aemon said, "five members of your own soturi can testify to his strength. Perhaps five who were set to guard during today's festival?"

Imperator Kormac smiled, descending to his seat. "I'm sure I will have the opportunity to see the great akadim slayer in action one day." His eyes fell on me. "We shall proceed with the ceremony. I know how eager tonight's participants must be. Especially the Lady Lyriana."

My throat tightened from the attention shift. Rhyan walked solemnly to the back pews, selecting a row at the end of the red ray. The ceremony began.

Kolaya moved so quickly, everything felt like a blur. I barely saw anyone's magic revealed. Every second it seemed white robes vanished from beside me. So many mages showed beautiful bursts of power—strikes of lightning, heavenly music. Soon the only initiates left were from the head families of the noble Kavim.

Lady Pavi from Ka Elys went next, revealing a dark purple dress as she became a soturion. Then Viktor Kormac approached the Chamber.

"Soturion," he said, dropping his robe on the floor. The Red Watcher was forced to walk around her table and retrieve it, her veil skimming the floor. He rudely shoved his hand at Kolaya and bled into the flames before snatching his dagger, still smoking with his name.

Then it was just me and Naria. She stood and dropped her robes beneath the flames.

"Soturion," she said loudly.

My jaw dropped. Naria was becoming a soturion? Since when? Naria had never shown any interest. Plus, she'd be under the orders of the Ready, and she hated him. When her father had rebelled, the Ready had been the one who'd slaughtered him on the street.

Naria bled into the fire and revealed her magic, leaping into the air. She twirled gracefully, levitating mid-spin, before landing with tiny blue sparks, earning a round of applause.

Then I alone wore the white robes of the initiate. All chatter stopped, and all eyes were on me, the youngest

daughter and Heir of Arkasva Harren Batavia and the late
Arkasva Marianna Batavia, the High Lord and High Lady of
Bamaria.

The Bastardmaker leaned forward, his hand stroking the
hilt of his sword as his eyes moved up and down my body.
Beside him, the Imperator shifted with a wolfish grin.

Eyes carefully averted from my father, fearing I'd give us
away, I took a deep breath.

But the air never came. I was cut off mid-inhale and left
feeling as if I would choke. My face tightened painfully, and
I was forced to look calm by an outside force. My feet
moved, stepping forward against my will, my right foot
heavier than the left. I couldn't turn my head or change my
pace. My father had already seized control of my body like
he had with Meera and like he had with Morgana a year ago.
I caught Tristan smiling at me from the corner of my eye in
his seat. He mouthed, "I love you." But I couldn't react,
couldn't smile or mouth that I loved him back. The light left
Tristan's eyes which filled with hurt and rejection.

Awkwardly, my foot stepped forward, unbalanced. My
heart skipped; I was fearful I'd trip. I wasn't in control of my
body. A sudden jerk of my head caused a spasm in my neck,
and my diadem banged against my forehead. My gaze fell on
Viktor Kormac. As if to compensate for my strangeness, my
father forced a silly smile across my lips—a smile aimed at
Viktor.

Auriel's fucking bane.

"Lady Lyriana Batavia, Heir to the Arkasva, High Lord of
Bamaria, what path do you choose?"

My father's control over me loosened, and I took a deep
breath.

"Mage." I let the word hang in the air before I slipped my
robes off my shoulders.

Ramia's necklace glowed beneath the eternal flames,
which flickered from purple to red. Batavia red. Each

diamond radiated starfire, sparkling and shimmering beneath the light. Hushed voices came with several noises of shock at its garishness, as well as awe at its splendor.

I could just make out the word "necklace" being whispered from the corners of the room. Even the Imperator's eyes were drawn to the jewels across my chest and shoulders, his mouth agape. Morgana gave the slightest nod of confirmation. My distraction was working. She bit her lip. We were close, so close to finishing this game. I just had to play my role a little longer.

I handed my robes to the Watcher and turned toward Kolaya's dagger. The cut came swiftly, shocking me. I nearly turned toward the soturion flames. The mage's bowl, once pure with ocean water, was now filled with blood. I held my hand over it, adding my own.

"My oath begins here."

And then my stave was in my hands. My stave! My heart leapt. The smooth wood felt cool as my fingers tightened around it. I hadn't realized until that moment how much I'd wanted this, desired it. I'd been so worried, I'd forgotten I would receive my stave, and I, too, would be able to perform magic. The golden sphere of light, blazingly bright and warm, descended, illuminating my body in a golden glow and blinding me.

My necklace heated against my skin, and in the distance, I thought I saw an image of the goddess Asherah, her red hair in long loose waves, a finger pressed against her lips. The image along with the golden light faded into the floor, disappearing beneath my feet. Fire erupted down my stave, and *Lyriana Batavia* was carved in bright red, flaming letters as smoke wisped around me. My heart pounded both with fear and anticipation. My Birth Bind was gone, but nothing had happened.

Meera had immediately fallen into a vision when her magic was revealed. Morgana's head had seared with pain as the inner thoughts of everyone in the temple pushed into her mind. I experienced neither. I hadn't traveled anywhere; I was still standing exactly where I'd been. No vorakh! By the Gods! Tears welled in my eyes. I was safe.

But as I stared out into the crowd of Lumerians, their faces a mix of scorn and suspicion, doubt crept in. I didn't have a vorakh, but I also felt no magic. No impulses or inspiration. I'd heard it described as a buzzing, pulsing, almost burning sensation inside, one you had to release. After nineteen years with the Birth Bind, the magic trapped inside could hardly be contained. Most Lumerians went stir crazy in the weeks before the Ceremony, unable to withstand the sheer level of power trapped within themselves. I hadn't noticed. But I'd been distracted.

I looked at the paintings of the Valya decorating the temple walls. Everyone else tonight had done so after their magic was revealed. The paintings should have come alive for me; the stories should have been moving and unfolding their secrets. They were still. Was my father's hold on me so strong I couldn't see our moving pictures or feel my magic?

Maybe that was it. Maybe his hold on me had even put a hold on my magic. And maybe I wasn't safe. Not yet. Heart hammering and vision blurring, I was aware of the silence turning to uncomfortable murmuring. Suspicion was growing. Something had to happen. My father had to do something. But my father was not acting. I could feel his power, but instead of showing magic, he'd frozen me.

I could just make out the faintest blue glow emanating from the stave in his black robes. My arm shot up, and then fell like a deadweight at my side. The light blinked out, his hold on me vanishing completely. I stumbled forward.

A soturion of Ka Kormac had bumped into my father, knocking his stave from his hands. The stave rolled across the floor to Imperator Kormac's sandal. He picked it up.

"How dare—" my father's voice rang out.

"Arrest the fool," the Imperator commanded, wiping my father's stave with his cloak. He took careful, measured steps across the temple, holding my father's stave close. "Arkasva Batavia, forgive Ka Kormac for this soturion's clumsiness. He'll be punished severely."

The Bastardmaker signaled, and the man was dragged away by one of his own men. The Imperator now stood right next to my father, too close for him to help me. Tears burned my eyes. Myself to Moriel. He'd known! He'd fucking known. He'd guessed what my father was up to, and he'd planned his own diversion to catch us in the act.

"My apologies for the commotion, your grace," the Imperator said, finally returning my father's stave. "Go on."

I lifted my stave, arm shaking as a new fear took hold of me, one I hadn't considered in my wildest dreams. Even without my father freezing my body, without the Birth Bind in place, I felt nothing. No sensations, no impulses.

There was no magic in me. Nothing was happening.

"Lady Lyriana Batavia...LADY LYRIANA!" Imperator Kormac's voice cut through me. "I don't know what game you're playing. But it ends now. By order of the Senate and Emperor Theotis, you will show your magic. Now." Anger tinged his voice, but there was also an excitement in it that made me sick.

His aura pulsed, unleashing his fury on me, two years of having been denied his prize and having his suspicions unanswered. A predator finally catching his prey.

"I...." Tears welled in my eyes as the realization began to take form. "I can't." My eyes fell on Tristan's. He was already red, leaning forward in his seat, his mouth half-open in fear. I shook my head at him. *It's not what you think.* But his nostrils only flared in response.

"By the order of the Senate and Emperor Theotis, you will express your magic now," said the Imperator. "If you do not, you will be arrested for attempted concealment of vorakh, and upon examination we will determine if you're hiding the first, second, or third."

Lumerians were standing up, shouting through the temple. Everything looked and felt like it had two years ago when Jules's vorakh had been revealed.

Arm shaking, tears blurring my vision, I held my stave high, but I knew it was futile. Nothing would happen. I was empty.

"Lady Lyriana Batavia, Heir to the Arkasva, High Lord of Bamaria, by the order of the Senate and Emperor Theotis, for the refusal to show your magic and the attempted concealment of a vorakh power, you are under arrest." His eyes flicked to the Bastardmaker. "Seize her."

CHAPTER EIGHT

I WAS LOST in panic, falling in and out of consciousness. Fuzzy, disconnected images tinged in darkness appeared as I sank beneath the weight of shadows.

A powerful-looking mage with a silver wolf sigil stalked forward, his stave drawn, before Tristan rushed at him, throwing the man to the ground.

"No!" he shouted. They wrestled, rolling across the floor until Tristan straddled his chest and punched him in the face. The mage drew his stave, thunder bursting forth, pushing him back. But Tristan met him with his own magic storm as he screamed, "I'll do it!"

Tristan knocked him out with another sweep of his stave before staggering to his feet.

I was yelling, screaming, begging and pleading for him not to. But Tristan stalked toward me, chanting in High Lumerian. *No, no, no, don't.* The burning hot ropes of a binding tightened around my body. I seized, barely able to breathe, and our eyes met.

"I'm sorry," he mouthed.

Tristan.

My skin burned. The ropes were so tight, so hot, I was barely holding onto consciousness. Then there was nothing.

More images came. Then darkness.

Arianna grabbing Morgana and Meera, rushing them out, surrounded by our guard.

Nothing.

My cousin, Naria, looking half-shocked, half-pleased.

Members of Ka Batavia jumping to their feet, eyes alight.

Fists waving and shouts crashing against each other.

Lord Viktor Kormac grinning as the Bastardmaker's hands wrapped around my wrists.

My feet dragging on the floor behind me, sandal laces coming undone.

The Bastardmaker's red cloak flowing behind him and falling on my body.

His sickening smell tinged with incense from the temple.

Rhyan rushing to my father's side as he argued with Imperator Kormac.

The Ready, sword drawn, starfire flaming, ordering his soturi to stand down.

Tristan shouting.

Shadows. Dark, thundering auras suffocating me, clawing at me.

And nothing.

I was drowning, fearing for my life, sick with terror for my sisters. I was supposed to protect them, save them the way I hadn't been able to save Jules. And now I couldn't, couldn't….

I couldn't breathe. I couldn't find air.

At last, one final wave crashed over me, and blackness dragged me under.

I woke on a small, stiff bed, head aching. Someone had covered me with a thin blanket. The material was scratchy, itchy, with the scent of dust and mold. The stench of old sweat permeated the air. I sat up, chilled as a cold breeze rushed in from above the darkened room of uneven stone-gray walls over three stories high. A circular window was open in the ceiling's center. No Lumerian could reach it without magic, though the window boasted several iron bars humming with power. They blurred the full moon beyond it.

I was underground in the cells of the Shadow Stronghold. They were a series of ancient caves that led miles underground, impossible to escape by design, with both physical and magical locks layered with the Shadows guarding it.

Part of me hoped I'd wake in my own bed, that it would all have been a dream—that my Revelation Ceremony hadn't happened yet. It was a feeling I'd had often the last two years —endless fantasies and daydreams that I'd wake and find Jules alive, Meera and Morgana healthy again. But those never happened.

This wasn't a dream.

I'd been imprisoned. Bound. The black glittering ropes, conjured by Tristan, still wrapped around my body, burning every inch of skin they touched. No matter how I moved my body, or shifted I couldn't find relief. My chest heaved as I felt the ropes cut sharply against me. Tears burned behind my eyes. While my body was feverish and raw where the binding touched, the rest of my skin was cold, shivering. There were Shadows in the walls. I couldn't see them. But I could feel them. Like ghosts.

I stared, afraid I might see one, that a Shadow might jump out to frighten me. Was this the cell Jules had been brought to? Had she woken like this, hot and cold? In pain? Terrified?

I searched for my stave—but that was gone. They would have never imprisoned me with it. I still wore my gown from the evening and my necklace, but neither was sufficient to keep me warm in my cell.

I took a deep breath. I'd already fainted tonight, but now I had to remain calm, to come up with a plan. Someone would enter those doors soon, and I had to be prepared for whomever it was and hold my own. At least I was in Bamaria, not on a boat to Lethea. As long as I remained in my own country, I had a chance of surviving.

Footsteps sounded down the corridor, and I stood, swaying on my feet with dizziness, my head heavy. I could feel them before I saw them, their auras in competition—the four most powerful men in Bamaria.

The Imperator entered the corridor, his black robe bordered in gold ominously floating behind him like a shadow. Limping slowly, my father followed. He looked weak behind the Imperator's strong stride. Next came the red-cloaked arkturi, walking in unison—the Bastardmaker and the Ready.

"How's the prisoner?" the Imperator asked.

My father broke protocol at the last second, rushing toward my cell before I could respond. "Lyriana, are you all right? *Me bat?*" High Lumerian for *my daughter*. He really was scared.

I scanned him, desperate for insight. But all I saw was his fear. Hair I swore had been black an hour ago now looked gray. The lines around his eyes had deepened, and new creases appeared beside his mouth.

Everything ached, and burned, making it hard to focus. I was more terrified than I'd ever been in my life. But I couldn't say that, not in front of the Imperator. I had to play this right. I just wished I knew what to do. Should I look meek? Angry? In agreement with my father? Against him? His face offered no insights, no indication of how to survive. Maybe he didn't know what to do either. He'd saved Meera and Morgana, barely. But he'd lost Jules, lost my mother, and nearly lost himself to the mob. Had he resigned himself to lose me as well?

I took a deep breath. I knew how to play one role well, and I was going to play it perfectly. I stood tall and threw my shoulders back. "My room isn't quite up to the standards of living that I'm accustomed to." I gestured at the ropes tied around me, swallowing a cry as they burned against my skin. "And these don't really match my ensemble."

Amusement shone in the Imperator's dark eyes as he laughed. "She's got spirit, this one."

I wanted to kick him.

"Well, luckily for you, we can remove that aspect of your outfit." He jerked his chin at the Bastardmaker. "Bring him in."

No.

"Tristan," I said as he appeared. His eyes were red, his face blotchy.

"Yes," the Imperator drawled. "He beat down my mage to do the honors. Go on." He used his shoulder to nudge Tristan forward.

Tristan snapped his head at the Imperator, fire in his eyes. His nostrils flared as he turned to me. "I did it so it wouldn't hurt you," he said quietly. "I'll be gentle."

It did hurt, I wanted to cry. *It still hurts.*

He unsheathed his stave and pointed it at me.

My throat tightened, and I closed my eyes, unable to watch. My hands began to shake. He was removing the bind, not attacking me, but fear still spiked in my veins.

Words spilled from his lips, low and full of emotion, and slowly the heat of the ropes around my body faded away. My shoulders slumped forward.

"Stand back," said the Imperator. "She'll prove her vorakh now."

But I didn't. As before, nothing happened. Tristan's jaw tightened.

"I don't have a vorakh," I seethed. "Release me."

"We can't do that," said the Imperator. "Give her grace her stave."

My eyes widened. The Bastardmaker pulled it from his belt and tossed it into the cell with me.

"Pick it up," said the Imperator. "Be ready to bind her again, Lord Tristan."

Teeth clenched at the indignity that my stave had been allowed to touch the floor, I obeyed, grasping it tight in my hand. Nothing happened. I couldn't help it. Tears rolled down my cheeks, burning hot with fear, and utter disappointment.

"Take the stave back, Lord Tristan," the Imperator ordered.

Tristan snapped his head at the Imperator, jaw still clenched, and walked toward the prison bars, but the Imperator clicked his tongue. "Use your stave, idiot."

Cheeks burning, I held out my hand, palm open with my stave resting on top. Tristan looked ready to cry himself as he pointed his stave at me. Mine flew in a rush through the bars into his hand. The Imperator grabbed it.

"We'll be holding this until further notice."

"She doesn't have a vorakh," Tristan said. "We'd know by now. Release her."

"You are dismissed, Lord Tristan."

Tristan remained firm, not moving.

"Lord Tristan," my father said pointedly. "Good night."

"She has no vorakh," Tristan snarled. "I won't rest until she's brought home."

"Be prepared to stay awake a very long time," said the Imperator.

"Lord Tristan," my father said once more, his voice cold, full of warning. It was the voice of the Arkasva, the one Tristan could not disobey.

He turned to me one last time, his head cocked, his neck red, his stance ready to fight. "I am so sorry," he mouthed. Then he nodded, looking away from me, and retreated through the door that closed off my hall. It slammed shut behind him.

Deep breath, deep breath. Don't cry. I was exhausted and scared and humiliated. I wanted Tristan to burst back through the doors and hold me. I wanted to punch through the bars and strangle the Bastardmaker for watching me so closely. I wanted my stave. I wanted my magic. I wanted to go home.

The Imperator's eyes ran up and down my body curiously. "I believe you're hiding a vorakh. There's no other explanation just yet. So you'll remain locked up for now. But, as Heir to the Arkasva, you're being afforded certain privileges—one of which is where you're to remain imprisoned."

"And how long am I to be imprisoned?"

"Until we understand what happened," my father said. "The findings will determine our next step. We've sent for an examiner from Ka Maras in Lethea. He'll evaluate you for power and vorakh and, by the Gods, explain what happened once his ship reaches harbor."

"But I'm not going to Lethea?" I asked carefully.

"No, your grace." Aemon stepped forward. His red cloak had been pinned over the shoulders of his golden armor. The exposed seraphim feathers were sharp as spikes, pressing against the flexed muscles in his arms. He was tense. "We're not sending you away."

Imperator Kormac raised his eyebrows, a gesture that clearly said *Not yet*.

"Ka Maras has an expertise on…non-magical Lumerians," Aemon said carefully.

I bit my lip to stop trembling. There were only two kinds of non-magical Lumerians: those who were under nineteen and hadn't taken part in the Revelation Ceremony and forsworn who'd been stripped. I was neither.

"So Ka Maras is coming to tell you why I have no power?"

"To tell us what power you're hiding," said the Imperator.

"I'm hiding nothing. You've had two opportunities to prove it and couldn't."

My father's eyebrows narrowed, and I took a deep breath, willing my tone to calm and sound even. *Control what they see.*

A memory popped into my head of a day not long after word had reached us of Jules's death. I'd been forbidden from grieving. Pavi, a noble girl from Ka Elys, was going on and on about how we were better off without Jules because of her vorakh. I'd nearly punched her in the face before Arianna had stopped me. She'd warned that if I acted out of anger, I'd reveal my true feelings that I was sympathetic to those with vorakh—a truth I couldn't admit in public.

"Pavi didn't even know her!" I'd shouted.

"Then her words have no weight. Lyriana, no one ever takes offense at a falsehood. Only at truth. Know your truth and own it, and if you do, no circumstances, no event, no person can take that away from you. A gryphon does not shed tears when it's called a seraphim. It knows what it is. Only a seraphim in the mask of a gryphon would be upset— for their truth has been revealed. Never show offense, or you reveal your truth to your enemies. Control what they see, and you control what they think."

A gryphon does not shed tears when it's called a seraphim. If I showed emotion, I'd give myself away.

"Will I be free after I agree to the examination?" I asked calmly.

"I didn't ask you to agree," said the Imperator. "But to follow orders. You may be third in line to the Seat, but I control your fate now. Until such a day when you are cleared of these charges, you'll be under my lock, my guard."

I shivered. The days were still warm, but at night I'd freeze. And I'd just discovered a second item in my room—a small bucket. Nausea at the thought of having to relieve myself in it, to use it without privacy, roiled through me.

"The Senate has agreed to allow you to remain in Cresthaven. Under guard until the examiner arrives," said

Aemon.

"I can stay at home?" I asked, my voice smaller than I liked.

Aemon nodded. "You'd be under house arrest, and there will be a rotation of guards." He paused to pointedly glare at Imperator Kormac.

"Protocol," the Imperator said. "By order of the Senate, I'm afraid."

Order of the Senate? I wasn't that naïve. This was an order from the Imperator. And it was kind. Kind to let me go home instead of force me to wait here.

The Imperator was definitely not kind. He was plotting.

"We can take you home now, Lady Lyriana, if it pleases your grace," Aemon said.

I got a whiff of the blanket again: stale sweat and mold. My eyes fell on the bucket and the indignity it promised. An old stink from some corner of the cell found its way to me, and I nearly gagged. "Who will guard me at Cresthaven?"

"As you are under arrest by me," said the Imperator, "it will be my men, of course."

"Your men?" I asked. "Ka Kormac? Inside Bamaria's fortress?"

The Imperator nodded, and my stomach turned.

That was why he wanted me home. To bring his army inside Cresthaven. It would be a symbolic conquering of Bamaria. If they were already occupying the city, allowing them inside the fortress...I couldn't allow it, I couldn't agree to it.

And even without the symbolic defeat, it put Meera and Morgana in danger. Cresthaven was the only place they were safe because we kept our wing empty—no maids, servants, or sentries of any kind were allowed upstairs. How long before Kormac's men saw Morgana with a headache or heard Meera's screams?

I imagined my bedroom. Large, warm, with beautiful windows full of sunlight in the morning. A balcony I could step onto, a view of the ocean, the rolling waves lulling me to sleep each night. It was private, comfortable, and mine. The carpet on my floor was soft and thick and infinitely more welcoming than the prison bed. And the smell of my room was clean and floral with a hint of incense. Not to mention I had my own private bath made of pristine white marble. I'd do almost anything to be back in my bed. With my sisters. With Tristan, even. My throat tightened at the thought of him walking out of here.

"Well?" The Imperator's black eyes remained expressionless and ever so slowly glanced at the bucket then back to me. Himself to fucking Moriel! He knew my weakness.

"No!" I shouted, afraid I'd change my mind. "I will not be prisoner in my own home, nor will I allow foreign soldiers in our fortress. Cresthaven hasn't been breached in a thousand years. I will not be the reason for it now. I will remain right here."

The Bastardmaker spat. "You think we want your little house?"

I pressed my hands against my hips to keep them from shaking. I had thought of my reasons out of pride. But now that the Bastardmaker had spoken, I knew it in my gut.

The offense was painted across the Bastardmaker's face. He was a soldier, not a politician like his brother, the Imperator. He could not hide his true nature, and all at once he confirmed my suspicions. My imprisonment in Cresthaven was not protocol. Ka Kormac occupied the city, but they'd invade my country if the opportunity presented itself.

"Come now." The Imperator's eyes flicked to the Bastardmaker, whose skin had turned an orangey shade of red. "She's a foolish girl, spouting nonsense. Refusing a generous offer."

But I knew I'd made the right choice, and the look in my father's eyes confirmed it.

"Let it be so," he said, offering the Arkasva's words of finality.

"Then it is done." The Imperator pointedly examined the dank cell.

I involuntarily followed his gaze, and my eyes landed once more on the bucket.

"I will require a change of clothes," I said, affecting my best Heir voice.

"Lyriana," the Imperator addressed me informally, "you're a prisoner, not vacationing in a summer home."

My fists clenched.

"It's fair what she asks," said Aemon. "Especially after the special accommodations offered by the Senate. We have a written request from the Master of Education, Lady Arianna Batavia, to ensure she is comfortable here. As her grace is still enrolled in the University of Bamaria, certain dignities are expected, even if they are not currently being extended to Heirs." He glanced around my cell, wrinkling his nose. "We'll make suitable arrangements for bathing."

I gave him a small smile, so relieved to have him on my side and grateful for Arianna's quick thinking. He winked in response.

"We'll have your things sent at once," my father said.

"We will also provide a privacy curtain," Aemon added, his eyes on the Bastardmaker.

"Only to be drawn when indisposed and a guard is present in the cell," the Imperator said.

Aemon swirled on him. "A female guard. Turion Brenna will create a schedule tonight."

The Imperator snorted, as if this was unnecessary and frivolous, but nodded. "Of course, the Lady Lyriana must uphold her upstanding reputation while in prison. But please do not pull your *best* soturi off duty for such a small task."

"All of my soturi are what I consider the best." Aemon glared at the Imperator, who offered a banal smile. "For tonight, we'll send in the guard we agreed upon."

Guard? Someone from Ka Kormac? Ka Batavia? Not an actual Shadow, I hoped.

"Lyriana," said my father. *"Me bat."*

I could hear the unspoken words. *Be strong.* I nodded, willing no more tears to fall.

The corridor emptied, and I returned to the bed. It was hard against my back, and the blanket itched. My palm stung where Kolaya had cut me, but I refused to move until I heard a single set of footsteps outside my cell. My new guard had arrived. A male.

Fear slithered over me, but I sensed no malice in his aura. I didn't see the silver armor of Ka Kormac nor the gold of Ka Batavia as he stepped out of the shadows. The soturion wore plain black armor and boots. His energy reached me first, not quite cold, but cool.

Rhyan.

CHAPTER NINE

THE BARS CUT shadows across Rhyan's face. Moonlight crowned his head with bronzed curls and silvered the scar slicing through his left eye.

"Look at what trouble you've gotten us into now, partner." He looked up and down the hall. "Not what I expected for the youngest Batavia's Revelation Ceremony." At my silence, he continued, "I saw Lord Grey rushing out of here." He leaned in conspiratorially. "You might not know this, but he seemed quite upset."

"Of course, he's upset," I snapped.

"Personally, I'd avoid assisting in the arrest of my almost-fiancée, but that's me."

"You would be joking at a time like this. *Partner*." I shook my head. "Why the fuck did they send you?"

"Fuck? You must be serious. Well then let me assure you, none of this is a joke to me." He examined his fingernails, flicking off a piece of dirt, and shrugged. "But as to why I'm here? Your father refused a guard from Ka Kormac. The Imperator denied a guard from Ka Batavia—fearing they'd attempt to free you or some other nonsense, since you refused to go home. Luckily, I was a neutral party."

"Right, send the forsworn."

He stiffened, his good eyebrow raised. "This may be a surprise to you, but forsworn these days are quite modern. We actually prefer it when you use our real names. It's Rhyan."

"Then stop calling me 'partner.' It's Lady Lyriana! Or your grace." I shook my head. "Why should I trust what you're saying when you didn't even swear?"

He stalked toward my bars. "Who said you should trust me?" he purred.

"Forget it, talking to you is a waste of breath."

"Because I'm forsworn? Or do you hold some other grudge against me?"

I folded my arms across my chest, shaking. I was suddenly so cold.

"If you don't tell me, I can't apologize or make it right. And if you're just prejudiced against forsworn, then you're like everyone else in the Empire."

I scoffed. "I took you with me today, didn't I? So clearly I'm not prejudiced."

"Aren't you, though?" he asked.

"I'm not!" I snapped. "It's you. You're impossible. You have to make everything so much more difficult. And for the record," I said, voice dripping with sarcasm, "you were a real prince today when I risked everything to pull you out of the street."

"Lady Lyriana," he said slowly, "your grace." He held his hands up in surrender, ducking his head like I was a wild animal. "Just as I'm not a lord, I'm also not a prince."

"If I could throw something at you, I would. Plus, you lied about calling me partner."

He scratched his chin. "If memory serves, you lied. I assume for Lord Grey's delicate feelings. I simply went along with it. You're welcome."

"Forget it. Forget I said anything. It doesn't matter." I turned away.

Rhyan sighed. "If you're so deeply unhappy with this arrangement, perhaps your father can arrange for another soturion to—"

"NO." I whirled back to face him. My eyes locked with his. A sense of panic at the idea of him leaving me alone down here rose violently inside me. I feared who would replace him before Turion Brenna made her schedule. I feared…I feared being by myself, alone with the Shadows. "I want you. No one else."

He seemed taken aback by my outburst, but then his good eyebrow lifted, and his lips curled. "You want me?"

I stepped back, not sure why those words had been the ones to escape my lips. I only knew I couldn't stand for him to walk away. I swallowed, composing myself. "You've already seen me here—it can't be helped," I said, carefully. "I will not allow anyone else to see me in this state."

Rhyan bowed. "As you wish." He stood back, gazing into my cell. "I'll stay."

I collapsed to a seat on the bed and closed my eyes. I needed to think, to try to understand what had happened, and why, and what it would mean. But it was too weird knowing Rhyan was there, watching me. So I stood again, and before I knew it, I was pacing back and forth.

"Every part of your cell will look the same on your hundredth stroll as it did on your fiftieth," Rhyan called.

I kept walking, my feet carrying me faster, back and forth, back and forth. I hit the wall, turned, and hit the one behind me.

"Oh, now look at this tile, I call this color *stone* gray. This exact shade gives it character, but oh, is that a stain! Don't recall that the last time we passed this way." He turned his head and changed the affect in his voice. "Oh really, and when was that?" He turned again, mimicking the voice of the first speaker. "A second ago!"

"Shut up." I continued pacing, hitting the walls, again and again. Every time I reached the end, I slammed my fist into the stone.

"The cell isn't going to get any bigger," Rhyan groaned. "And you're going to break your hand if you keep doing that."

I punched again. "So what?"

"At least wrap your thumb over your fingers, your grace."

"You really love the sound of your voice, don't you?"

"I've been told it's quite lovely in the past," he said, exaggerating his accent. Rhyan rolled his shoulders back, stretching his neck from side to side. "I wasn't kidding. Wrap your thumb around like this, or you will break your hand if you keep punching like that."

I turned away from him and continued pacing, refusing to reply.

"I'm bored," he said.

"At least I'm doing something. Isn't this more entertaining than watching me on the bed?"

He lifted an eyebrow. "Depends on what you're doing on the bed."

"Pig! You wish!"

Rhyan scoffed. "Trust me, my wishes have nothing to do with you and a bed in the Shadow Stronghold."

"So you just prefer me with my back up against trees?" I asked.

He froze, and plucked at his cloak again. "I have no idea what you're talking about."

"Of course not." I turned on my heels, beginning another round. And then another.

"Auriel's bane. You're exhausting. Thumb over your damn fingers!"

"Ugh! Just stop! Stop talking to me. Stop watching me. You know what? Just go! I swear I won't escape. I'm third from the Seat of the Arkasva, and I'm in a fucking prison cell surrounded by Shadows on my birthday. My almost-fiancé— as you like to put it—helped imprison me. And my own father, the Arkasva himself, left me here." I choked on the words as the reality began to sink in. I was moving past shock into fear. "The Imperator should have known my father wouldn't break the law for me."

"You're his daughter." Rhyan's voice sounded sincere for once.

"So? He walked right out of here tonight, leaving me behind bars." He'd had to, I reminded myself. And he *had* broken the law to protect me tonight…just not enough. We'd been caught.

"He loves you. Sometimes that compels action against reason."

I shook my head. "They imprisoned my cousin here two years ago for having visions. My father didn't step in then either. He'd raised her as his own daughter." And then it hit me. The Imperator knew I wouldn't escape—couldn't escape. No one escaped the Shadow Stronghold alive. Not with all its ancient magic and its Shadow guardians haunting the walls. Keeping me in prison wasn't the goal. It was humiliating my father, forcing his hand in his own country—against his own daughter. That was why Rhyan was here—my escape had never been in question.

Rhyan frowned. "The Lady Julianna, you mean?"

I bit my lip, tears welling behind my eyes. "Yes." My voice came as a whisper.

Rhyan took a step forward. "I was sorry to hear when that happened."

I stopped, wanting to laugh and cry at the same time. My heart felt like it was being squeezed too tight. I hadn't expected that. Hadn't expected him—of all people—to be nice. And certainly not about Jules.

"Most tell me to forget her," I said, throat raw. Tristan was among those people. "That I should be glad she's gone."

"Vorakh doesn't make a person who they are. And even if she was...bad, or whatever, she was still your cousin, and you have a right to grieve. But, for the record, she was a good person," Rhyan said quietly. "At least from my interactions with her, she was kind. I'm sorry for your loss."

A sob built deep inside me, one I had to swallow. For years I'd needed to hear that, needed one person to say they were sorry, to remember Jules with me—the way she was.

Two years. Two years had passed since her death, and Rhyan was the first who ever offered me condolences.

I wanted to ask him more—ask him what his every interaction with her had been like and tell him how amazing she'd been, and how much I'd loved her, and how much fun we used to have, and how hard we used to laugh. But the walls around me were closing in. She'd been brought here on this night two years ago, screaming and under the thrall of her vorakh before she'd been bound. How had she felt down here? Had she been scared? Had she been alone? Had she suffered under the Bastardmaker? Had anyone done anything? Stepped in? Cared? I shivered, my chest tightening. I didn't even know the full circumstances of her death, of how exactly she had died, and the not knowing...it ate at me every day.

Bells rang as the timekeeper called the hour. I glanced up, just catching the flash of blue light from ashvan galloping beneath the moon. That was when I realized the moon's position.

It was the middle of the night.

"How many hours since my arrest?" I asked urgently.

Rhyan gazed up, squinting. "Three."

"Three! Is that all? Are you sure?" I asked.

"Is the time not passing quickly enough for you?"

I'd seen my father and Tristan, but not my sisters. Surely if my father could come, they could have, would have...but they hadn't. Panic gripped me over their absence. Perhaps they'd thought it best to go home for appearances...but what if they'd been kept from me? My chest tightened.

"Any other scandals tonight? Was anyone else arrested?" I asked anxiously. Was that why my father had looked so scared?

Rhyan scrunched one eyebrow in confusion. "No. Your sisters were briefly detained for questioning."

"Who took them? Where are they?" I clutched at my chest, the tightness around my heart suffocating.

"They're fine," he said. "Already released, home at Cresthaven. Are...are you all right?"

They were home. Safe at Cresthaven. But for how long? Meera had just had a vision, which put her in a safe window for the next few weeks, but Morgana...she'd need my help, especially after being in such a large crowd. Plus, the examiner was coming from Ka Maras to investigate me. What if they extended the investigation to Meera? To Morgana? Would the Imperator suggest it? Or would Tristan —in some weird attempt to prove our innocence? I thought of all the things I needed to do at home for them and felt the desperate clawing instinct to protect them, to keep my family safe, to not let another member of my household be lost. To do all the things I couldn't do for Jules, that I should have done for Jules. But I couldn't—I couldn't protect them. I couldn't even protect myself. I was here. Like Jules had been. And they were....

I was spiraling. Each breath felt like an unreachable mountaintop, the next cliff too far away. My vision blurred, and the blackness threatened to drown me once more. The cell looked increasingly smaller, the walls unstable, the ceiling lower. I was losing it, losing all sense of reality.

"Your grace?" Rhyan gripped the cell bars. "Lady Lyriana."

I couldn't respond. I clutched my chest, nails digging into my skin. I'd worked so hard to hold it together, to appear strong before the Imperator. But I wasn't strong. I was weak. I was a seraphim barely concealed behind the mask of a gryphon. I'd let Jules die, and now I was here, and I....

"Lyriana!"

Rhyan was calling my name, but I couldn't respond. His voice sounded far away, like there were walls between us. Walls that were crumbling, crashing down on me.

"Auriel's bane. Lyriana!" Rhyan stretched his arm inside my cell. "Take my hand."

The gesture was so at odds with every interaction I'd had with Rhyan, I stared, incredulous. "What?"

"I'm not having you shatter on me. You need something to hold onto. Now, take my hand," he said again.

Take my hand.

Rhyan said the words in my mind. A nineteen-year-old Rhyan standing beneath the starlit sky of the summer solstice, his face unmarked by scars, while music swelled around us.

I hadn't realized I'd taken a crouched position on the ground, my arms like a shield around myself. Shakily, I stood and made my way to the bars. He nodded as I reached for him.

"That's it." His fingers closed around mine, calloused but warm. "I've got you. Deep breath." His other hand lay on top of mine, cocooning, soothing. I squeezed his hands, willing my breaths to slow. "Squeeze as hard as you want," he said. "You won't break me. Good. Look at me. Look!"

Our eyes met.

"I'm going to breathe with you, all right? Inhale...."

I breathed, inhaling on his command and following his exhale. Again and again.

"Good. Inhale…exhale…."

Moments passed slowly as our breathing synced.

"How do you feel?" he asked, watching me carefully.

"I don't know. I…tight in my chest…bad…."

"Panic attacks?" he asked quietly.

I nodded.

"Does this happen a lot?"

"For the last two years. Since…." A shudder ran through me. I couldn't say it. But I could see the understanding in his eyes. Since Jules.

"Right," he said. "Feel my hand."

"What?"

"You need to concentrate on your physical surroundings, small details. It'll help focus you here and now. Tell me what my hand feels like."

"It feels…." I gulped. "W-Warm."

He nodded encouragingly.

I shrank my world down to just my hand in his, the feel of his skin, our fingers entwined, the firm steadiness with which he held me. His other hand, a soothing weight, comforting.

"Rough, calloused."

"Good. Something else now," he said, and I looked up, trying to find another anchor. "More details."

"Your eyes," I said without thinking. "They're so green, like emeralds."

His jaw tightened. "Try another sense. Something else you can feel."

"The…the wind," I said. "I can hear it blowing. Feel it on my back. Cold."

"Good," he said. "Stay with me. You're safe. All right? Your sisters are safe at home, your father, too. Nothing can hurt you right now, Lyr. Nothing. I'm right here."

I didn't know why, but I believed him.

My chest still hurt, but breath came. "Why are you being so nice to me?"

"You'd be pretty boring to guard passed out on the floor, and I forgot to bring a scroll to read." His lips quirked, but the softness never left his eyes. He was trying to distract me. I think...I think he'd been trying to distract me since he arrived.

A long moment passed before I spoke. "Rhyan?"

He leaned his forehead against the bars. "Lyr?"

I exhaled sharply, a tear rolling down my cheek. "I'm scared."

He nodded. "I know." His thumb circled soothingly over my hand. "It'll be all right."

"No, it won't." I shook my head, more tears falling. "I'm not hiding a vorakh," I confessed. "I have no magic. No power."

"Are you sure that's what happened?"

A choked laugh came out. "Do you think I'd be in here if it wasn't? If I'd had a vorakh, it would have been obvious by now, and if I had power, I'd have expressed it and gone home."

"But everyone...." he trailed off, not saying what we both knew to be true. Everyone born of Lumeria had magic, even if one parent did not. The ability was strong; it always, always passed down. He shook his head. "That's not possible."

"These prison cells say differently." The tears escaped, freely flowing down my cheeks.

He flinched watching.

"You don't have to do this," I said. "Why are you really helping me?"

Rhyan pulled back, but I held tight to the fingers entwined with mine, refusing to release his hand. Our eyes met again.

"Please," I said. "Don't go."

His fingers tightened around mine in response. His breath deepened, like he was settling into his spot there before me.

"You didn't answer my question," I said.

Rhyan's jaw clenched, his hold on my hand steadying, though his eyes shifted, glancing nervously around the cell before focusing once more on me. "Because I've been where you are. More or less."

"Imprisoned in your own home?"

"I'll spare you the gory details." The muscles in his jaw tensed. "The cells in Glemaria are...well, they make this place look like a palace."

I shuddered. "When did you become forsworn?"

"A year ago. Right after," Rhyan swallowed, his features hardening, "my mother died."

"I'm sorry."

"You're not going to accuse me of killing her?"

"No."

"You should. That's the reason I was named forsworn. Her death."

"I don't believe that's the truth." Growing up in the court of the Arkasva, I'd seen killers, liars, two-faced courtiers, and worse, like the Bastardmaker. Rhyan wasn't like any of them. Murderers didn't hold your hand and breathe with you through a panic attack.

"You'd be the first." He bit his lip, his free hand rubbing the back of his neck.

We were silent, and the steady rhythm of his breathing mixed with the crackling flames in the corridor until my own came easily and matched his.

"That's new." His eyes darted to my tattoo.

But before he could ask any more about it, there was a commotion in the hall. We both turned, breath sucked in.

He slid his hand away, stepping back from the cell. His fingers lingered an extra second against my skin.

"Sorry," he said.

I folded my arms around myself. I'd somehow forgotten we were still touching—it had seemed natural, as natural as breathing. "No, it's probably best no one sees us like that."

He winked. "They might take away my title of neutral party."

A door at the end of the hall burst open, and Tristan strode through, his stave held high and emanating a white glow to light his path. Thunder rolled off his aura with such force, I swore I saw lightning strike in the corner of my eye. Four Grey escorts followed with staves drawn.

"Are you leading a parade, Lord Grey?" Rhyan leaned against the other side of the hall, as far from my bars as possible, arms crossed and one knee bent with his foot resting against the wall like he'd been there all along. How had he moved so fast?

"Shut your mouth, forsworn." Tristan swept past Rhyan to my cell. He jerked his chin at his escorts, and two approached Rhyan, staves aimed at his throat.

I froze, chest heaving. "What's happened?" I asked.

"Seriously," Rhyan said, "you don't need to point so close. Just doing my job."

The escorts sneered.

"Lyr, stand back from the bars. We have one minute before the Shadows come," Tristan said. "I paid them to close their eyes." The remaining two escorts flanked him.

"What? Tristan!"

He began to chant, his stave glowing blue. These cells were well protected; I didn't believe he'd actually succeed. But what if he did? Where would we go? What would we do?

What would happen to Meera and Morgana? I couldn't leave them behind. I couldn't run.

I shook my head, my eyes filling with tears. "Tristan, no."

"Lyr, I'm almost there—just hang on." And indeed, the lock was starting to grind, the metal pushing against itself, his power fighting through the magic. His face was red from exertion. Something clicked. The first level unlocked, but there were more. The walls seemed to breathe behind me, the

Shadows growing restless. But Tristan sent out a blast of light that hushed them.

By the Gods. He was going to do it. He was going to get me out of here.

"Come on," he muttered, twisting his wrist, his arm shaking as he pushed more magic through.

I looked to Rhyan, my expression pleading, desperate. He had to help me. He had to save me—by keeping me in prison. Of all things.

If I left, the Imperator would search for me. He'd turn his eye on Meera and Morgana. Even if I got to safety, I'd never let that happen. I'd never let them be exposed.

Please, I thought, staring past Tristan to Rhyan, still against the wall. *Stop him!*

Rhyan's eyes met mine, his jaw tensed.

I pleaded, desperate for him to understand. *Don't let Tristan take me.*

One eyebrow lifted as he frowned, asking if I was sure. I could barely move for fear Tristan would notice and gave Rhyan the barest of nods.

And then, just like that, he spun into action. Silent. Deadly. He moved so fast, I couldn't make out what body parts had gone where. One second, Tristan's escorts were holding their staves to his throat, and the next, they were both flat on their backs, unconscious.

He raced for the two by Tristan's side.

One saw Rhyan first. He whirled on his heels, his stave already emanating magic—magic he turned on Rhyan, wrapping it around his body. Grunting, Rhyan burst through it as though the magic were a flimsy piece of parchment. The escort joined the others on the ground.

Only then did Tristan realize what was happening.

"I will end you," Tristan seethed.

Rhyan only smirked, even as Tristan raised his stave in time with his final escort, both ends pointed at Rhyan. A thunderous blast shot forth, the magic from the two staves joining and entwining, creating a hurricane-like gust of wind. Rhyan ducked and rolled. Lightning flashed, and there was a scream and a grunt of pain. When the light returned, the final escort lay unconscious.

Tristan leapt back, snarling at Rhyan, who ran for him, dodging each burst of power that shot from Tristan's stave until they collided. Rhyan knocked Tristan's stave from his hand before pushing him to the ground.

"No!" I yelled. "Don't hurt him!"

The lights flickered again as they rolled, kicking and punching at each other. Rhyan swore.

"Tristan!" I screamed. The hall had gone black. His time was up. The Shadows were coming. "You have to go! Now!"

"If you hurt her...," Tristan snarled.

"Tristan! They're coming," I said.

The room grew cold, and I could feel them hissing puffs of ice at my back. The Shadows. They pulsed in the walls, breaking through, sweeping past me in cold rushes, brushing against my chilled skin. I clutched my chest, terror rising inside. My teeth chattered. There were more grunts of pain, and then a door swung open and slammed shut.

The torchlights in the hall flickered back to life. I was alone again with only Rhyan outside my cell.

"Lyr? You all right?" he asked, straightening his green cloak back over his shoulder.

I burst into tears in response. "Fine. Did they hurt you?"

"No." Swallowing, he approached the bars.

I shivered. I'd never actually seen the Shadows in action; they were more frightening than I'd anticipated. "Do you think he's hurt?"

Rhyan shrugged. "He paid his minute. I'm sure management wouldn't risk harming a potential repeat customer. He almost pulled it off. Impressive for what must have been some half-cocked plan." His eyes met mine. "You didn't want to be rescued, partner?"

My heart squeezed, my lip trembling. "I have my reasons."

His jaw tightened in response.

"Please," I said, "don't tell anyone."

Rhyan lifted an eyebrow. "I was just doing what the Arkasva and Imperator commanded."

"Thank you," I said, voice rough.

"You should get some sleep. Before any other excitement barrels through these doors."

"I can't."

"Sleep. It's been a long day. You're not going to be able to feel better unless you get some rest. I'll be right here. You won't be able to get out, I promise. And no one else can get in."

I swallowed. "Won't you be bored?"

Rhyan's lips quirked. "Terribly. I'll be counting down the hours until you wake and can entertain me again with your pacing and poorly formed wall punches." Then, more seriously, he said, "For what it's worth, you chose bravely tonight. Most Lumerians would have gone home in an instant, charming as these caves are." He wiped dust off the wall and frowned. "Or when their almost-fiancé so gallantly pays their way in here." His eyes searched mine. "I know I didn't swear to your father tonight. But your Ka has given me shelter. And while I remain, I swear, no harm will come to you. Not just here." He gestured around the Stronghold. "But anywhere in Lumeria. If I'm there, you're safe. I swear it." He pressed his fist against his heart, tapping it twice before he flattened his palm over his chest.

"I thought you said not to trust you."

Rhyan paused, his posture stiff before he retreated from my bars, stationing himself on the other side of the hall. "I said no one told you to trust me." His nostrils flared. "Now lay down." He gave me a small smile. "Don't worry about me. I'll manage the night without your charming conversation. I'll count floor tiles."

I stared at the high ceiling, listening for the steady rhythm of Rhyan's breathing. I couldn't process anything else: that Tristan had tried to rescue me; that I was here; that Rhyan had intervened. I squeezed my eyes shut until all thoughts left.

"Arrest her!" The Imperator stormed up the dais of Auriel's Chamber, his mage snaking behind him, casting the binding over Jules.

The Bastardmaker hauled her over his shoulders, his grubby hands pushing up her dress, exposing her bare legs.

I stood in my chair, screaming as Tristan grabbed my waist, holding me back. Aunt Arianna watched from a distance, her blue eyes devoid of feeling.

"Let me go! I have to save her! Let me go!" I beat at Tristan's chest, but he wouldn't move. His brown eyes were cruel, blackening, until I saw it was the Imperator who held me, his lips curled into a snarl, canines elongating like a wolf's.

"Asherah," he hissed. "We'll have our way with you yet."

I screamed for help, but everyone in the temple sat busily staring at their scrolls, not noticing that the Imperator was trying to steal me away or that the Bastardmaker had Jules. My father seemed to be asleep on his chair, his Laurel askew.

I twisted away from the Imperator, wrenching myself against his arms. The Bastardmaker was nearly at the door, his red cloak swinging out behind him. Jules's dress lay discarded on the floor of the temple. But Jules was gone. In the Bastardmaker's arms was Meera. Her diadem fell to the floor, smashing into a thousand pieces, and then Morgana appeared in his arms.

And then me. I was screaming. I knew I was screaming, I could feel the vibration, the anguished rage rising inside of me, but no sound came out. I had no mouth. Only a black hole. I was trapped in Meera's painting. Tristan pointed his stave at me, his face full of menace.

"I'm sorry, Lyr. I have to do this. It has to be me."

No!

The Bastardmaker threw me on the floor, his body pressing over mine.

"Lyr!"

I bolted upright on my cot, my hair coated to my cheek in sweat. Rhyan was wide awake, sitting up against my prison bars, his arm stretched all the way inside. His gaze rolled over me as I stirred, halting when he met my eyes, one brow lifted in question.

I looked down, only then noticing his hand wrapped around mine.

I lay back down, feeling the scratchiness of the blanket over my arms, the rush of cool air as I pulled my hair back from my face, and Rhyan's eyes, bright and emerald, watching me. Our eyes locked, holding each other in silence. Our hands still touching through the bars.

"I'm here," he said again, squeezing my hand. "Sleep."

My lids finally closed. Only then did I hear him shift, though his hand remained in mine.

CHAPTER TEN

DAYS PASSED, DREARY, endless, full of seemingly impossible moments to survive. Nights were worse—longer, restless, and what little sleep I managed came with disturbing dreams. The Imperator ordering me to be arrested. The Bastardmaker taking me. Taking Jules. Taking my sisters.

My only entertainment was to pace my cell and practice making a proper fist. Rhyan hadn't been on duty when I'd awoken that first morning, and every guard I'd had since had been silent, refusing to speak to me beyond basic grunts if I needed to use the bathing room to relieve myself. No one else came to visit, not even my father. And so I paced. And I punched. For days.

The seventh morning I woke in prison, Turion Brenna took over guard duty. She'd come into my cell with me, the first of my guards to do so. Word had come that the examiner had arrived. When the timekeeper called for late afternoon, a message came through her vadati stone, glowing blue in her palm. She nodded toward the corridor's entrance. "They're ready for you, your grace."

My throat tightened. "Do you know what will happen?" I asked.

"The examiner will explain. I'll fix your hair." She sat behind me, gathering my locks into a braid.

Brenna had coarse black hair she wore in a regulation soturion braid down her back. I could feel from her sectioning that she was creating a similar style for me.

I tried to relax into the soothing feeling of having my hair brushed and braided, but my stomach was twisting. "Should I be worried you didn't answer my question?"

Brenna gathered another section of my hair, her fingers working the braid tightly against my scalp. "I've heard stories, your grace, but I can't say for sure." It was a bad sign when my father's Master of Peace was lying to me.

My eyes closed, and I tried not to lean too much into her touch. She was my first human contact in a week. My last touch had been Rhyan, holding my hand. She sealed off the braid and patted my back.

Footsteps pounded against stone, and the doors creaked open, revealing my father, the Ready, Imperator Kormac, and the Bastardmaker. The last to enter was the examiner from Ka Maras. The only way to describe him was in triangles. Black pointed eyebrows loomed over a sharp triangular nose. His mustache fell below his lips in a long upside-down V, and his black beard tapered to a sharp point.

I stood as the men approached, my father moving slowly with his limp. The examiner nodded at Brenna. She unlocked my cell, and he stepped inside. The bars clanged, echoing down the corridor, as she sealed the two of us within.

"I am Kunda Lith, the examiner. Lie down." Kunda carried a large black box and set it down in the center of my cell. He watched me intently with a hungry look in his eyes as his aura pulsed with a slippery, slimy energy: curious and invasive. He wasn't standing close to me, but the bars of my prison were suddenly too near, the cell too small.

I shook the feeling off, and my eyes landed on the box. "What's that for?"

"Remove your dress and lie down."

"Father!" I turned, nearly reaching through the bars for his hand like I was a child.

"Kunda?" my father asked. "Is undressing necessary?"

The examiner coughed. "It's protocol. I need to be able to see the exam process thoroughly. Otherwise, if there's a mistake, it will have to be repeated." He clicked the box open, and I heard movement, like skin sliding against skin over a quiet hiss.

I remained focused on the box. What in Lumeria was inside?

"Remove your dress," he repeated.

"N-No." My breath was starting to shorten.

The Imperator's lips twitched, but I turned to my father and Aemon. "I will not undress without my privacy curtain drawn. And I demand a female escort present. Why isn't Arianna here? She would serve as a proper escort."

It had been a week since I'd seen her. I missed her. And I hoped I could buy myself some time while they went to get her.

"Your father is here to ensure you are treated fairly," the Imperator said. "There's no reason to make this an extended affair. As Master of Education, your aunt is otherwise occupied."

"Then Turion Brenna remains with me." I would not submit otherwise.

"This is beneath the Master of Peace." The Imperator's black eyes flared.

"It would be my honor to stay with her grace," Brenna said quickly.

I shot her a grateful smile, but the Imperator frowned.

"And with the curtain drawn, how may we be sure the examination is not cheated in some way?"

Kunda sneered, deepening the triangular shape of his mustache to a point. "Are you saying you do not trust Ka

Maras, who has perfected the art form since before the Drowning?"

Imperator Kormac's nostrils flared as he stepped back.

"Let it be so." My father waved. He shot a quick look at Brenna, telling her to remain by my side before she locked the cell and closed my curtain.

The thick black material cast the walls in black shadows. It had been dark and stormy all morning, with little light coming through the ceiling. At least the examiner would have less light with which to stare.

My hands shaking, Brenna helped me undress. My gown slipped to the floor, a puddle around my feet. I stood practically naked in a thin shift covering my breasts to the tops of my thighs. Beneath that my underclothes, thankfully secured around my waist, gave me an extra layer of dignity. For now.

Kunda looked at me with hunger, but it was different from what I'd seen before on men and women when they watched me. He wasn't interested in my body sexually. Kunda the examiner was excited over what he was about to do. I was something new for him, something mysterious—a fully grown Lumerian who'd been unbound and still had no magic power. He'd never seen anything like me before; this excited him.

He bent low, uttering soft, soothing sounds as he removed the contents of the box.

Nahashim. Two of them. I should have known. The sigil for Ka Maras was two undulating nahashim, but I had not prepared for the shock of seeing them in person. These were creatures of the old world, Lumeria Matavia, one of the few species to survive the Drowning along with the seraphim, ashvan, and gryphons. The nahashim were thin as the parchment for scrolls, their scaly skin black and shiny. They had the ability to find anything one was looking for and lived exclusively on the island of Lethea, where they were bred by Ka Maras.

The nahashim's slippery bodies stretched and curled in the examiner's hands as he approached. They shifted from the size of a thumb to the length of an arm, slithering around him, expanding and contracting in length, like deep inhales and exhales.

The examiner eyed my undergarments, what remained of my dignity. I reached beneath my breasts for the fastenings of my nearly sheer shift. My stomach twisted, but Kunda shook his head.

"You may keep those on. Lie down."

I did, staring at the ceiling, willing myself not to panic. But the nahashim were hissing, and I was lying on a bed before a strange man in my undergarments.

This was a procedure, I told myself. It was simple, and it would be over soon. I repeated these thoughts in my mind like a prayer. *It's only a procedure. It will be over soon.*

"The nahashim will go through you, searching for any sign of magic," he said.

I froze. "Through me?"

His eyes lit up. "Magic exists in physical form within the body. Inside your muscles and bones. It's why you feel like crawling out of your skin when you're bound, why stripping almost always kills. The magic must be extracted from every inch of the flesh, and the process—painful, yes—causes organs to shift from each other. I am close to finding a method that will allow the Lumerian to live, though I can't yet deny the pain." He looked proud of his achievement.

My mind had latched onto one thing. "Is there…a chance I could die?"

"No," Kunda said. "We're not removing anything, only hoping to find what is or is not there." His eyes turned into snake-like slits to match his nahashim. "They so rarely get to search for magic. So few come in such a state." He spoke dreamily. "Relax."

With effort, I unclenched my fists. "Is this painful?"

The examiner smiled. Even his lips had sharp edges.

The black nahashim's bodies were pulsating, and their hisses came more rapidly as their bodies lengthened and retracted—excited, eager to begin.

My stomach twisted as Kunda sat beside me, the nahashim vibrating in his hands. His face came within inches of mine, his eyes moving rapidly as he placed the nahashim on my face, one on each cheek.

I sucked in my breath and squeezed my eyes shut. Their scales were surprisingly hot, almost burning. My hands clenched again. The nahashim were scalding my skin as though I were holding my face over an open flame.

"Why are they so hot?" I was beginning to sweat.

"Open your eyes," Kunda said.

"No." I didn't want the nahashim anywhere near my eyes. I wanted them off my face, out of my cell, back in their box, and on a ship to Lethea.

"They're hurting her," Brenna said.

"They do that," Kunda said. "Once your eyes open, they'll begin. It won't take long."

My breath came in quick hot spurts, and I kept my lips screwed shut, fearful they'd slip into my mouth. *Stay calm, stay calm, stay calm....*

But when I felt Kunda pull my shift up to my chest— without warning—exposing the length of my stomach, my eyes flew open in surprise. The nahashim lifted their paper-thin heads, and with sharp hisses, dove between my eyelids, slipping in.

Everything went black as fiery tears welled. The burning sensation moved, traveling down my cheeks to my neck. But the fire wasn't on my neck.

It was inside. The nahashim were inside of me, sliding, slithering, and hissing past my throat. I sat up on my elbows and screamed. My skin was translucent against their dark bodies stretching and slithering in every direction. Every place they moved within burned, and my skin outside turned black.

I cried out in pain. I couldn't stop myself.

"What's happening?" my father called. "Kunda!"

"We are nearly finished with the first stage of the process," he said.

Two black marks slid down my chest, their bodies disappearing beneath my shift, inside my breasts. I could feel them descend deeper, wrapping around my heart, squeezing, burning, casting their shadow over it.

"Please," I said. "Get them out. Get them out. Gods! I can't stand it!"

"Not much longer." The examiner's eyes watched as they slid from my heart to my belly, sliding down my torso and curving around my back, until they moved between my legs.

I threw my head back and clenched my teeth as the burning moved lower and lower, intensifying. I lost control, whimpering and sobbing, pleading for it to be over.

As their heat singed my toes, I clenched my teeth. "Is it done?" They'd passed through my entire body, so now it was time to leave. He could cut off my feet for all I cared—so long as he took them out.

"They must search deeper," Kunda said.

"Deeper?" They slid further inside me, into my muscles. I imagined their slim, burning bodies wrapping around my bones.

I closed my eyes, my entire body shaking, raw and burnt as they continued moving inside of me. I tried to breathe, to stay calm, but my next breath turned into a keening wail.

"They'll exit now," Kunda said.

I opened my eyes as wide as I could, chest heaving.

The examiner shook his head, and it was only then I saw his eyes were glowing blue. The blue of Lumerian magic. "Not through there."

I started to ask where, but my answer came swiftly.

The nahashim hissed, making my throat rumble and burn as they slithered onto my tongue. I gagged as the examiner pulled them from my lips. He quickly rolled me to my side just before I threw up all over the stone floor.

"Help her," Kunda told Brenna. He shoved a glass of water into my hand as I sat up. "Drink."

I took a sip, my throat scratchy and irritated. Kunda held the nahashim in his palm, staring at them intently, before he replaced them in his black box, his eyes returning to their natural, darkened color.

"Wha—" I coughed, my throat still too dry to speak. I was ready to throw up a second time, but I had to know. "What did they find?"

The examiner was no longer paying attention to me. His job was done, and he turned to Brenna. "Turion, I'll need you to release me. Help her grace dress and offer moonleaves. The burning and the dryness will cool by evening." He bowed. "Your grace." The hungry look in his eyes returned as he carefully locked the box. "This was fascinating. I must speak to your Arkasva and the Imperator."

"Wait!" I reached an arm helplessly, as if I could stop him, force him to tell me what they'd seen and what it meant. What was wrong with me? Was I safe? Had this implicated my sisters in any way?

My heart pounded as the men exited the Stronghold, leaving me alone and in the dark once more. I rolled onto my side, my stomach roiling as I heaved and vomited.

Brenna helped me dress, and I sipped slowly on water, followed by tea treated with cured moonleaves. Everything ached. Every breath and every movement shot pain through my limbs. I waited, slumped over, Brenna standing guard outside. An hour passed, then another. The timekeeper rang the bells calling midday, and as the final ring faded, Aemon returned.

"Lady Lyriana," he said, "come with me."

"Where are we going?" I asked.

"To hear the Imperator's verdict."

"You can't say more than that?"

Aemon shook his head slowly. "Come, your grace."

I stepped into my sandals, though I couldn't bend over to lace them and needed Brenna's assistance again. I took Ramia's necklace, which had been sitting on the night table since my arrest, and clasped it around my neck. My chest ached when the metal made contact, but the coolness of the piece soothed my burning skin. My diadem had been with me since my imprisonment, and Brenna helped arrange it over my forehead.

For the first time in a week, I stepped outside just as the sun emerged from the storm, fiercely retaking its reign in the sky.

"There's the red again," Brenna said. "Batavia red." She tugged at my braid, bathed now in sunlight. "I think of your mother, *Ha Ka Mokan*, every time you're in the sun."

"Her soul freed," I said, throat still dry. I tried to smile, knowing she meant to be kind, but my stomach sank. I'd always thought the red meant something special, that the color gave me some deeper connection to my mother, to my bloodline. I thought it meant I was destined to be powerful like her and my ancestors. It meant nothing.

Brenna, Aemon, and I arrived at a seraphim port. The giant bird lay on its belly, its bright blue carriage doors open. Brenna helped me inside, and then we were launching into the sky and soaring over Bamaria across the city of Urtavia to the Temple of Dawn. We approached the nearest entrance through the red ray, and the Red Watcher of the Light stood waiting to bring us to Auriel's Chamber in the Temple's center.

Aemon stepped onto the stage, his expression darkening, and all at once, he was the Ready, the deadliest warlord in Lumeria. My father sat on his Seat of power, his golden wreath around his head, his black Arkasva robes elegantly falling to his sandals. Arkmage Kolaya and Aunt Arianna stood on either side of him. Arianna's eyes lit up when she saw me, her arms lifting as if she meant to wrap me up in them. But she neatly folded her hands before her waist.

Walking up onto the dais from behind was the Bastardmaker and then the Imperator.

"At last," he drawled.

CHAPTER ELEVEN

I SANK TO the ground, meaning to curtsy, but I didn't have the strength to hold myself up. Instead, my knees hit the floor in a blindingly painful smack.

Turion Brenna bowed low beside me. The sun danced patterns of color and light on the floor as she reached for my arm and helped me to stand. My legs shook with the effort, my feet wobbling forward.

The eternal flame crackled, appearing white over Imperator Kormac's blonde hair. He leaned forward, his chair creaking beneath him. "Already falling to your knees?" he asked with a smirk. "Before I pass judgment?"

"Your highness," I said, through gritted teeth. I could feel his aura clawing at the walls, lupine, feral, ready to strike.

"Arkmage Kolaya confirms the Birth Bind has been removed," he said. "Which means your power is unbound, and yet you failed to produce any signs. Considering the taint in your bloodline of vorakh, we had reasonable suspicion to believe you were concealing your magic." His eyes flicked toward my father, accusation in his expression. "Or you had someone concealing your vorakh for you. But we now have the results from Ka Maras. I witnessed the findings of the nahashim's search myself. And it has been concluded that you have no power."

I bit my lower lip. The urge to cry was overwhelming. I'd known this for a week and had been unable to think of anything else, but hearing it now from the Imperator's mouth made it somehow more real. I realized what I was about to lose. My body numbed. The truth seemed to come like the rising tides, flowing again and again.

"Don't look so sad, Lady Lyriana," he crooned. "All the charges against you have been dropped."

"Is there…any explanation?" I asked. "Could anything have affected me to cause this?"

"Nothing more than an anomaly," said the Imperator.

Something broke inside of me. I was an anomaly. Powerless. Weak. A failure.

"And this ends the investigation?" I asked, my heart breaking. I wanted him to say no, say they'd find the reason, fix this. And, I needed him to say yes. To know his eyes were no longer on my family. On my sisters.

"Yes," he said. "We're done."

I swallowed, pushing back tears. "Am I free to go?" I asked, my voice so much smaller than it had ever been.

"That is where things become complicated," he said. His lips turned up, his mouth feral with delight. "Now what happens to you?" he asked, tapping his chin. "Well, that depends on what we all decide here. Lady Arianna, I believe this brings us to your role in all of this."

My heart pounded as Arianna stepped forward, face solemn.

"Lyriana, my dear. I'm so sorry this happened to you."

I bit my lower lip again, sure I was going to start crying.

"I've thought this through a hundred ways, over and over. But without magic, it's impossible for you to attend the Mage Academy. There is not one single course of study that can be completed without it." She wrung her hands together and shook her head, looking near tears. "Lady Lyriana Batavia, as Master of Education on the Council serving Arkasva Batavia, High Lord of Bamaria, and the University of Bamaria...." Sorrow filled her eyes.

"No, Arianna...." My voice came out in a strangled whisper.

"You are hereby expelled," she said.

"Arianna, don't...."

She removed a stave from her belt. My stave. My name flashed in a brilliant shade of gold along the light and dark moon and sun wood twining together. "Forgive me, Lyr." She sniffled. "I have no choice." Arianna snapped the stave in half.

"NO!" I reached forward, desperate to grab it. But I was too late.

She handed the destroyed halves to the Red Watcher, revealing a clean break—Lyriana on one side, Batavia on the other.

The Watcher gently placed them in my hands. Worthless now. Just pieces of wood.

My fingers curled around them so tightly the halves dug into my palms.

I'd spent two years worried about what kind of power I might have, which vorakh might plague my family next. The idea that I'd have none had never occurred to me. It had never happened before. The ability to use magic always passed down with Lumerian blood. Always. Even bastards born of human mothers had magic, and I was no bastard. I was the daughter of two Arkasvim. I should have been amongst the most powerful.

I took a deep breath, dizzy. "If I'm not to become a mage, what becomes of me?"

The Bastardmaker's beady eyes wandered up and down my body like he had some ideas.

The Imperator stepped forward. "I am sorry to say, Lady Lyriana, but the law of the Empire states that Lumerians who cannot function in our society cannot remain within."

My body felt hollow. Surely, he couldn't mean...they would not take me from Bamaria? From my home? My country? My father's eyes were red, his mouth open in grief.

"According to Lumerian law," the Imperator said, "adult Lumerians, those who have reached the age of nineteen, having completed the Revelation Ceremony but living without power, must be banished."

"That law applies to criminals stripped of their magic." My father gripped his Seat, his knuckles turning white.

"It applies to anyone without magic," said the Imperator. "It just so happens that it's only been practiced for criminals who've been stripped of their power. But the law is the law. The language makes it clear. It applies."

I squeezed my eyes shut, trying desperately to picture the scrolls I'd read on Lumerian law. All of my research had been on vorakh powers, on every law concerning them, on any loopholes I could use if my sisters were ever caught. But I couldn't recall anything on this ruling. It was so hardly used. Stripping was amongst the most severe punishments in the Empire. Most who were exiled were simply forsworn— maintaining their magic but forbidden from crossing back into our borders.

"It's a gross application of the law." My father's voice rose, red rising up his neck. "Consider what you're doing and to whom."

"I am considering, and it is a fair application," the Imperator said calmly. "We abandoned the kings and queens of old who had one rule for themselves and another for their subjects. Lumeria Matavia sank under such leadership. Ka Azria broke the rules, and they suffered as any other Lumerian would have. You will get no exceptions from me. I have always ruled fairly across the Southern Empire."

My breath came up short. The mention of Ka Azria, here, now, and the idea of the Imperator being fair.... I sucked at the air, grasping for my next breath.

"We can arrange for her to travel to another country out of the Empire—one of her choice—and we will happily provide her enough money to settle into a new home," the Imperator said. "The Senate is willing to be charitable here. But after that, I'm afraid, you will no longer be considered a Lumerian or welcome to communicate or visit."

My breath left me at that, and I stumbled back, my hands searching for a pew or wall, something to hold onto, to keep me from falling over. The cruelty of it, the unfairness. I was no criminal, no threat to the Empire. And he knew it. This was a power play designed to hurt my father. To weaken Ka Batavia and our claim to the Seat.

My breath hitched, and I focused on my broken stave, its gold and silver colors, the smoothness of it in my hands, the shallow but fresh scent of the trees it had come from, desperately trying to stay present and not faint.

How could I be sent away from my home? From Tristan? My family? My future? They might as well have sentenced me to death. My heart was shattering, splitting open and spilling its contents out.

And as it did, one small secret came to light. A secret truth that had settled deep inside my heart amidst the darkest of nights, tucked out of sight and locked tightly away.

One day, I would be Arkasva Lyriana Batavia, High Lady of Bamaria. Meera couldn't rule, not with her vorakh. Neither could Morgana. We all knew it, even if we never dared speak it aloud. And on the day Meera was named Arkasva Batavia, the day she was set to take the Seat of power and place the Laurel of the Arkasva on her head, she'd abdicate and step down. To me. The third daughter.

The secret I'd held onto for so long was this: I wished for it. I desired and longed to rule with all my heart. I loved

Bamaria. I loved our people, history, and traditions. I wanted to take the Seat like my mother had. I wanted to replace my diadem with the Laurel, to name my Second, to rule and preside over society, to improve it with a voice on the Bamarian Council. I wanted all of it.

But that future was slipping away.

A Watcher of the light shifted her position. The Bastardmaker coughed. I pressed my hands against my hips. A stream of light through the colorful temple windows cast a rainbow of color onto the floor. Dust particles danced in the streaming light. My left arm itched. Small details. Stay present. Keep breathing.

"Please," I said, blinking back tears. My voice broke, and with my throat still so dry, I wasn't sure anyone had heard me. Maybe my dreams were lost, but if I could buy myself time, if I could find a way to stay, I could find out more. Maybe change things. I'd found a way to manage Meera's symptoms when I'd been told it wasn't possible. I'd discovered ways for Morgana to find pain relief when her vorakh was supposed to cause constant suffering. Who was to say I couldn't find some answers for myself? I could do research, see if the library had any information or scrolls that had been overlooked or not considered since circumstances like mine had never happened before.

"Please don't send me away. I...I'll do anything. Renounce my title, my home...." I nearly choked on the words. I had to abdicate my dreams, to do whatever it took to stay. Not just for me. "Please, your highness. Let me stay with my family."

"The law is the law, and it applies to every child of the Empire."

The Ready's hand snaked toward his sword, and my eyes caught the hilt of his ceremonial dagger tucked into a small black leather scabbard and glinting from the sunlight streaming through the windows. If I'd chosen the soturion path, what would they have done? How would Arianna have destroyed my blade? Melted it down?

I'd never touched a dagger before, or a sword.

But I could.

I'd been expelled from the Mage Academy because I couldn't use a stave. But I didn't need magic to lift a sword or fight. Blades cut flesh whether their owner possessed magic or not. Akadim didn't respond to magic. All Lumerians had magic, but not all used it on a daily basis for spells or work. Some kept it contained in their bodies. They trained and channeled that force into becoming warriors.

I stared at my palms, at the freshly healing scar. Right for mages, left for soturi. I glanced up to see Aemon watching me closely.

"I understand the law, your highness," I said. "Without magic, I cannot be a mage. I cannot contribute to society in that way. But I believe there's another option." I swallowed. "I could become a soturion."

Aemon's eyes brightened, his lips curving into a smile, and I knew I'd stumbled on my answer. He shared a quick look with my father, who breathed a sigh of relief.

"A soturion?" the Imperator guffawed. "You? A girl without magic? Do you even realize what soturi do, girl?"

"I grew up with them in the halls of Cresthaven," I said, lifting my chin. "They've trained in my backyard and shadowed my every step. No magic is needed to throw a punch." Rhyan had even given me a start on how to give one.

"It is not as simple as that," Aemon said, but he gave me a conspiratorial grin.

I continued, "Soturi fight akadim, the one thing in our world impervious to magic."

"We have already reached our verdict." The Imperator turned the full force of his anger toward me. He was a trained soturion, and even through his robes and armor, I could see the powerful muscle covering his body, muscles that had been empowered and enhanced with magic. "Now you're just encouraging the fantasies of a delusional child." His voice grew cold. "My son and future soturi are enrolled in this Academy because of its esteem."

The Ready snarled. "Your soturi come here because they need our proximity to the ocean for proper training. You rely on our magic, on our source. It's the folly of your people who retreated too far into the hills! Too far from the water."

The one weakness in Lumerian magic: the farther one went from the Lumerian Ocean, the weaker their magic became, and the harder it was to draw on. It was the one reason why our Empire had not conquered the entire human world.

"Even so," the Imperator drawled, "even our weakest warrior on the outskirts of the Empire outmatches her on his worst day. Look at her. Just because she's wearing her hair like a soturion doesn't mean she can be one."

I self-consciously felt the braid Brenna had created for me.

"Can you imagine her taking on one soturion?" the Imperator asked. "Forget five. She'd be slaughtered."

All at once, my plan seemed childish. I took a step back, but the Ready gave me a look that ordered me to stand tall, not to back down. He was on my side. Knowing that, hope surged. If the most powerful warrior in the Empire supported me, that had to mean it was possible, had to mean this could work.

Aemon gave me a small nod. "At this moment, without training? No," he said carefully, looking to the Imperator. "I wouldn't expect her grace to perform well in a fight."

"But you're considering it! You'd let the standards sink so low, Aemon?" the Imperator spat. "This is what the Soturion Academy of the esteemed University of Bamaria has become? Little girls playing dress up as soldiers? Enough. She's been found without magic, without the ability to attend either Academy properly. The law is the law. She goes."

"The law says a Lumerian over the age of nineteen, having taken part in the Revelation Ceremony without magic, is to be banished," Aemon said. "But we all know the legal interpretation is a Lumerian who has been stripped of their magic, punished for being a disruption to society, unable to contribute to it. Lady Lyriana is neither. She may be able to attend the Soturion Academy, in which case she would be contributing. We are still the country of education and I won't have an ignorant, base reading of the law determine her future over its true meaning as interpreted by actual legal Scholars."

"You're playing a dangerous game," the Imperator sneered.

"Life is a dangerous game." Aemon looked me up and down, his expression studious, before his eyes softened, and he nodded. "We can come to an arrangement, I believe. One that would satisfy the law and not tear an innocent girl away from her home and country."

The Imperator folded his arms across his chest, his muscles rippling. He leaned his weight back onto his heels, his expression full of derision.

"Lady Lyriana, your grace, you must understand what you are agreeing to first," Aemon said, offering a quiet nod to my father.

The Imperator's eyebrows narrowed into slits. "She will always be at a disadvantage."

"Everyone has one disadvantage or another," Aemon said pointedly. "Hers is only more visible to the naked eye. Lady Lyriana, please know that if you say yes, there will be no exceptions, none at all. This should satisfy not only the law, but also our Imperator. If you are willing to do anything to stay, even going so far as to become a soturion, then that is a strength I am willing to bet on. I am willing to make you an offer."

I nodded, pressing my hands together to keep them from shaking.

"A girl without power will become a soldier? A girl without an ounce of strength when we are at war with the akadim? When the demons move closer to our borders in greater numbers every year," the Imperator said. "Do you think she'll be able to kill one? To defend herself? Do you hear how this sounds? We can't afford such weakness in this fight."

"No," I said. "You're right. I'm not a warrior. But I have two arms, two legs. Just like you." I turned my gaze to Aemon. "My feet can run, my muscles will build stamina. My hands can learn to hold a sword, and my arms will strengthen to withstand its weight. Give me time. My strength will grow."

Aemon narrowed his eyes. "Stepping into the halls of the Soturion Academy will immediately place your life in danger," he said gently.

I nodded, taking in his words. I'd be the weakest in a group of magically powered warriors. As an Heir facing the political unrest in Bamaria, I'd be an instant target, especially from the soturi sworn to Ka Kormac—the Imperator would make sure of it. But...it was better than the alternative. I had to stay for my family, my sisters, Tristan. And for myself. To reclaim my title, reclaim my destiny.

"Leaving the borders of the Empire is the equivalent of death for me."

"Arkturion Aemon," the Imperator said, "no exceptions can be made. I will not have her lowering Academy standards or causing my soturi to fall behind. Are you sure it's not...a kindness to send her away now?"

"Kindness to whom?" Aemon asked.

"She will suffer in the Academy," the Imperator said. "And who will train her? What poor apprentice will you sentence to her? I tell you now, I will not have my men linked to her—

lowering their ability to call on kashonim. And let's not forget she won't have access to that either."

"Kashonim is blood magic," Arianna said, breaking her long silence. "It's been used for centuries by soturi who have no study in spells. Like blood oaths and sensing auras. She'll be able to use it just fine if needed once bound to her apprentice."

My heart pounded. I hadn't considered my apprentice. Whoever was assigned to me was going to be resentful...and was probably going to make my life miserable. Unless I found a solution.

"It's decided," my father said cautiously. "The right apprentice can be found." He looked again to Aemon, who gave a small nod. "We have satisfied the Emperor's law, and we have satisfied decency." He turned a steely gaze on the Imperator. "Agreed?"

The Imperator pressed his fingers beneath his chin. "Never let it be said I'm not merciful in my rulings. Her grace may remain and attend the Soturion Academy as a novice."

I swallowed hard. The Imperator wasn't merciful. If he was agreeing to this...he had some other motive.

"But I do believe the Emperor will want to know about this little arrangement. He'll also want final say on whether this experiment is successful before long. We shall have a test, one the Emperor shall determine. Pass the Emperor's test, and we will know if we've made wise council. Fail, your grace, and you'll go immediately into exile as the law demands."

A test from the Emperor—the Imperator's uncle. The monster who'd ordered the execution of every last member of Ka Azria...even their children, because they'd hidden a family member with vorakh. Was it possible to pass a test set by such a man?

"Well," the Imperator said impatiently, "do you accept these terms?"

"When?" I asked. "How long will I have to prepare?"

"I think the spring equinox should suffice. The Emperor does enjoy Bamaria in the spring. That gives you seven months."

Seven months. "And the nature of this test?"

"Will be at the Emperor's discretion and pleasure."

I sucked in a breath.

Seven months. Seven months to train amongst the soturi, to master wielding weapons, to learn how to run and fight, to grow strong. I'd seen the soturi in action, knew what they could do. And I knew what I was physically capable of. I wasn't even close to their ability. Plus, it was entirely possible the Imperator was only playing with me, like a wolf who'd decided to torture and taunt his prey before going in for the kill. But trick or not, it bought me time.

My heart pounded as I stepped forward. My stomach twisted, but I forced the words out of my mouth, my voice loud and clear. "I accept."

Arkmage Kolaya nodded, stepping forward. She guided me to the center of the Chamber beneath the eternal flame. The Red Watcher of the light joined us, holding the golden ceremonial soturion bowl, now burning with fire. I held out my left hand, my palm up. The arkmage held her dagger and slashed.

My blood dripped Batavia red into the fiery flames of my fate—the flames of the soturion, the warrior. A ceremonial dagger was produced, smoking with black lettering. Lyriana Batavia blazed across the steel in black ash. I'd been broken inside, just like my stave, but this dagger made me new. I wouldn't let them destroy this one. I would not let them take it from me. I was going to fight and stake my claim—my destiny—or die trying.

"My oath begins here."

CHAPTER TWELVE

I RACED TO Cresthaven and immediately called for Meera and Morgana. They were already running to greet me when I entered the fortress walls. Morgana had *heard* me coming home.

"Lyr!" Morgana threw her arms tightly around me. "Oh, Gods, Lyr! We were so worried. What happened to you?"

I burst into tears and stumbled from Morgana's arms. Like a snake striking its victim, her arm whipped forward, turning my left wrist to expose the cut, bright red above my tattoo. Then she retrieved the dagger from my belt, her eyes widening as she read my name.

"Soturion Lyriana? How in Lumeria did this happen?"

I shook my head, exhausted and too aware of Euston and Rhodes eyeing me with curiosity from their posts.

I edged my sisters inside the Great Hall for some privacy. The double doors closed behind us. "How are you both? I was worried all week."

"Lyr, you're the one we're worried about."

"I know, but—"

"First, you need to tell us what happened," Morgana said.

"Out loud, please," Meera said.

Morgana nodded, her arm around me. "Upstairs."

Meera was still shaking her head after I'd explained everything about the examiner from Ka Maras, the nahashim, my examination, and finally my deal with the Imperator.

"But how can you not have magic?" Meera asked.

I rolled my neck, my scalp tingling as Morgana took out the last of Brenna's braids. I ran my fingers through my hair, now loose and wild around me.

It was the one question I most wanted answered and the one no one seemed to be acknowledging. The Imperator had called it an anomaly. A rare occurrence. After Jules and Meera, I'd tried to search our family history. Was there any pattern of vorakh, of unusual power? I'd asked Aunt Arianna, and I'd buried myself in the scrolls underground. There was nothing. Only mentions of my lineage having an exceptionally strong bloodline. Every mage was powerful, every arkasva, and until my mother and Aunt Gianna, the women of Ka Batavia all lived to old age—well over a hundred.

"Lyr, don't give up hope," Morgana said. "There may be an explanation—something no one has considered."

"Like what? What hasn't been considered?"

Morgana shook her head. "I don't know, you're the one always looking for possibilities. Go to the library. Maybe there's a scroll that will help. You figured out how to soften my pain. You learned how to shorten Meera's visions. You may find answers that no one was looking for because no one else ever needed to look for them. Answers don't appear until the question is asked. You have time—research."

I shook my head. "That was my first thought. But I'm not going to be just lounging around Cresthaven. I have soturion training, and you know what that means. I won't have time for both. And all of this is dependent on if I even survive these seven months."

"You'll survive," Meera said firmly. But her eyes were distant.

"There may be another option." Morgana winced, rubbing her temples.

Are you all right?

She lifted her head, grimacing as she pushed back her black hair. "I was out more than I should have been this week, hoping to find answers for you." She leaned against Meera, who resumed rubbing her temples for her. Her expression relaxed.

"Morgs." I was touched by her efforts, but I hated to see her suffering.

She rolled her eyes, reading my thoughts, and winced. "I just need a smoke, and I'll be fine. I may have found some useful information."

I sat forward.

Meera stilled, eyebrows narrowed. "You didn't tell me this."

"I'm telling you now," she snapped.

I squeezed Meera's hand in reassurance. Morgana was likely to bite someone's head off, but Meera could instantly dissolve into a puddle of tears. "What did you hear?" I asked.

"Don't speak and don't think until I finish telling you," Morgana said. "It's—" She paused, squinting, pinching the bridge of her nose. Her face was screwed up in pain.

Meera turned to me, her mouth open in concern.

"Just a fucking spasm!" Morgana snapped. "Myself to Moriel! Stop fussing! I hear everything, you know!" Morgana took several deep inhales as Meera and I waited, still, not looking at each other and nervously trying to quiet our minds. Morgana's condition was getting worse, something I didn't want to think about in that moment and absolutely couldn't—not without upsetting her again.

At last, she exhaled, her eyes opening. "There's one other option. But it's dangerous, and you must swear not to act on it until I say. If we get to spring and aren't any closer to solving it than we are now…it's our last resort. Swear. You won't do anything with this yet."

"I swear it," I said quickly. Meera narrowed her eyes.

"An ambassador from the Star Court is visiting. He just arrived to meet with the Ready for contract renewal negotiations regarding the starfire trade. He's Afeyan."

"No," Meera said automatically. "You can't. You mustn't."

"Of course, she mustn't. I'm only saying he's here."

"Gryphon-shit. Why bring it up then?" Meera turned to me. "Absolutely not. You cannot speak to an Afeya. You know the rules."

I did, as did every Lumerian. We learned them as soon as we could walk. First: Akadim attacked at night. Second: Never make a deal with the Afeya.

There was one exception: Ramia. And that was only because she was half-Afeyan, lacking their worst, most dangerous qualities. Though…I did still owe her a favor. My fingers ran over the necklace secured like armor around my chest and shoulders.

The Afeya came from Lumeria Matavia, just like us. Both of our races had lived peacefully together for a time before the Drowning. We had many similar traditions and histories, but they were immortal and able to draw from the deepest wells of magic anywhere in the world. It was said the Afeya could move Heaven and Earth; they could do anything one dreamed of, answer any question asked. But there was a catch. No Afeya could use magic of their own free will. The immortals had to act on the request of another, their curse after the Drowning. They eagerly granted any wishes made, but at a price. The price was always too high.

Still, part of me was tempted. Afeya had living memories of Lumeria Matavia when visions, mind reading, and traveling were not vorakh, but common abilities for everyone. They remembered the forming of the world when the Gods and Goddesses were descending and becoming mortal. All I had to do was ask for what I wanted, and their magic would answer. What if I could ask for the source of my power? Or to be made a mage?

"Lyr," Meera said. "I can't read your mind, but I still know what you're thinking. Stop thinking it. Don't."

"She needs to know all of her options, and so do we. We're rolling closer to your coronation, Meera," Morgana said darkly. "So unless you want to be having visions on the Seat of the Arkasva, just long enough for the Imperator to see... we need to figure this out. We're in this together." Morgana held out her left arm, flashing her tattoo of the phases of the moon—the tattoo that concealed her own blood oath. She grabbed my arm and then Meera's so all of our tattoos came together. The sun, the moon, and the stars. "We all swore, and we all stick together. And that includes knowing the last resort."

"Enough," I said, snatching my arm back. "I'm not going to find any answers. Not tonight." I sank back on the bed. "Have either of you heard from Tristan?"

"Why?" Morgana asked carefully, her voice dangerously low.

Meera looked conspicuously away.

"What do you mean 'why'? We've been apart for a week. I need to see him."

"So the bastard can bind you again?" Morgana snarled.

"He did that to protect me." I had to believe he'd done it to protect me. He'd looked so sad, so heartbroken, so determined to be the one who went with me in place of that nameless Kormac mage. "And he tried to make it up to me. To rescue me."

Morgana scoffed. "And he would have gotten one step outside the Stronghold before he was locked up in another prison beside you—idiot. He bound you, Lyr," Morgana seethed. "You're delusional if you think he was protecting you."

"He spent a fortune to get the Shadows to look away."

Morgana clapped slowly. "What a fucking hero! Maybe he should have spent a little more money so he had time to actually save you and not just make a spectacle. Or better yet —not fucking helped those bastards arrest you in the first place!"

"It's not so black and white," Meera said. "I still hate him, though."

"You can't hate your future brother-in-law," I said.

"Like you ever stopped hating Markan?" Morgana asked. "He was just doing his job."

"Stop. I need to see Tristan," I said, voice shaky. But I was losing confidence.

A part of me missed him terribly. He was so familiar, and he had seemed truly sorry that night. And yet...he had attacked me—and done so on behalf of the Imperator.

There was something else, too. I was afraid he wouldn't want to marry me anymore. And even more afraid that I needed him to marry me. For if we did...perhaps that was another way out of my predicament.

"Where are you going with this thought?" Morgana frowned.

I sighed. "We were going to be engaged. He'd have become a Batavia per tradition of the ranking Kavim. But...if he'll still have me...maybe I should become Ka Grey."

"NO!" Morgana leapt from the bed.

Meera remained still, her expression thoughtful.

"I have no guarantee I'll survive a week, much less until spring," I said. "And what if the Imperator changes his mind before my test? Or the Emperor ends the arrangement on a whim? Then I'm banished into exile, and there's nothing I can do! An alliance between Ka Batavia and Ka Grey sealed by marriage may buy me more time. Keep me safe. Father must hold back for the sake of politics. He can't be seen evading justice, especially for his own blood. He—we know he had to let Jules go to protect us. Now I need to do what I must to protect you."

"You're farther than Lethea!" Morgana said, shaking her head.

"I'm not," I said. "Ka Grey has less power in politics but more power in the financial sphere. They have money—more than we do. Money that would be mine if we married. Father's hand might be forced, he might have to give me up. The name Batavia isn't enough to keep me safe anymore. But as a Grey, their Ka's pride would hardly allow them to lose a daughter-in-law. Or..." I swallowed, "a grandchild."

"Stop it, Lyr," Morgana said. "This is utter nonsense. You think money and politics are two separate worlds. They're not. Don't do this. It's not the time to make some brash decision."

"Brash? This was decided two years ago! Maybe even longer. Tristan was always my destiny, that's why no one blinked for more than a minute when he started courting me."

"But you weren't going to take his name! He was going to take yours! And you certainly weren't going to be pregnant at nineteen without finishing your studies!"

I threw my hands up. "Morgana, I was expelled. Finishing my studies is already lost at sea. Soturi have the strength of twenty men, and I've never trained a day in my life. How am I going to survive without magic?" I shook my head, tears forming. "What does it matter? You knew I was going to marry Tristan. This was always the plan."

"No, it wasn't. Not like this. You're not going to throw away your birthright and hide as Tristan Grey's fucking wife, acting like some breeder for Ka Grey!"

"Gods, Morgs! I love him."

"You love him?" She was yelling now, her cheeks red. "You've been lying to everyone for so long, playing your part so perfectly as the virtuous Lady Lyriana, you've convinced yourself. Wake up! He assisted in arresting you! He called for Jules's death. He regularly arrests and hands our kind over to monsters. And you! You have to psych yourself up just to kiss him! It's been two years, Lyr, and you're still not fucking him. Because you don't want to, even if you won't admit it. What kind of life is that?"

"And who do you think I do all of that for? For you! For Meera!" I scoffed. "How dare you attack the choices I make with Tristan! Are you in love with every single person you fuck? What's your latest total? Huh? A hundred?"

"Fuck you!" Morgana pulled a flask from her belt and sucked down a sip.

"Enough! Both of you. We're all on the same side here," Meera said, her voice unusually commanding. She held out her arm, flashing her tattoo of the sun.

"Put your Godsdamned arm down. I'm not flashing my tattoo every time you want unity," Morgana snapped.

I took a deep breath. "I'm sorry, Morgs. I didn't mean...."

"It's fine."

But it wasn't. Morgana had gone from being jealous of me having had my first kiss before her to sleeping her way through half her Mage Academy class. Sex, it turned out, had a similar effect to drugs and alcohol on her vorakh, taking her pain away. And between her mesmerizing beauty and mind reading, it wasn't hard to find willing partners, male or female. I knew she enjoyed sex, but she didn't enjoy needing it to ease her pain. I had been wrong to throw it in her face.

"I just...I don't know what to do. I know our relationship isn't perfect, but despite our problems, I'm going to take the chance to be with him. If he'll still have me." I stared at my hands, hating myself for saying that.

"If he'll have you?" Morgana laughed. She sounded almost hysterical. "Myself to Moriel. Of course, he'll have you! But you are so naïve if you think you can fix this by marrying into his Ka. Even more naïve if you think his grandmother will accept an alliance that doesn't advance Ka Grey's rank. And do not even think of becoming pregnant. Tristan still loves you, but Lady Romula may not be so keen when you can't offer a worthy exchange. She has his balls tied to a leash, especially after his stunt last week. So stop thinking that you need him. You're destined for greater than this."

"Greater than Tristan? Greater than being the worst soturion in all Lumeria? Whatever destiny I had is lost, was stolen the moment Kolaya called my name! I'm out of options, and I need to do whatever it takes to survive!"

Meera shuddered as I yelled, but Morgana only looked more determined, sticking her face in mine.

"Mother would roll in her grave," she said. "As would Jules!"

"How dare you—" My hand flew up.

"I thought we called a truce!" Meera reached for Morgana's arm, tugging her back.

"Maybe you did, but I didn't!" Morgana freed herself from Meera's clutches.

I stood, glaring at Morgana, my chest heaving.

Her nostrils flared. Then she flinched, reaching for her temples in pain.

"Morgana," Meera said, her voice soft and soothing. "Lyr and Tristan have been apart for a week. They do need to talk. But, Lyr, not tonight. You need to get your head on straight. You need to eat and rest, recover from the past week, recover from what they forced you to do today. I'll have the cook prepare a meal and send it up. In the meantime, draw yourself a bath."

"I'm going to smoke." Morgana slammed the door.

Meera smiled faintly. "She'll calm down, Lyr."

"Sure," I said, but we both knew that was a lie.

An hour later, I was summoned downstairs when Euston announced, "Lady Lyriana, Arkturion Aemon is here to see you."

I moved slowly through the Great Hall, stepping outside and breaking into a sweat. Had the Imperator already changed his mind? Or the Emperor?

Aemon strolled purposely down the waterway. His blood-red cloak floated in the wind behind him as the sun set, lighting the path in gold and silver sparks. His golden armor shimmered with the reflections of the glass beneath his feet.

"Soturion Lyriana," he said, bowing his chin in respect.

Relief washed through me. Nothing had changed. I held my chin up high. "I prefer lady."

He smiled. "You're both now, your grace. And that begins with moving into your new quarters. I've come to escort you to the Soturion Academy apartments. You need to move in tonight."

CHAPTER THIRTEEN

"THE APARTMENTS? BUT...I just got home to Cresthaven. I'm to complete my studies here."

Aemon frowned. "Mages may study at home, but all soturi live in apartments by the Katurium. The training exercises require you to be in proximity. The mornings start with a run, followed by a full day of classes and training. After dinner and a brief rest, you return to the Katurium for combat clinics —fights you must observe, critique, and take turns participating in three nights a week."

"Three! No...I...I need to be home." Who was going to help Meera through her visions and care for her after? What about Morgana?

"You need to fulfill your end of the deal with the Imperator. No favors. No exceptions."

"I know. But the Heirs of Ka Batavia have always resided in Cresthaven through their studies. It's tradition."

"Yes, and tradition in Ka Batavia is studying at the Mage Academy, but you're not. You must adapt to our ways, your grace. They're going to be watching you, taking score, noting every favor and bend in the rules, and using it against you. The Imperator won't play fair in this bargain. He's going to make sure he wins the upper hand in this deal in the end. We can't let that happen, so we must do everything in our power to prevent that—adhere to every rule and follow the law precisely. You are to be the most model student we've ever had. This is step one."

I stumbled back, staring at the entrance to Cresthaven. My heart hurt. I thought I could pretend everything was normal. I could still marry Tristan. Still live here and protect my sisters.

But Aemon was right.

"I assume my father already knows."

"Of course."

"Very well," I said. "I'll need a few moments to pack."

Aemon bowed. "I'll be waiting."

I excused myself upstairs, quickly gathering my essentials. A few minutes later, I was off with Aemon, having avoided saying goodbye to my sisters. I was still furious with Morgana and knew Meera would take my leaving again so soon badly. The only upside to this was getting to walk away from Cresthaven and leaving Markan behind. I would still have access to escorts and soturi when moving through Bamaria, but not in apartment housing or when in training at the Katurium. I took some satisfaction in glaring at Markan as I walked out of Cresthaven while he remained still. He'd follow me, of course, but not as closely as before. I gave him a dirty gesture when I reached the outer wall.

I suppose had this been planned, I would have settled into a luxury apartment. But seeing as how all the apartments were already rented by those who'd planned to be a soturion, I was stuck with what remained.

My apartment was small, dark, and bare, not befitting a lady of Ka Batavia. There was a living room along with a kitchenette, bathroom, and bedroom. I walked through slowly, taking stock of my new surroundings and modest furniture. The living room was the barest with only a small couch and table. Candles had been set up around the room. I lit them one by one. The kitchenette had a wooden stove and a pantry with a handful of spice bottles. The bathroom included a toilet, sink, and a shower—but no bath. I lit more candles as I walked around, carrying one into the bedroom and setting it on the nightstand. The bed was single-sized and directly across from a small wardrobe and a desk—all familiar pieces, if slightly more used and plainer than I was used to. But what made my new reality truly sink in was the dummy by the bedroom window. It was dusty and naked, waiting to hold armor—my armor. It still sounded impossible. I coughed and opened the windows, but the air outside felt stagnant and hot from the surrounding city. I was used to the cool breeze from the Lumerian Ocean caressing my bedroom in Cresthaven. The comforting sounds of the waves as they lulled me to sleep each night. There was nothing at the Soturion Academy beyond the noise of soturi shouting outside, and the scent of stale sweat and body odor drifting from the Katurium.

There was a sudden knock on my apartment door. I froze, not sure I wanted to see anyone, or who besides Aemon even knew I was here. The knocks persisted. Louder, more urgent.

Straightening my tunic, I pulled the front door open to find a distraught Tristan stumbling inside, arms already reaching for me. His hair was mussed; for once, he looked disheveled.

"Lyr! Gods."

I took a step back. Fear gripped me. The sensation started in my toes, rising rapidly through my body.

His face fell, arms dangling uncertainly at his sides. "You're afraid of me?"

My lower lip trembled, and I hated myself for it. I was afraid of him. I'd been afraid for two years.

"Because I bound you?" he asked, the shame and anguish surging through his voice.

"Yes," I whispered. *And because you'd bind my sisters if you could. If you knew.*

"I...." He ran his hands through his hair, shaking. "I see you in my mind every time I close my eyes. The look on your face when I—it's been killing me." He shook his head, his hand reaching for me before he pulled it back, hugging himself. "Damnit, Lyr, it had to be me. I couldn't let someone else do that to you." This time he did reach for me, his hands on my shoulders, the pressure light. I tensed. "I knew they'd need the binding removed at some point—and hoped they'd need me to do it. It was the only way I could make sure I saw you again."

I stepped out of his touch, backing toward the couch. "You paid a small fortune to do so barely an hour later. If you really meant to rescue me, why bind me to begin with?"

He closed his eyes, his hands fisting at his sides. "I-I don't know. I panicked. I'm sorry. I'm so fucking sorry. When I saw you being arrested, I just...I did whatever I could to stay at your side. In case...." He snapped his mouth shut.

"In case what?"

"In case the charges were true."

My chest heaved. In case I had vorakh. Did that mean... had he wanted to be the one to kill me? And add another notch on his vorakh hunting belt? Or...was his mind changing about them?

"But then you didn't see me again all week. You left me alone for seven days. Why?"

He shook his head again. "If that damned forsworn bastard had just stayed out of my way. Lyr, I wanted to see you. So badly. I was forbidden."

His grandmother. Lady Romula. She still ran Ka Grey, still had final say in all of Tristan's decisions. I shook my head.

He stepped forward, submissive, his palms open. "Please, don't be afraid of me. I-I need to touch you."

My chest hammered. Something coiled inside of me, tight and pressing. I'd been left alone for a week, untouched until today when the nahashim had snaked through my body, violating me to reveal my secrets. I shuddered, the ghost of their horrid embrace still reverberating inside.

"Please," he begged. "Lyr. Let me hold you."

I closed my eyes, inhaling and exhaling. This was Tristan. He loved me. He'd never hurt me....

Except he did hurt me. Again and again. More than he ever knew.

I took a step forward, and then another, until we were face to face, close enough for me to feel his breath on my cheek. My hands balled into fists at my side.

His hand snaked out, fingers curling around my waist, and I stumbled back from his touch. "No. Not yet."

His eyes widened, hurt and shame clouding them. "Lyr, I love you."

"What if...what if I'd had a vorakh?" I said suddenly. My throat went dry. "What would you have done?"

Tristan cocked his head to the side. "I would have killed anyone who tried to hurt you. I would have protected you, kept you safe with every last breath in my body."

A shudder ran through me, and my heart lifted. "You would have defended me?"

"Lyr, I'd do anything for you." His aura warmed, cocooning me with the truth of his words.

And just like that, the thing coiled tightly in my core unraveled. I didn't feel any hesitation. I wanted Tristan. I wanted to touch him. I wanted him to touch me. All the doubt, all the fear I'd felt, ebbed away. He had changed, he was different. And he was mine. He would protect me. And if he'd come around on that, he could come around to my sisters. If not today, then soon. There was hope.

But right there in that moment, I needed him. I needed him so badly to erase the violation of the nahashim. I needed to be touched softly, needed a touch that wouldn't tear through me but would make me feel good.

I pulled his hands onto my waist, breathing the familiar scent of him—mint and the salt of the ocean, like the shore outside my bedroom window at home. He sucked in a breath.

"Touch me," I said.

I barely breathed as his hands flattened over my hips, fingers digging into my flesh before he pulled me forward, our hips flush. "Like this?" he asked, voice hoarse.

Swallowing, I stared up into his brown eyes, so deep, already hooded with desire.

I brushed my lips against his. He stilled, letting me offer one kiss, then two. On the third, his lips crushed against mine, hard and desperate for me to open to his mouth. He groaned, pressing me closer. My hands rushed up the muscles of his back, tangling in his hair, grabbing his face, then sliding down his stomach to the silver belt buckled low on his hips. His scabbard poked out to the side.

I withdrew his stave, seeing him again in my mind's eye as he bound me. I could feel the burning of the ropes he'd conjured as I pointed the stave at his heart.

Tristan froze.

"Never use this on me again," I said. "No matter what."

"I swear." His brown eyes widened, sorrowful.

I pushed it into his chest, hard enough that if it had been my dagger, I'd have drawn blood. Then I tossed it on the floor, watching it roll under a table—revenge for the indignity my own broken stave had been afforded. My hands played with his belt buckle, unfastening and letting it drop to the ground so I could pull up the hem of his tunic. I traced the length of his thighs and hips. My fingers splayed across his stomach and then up his chest. He pulled the cloth over his head and shucked it onto the couch.

"Blow out the candles," I said, backing away. Within seconds every flame and torch was extinguished. Only the waning moonlight and the torchlights from the city remained. I removed my own top next, secure in knowing he couldn't see any scars, or bruises left on my skin. His hands rose up my torso, cupping my breasts, thumbs rubbing over my nipples through the rough material of my shift until I gasped.

"Lyr," he said, kissing my neck.

"Take me to bed." I grabbed his hips and walked us backwards, steering him into the bedroom, past the naked dummy.

The backs of my knees hit the mattress first, and I fell back onto it, Tristan's weight on top of me. I opened my legs, sliding up to the headboard, and he followed, settling on top of me, pulling the straps of my shift off my shoulders as he kissed his way down my jaw and neck.

I arched my back, wrapping my legs around him. The contact was almost too much, too much after a week where no one had touched me once. "Take it off," I said.

Clumsily, he untied the bow beneath my breasts, sliding the material off, baring me to him.

"Gods," he said. "Beautiful." He kissed the corner of my mouth before pulling back, palming my breasts, bending down to kiss them.

I undulated beneath him as he took one peaked nipple in his mouth, his fingers teasing the other. His other hand rose up my neck, his fingers caressed my lips. I froze as something silver caught my eye.

His signet ring, the sigil of Ka Grey. Silver seraphim wings beneath a silver moon. He'd worn that ring since he was a boy, inherited it from his father after he died.

"Tristan," I said breathlessly. "What are we doing?"

"Whatever you want." His palm moved down my belly until his fingers skimmed the edge of my riding pants. His mouth sucked harder, drawing ripples of pleasure through my body, until heat coursed through me, pooling between my legs. "I know you wanted to wait, and we can, or...whatever you want."

I pulled away from him, scooting into a seat, and took his hand. I'd said I'd wanted to wait until we were engaged to have sex—not that I actually cared about that sort of thing. I'd wanted to buy myself more time to mentally prepare before I fully gave in, and I'd known I'd needed to lessen the times he'd see my naked body when it carried cuts and bruises. But now...now that we were here, now that I felt actually ready to complete our relationship—it was hitting me. I still had no ring on my finger.

"You were supposed to propose to me last week," I said.

He squeezed his eyes shut. "I know."

I threw my hands up. "You know? What does that mean? Are you still proposing?"

He sat back on his heels, swallowing hard, before shifting awkwardly to adjust his pants. "She won't allow it."

"Your grandmother won't give you permission?" I snapped.

"Gods, Lyr. Don't say it like that. She's not just my grandmother. She's the Lady of Ka Grey. She sits on the Bamarian Council. You know Godsdamned well this is bigger than us."

"So now because your grandmother won't let you, you don't want to marry me anymore?"

"Of course, I still want to marry you."

"Then do it!"

"I can't!" he snarled. "I don't even have the ring."

I tensed. "Don't have it anymore...or never had it?"

He lifted his hands up helplessly. "How do you think I got the money together so fast for the Shadow Stronghold?"

Gods, he hadn't!

"Lyr, I gave the Shadows my mother's ring. My grandmother won't forgive me. She's frozen my accounts over it." He pushed his fingers through his hair, looking miserable. "If I ran our Ka, I'd have bought you ten rings by now, one for every finger. You're my love. But I can't, not yet, not while she's still in charge. When the Imperator accused you, she got spooked. She's scared."

"Scared of me?" I grabbed the covers and pulled them over my breasts. I couldn't be half naked for this conversation. Even in the dark.

"Scared for me." He groaned. "I know you don't have vorakh, but…well, it runs in your family."

I stiffened. Jules. He meant Jules. Not Meera. Not Morgana.

"We just need to give her some time." He squeezed my hand. "Just a little. It's not easy for her—it never has been."

I stared up at the ceiling. Numbness seeped through me. Lady Romula was terrified of vorakh, but not in the way most Lumerians were trained to hate and fear them. The feelings went deeper for her, for Tristan. There was a reason they hunted vorakh. It was personal.

Tristan had been three when he'd witnessed his parents' murder. A mage with visions had gone mad and attacked Ka Grey. In their panic to protect Tristan, his parents had been overpowered, ripped to pieces. He'd seen the whole thing.

He never really recovered from the trauma. All Lumerians learned a wretched song about vorakh as children. We'd hold hands and sing, dancing in a circle until the song ended with everyone falling, pretending to drown. Tristan always turned violent at the end, pushing down the others as if they were his parents' murderers. We quickly learned not to sing that song when he was present.

I, of all people, knew intimately the pain he carried. I'd seen him cry for his parents, had held him in my arms the last two years on the anniversary of their deaths. It was why he couldn't stand the sight of blood. It brought him back to that night.

"So what?" I said. "We give her time to realize I'm not scary and not going to hurt you?"

Tristan shook his head. "She's not going to be so easily convinced. Plus, you're…. How would it look to Bamaria if a lord of Ka Grey married a Lumerian without magic?"

My mouth opened. "A Lumerian without magic? That's what you think of me?"

"No! Those aren't my words. They're…."

"Your grandmother's? You bound me, gave away my engagement ring, left me alone in prison for a week, and then planned to fuck me."

"Lyr!" He reddened. "No…no! Gods. I am so sorry. I will forever be sorry. But I didn't know what to do! And I didn't come here to sleep with you. I came to see you. To hold you. To make sure you were all right. I came as soon as I found out you were free. I wish…." He groaned. "I wish it were simpler. If I were just some boy, and you were just some girl, none of this would be a second thought. But we are who we are. Our engagement has political ramifications." He shook his head, brown eyes pleading. "Don't attack me for the same golden bonds that forced your father, the Arkasva, to leave you behind bars. I know what role I played, but whether I'd been there or not, the outcome was going to be the same, some other mage would have bound you, and you know it. I didn't cause this. Stop blaming me!"

I looked away, still so angry. Angry at him. Angry he was right. Angry at everything.

His voice softened. "Our stations in life come with privilege, but they also weigh us down with golden chains."

I glared. "Don't patronize me. You think I don't know that? I was imprisoned for those chains. I sat still while my own cousin was taken before me and murdered for those chains."

Tristan was silent. A moment passed, my words hanging in the air. "Lyr," he said quietly. He shook his head very slowly, his brown eyes widening with concern. His energy shifted, his aura stilling to an unsettling calm, like the sea, too still just before a storm. Carefully, he leaned forward and took my hand in his. "Jules wasn't murdered."

"Yes, she was," I spat, my blood boiling.

He turned pale, his brown eyes searching mine. "Lyr."

I slapped his hand away like I'd been burned. "You said you'd protect me if I had vorakh."

"I'd do anything for you. But that doesn't change—Lyr, it had to be done. Jules had to be executed."

There were spots in my vision. My anger was so palpable I could barely see straight. I'd been so fucking stupid. He would have protected me because I was his. He hadn't changed his mind at all, he hadn't evolved. If he knew about Meera or Morgana, he'd turn them in, have them arrested, probably bind them, too. And I'd been ready to have sex with him.

I clutched my wrist, my hand squeezing over my blood oaths. The skin burned raw there with the new scar, my soturion oath.

"Lyr, do you understand?"

"Get out."

"Lyr."

"GET. OUT." I didn't care anymore. I didn't care how I sounded or what he thought.

"I'm sorry, Lyr, but—"

"If you won't leave," I sneered, "I will." And when Tristan still didn't move, I jumped from the bed, grabbed a tunic and sandals, and slammed my bedroom door on him. Then I flew out the apartment before he could follow.

CHAPTER FOURTEEN

I'D JUST PULLED the tunic over my shoulders and laced my sandals when the gravity of what I'd done hit me.

Fuck! Fuck! Fuck!

I'd admitted my feelings about Jules. I'd admitted I believed she'd suffered unjustly, that I was sympathetic to people with vorakh. I'd left my feelings out on display, been too open. I'd forgotten my place, forgotten the role I had to play.

I had half a mind to run back upstairs and fall on my knees and tell Tristan I'd been an idiot, and I was sorry, and he was right about Jules, and I'd have him any way I could.

The other part of me worried I'd pick up my dagger and stab him. I couldn't go back in there, couldn't face him when my stomach was twisting, my heart pounding, and my grief for Jules—a living, breathing wound inside my soul—was about to explode. That was what kept me running from the apartment; I just needed to keep moving. To think. To calm down.

Falling rain drops quickly gave way to pounding thunks against the waterway. I had to find shelter. Cresthaven was too far, but the Temple of Dawn was near. Tears mixing with the rain, I ran, bursting through the temple doors.

The Orange Watcher of the light sat atop Auriel's Chamber staring in adoration at the flame, his hands clasped in prayer, his orange veil covering his head. I entered slowly, hoping not to be noticed by the Watcher or the one late night guest in the pews. I tried to move silently and find a seat in the back, but thunder crashed, followed by a flash of lightning. I jumped in surprise, and the visitor turned toward the disturbance.

Rhyan.

With a small nod, he leaned back and stared at the ceiling, waiting as I made my way to his row. I wasn't in the mood to talk to anyone, not after Tristan. But he'd seen me, and it felt awkward to avoid him when we were the only two here. I made my way down the aisle.

"Did they let you out on bail, or have you escaped from prison, your grace?" Rhyan smirked as I entered his pew. Raindrops shattered against the stained-glass windows, blanketing the temple in a soothing pattering. His voice echoed into its emptiness.

"Your grace?" I countered. "What? No 'partner' tonight?"

"Would you rather I called you lover?" He smirked.

"Are you admitting to it?"

"Are you asking me to?"

I collapsed into the seat beside him and groaned. "You always know exactly what to say to make me feel better."

"It's a gift."

"You might want to return it to the shop," I said.

"Damn, I lost the receipt. Instead, I'll offer you some of my own wisdom regarding prison," he said, eyes twinkling. "Don't go back."

"But it feels so good to be bad," I purred.

He chuckled. "And she makes a joke! At last. I knew you could do it. Ladies and gentlemen...." He swung his arms out wide as if greeting an audience. "Well, single Watcher of the light. Unfortunately, quite a small audience for your comedic debut."

"I'll live."

"I could try and book you a show, make a tour schedule...."

"Or not."

"Or...you could tell me what brought you here so late."

The Orange Watcher stood, adding a sun tree branch to the pyre. The flame, weakened from the storm, flared back to life, glowing bright white. Burning embers popped, vanishing into the smoke.

I squeezed the excess water from my hair, pulling the wet locks off my neck. "I'm becoming a soturion tomorrow, and considering all the punching and push-ups I'm about to do, I thought it best to start praying now."

"You're what? Are they farther than Lethea?"

"Thanks for the vote of confidence."

"It has nothing to do with my confidence in you and everything to do with...how difficult training is—especially when you're unprepared."

"How about a new topic?" I suggested, my stomach twisting. "How are you?"

"Nice deflection." But he shrugged in response. His hair, curling from the rain, fell wildly over his scar. He pushed his locks back, but they immediately opened into loose waves, sprouting over his forehead. He didn't seem to know what to do with it at this length. I doubted he'd ever had hair this long before. Most soturi kept it cut short to avoid it being pulled by opponents.

"Are they treating you all right here?" I asked.

"I'm forsworn. Lucky not to be killed in my sleep. At least the lock to my apartment works."

"That sounds like a no, then."

"I have a roof over my head, food to eat. I can take care of myself." He shrugged again, and his gaze shifted, scanning the high walls. "Now, no more questions. I'm here to take in the art."

"You came here for the art?" I asked.

"I did, actually." There was a vulnerability in his eyes, one I'd seen when we danced. He was telling the truth. "Don't look so surprised."

"I…I didn't realize you cared for art."

"You know, if you're going to be one of us, you really need to learn we're more faceted than just punching and push-ups."

"Right," I said and looked up.

Seven stories high, the temple was full of depictions from the Valya, our most sacred text, telling the story of the creation and loss of the Valalumir. Paintings adorned the high windows and walls that surrounded us.

In the first scene, the god Canturiel in Heaven was seen dreaming in his garden, his hands shaping the light into existence as he sang. The Valalumir was a light, a pure white flame simultaneously revealing and concealing every color of the rainbow within it. Canturiel had sung all of his love and power and magic into it, and so the light burned brighter than any other in Heaven, even brighter than the sun. With all of the love poured inside, one could stare directly into it without harm. The Valalumir offered heat but did not burn. It offered light but did not blind. It healed those who were ill and strengthened those who felt weak. It enhanced beauty and skill, calmed upset minds, and improved the lives of all who gazed upon it.

The next painting showed the battle for the light in the Celestial Realms. Akadim, created from Gods and Goddesses who'd fallen to corruption, planned an invasion to steal the light, breaching Heaven. To keep the akadim from ever existing in the Celestial Realms again, an army of Gods and

Goddesses imprisoned the monsters on Earth. That was how evil came to Lumeria. For a millennium, Gods and Goddesses incarnated there as humans in an attempt to protect Earth from the blight they'd sent. They continued fighting until mortality trapped them.

Though the akadim were now banished from the Celestial Realms with no chance of breaching Heaven, the Council still feared for the Valalumir's safety, moving the light from Canturiel's garden to the Hall of Records. Seven guardians, including the red-haired Goddess Asherah and the golden-haired God Auriel, were chosen to protect the light, to take shifts watching it day and night.

The guardians were forbidden from any and all affairs that might distract from their duties, especially affairs with each other. They were not allowed to marry and had been sworn to remain chaste. But as the years passed, Auriel and Asherah fell in love, and as much as they tried, they could not resist each other.

When Moriel, one of the seven guardians, discovered the affair, he reported them to the Council. Asherah was banished to Earth in the body of a mortal. It was after the age when Gods and Goddesses had willingly descended, since almost all had fallen into the mortal coil. But they made an exception for her as punishment. Asherah joined the wars against the growing force of the akadim. She became an arkturion, the general of her own army of soturi, but her weakened state put her in increasing danger. That was when Auriel made the decision that changed everything. Asherah was his soulmate, his true love, and he was going to bring her every ounce of aid he could.

He stole the Valalumir from the Hall of Records and fell from Heaven. The fall changed Auriel, and it changed the Valalumir. The beloved golden-haired God was now mortal. The once great and powerful light materialized, its flames hardening into a star-shaped crystal. But just before the light finished its transformation from ether to crystal, Auriel placed a spark inside Asherah's heart in an attempt to save its essence before dying. And so a flicker of light of the Valalumir in its purest form lived inside her until she died.

Rhyan watched the paintings reenacting the story. I'd never seen the moving art of Lumeria come alive. Not without magic.

"It's different from my temple at home." His eyebrows furrowed. "Yours tells the story the way my mother used to tell me."

I watched him carefully; he was truly absorbed in the art, a look of awe on his face.

"How did she tell it?" I asked.

He shook his head. "You're not going to get me to play storyteller."

"How do you know?" I quipped. "I can be quite persuasive."

"That I'd like to see." His eyes locked on mine, intense, holding me fixed in place. Then he looked away, a small smile on his lips as he shrugged. "I don't think you'd get the full effect. She was..." his jaw tightened, "a better storyteller. It all ends the same. Asherah's banishment, Auriel's theft, Moriel's betrayal, the war, the Drowning...but she told it like your temple—the story starts the way it's supposed to." He pointed at a painting of Auriel and Asherah watching the light in the Hall of Records behind us. I had to strain my head, leaning into him to look. "See? From the first moment Auriel saw Asherah, he was completely in love with her."

I stared at the painting. The God and Goddess were frozen. I couldn't see any of what Rhyan described. I desperately wanted to. Seeing the paintings come to life had always been something I'd looked forward to.

"Rhyan," I said, biting my lip. My heart hammered in my chest as I mustered my courage. "Without magic, I...I can't see the paintings move." My cheeks reddened with embarrassment.

His mouth fell open. "I forgot. Sorry."

I shook my head. "No, I just…um." I stared at them, the still moments frozen in paint.

One eyebrow furrowed, he asked, "You just what?"

I groaned. "Would you describe them to me? What they look like when they move?"

Eyes searching mine, he nodded, then pointed back to the first picture of Canturiel, describing how he seemed to dance as he sang existence into the Valalumir, the way the light shifted and changed, pulsing with life and brightening.

"This is the moment the seven guardians are picked. They —actually, here, I'll show you." He paused, eyes searching the room, and took my hand, his fingers warm and calloused against my skin. "Auriel walks into the Hall of Records, and his eyes widen. He's basically in awe of the light's brilliance." He moved my hand in smooth movements across the picture, showing Auriel's reaction, describing the choosing of the other guardians, including Moriel who would betray them. "And then Asherah walks in, and…." He released my hand, looking away from me. "He's immediately in love with her."

I peered at the painting, dull without his guidance, my hand already missing the warmth of his. "How can you tell?" I asked. "What does he do to show that?"

"It's not something he does," Rhyan said, squinting at the painting. "It's the way he sees her. See, when he first walked in, the Valalumir was the brightest, most beautiful thing he'd ever seen—it's almost too much to look at it. But when Asherah enters, the light dims. The most powerful light in Heaven ever to be created, and it dims from merely being in her presence."

I turned to him. He was staring at me, his eyes bright and emerald—brighter than the eternal flame. I held onto a breath, my heart pounding. The ache inside of me that had kindled with Tristan, the need to feel alive, now seemed to burn.

"I've never heard of Asherah having the power to dim the Valalumir."

He shook his head. "She doesn't. But the painting's in Auriel's perspective. The light weakens when she's around—but only in his eyes. Because he's in love with her. For him, she's brighter than the brightest star in Heaven."

He pointed to the painting of Auriel preparing to steal the light. "There, without her, the light is brighter, as bright as others see it. But when Auriel sees Asherah again in Lumeria, even as a mortal, she's brighter than the sun."

"All of my lessons seemed to shift from the two of them being soulmates to her being nothing more than a seductress, a demon who'd deceived him and cheated Heaven of its most prized possession. Lately, it seems her reputation as an evil seductress is the only acceptable one." Ka Kormac had seen to that.

"Well, sure, with the disputes over the translations of the Valya from High Lumerian," Rhyan said, excitement in his voice.

I laughed. "You studied High Lumerian?"

"All proper lords do." He sounded incredulous. It was the first time he'd owned his title.

"I know all proper lords are *supposed* to, but most have a way of avoiding their lessons or forgetting everything they memorized the day after tests." Tristan was a prime example.

"I am not most. Nor are you. I remember last time I was here," he continued, "you were always carrying scrolls everywhere and dropping them." He laughed. "I picked some up and helped you carry them to the stairs in Cresthaven. Remember? Every single scroll was in High Lumerian."

I blinked, remembering that day. I'd just returned from Scholars Harbor, planning to reread my favorite stories translated in High Lumerian to test myself. When I realized Rhyan was nearby, I'd tried to walk past him, to see if he'd notice me. I dropped every single scroll. It had been right after we'd danced, after we'd kissed...I could still feel his lips on mine. I hadn't gone more than a minute without replaying it in my mind or thinking about seeing him again.

I met his gaze. "I thought you didn't remember the last time you were here."

There was a pause as his green eyes, lined in dark lashes, searched mine. "I remember. I remember...everything."

My stomach tightened, the feeling moving lower.

He broke eye contact first and glanced at my arm, at the Valalumirs between my elbow and wrist concealing my blood oaths. "Didn't think you were the type to get a tattoo."

"I wasn't. I'm not the same person I was before." Before, I had been careless, privileged, free. My greatest worry had been dancing with the cold, handsome future High Lord of Glemaria who'd been on my mind and in my fantasies all summer.

"No," he said, ruffling his hair and pulling it over his scar. He wasn't the same either. We'd both changed. Both lost people we'd loved.

He coughed. "So, tell me your best academic observations of the translation debate."

I sat up. "Are you serious?"

"After you guiled me into an art history lesson, you still think I have no interests outside of push ups and punching people?"

"No. I...I just never knew anyone else who cared about the debate."

"Now you do. So tell me."

Excitement bubbled inside me. "Well, the Valya reads *Auriel janam Asherahdia*. Auriel knew Asherah's body. And that comes from the Mar Valya—the first Valya to be found and preserved after the Drowning. Everyone's used that translation without thought."

Rhyan sat forward and nodded, his emerald eyes alight. I'd never seen him look so excited. "I know. I've read it."

"Right, of course," I continued. "Anyway, I viewed the scrolls of the Valya recorded before the Drowning in the Great Library, and I checked the scraps of destroyed Valyas under glass at the Museion. I've seen dozens of full copies predating the Drowning housed in the underground levels of the pyramids, including the Tavia Valya—the scroll that had been preserved in a chest and washed ashore a hundred years later. Every Valya recorded before the Drowning includes an M in their scrolls and reads *Auriel janam Asherahdiam*."

"But it's missing in the Mar Valya because of water damage," Rhyan added.

"Right! In the scrolls I viewed, the translation reads, 'Auriel knew Asherah as two.'" The High Lumerian for two was diam. Body was dia. I was convinced "two" was the proper translation, but the Mar Valya had become the standard for copying thanks to an edict from some Emperor centuries ago.

Rhyan nodded excitedly. "Yes! And I read the Scholars originally translated janam as 'recognize.' So the translation should be, 'Auriel recognized Asherah as two.' Two bodies that were one. Mekarim."

"Soulmates," I said.

Rhyan's eyes filled with light. "I haven't had an academic discussion in...." He shook his head. "Well, it's been a while."

Warmth spread through me. I became aware of his every detail. His dark lashes, the strong bridge of his nose, the curve of his lips, the stubble shadowing his jawline. I'd had the biggest crush on him when I was younger despite the fact that he was cruel and aloof. But then we'd danced and we'd kissed, and it had felt like destiny. I'd taken his hand, and we'd swayed in the night, his eyes on mine, his arm around my waist. My desire for him had taken me captive. Sitting here now, I knew that desire had never let me go.

The doors to the violet ray opened.

Rhyan turned, his posture tensing. A muscle in his jaw twitched. His right hand snaked toward the hilt of his sword. My mouth went dry.

An Afeyan of the Star Court walked languidly through the pews. His skin was tinged blue, glowing faintly beneath gold and silver coils tattooed across every inch of his body. He wore only a silver loincloth between his legs. The golden silk cape draped over his shoulder fell in elegant folds to his feet. Diamonds centered the metallic coils and whorls across his body, glittering and sparkling with every step he took. A crown of silver stars lay atop silky black hair braided down to his hips.

He was beautiful in a way I'd never seen. Delicately feminine and strongly masculine at the same time. With every step he took, he sparkled as the diamonds adorning his body caught the light of the eternal flame. It reminded me of my necklace, embellished with diamonds infused with starfire. He held a Valalumir, glittering like a star, in his hand.

Lumerians had auras, invisible energy colored by their feelings, visible if they were using an extreme amount of power or emotion—but their auras were closely tied to their bodies. The Afeyan's aura was cast out, completely separate from him. The ceiling of the temple, full of paintings, blacked out into an endless sky of twinkling stars.

The Afeyan stood before our row and bowed abruptly. "At your service, Lady Lyriana Batavia, Heir to the Arkasva, High Lord of Bamaria. And to you, Lord Rhyan Hart, Heir Apparent to the Arkasva, High Lord of Glemaria, Imperator to the North." The Valalumir rolled between his fingers, a golden halo around it, as his eyes moved between us. He tossed the star into his other hand like a ball and burst into laughter. "I am Mercurial, First Messenger of Her Royal Highness, Queen Ishtara of the Star Court, High Lady of the Night Lands. I am at your service. What can I do for you?"

"Nothing," Rhyan muttered, "as I am not Lord Rhyan Hart."

"No, not today." Mercurial shrugged. "It matters not to a First Messenger when over the course of a tiny Lumerian life you are one thing or another. Someone strips you of a title, someone says you broke an oath. Why should someone else's words change who you are? A man may be a lord one day and bleed when you cut him, and he may become Arkasva the next. He bleeds the same. Change your name, change your face. Your soul remains. You are still you, *Lord Rhyan.* You do have another name, but you're not ready to hear it."

"Forsworn?" Rhyan asked. "Traitor? Murderer? Bastard? I've heard them all. And if you run out of names, I'll supply you with more."

"Fire, this one has." Mercurial laughed and held his hands before him. The glittering Valalumir floated between his palms, the golden halo waxing brighter. "But you know not of what the First Messenger speaks." His voice had taken on a conspiratorial tone, and his eyebrows narrowed. "You do have questions, I see. Both of you. Questions to which you need answers. Answers I have—even answers for questions you've not yet asked but will. All one has to do is ask the question. Answers are always available."

"No, thank you," I said quickly, suppressing every traitorously tempting thought. I had to remember Morgana and Meera's warnings, the warnings I'd known my whole life. Still, there was something hypnotic about Mercurial, and I found myself mesmerized by even the tiniest of his movements—a blink, a turn of his head. He knew what I wanted, and he could give it to me. All I had to do was ask. I could go home, enroll in the Mage school, restore my stave....

I can do all those things. All those things and more. It would be so easy. Nothing at all….

His voice. His voice was in my mind. Or was I imagining it? My eyes widened, but he didn't react, as if nothing had happened.

"Are you sure?" He extended his hand. The Valalumir spun in his palm, glowing brighter and brighter. On second glance, I realized he hadn't moved at all. I had. I leaned forward still; my chest lifted. I wanted to touch the Valalumir, to feel it, hold it, possess it.

Rhyan touched my arm. His fingers pressed into my tattoo, hitting the scarred skin.

I blinked, coming out of my trance, and Mercurial pulled his hand back, the star rolling across his fingers. It was in the ancient style, like my tattoo and my necklace from Ramia.

"We're quite all right," I said, voice dry. "It was a pleasure to meet the First Messenger of Queen Ishtara."

"First Messenger of Her Royal Highness, Queen Ishtara," he corrected, his head rolling side to side, eyes watching us. "The pleasure's mine. I didn't expect to see you again so soon, your grace." He winked at Rhyan.

Rhyan smiled tightly. "We've not met before."

"You wouldn't remember," Mercurial purred. "You'd understand so much more if you knew what I could see. And I can tell you. All you need to do is ask the First Messenger." He stretched his neck, rolling his head like a snake about to strike.

"See what?" The words spilled from my lips before I could stop them. Rhyan grabbed my arm, but he was too late. The question had been asked.

"Aha." Mercurial smiled. He held out his palm, the star glittering and spinning in its center. The golden light pulsed around the star. "I know your questions. Where is your magic power? How do you find it? How do you help…them? They all connect, but not in the way you expect. And, Lord Rhyan Hart, why do you—"

"Good night, Mercurial." Rhyan was on his feet, sweeping his cloak over his shoulder. He still wore his tattered uniform, but in that moment, he appeared as powerful as an Arkturion. His aura vibrated with power and strength. Any opponent would have cowered before him, but Mercurial seemed only more determined.

I stood, my stomach twisting. I'd never been this close to an Afeyan before, much less spoken to one. The fullness of his aura was overwhelming, along with his sinuous, seductive movements. I knew it was wrong, but I was so deeply entranced. It was unsettling.

"You dare walk away from the First Messenger of Her Royal Highness, when I have so generously offered my help?" He tossed the Valalumir into the air, the light vanishing before it fell and nestled into his hair. "It was you who destroyed my home. Your greed for starfire, your desire for war, your mortal folly. You left my people with nothing but rocks in an ocean of death that swallowed your land whole. Then you have the audacity to name your homes Cresthaven and Sea Tower, as if you were victorious. You're descended from the Gods, but you can't walk on water without glass beneath your feet. You've forgotten how to fly without borrowed wings and can't even remember the secrets within the Guardian of Bamaria. You're nothing more than children of a drowned empire. Your prized light was shattered into pieces. Betrayed by your own. While your home...your true home lies beneath the ocean. And it is all..." he stepped closer, "your..." another step, "fault."

Rhyan stiffened. "Her grace and I must go. We have to prepare for the Oath Ceremony."

Mercurial burst into laughter. "Oh! The oath you shall swear. Swear and forswear again."

Gripping my arm, Rhyan led me outside. Thunder crashed, and lightning lit the sky. The ashvan horses took flight, circling amidst sparks of blue light. The timekeeper rang the bells, marking an hour that signaled dawn on the horizon.

For a moment we stared at each other, our faces drenched. Then Rhyan yelled, "RUN!"

We ran without stopping, his hand reaching for mine, helping me navigate the watery ground without slipping, until we reached my apartment building. He released my hand, and I leaned back against the wall to catch my breath, my heart racing.

"Do you think he really had answers about my power?" I asked.

Frowning, Rhyan brushed raindrops from his hair, letting them splatter with the rest of the rain on his cloak. "I don't think it'd matter after hearing his asking price. I know you have questions. I do, too. But I've gotten this far without answers." He folded his arms. "It took me a while to learn that. I don't need to know everything. Answers are nice, but they don't solve your problems. You do that."

"I suppose," I said slowly. "But magic would really help."

Rhyan shook his head. "Leave immediately if Mercurial approaches you again. He knows you're desperate. He'll use it against you. I've seen it happen—forsworn who went to the Afeya for help out on the road. They prey on forsworn all the time. But no matter what he offers you, it's not worth it— never is. Find a way to get through the next five minutes without answers. When you get through them, get through five more. Enough of those minutes become a day, and before you know it, those days become weeks. I've survived for months like this. It's enough."

"Enough for me to survive training?" I asked.

He bowed. "Get a full night's sleep first."

But that wasn't going to work, not this time. I was too full of energy, too on edge about my Ka and sisters and training and Tristan—fuck! I'd forgotten what a mess I'd made.

Heart pounding, I rushed upstairs and checked my apartment, but he was gone.

Meera had been right—I shouldn't have seen him tonight. I hadn't been thinking straight. But I couldn't let this fight between Tristan and I go until morning. I had to erase my actions. I had to erase what I'd said.

I turned abruptly, walked out of the apartment, and snuck down the Urtavian waterways to the nearest port. I dodged the glimpses of silver and gold hiding in the bushes—the camouflaged soturi in wait.

Markan was nearby. I always knew where he was better than he knew where I was. And as I climbed into my carriage, he emerged, scowling, realizing his mistake. I flipped him off and took to the sky.

My seraphim soared over the city into the greener, lush fields of Vertavia where Ka Grey's central villa stood.

We landed in a port not far from Tristan's home, and I rushed through muddied lands onto the waterway until I reached the walls of the villa and found him sitting on a stone bench, back hunched over, elbows on his knees.

I sat beside him. "I'm sorry," I said. "I don't know what came over me tonight."

"Lyr," he said, his voice full of surprise. He sat up, staring at me. Then he nodded. "It's all right." He wrapped me in his arms, and I willed my body to relax beneath his touch. "You've been through a lot. Do you want to come inside?" It looked like another burst of rain was about to fall.

I took his hand, silent as he led me toward the entrance, past the sentries on duty and quietly up to his bedroom. He closed the door behind him. My heart pounded. My body was so alive, so irritated and desirous...too many things. But I had to make things right with Tristan.

I kissed him without hesitation, running my hands through his hair. My arms wrapped around him so tight there was a sound of anguish and relief from his lips, and our kiss deepened. Before I knew it, I was pushing him backwards onto his bed and straddling his hips. "I'm sorry," I said, writhing against him, sliding his tunic over his head, my hands exploring his bared chest. He was so lean, just enough muscle to prove how easily he could overpower a vorakh. I ran my hands over his belly, moving lower, and lower.

And just as I could feel him tense, unsure of my intentions, I gripped his shoulders, pressing them down.

"We'll wait," I said, biting his lower lip roughly, angrily, despite my words. He was already hard beneath me, straining through his pants, his breath heavy. "We'll wait just a little while longer for it to be right. For her to agree. But tonight, I need to feel you. Just like this."

He nodded, and his hips rose to meet mine, thrusting against me. I moved over him, closing my eyes, my body moving faster and faster, building to my release. Tristan pressed his hands into my hips, steadying me as I rocked over him, the friction of my clothes against his pushing me over the edge. I closed my eyes, biting my lip, tears welling in my eyes as I came in silence.

Tristan watched me wordlessly, his thrusts now rabid until he came as well beneath me.

Catching my breath, I crawled off of him, and curled up by his side. He got up silently and changed, offering me a fresh tunic to change into and a towel.

We didn't speak as we prepared for bed. Only when I was in his arms, my head on his chest, his heart pounding against my ear, did he push my hair out of my face and ask if I was all right.

I didn't answer, only closed my eyes, breathing steadily until I fell asleep.

I snuck out just before sunrise. Just before the Lady of Ka Grey awakened.

CHAPTER FIFTEEN

I SPENT THE following day in meditation at the Temple of Dawn, sitting before Auriel's Chamber with the novices and apprentices preparing to finalize their oaths. We were in nearly the exact same formation as we had been when the Revelation Ceremony began, but this time there was no audience.

Kolaya circled us, the crystal tip of her stave swelling with light. Her long white robes trailed behind, whispering with the soft steps of her bare feet. With each turn her light grew brighter, absorbing energy from us. Every so often her crystal reached its capacity, and she'd step up onto Auriel's Chamber and deposit light from the crystal into a silver bowl full of glittering water that had been drawn from the Lumerian Ocean that morning.

Aunt Arianna, resplendent in her blue robes, stood off to the side with the Ready. The meditation offered insights into the creation of the lineages we'd join, sealed in blood with the oaths we'd take tonight. Though we'd attend lectures at the Mage and Soturion Academies, most of our training happened one on one with an apprentice. After the Oath Ceremony, we'd be magically linked to them and their lineage—connected to their apprentice, their apprentice's apprentice, and so on.

Part of the recommendations for whom to match came from Kolaya and the work she performed here. But the recommendations of the Ready overseeing the soturi and Arianna observing the mages were also taken into account. They attempted to match novices and apprentices according to skill sets, but there was also an attempt to make assignments across country and Kavim. Mixing lineages united the tribes across the Empire and kept civil wars from breaking out. If relations flared, the cross-lineages often kept the peace.

As a novice, Tristan had been linked to a mage from Ka Elys. But since he'd become an apprentice, he now trained another mage from Ka Grey.

My knees and back ached from hours of sitting cross-legged, and the incense burned in my nose and eyes as the seven Watchers released fresh puffs of smoke. I could feel everyone's eyes on me. I could feel their questions, their ridicule, and their glee over the fall of Lady Lyriana Batavia, daughter of the *shekar arkasva*. I sat taller; my chin lifted. I would control what they saw. I would not show fear or worry. I would not allow even a small slope of my back.

At last, we were dismissed to eat, bathe, and change into our ceremonial robes, black for the Oath Ceremony.

All around me were excited whispers and speculations of which apprentice they'd be assigned. Certain ones were highly sought after, known for their prowess, while others seemed desirable simply because of their Ka. I felt sorry for whomever was forced to pair with me.

A small group of apprentices from Ka Kormac rushed past me, catching up to Rhyan, who was nearly out the door. They surrounded him. A tall blonde boy shoved into Rhyan, and another pushed him to the side. But he kept his balance, staring ahead, until he reached the temple doors. The soturi snickered, jovially punching each other's backs, and ran ahead.

Something tugged inside of me, a need to go to him, to see if he was all right, but Haleika and Galen caught me, excitedly chatting, intent on filling me in on every detail about training.

Haleika's curly hair was the same exact shade of brown as Tristan's. It bounced excitedly as she talked about her future lineage. Galen, quiet and stoic, just folded his arms and smiled, listening to her.

She eyed an apprentice soturion from Ka Daquataine while Galen wasn't looking. He was almost as tall as Rhyan, was full of muscle, and had dirty blonde hair. His features weren't necessarily attractive on their own, but he was so animated and expressive as he talked to his friends that he seemed to become more handsome the more he moved. Haleika bit her lip.

"Hoping to get him?" I asked.

She blushed. "Not as my apprentice…since, you know, it's forbidden."

I raised my eyebrows. "You have a crush on him? What about Galen?"

She smirked. "It's that obvious?"

"Either Tristan or I will be coming into a large fortune over your decision soon."

Haleika laughed, eyeing the apprentice one last time, and shook her head. "Keep betting." She grabbed Galen's arm and winked at me over her shoulder as they joined a group of novices from Kavim sworn to Ka Batavia. A few were distantly related to Aemon, belonging to Ka Melvik, and there were more of Tristan and Haleika's Ka Grey cousins. Most weren't noble, and none were on the mage track, so I'd paid little attention to them over the years as we grew up.

Naria joined the group, and I knew in that moment I'd made a grave error. I'd been so focused on who would be of benefit to me politically and on how to keep Meera and Morgana safe, I'd grown distant from my own people. I needed allies and friends in this new world.

I inched closer to the group, but their ranks closed in, their circle tightening. Heads turned rapidly as whispers rose through the crowd. They were talking about me, about my arrest.

I'd never been denied access to any social circles before. As Heir, I'd been the center of them whenever I'd chosen to be. Now it looked as if Naria was the most important Lady of Bamaria.

Most surrounding Naria were from the Bamarian branch of Ka Elys, though a few from Elyria were there as well. Their jewelry all featured their sigil, the ashvan horse galloping over a golden sun. Most of their dresses were deep purple, the traditional color of Ka Elys. Those from Elyria wore orange. But Bamarian or Elyrian, all members of Ka Elys had the same golden-brown skin, silky black hair, and long faces.

Standing closest to Naria was Lady Pavi Elys, who would one day lead Ka Elys in Bamaria. Her aunt was Senator Janvi Elys, which made Pavi someone I should have paid much more attention to a long time ago. Naria hadn't made my mistake.

"Lady Lyriana," Naria said. Her voice was mockingly sweet. With a wave of her hand, the crowd parted before her. "I'm so glad to see you here."

All eyes were on me. But they always were, I reminded myself. I stood tall, allowing my arms to fall neatly at my sides. "And I you, cousin."

Naria showed off a wide grin, but her eyebrows narrowed. "After your imprisonment in the Shadow Stronghold and your expulsion...." She paused, letting the words hang in the air, tossing back her blonde hair. Her features were all Ka Kasmar, like those of her father Tarek Kasmar, the traitor. "Forgive me, but we're all so curious how you pulled this off.

No one without magic has ever been admitted to the Academy before. What did you promise the Ready?"

Hushed gasps sounded around me, followed by a few fits of giggles.

"I can't decide," I said slowly, forcing my voice to remain steady, "who should be more insulted by your false allegations. Tristan, for your insinuating I'd be untrue, the Ready, for your suggesting he could be so manipulated, or me."

Naria glared in response. No one had objected to her insult; the crowd behind her had barely reacted. Rumors and gossip amongst lords and ladies were common, and I wasn't surprised she'd attacked me and Tristan. But how strong was the unrest toward my father's rule if the Ready could be openly insulted by soturi?

"You may leave." I waved her off. Prolonging conversations only brought more life to rumors. The less of this conversation people witnessed, the less to discuss later.

"Of course," she said. "I hope this new chapter in your life doesn't interfere with your engagement. I'm sure Tristan and all of Ka Grey still support you."

"Now," I commanded.

Naria bit her lip, her eyes alight. I could almost see her mind turning. She knew exactly how to upset me—she'd known since we ran barefoot in the halls of Cresthaven. But in public, her actions had consequences. And she knew it. She bowed too deeply—a mockery of the gesture—and with a final death glare, she left the group. Several of the novice soturi followed her, including every purple-donning soturion from Ka Elys, dutifully following Pavi. Naria looked back one last time, and then to my shock, she greeted Viktor Kormac with a kiss on the cheek. She slipped her arm through his. Several silver-wolfed soturi followed them into the night.

I'd barely been home long enough to bathe and change before I had to return.

I stood outside the temple in my black robes with the rest of the novices. In the Oath Ceremony, we entered the temple one by one when it was time to swear into our lineage.

My palms were sweating when my name was called, and I stepped into the red ray once more, this time alone. Black shadows and incense permeated the air, thick and heavy. The Red Watcher of the light placed a black veil over my face, further blinding me. I stumbled forward, disoriented in the dark.

"Let the novice walk in shadows, let them walk through the darkness, not yet strong, not yet powerful, not yet a soturion," intoned Kolaya. "*La ha nuha vrata chayate lyla, la ha nuha vrata el ha lyla, aisha, ashukroya, asoturion.*"

The eternal flame flickered purple, and I saw the shadow of my apprentice standing on the dais, waiting for me beside the Ready. Fear of who stood in the shadows pulsed through me.

Kolaya continued, "And when the novice meets their apprentice, their training brings them into the light of the Valalumir, and in that light they grow and find their strength."

"There's a step," the Watcher whispered, squeezing my hand as I reached the Chamber.

My apprentice stepped forward to remove my veil. Black filled my vision as hands reached for my face and pulled the cloth above my eyes.

Rhyan.

No. Not him. The thought struck me without warning. But why not? He was an accomplished soturion, and he'd trained at one of the most brutal schools. We already had something like a friendship. Still, my stomach churned with something I didn't have words for. Relationships between novices and their apprentices were forbidden. And I was with Tristan.

Take my hand.

The eternal flame scorched, illuminating Rhyan in gold. He was so bright, almost too bright to look at.

Rhyan betrayed no emotion—no joy at seeing my face but no horror either. There was only the slightest lift of his uninjured eyebrow. Someone had trimmed off his curls. He looked older without them, more severe.

His ruined uniform had been replaced with a newly pressed green cloak. He had elegantly skirted the pleats around his waist and draped the extra material across his shoulders in perfect folds. His belt shined with seven leather straps adorned with freshly sharpened Valalumir stars. And his newly forged armor was simple and elegant, black leather with a sigil I didn't recognize—the face of a golden seraphim in profile opposite the face of a silver gryphon. The tips of their wings met above their heads, framing the sun, and beneath their faces was a full moon. The gryphon and the sun represented Ka Hart, and the seraphim and moon Ka Batavia. This new design showed his past and his future. The start of a fresh lineage here. A kashonim. His line in Glemaria had been broken when he'd been named forsworn. He headed a new kashonim now, could forge a new link. Ours. A lineage of just the two of us. We truly were partners now.

"You are no longer a child of Lumeria," said the Ready. "You are reborn a soturion."

A lump formed in my throat. I could barely breathe. I knew what was coming next.

Rhyan untied the belt at my waist, his hands brushing against my hips. His jaw tensed as he pushed my robes open, revealing a white shift barely concealing my breasts and short-pants.

In Lumeria Matavia, before the Drowning, the Oath Ceremony was completed with full nudity. A part of me was imagining it now—being naked before Rhyan. I was nearly there. And even with a temple full of people watching, even knowing Tristan sat out there, my heart felt like it would drum its way out of my chest as I watched Rhyan. I'd made sure my hair was full and loose to cover my back and hide my healing wounds and that my cuffs and bracelets were arranged just so. I'd expected my nerves to jump.

But I hadn't expected this. This look from Rhyan. This heated feeling inside of me.

Rhyan's eyes were on me with a fiery intensity that warmed me from the inside out. I could feel each place his gaze lingered. Jaw clenched, he grazed my shoulders. His fingers, so rough and calloused, so unlike Tristan's, against my now bared skin. The word janam ran through my mind. Recognition. Knowing.

The Ready gestured to a burning pyre behind us. Rhyan had fully removed my robe and tossed it into the fire.

"You are reborn as one," he said louder. "Apprentice and novice. Soturi."

The Ready presented my new uniform to Rhyan. "As the apprentice trains the novice with knowledge, so the apprentice outfits the novice in the clothes and weapons they will need."

Rhyan pleated the green cloak around my waist, draping the ends over my shoulders the way he fashioned his. He strapped on my armor, golden with sharpened seraphim-shaped feathers curling over my shoulder. He cinched my belt around my waist; the seven straps full of Valalumirs weighed heavy against my thighs. Last, he sheathed my starfire sword.

The Ready grabbed our hands, holding our wrists together. His dagger struck swiftly, slashing our wrists. Our blood mixed and dripped into a silver goblet, and with a quick slice to my armor and Rhyan's, our blood flowed through our sigils, turning them red. We were now linked. The magic which sealed our fates would allow us to draw strength from each other.

Now all that remained was the oath, made as one.

"I am a soturion. I pledge my heart and soul to the fight against evil, to the protection of the innocent, to the promise of a better world. And in my pledge, I will forsake everything and everyone that should come between me and my fight...."

Rhyan's fingers brushed against mine, our wrists still bound.

"I shall fight beside my fellow soturi, I shall honor my Ka and all my vows. And I shall fight with my lineage always working to end all evil. And if I shall be forsworn...." Rhyan's jaw clenched. His eyes found mine.

"If I should put others before my duties, if I should love those whom I've sworn to not, then I will no longer be a soturion. I will gladly accept my death. And so my oath is complete."

At the final words of the oath—*If I should love those whom I've sworn to not*—my stomach tightened, and a sense of wrongness swept through me. The words felt poisonous, like I'd be sick if I spoke them. I'd loved Jules when I shouldn't have. And my sisters. The oaths of Lumeria were starting to suffocate me. But I had no choice.

I had to swear it. For my sisters. For my life. For a future in Bamaria.

My voice came as a rasp before I managed to say with Rhyan the final words. "I will gladly accept my death. And so my oath is complete. *Ani Dhara Me Sha El Lyrotz.*"

The Arkmage stepped forward with the silver goblet, sprinkling what remained of our blood over our heads as she blessed us in High Lumerian. One drop of blood rolled down Rhyan's forehead, down his scar. He closed his eyes.

"Your oath begins with the flow of blood, your oath will end when its flow may cease. *Ra sha se ledah o ha vrania d'lyrotz, ra sha se lavra ru ha vrania halavra.*"

The Ready slashed through the binding, releasing our wrists, and we found our seats below the Chamber. The next novice entered, cloaked in black, and a new apprentice stepped up, their face crackling under the flames, now a deep purple.

It was finished. We had sworn to be apprentice and novice. To be kashonim. To never be more than that.

What had I done?

THE THIRD SCROLL:
KATURIUM

CHAPTER SIXTEEN

"THEY BOUND YOU to him!" Tristan cocked his head to the side, fury emanating from his aura. "To him! That bastard forsworn."

"Tristan, calm down." I stepped back. The heat of his anger was irritating my skin.

"Calm down? How can I calm down when you've been blood-tied to a murderer? I don't care that your father and Aemon let him in. There's a reason he's forsworn, a reason no other country will take him in."

"I don't think he's a danger to me."

"No? He got in my way that night. I almost had you free."

"Tristan, he was doing his job. I had a guard on me to prevent exactly what you tried. And don't forget he was put there by the Imperator."

He shook his head. "I don't like it."

I sighed. "You don't have to. I don't exactly like the novice mage you're assigned to train either, nor do I like the fact that I'm a soturion, but I'm dealing with it. Tristan, please. I don't have the energy to convince myself it'll be all right and convince you, too. Can you just drop it?"

His nostrils flared. "I'm never going to like this. Or him."

"Fine, but for tonight...let's just go to the after party. I need some fun after the week I've had." I took his hands, pulling them onto my waist, and kissed him. "Come on."

He remained motionless, fire dancing in his dark eyes.

"Please?"

Tristan exhaled sharply. "You're right. Let's go."

We walked to the fields where everyone had gathered for the Oath Ceremony's after party. It was a celebration of the newly formed lineages and the last night of freedom for novices before classes and training began in the morning. A soft breeze tickled the night, whispering the echo of drums beating in time to the notes of lyres and flutes. Fires sprang to light, and novice mages, drunk on their new powers, sparked dazzling fireworks in the starlit sky.

Someone conjured a dance floor in the clearing's center. Wanting to vanish into a crowd, I dragged Tristan in. His hands snaked down my ribs and waist still covered in golden armor until he dug into my hips and pulled me close, our bodies in rhythm as we danced. Fireworks exploded above, and water dancers performed beside the drummers, their blue ribbons shimmying across the ground. There was still an edge of fury in his aura. I danced closer to him, even more seductively, grinding my ass against him, snaking my hips up and down in the way I knew drove him mad. But he wasn't going to forget I was now linked to Rhyan so easily. Not with the armor between us.

I certainly couldn't forget.

Even as we moved, I couldn't stop seeing Rhyan's face in the temple. I couldn't stop seeing the intensity of his eyes as he'd undressed me. I couldn't forget the way his hands had felt against my skin.

But the hands now playfully pulling me back were smooth, not calloused. Tristan spun me to face him, pulling my body against his. I buried my face in his neck, worried he'd read my mind and know it was on Rhyan.

We continued dancing as more shows of magic erupted around us. As always, those drunkest, or most foolish, chanted the incantation for kashonim, invoking the full power of their lineage. It was easy to tell who'd done so. There'd be a hurricane of energy around them, a minor earthquake from a single jump, lightning as bright as the sun nearly leaving their stave in ashes. Patrols were doubled the night of the Oath Ceremony just to account for the idiocy.

As the music sped up, Tristan twirled me while one soturion uprooted a tree. More began to call on kashonim, and every single one of them began to fall, keeling over and collapsing, unable to sustain so much power at once. We'd barely been out there half an hour, but the celebration was already littered with passed out mages and soturi either being stepped over or arranged into compromising positions by their friends.

The music slowed again, and fewer couples remained on the dance floor. Some of the new soturi were getting into brawls while their friends cheered on the sidelines.

I wrapped my arms around Tristan's neck, and he leaned in, his lips on mine.

"Do you want to go somewhere?" His voice was husky with desire.

"By those trees," I said, squeezing his hand.

We weaved our way through the crowd—most of the party attendees were too drunk to notice. We weren't the only ones suddenly caught up in the frenzy and lust on the field.

There was a scream, and I turned to find another brawl had broken out. Not a brawl, a five. Five soturi taking on one soturion.

Naria.

She was unskilled, taking hits and punches in the belly or on her back. Punches that would have left me on my knees and bawling in unimaginable pain. But she seemed unfazed, as if she'd merely been slapped. She easily missed her targets with her poor aim but happily laughed in response, even after taking a punch to her jaw.

I leaned back against the tree I'd found, away from the other couples. Moans of pleasure whispered through the leaves rustling around us. I closed my eyes as Tristan fumbled with my armor, loosening the unfamiliar straps until he could fit his hands inside, pushing aside my cloak and pawing at my breasts. His thumb brushed against an already hardened nipple, and I gasped, pulling him closer. Gripping his belt, I wrapped my leg around his hips. Tristan unhooked my golden plates, his hands sweeping over my shoulders, baring me to him.

I closed my eyes, head falling back.

We were pressed against a sun tree. His jaw was clenched, and his hands were rough on my hips. I wanted him so bad, I ached. He leaned in, his cheek pressed against mine the way it had when we were dancing. I could feel his breath in my ear and my knees weakened.

"I want to kiss you," he said, with that beautiful northern lilt to his voice. "Can I?"

"Yes."

His lips brushed against mine, soft, tentative, testing. He pulled back, and his emerald eyes met mine. They sparked with desire, and his mouth was on mine again, his lips moving with a fierce softness as he deepened the kiss, tasting me, moaning into my mouth. The sound drove me wild, as did his taste and the feel of him. My core heated, and I pulled him against me, his hips settling against mine. One hand wrapped around my waist, traveling down my hips and around to cup my ass. His other hand rose to cup my chin, his fingers caressing my cheek.

"I want you," he growled in my ear. "I've always wanted you."

Then he pulled back, removing my robe, baring me to him. His blood was my blood, running through the enchantments of our armor, through my body. He was under my skin. There was a new scar on my wrist to accompany my blood oaths, linking us together forever.

"You feel so good," he breathed, his aura swirling around me, cocooning me, claiming me. I couldn't catch my breath.

Rhyan's hand grazed my hips, his breath hot on my shoulder as he kissed his way to my collarbone, his other hand sliding between my legs. I was so wet, so ready for him, I was pulsing. I thrust my hips forward to meet him. Yes. Gods, yes.

"Lyr," Tristan moaned my name. Tristan. Not Rhyan.

My eyes snapped open. Brown eyes, not green, stared into mine. I shuddered. I'd fallen into a full fantasy of Rhyan, a memory of our actual first kiss mixed into what Tristan was doing to me now. Gods. I'd been so absorbed...I had no idea I was still kissing Tristan. My entire body felt cold as I tried to blink the images away.

"Are you all right?" Tristan asked, nipping a soft kiss on my cheek.

I nodded and sucked in a shaky breath. "Don't stop."

Tristan kissed his way to my neck, and I stared out at the field, afraid to close my eyes again, afraid I'd forget whose arms I was in.

Naria had spotted us in the distance, finding our location even through the trees, and watched with vitriol in her eyes. She didn't see Pavi coming. The soturion jumped, her body colliding into Naria with such force they flew several feet across the grass, crashing onto the ground. Naria landed roughly on her back with Pavi over her. I winced, but Pavi easily rolled off, and Naria bounced to her feet.

These were unskilled novice soturi—without any training. But their strength was clear. If they decided to attack, they'd kill me. If I suffered a fall like that, it would kill me.

I felt cold all over with fear over what was waiting for me in the morning. My first option of becoming Ka Grey was on hold, and I couldn't approach the Afeya for answers. Mercurial terrified me too much.

That left one last option for help. The library. Thousands of scrolls were above and underground in the pyramids... somewhere in there had to be answers.

I couldn't wait. I couldn't stay at this party any longer, not when I'd just be counting down the hours until I'd be in the arena with Naria and Pavi and Viktor and the other soturi. I needed more information, and I needed to start now—even if it was almost the middle of the night. Either way, I wasn't going to get any sleep.

"Tristan," I said. "I think I'd better go." I pointed his face toward the five still going strong. Another girl from Ka Elys entered the makeshift arena, standing proud in the center. Tani Elwen. She wasn't noble but seemed to have latched onto Pavi.

Pavi threw a brutal punch into her stomach. Tani stumbled, gasping for breath, but quickly recovered.

"That's what I face tomorrow," I said, watching his eyes widen.

He turned to me, pressing his forehead against mine, and exhaled slowly. Wordlessly, he nodded, our heads still touching until he pressed a kiss to my forehead. Deftly, he began to reassemble my cloak into the pleats and folds Rhyan had created.

Hand in hand, we crossed the field, stepping over the bodies of the passed out soturi who'd called on kashonim and worn themselves out. We passed the shows of magic from the mages. Viktor stood off to the side of the excitement with several of his wolves, all clearly drunk and sloppily holding goblets in their hands, sloshing wine onto the ground.

"Lady Asherah." He howled like a wolf. His men howled in response. "Don't ride him too hard tonight. Save some for us in the morning! Arrrooo!"

Tristan tightened his grasp on my hand, and we hurried along. I wished he'd leave me to go to the seraphim port on my own, but I couldn't explain where I was truly going. He'd try to convince me to stay in my apartment and rest, and I'd lose time arguing with him.

At last, I left him at the front door with a long, deep kiss.

As soon as he turned, I made my move. Quickly, I pulled the excess material of my cloak over my head like a hood—Ka Batavia style—and disappeared into the night. One benefit to my situation: I now had the ability to camouflage into my surroundings, and Tristan had never been good at spotting soturi.

Only one available seraphim remained at the port, looking a little sleepy. I grabbed a treat from the attendant and fed her, giving her wing a long stroke before I climbed aboard the carriage. We were airborne instantly.

My nerves were jumping as I arrived on Scholar's Harbor, the site of the Great Library. Every scroll that survived Lumeria Matavia after the Drowning and every scroll that had been recorded since were stored here in three pyramids made of golden bricks. The Scholars, a Ka that had remained mostly isolated since the Drowning, were completely committed to the preservation and sharing of knowledge. Very few left the pyramids or Harbor to seek other passions. Arkmage Kolaya was one exception. Galen was another.

Soturi of Ka Batavia stood guard outside the golden pyramids, and Scholars raced across the golden beaches that surrounded the pyramids on the backs of ashvan horses, scarves covering their faces and scrolls tied to their backs. Some raced on the wind, soaring above the tops of the pyramids, while others raced across the sand, dust clouds exploding behind them. This was where ashvan came when they grew too old to fly high. The oldest ashvan were grounded on the beach, shooting blue sparks from their hooves as they galloped across the sand dunes, lifting their heads and throwing back their manes as the younger horses ran across their backs.

The golden pyramids glowed bronze beneath the waning moon. The first had been built when the Scholars arrived on these shores. It was over three stories tall above ground. Beneath it was a second underground pyramid where the most ancient and delicate scrolls were kept. An inordinate amount of magic had been needed to construct it. Because magic often changed the land, it was actually the construction of the first pyramid that had transformed the landscape into a desert. When my ancestors arrived, the ground was lush and green. The first pyramid had seemed overly spacious for what scrolls existed at the time and had been mocked as a ridiculously large, indulgent structure by the Senate. But soon the pyramids both above and below ground were bursting with newly written scrolls, and a second pyramid, even larger, had been built, drying the land even further as they dug deep. The third had only been built in the last hundred years, and it too was already running low on space.

I needed the smallest, most ancient pyramid, the one which housed the texts in High Lumerian. Two soturi, each over six feet tall with nearly black skin, stood on either side of the doorway, their swords crossed. Eger Scholar and Apollon Scholar, brothers who'd trained under Turion Brenna, now dedicated their lives to the protection of knowledge. They both tended to guard late at night—when I'd made many of my research visits in spite of Markan's grumbling.

Eger lowered his chin. "Welcome, your grace."

Apollon nodded in welcome. If they were surprised to see me tonight, knowing I was a novice about to begin soturion training in the morning, they did not show it. They pulled back their swords, allowing me to enter.

I smiled in return, greeting them each as I crossed the threshold, surrounded by the golden bricks of the ancient pyramid.

Nabula Kajan, one of the lead librarians, jumped from behind a long table overflowing with scrolls. She'd been closely reading a tiny parchment, still stiff in her hand. Quickly, she rolled it up and sealed it into a small leather case tied around her right arm. Several more cases appeared on her left arm, and larger cases hung from her waist, belted over a flowing white gown. In my arm cuff, I wore the parchment keeping Meera's secrets. But the librarians wore scrolls all over their bodies, letting knowledge adorn them like jewels.

"Lady Lyriana, congratulations." Nabula bobbed her head up and down, grinning in a way that accentuated her pointed chin. Then her eyes took in my attire, and she gasped. "You chose the path of soturion!"

My chest seized as the realization hit. She didn't know. Typical. Lumerians from Ka Scholar rarely left the Harbor and sanctuary of their texts. They spent so much time in the past that current events reached them in a delayed manner.

"Thank you, Nabula." My voice was stilted, not yet sure how to form the words to tell her the truth—that I hadn't chosen this, not willingly.

She reached overhead, pulling a long golden lamp from a cluttered shelf. An amethyst nearly the size of my head dangled from the hook of the lamp rod, its multifaceted edges catching tiny glimmers of light from the doorway behind me.

Smiling proudly, Nabula handed the lamp to me. Its weight was heavy in my hands. I watched the amethyst swing from side to side as I steadied my hold.

"Are you ready to light the crystal for the first time?" Magically lit amethysts were the only source of light inside the pyramids. Fire was strictly forbidden near the scrolls.

Nabula had been lighting my lamp for years, and we'd often talked about the day I'd have my own magic and could light it myself.

But I couldn't. My heart sank as I handed the lamp back to Nabula. Her small hands closed around the golden rod as her dark eyebrows scrunched up in confusion.

"That's why I'm here," I said, voice quiet with shame I could no longer conceal.

Nabula's face fell. "I don't understand, your grace."

"I didn't manifest any magic." I watched sadly as her mouth fell open. "None at all."

"Your grace!" Nabula's eyes widened, but she had enough sense to close her mouth. "But...such a thing is not possible." She shook her head and straightened, her entire expression returning to one of neutral formality. "My apologies. I did not mean to offend."

I waved her off. "It's all right. I'm hoping I might find answers as to why this happened. And quickly. I must return to the Soturion Academy tonight."

"Yes, your grace, I'll pull some titles for you."

I nodded, swallowing. "Would you?" I gestured to the lamp.

Nabula lowered the base of the rod to the floor, causing the giant amethyst to swing precariously above her head. Her eyes closed, and she waved her right hand in a sweeping motion three times before repeating the gesture over the stone, whispering the spell for light. A luminescent light swelled within the base of the purple crystal. At first it was a tiny ball coiled tightly before it unraveled, snaking its way through the amethyst with light shining out in purple rays so bright, Nabula's dress turned lavender.

"Follow me." Nabula returned the lamp.

My fingers tightened around the rod as I pushed away my grief. It was just a lamp! I took a deep breath and walked behind her.

Nabula pulled a thin scroll from the cuff around her biceps and unraveled the parchment. Her eyes raced across the script until she brightened. "I know where to begin the search." We turned down a dark corridor lit by small floating crystals before climbing up two flights of stairs.

She left me in the center of the pyramid beneath an opening to the ceiling that revealed the pyramid rising to a point just over my head. A glowing amethyst shaped into the seven-pointed Valalumir hung from the peak. Purple Valalumirs had been painted onto the golden walls along with the sigil for Ka Scholar, a white scroll rolled before a glowing golden pyramid.

I sat at a table surrounded by golden walkways and shelves, inserted the rod of my lamp through a hole carved into the wood, and waited. Within minutes, Nabula returned and laid several scrolls across my desk. Quickly, she conjured scroll-stops on either side before they rolled onto the floor, and then she left me to my reading.

I unraveled the first scroll.

The History of Birth Binds by Vora Mazda of Ka Scholar. I rolled the yellowing parchment over until chapter one lay flat before me.

When in Lumeria Matavia such things as the Birth Bind were unconsidered and not yet conceived, for it was some two hundred years after the Drowning that the need for such measures arose. Our ancestors were blessed with more powerful magic than now, gifts from the Gods, or as the Scholars now believe, a result of the magic within the earth of Lumeria, a deeper magic now found in, or perhaps having leaked from, the waters that conceal it. It was common for Lumerians in the motherland to see visions with ease, connect to another mentally and communicate, as well as travel by disappearing and reappearing at will. Such magic was common, comfortable to use, and most importantly, well respected and easily regulated, making it difficult to abuse.

I rerolled the scroll, angrily shoving it aside. I'd read this before when Meera's visions began. It called for the Birth Bind to sniff out those with vorakh powers. Usually, vorakh powers had a tendency to burst out of a Lumerian in their first show of magic, so Birth Binds caught many—including Jules. But not always. Some vorakh strengthened over the first year a Lumerian was unbound. Otherwise, no one would survive the Revelation Ceremony...and Tristan wouldn't have become the hunter he was.

Rummaging through Nabula's selections, I found I'd previously read and taken notes on many of the scrolls before, from beginning to end, all of them connected to vorakh and the initial shows of magic power.

A shadow, tinged in purple, loomed over my desk.

"How was your stay in Shadow Stronghold?" Ramia glided toward me wearing a silky black dress. It wrapped around one shoulder and hugged every one of her curves. She dropped into the seat opposite me, fixing the bracelets adorning her arms. Her long red hair had been tied into a thick braid that fell over her shoulder into her lap. "Ironic, no? I worried I'd be thrown in, and yet, it was you. Though, not for ancient artifact theft." She winked. Right. I'd nearly forgotten the other crime I'd committed that day and the favor I'd promised a half-Afeyan.

I swallowed. "I take it you've been keeping up with current events?" I'd wondered, based on Nabula's reaction, if anyone on Scholar's Harbor knew what had happened to me.

Ramia laughed. "Past, current, future." She lifted an eyebrow, her gaze pointed at a Scholar hunched over a scroll. "They expel me from library to say so, but there's more to life than inside scrolls."

"Maybe," I said. "But I need to start somewhere."

"To find magic." Ramia rolled Nabula's selections along the table, her eyes sliding across the titles. "You not find answers here." She opened a leather pouch hanging from her shoulder and retrieved a set of white gloves, a slab of viewing glass, and a dark leather case. She unscrewed the lid, carefully sliding the ancient, weathered scroll onto the table.

It was from Lumeria Matavia. Over a thousand years old, written before the Drowning.

"You prepared this for me?" I asked. Nabula had only given me copies, nothing so ancient I had to read it under glass. These sorts of scrolls were usually reserved for reading beneath the pyramid in the underground levels. "Ramia, how did you know I was coming?"

"A guess," she said. "You're smart girl. Problems? You come to library."

I eyed the scroll again, suspicious. "Aren't you the Afeyan librarian?"

With a shrug, Ramia smiled. "What? I can't read outside my genre? How boring!"

"Ramia," I asked, "do you know the Star Court ambassador? Mercurial?"

She pushed her chair back to stand. "I know every Afeya who step foot in Bamaria." Her eyes roved over my soturion cloak and armor, the dagger at my waist. I felt like an idiot dressed up this way. But then a comment Ramia had made on my birthday struck me. She'd said I'd looked like the Goddess Asherah. Like a warrior. Like a soturion.

"Did you know I would become a soturion?" I asked.

Ramia wrinkled her nose. "No. I only know necklace make you look fierce. Fierce and beautiful. Wear it." She tapped the scroll. "In meantime, start here. High Lumerian."

"I will," I said.

"Find answers," she said with a shudder. "Arena is no place for the weak."

I stiffened at the warning, watching her collect a stack of scrolls and head down a dark aisle of shelves. I waited until she was gone, uneasy with the way she seemed so invested in me lately. But once I was alone, I slipped the gloves over my fingers and slid the scroll between the glass plates, gently pulling the edges of the parchment through. My amethyst flickered momentarily, brightening and then calming to a soft purple haze.

The Fall of Asherah and Her Loss of Power by Sianna Batavia.

I stared at the title, and my heart skipped a beat. *Her Loss of Power.* Excitement surged through me. I reread the author's name. I'd never heard of Sianna Batavia, but I suspected we were related. How then had I never heard of her or her scroll?

I pulled the parchment farther through the glass, the ends curling and rerolling, until I had a clear view of the first chapter.

My name is Sianna, and I take the name Batavia, for I am a daughter of the land. I come here to write what I know about the Goddess and Guardian of the Light, Asherah, and her Fall, in the hopes of preserving such information for prosperity. These times are uncertain. The waves on our shores grow higher each day, and I fear for the future. I sense a coming doom, and my own sister has dreamt of waves rising from the oceans to fall upon our heads and drown us in her waters. Some speak of leaving, believing there is more land beyond the sea. I do not know of any lands beyond Lumeria. I only hope. Thus, I take the name Batavia with the desire that I will truly become a daughter of land, and by the Gods be kept safe.

Sianna rambled on for chapters and chapters, speaking of her fears that the knowledge she spoke of would be lost. After hours of reading, I came to the chapters on Asherah, but it was all information I knew. How Asherah had been a young Goddess in Heaven, chosen as one of seven to guard the Valalumir after Canturiel's creation was nearly stolen by akadim in the Celestial Realms. How she reported daily to the Hall of Records to guard it until she fell in love with the golden-haired God, Auriel. And how their affair led to her Fall. How she was banished to Earth to live out her days in

Lumeria Matavia, mortal and weakened, until Auriel stole the Valalumir and fell to be with her and save her, forever changing the light to crystal—and forever hiding some of that light within her body.

I was nearing the end of the scroll, growing frustrated with Sianna's wordiness, when the writing shifted dramatically.

We've lost. The waves have come. My sister's dreams and visions foretold this. She was right. Water everywhere. Waves so high. The summer gardens dried up. The Valalumir has shattered. The pieces gone. All is lost. Akadim have overrun our lands, Moriel's forces have won.

And then the scroll ended. I pulled several more pages of parchment through the glass, but they were all empty. She'd never finished writing.

I took out my lamp and returned to Nabula's desk.

"Were any of the scrolls helpful, your grace?" she asked.

I shook my head, clutching Sianna's scroll. "Nabula, another librarian offered me *The Fall of Asherah and Her Loss of Power.*"

Nabula's cheeks darkened. "Auriel's bane. I should have thought to pull that title for you—it's just so rarely read. Sianna has trouble remaining focused. Many who've read it found it unhelpful. Did it give you any insight?"

I shrugged. "I don't know yet. The scroll cuts off before the end. Are there any of her other works in the library?"

Nabula removed the scroll on her arm, quickly unraveling the parchment, until her eyes narrowed. "Ah, yes, *The Fall of Asherah*. That was only part one of Sianna's writings."

"Part one? How many more scrolls did she write?"

Nabula cross-checked two scrolls on her desk, her eyes rushing back and forth. "One more."

"Can I borrow it?" I asked, heart skipping. "Or reserve it?" Maybe I could return tomorrow night.

Nabula's eyes raced across a parchment on her desk. Fingers racing across a second scroll as she cross-checked its availability, she frowned. "I'm so sorry, your grace. All but one copy is downstairs in restoration. And it's already being borrowed."

"Borrowed? By who?"

"The Afeyan Ambassador to the Star Court."

My stomach twisted. Mercurial. Suddenly Ramia's insistence on my reading part one left me uneasy…I needed part two. And Mercurial knew that. Had he anticipated this? Or sent Ramia to offer part one in an attempt to lure me to him to make a deal? I shivered. Did Ramia know what she was doing? I wasn't going to be bought this easily.

"Will you please alert me the moment it's returned?" I asked. "Or when the second copy returns from restoration?"

"Of course, your grace. It will be reserved and prepared for you immediately."

"Thank you, Nabula." From a distance, I caught Ramia climbing down the stairs, watching me, and turned on my heels, ready to get out of there as quickly as possible.

Blue streaks lit up the night sky as the bells called the hour. It was so late, it was practically morning. I had to be awake in mere hours. I raced back to my seraphim and spurred her to flight. And though I knew I was playing with fire, I called out to her, "Cresthaven." I just had to check on my sisters.

Morgana had passed out on top of her covers with a cooling pillow filled with lavender and moonleaves on her forehead. It had warmed to body temperature, leaving her sweating and scowling in her sleep. I traipsed down to the kitchen's ice room to switch her pillow out for a cold one and checked on my moon oil supply. We were almost out. I spent the next hour brewing a fresh batch, gathering herbs from the gardens and crushing moonstones until I had a new bottle for Morgana and Meera each. I laid the fresh, cooled pillow on Morgana's forehead, smoothing her hair back with moon oil and leaving an extra dose on her temples until her expression softened.

Meera looked at peace when I found her, so I left her jar on her nightstand. Her bedroom was in complete disarray, leaving me feeling guilty for having been away so long. I folded up her clothing and cleaned up her paints, lining them up beneath her newest masterpiece—the painting of a red-haired girl who'd turned into a black seraphim, missing her mouth. Shuddering, I left for my apartment.

I stood at the red ray's entrance to the Temple of Dawn wearing a silvery white gown, sparkling with starlight, twinkling with every breath I took. The dress swept behind my ankles into an unending train that flowed outside, streaming over the blue waterways of Bamaria and rippling through the city, past the green fields of Cresthaven, into the rolling waves of the ocean.

The moon was full, and my watery dress glittered as I stood before the temple's threshold. The sanctuary was dark, nearly black with shadow. The eternal flame burst to life with a popping sound; the scent of smoke burned my nostrils as flames crackled and echoed around me. Golden red light filled the temple, lighting each of the seven rays. I walked forward knowing I needed to touch the fire, feel its heat. I was made of water, and fire couldn't hurt me. But as I reached Auriel's Chamber, stepping onto the first level and then the second, my hand inches from the flames, the train of my dress tore away. The remaining material rose up my legs.

The flames brightened, the fires licking higher, farther from my outstretched hand. Thunder cracked, and the ceiling vanished, revealing a night sky, as Rhyan fell from the flames naked. He pushed onto his hands and knees and sat back on his heels, staring at me with bright emerald eyes. No soot or ash touched his body. But his bare skin, taut over muscle, was red as smoke swirled around him.

"Did the fire hurt you?" My voice sounded distant and echoed throughout the temple. Wings fluttered above,

drawing my attention to the paintings of Asherah and Auriel springing to life. Asherah wore my necklace from Ramia, the starfire diamonds glittering pure white, but I still wore it, too. Auriel poured pure red light into Asherah's chest. The God and Goddess embraced, and their clothes fell off as a warm light grew out of Asherah's heart and surrounded them. They were too bright to look at, but I could hear their soft gasps and moans as their bodies came together.

I turned to Rhyan. His skin was still red as the eternal flame. His emerald eyes burned as they watched me. His hands balled into fists on his lap, hands opening and closing, his expression pained.

I stepped closer. "I can cool you with my waters. You don't have to burn."

"You're the fire," he said darkly and stood, his face in anguish. He reached for my dress just as he'd reached for my robes in the Oath Ceremony. The cloth turned to water, dripping down my skin, leaving me naked. My nipples peaked, my skin flushing as desire coiled deep inside of me.

He looked me up and down. Desire hooded his eyes, as some force of power within him called out to me. An inexplicable force inside of me sang in response.

"I want to kiss you," he said with that beautiful northern lilt to his voice. "Can I?"

"Yes."

His aura trembled around me. "I know you." He spoke simultaneously in High Lumerian and in Common, like he had two voices. "Ani janam ra."

"I know you," I repeated. I heard my voice, but my mouth hadn't opened. The words echoed around us.

His fingers uncurled, hands rising to touch my face, turning it up, his skin heated against mine. He pulled me toward him, water into fire.

"You're mine," he breathed. I couldn't catch my breath. "Mine. Since before the dawn."

Our lips met, and we sank to the cold floor. He slid over me as desire hot as flames rippled over my body. Darkness and shadows covered us like a blanket. I opened my legs, pulling him closer to me. He settled against my hips, his length hard against me. I gasped as he wrapped his arms around me, pulling me closer, kissing my neck.

"Rhyan." I writhed against him, already wet for him.

His calloused fingers trailed up my thigh, between our hips, and stroked between my legs, deepening my desire before he positioned himself against my entrance.

His face hovered above mine, and I reached up to touch his hair. I hit a cold, hard surface, and then another, and the darkness grew. Rhyan flattened his body against mine. We were trapped. Buried underground.

Gold light exploded.

I sat up in my bed shaking as the golden light of dawn streamed in through my window. My head ached from too little sleep; my body was exhausted and still recovering from the nahashim. The bells rang. It was time to start my first day of soturion training.

CHAPTER SEVENTEEN

I PULLED OUT my practice uniform, ignoring the shining golden armor I'd managed to place on the wooden dummy before I passed out. The underclothes were familiar, like the shifts I wore, though the material was thicker and stretchier. I secured them around my waist then tackled the strappy material designed to support my breasts. Most shifts allowed for breathing room, but as a soturion, I needed to almost flatten my chest—no easy feat. After several frustrating tries, I finally managed to wrap and lace the strings together. This was followed by my black practice tunic, which also laced up the back, though it came with a pull that made it much easier to get on. I added a pair of black short-pants, a belt, and my new soturion-issue lace-up sandals—heavier than any shoes I'd worn before—and hoped I'd put everything on correctly.

There was far more grandeur, history, art, and culture in the Temple of Dawn and Cresthaven, but the Katurium was the largest building in Bamaria. Seven stories tall and seven times as wide, it was shaped as a perfect circle. In the Katurium's center was an open arena with a track and stadium seating. Red and gold spiked rays jutted from the top. From a seraphim's eye view, the Katurium looked like a flaming sun. Inside the rounded hallways and levels were classrooms, training rooms, armories full of weapons, and stores of starfire swords.

I joined an excited Galen and Haleika on the first level for breakfast. Haleika was going on and on about her apprentice, the attractive dirty-blonde soturion from Ka Daquataine, Leander Abden, who'd caught her eye. He was a lower-ranking noble in Damara. Haleika offered an in-depth rundown of his physical achievements but continued looking dreamily at Galen. I half-listened, barely able to focus or touch my food. We were about to engage in the soturi's first daily exercise—an hour-long run.

Out in the open arena, the morning was unusually hot. The Ready stood in the center with Turion Dairen, Aemon's Second and cousin. Dairen also served on my father's Council. He'd been a young soturion during my uncle's rebellion. While the Ready had killed Uncle Tarek and struck down the conspirators, it had been Dairen who'd saved my father from death—absorbing a killing blow after his leg had been injured. Dairen had been promoted immediately to turion, and despite being a sour prick, he was a hero at home.

We were all instructed to find a place on the track lines and mark them. Hundreds of daggers, all silver steel glittering with golden letters, flashed beneath the sun. We stabbed them into the ground to the hilts, marking our starting points. The run would begin when the new hour was called and would continue until the timekeeper rang the bells. Aemon's instructions filled me with dread. I'd never run for half an hour, much less a full one. But even worse, when the hour was over, we couldn't stop running until we retrieved our daggers. The track was half a mile in length, which meant I had to be very near my dagger when the hour was called, or everyone would be watching while I ran the extra half-mile to finish.

Haleika was already bouncing on her heels while simultaneously tying her curly brown hair into a ponytail. Leander, her apprentice, gave her a nod and stretched a few feet away. Galen also got a nod from his apprentice, a soturion from Ka Scholar, dark and extremely well-muscled.

Rhyan appeared, wearing only a half-tunic, leaving him naked from the waist up. His practice belt, plain leather with seven straps falling to his thighs, held it in place. But my focus was on anything but his belt.

I'd known he was muscled beneath his clothes, but seeing his torso bare and up close left my throat dry. Black gryphon wings were tattooed across each shoulder. The wing tips ended sharply below his collarbone, tapering to points on either side of his chest. My dream flashed like a bolt of lightning. Me and Rhyan in the temple, naked. The anguish in his eyes, the way he'd touched me. The unleashed desire I'd felt, and seen reflected in him. I looked down, unable to withstand the odd intimacy that came from dreaming of someone you knew, and feeling like they had to know what transpired, even though it was all in my head.

I fixated on his feet, unable to shake the image of him naked in my mind. He'd switched to the southern style of sandal, laced to just below his knee. The leather was shining and stiff with newness.

"Follow me." He was already walking away, not even looking over his shoulder to see if I'd follow. "Quick. The hour's about to call."

I squeezed my eyes shut, willing the images to dissolve, and followed behind Rhyan. The gryphon wings tattooed on his shoulder and chest connected to one large tattoo that had been inked across the expanse of his upper back. It was an intricately detailed gryphon, wings spread, soaring up into the sky beneath the sun. The sigil for Ka Hart was a gryphon beneath the sun—geometric, simplistic. Rhyan's tattoo was lifelike, with incredible detail, each wing shaded and unique.

The gryphon's leg had a piece of rope tied around it, a rope that had been severed. The edges were tattered, and the remains of the rope were below, amidst snowy mountaintops.

"Good luck, Lyr!" Haleika called, snapping me out of staring at the gryphon whose wings rippled with Rhyan's muscles.

I waved back, and Haleika turned toward Galen as Rhyan led me to the outermost track.

"Ever run before?" he asked, now facing me.

"Only when being chased."

He exhaled sharply, folding his arms across his chest. "Just as I suspected."

"What do I do?" I asked.

He cocked his eyebrow, the uninjured one. "Put one foot in front of the other. Quickly."

"Wow, thanks. You're a real help. I'm going back to Haleika."

"Set your dagger beside mine," he said, an unmistakable command in his voice. "If you want to get through this run, listen to me. Stay on the outermost ring. The others will favor the inner rings, hoping to gain the Ready's attention. You'll have more space and be left alone out here, so you can keep to your own pace. It also offers you an exit plan if you get crowded, you can step off the track and back on again when it's clear."

I nodded, surprised at how sensible his advice was. I stabbed my blade into the ground, marking my new starting point. The golden hilt shined next to Rhyan's, covered in worn black leather.

"Reach your arms up." He stood back, one finger resting on his chin, his eyes studious, roaming up and down the length of my body. His lips pressed together as he stepped forward, pressing my shoulders down. "Relax."

And just like that he was fully naked again in my mind, his hands on my shoulders. I mentally added in the details of his tattoo, the wing tips spreading across his shoulders and chest. The detail of the muscles, the flex of his arms. My dress dissolving beneath his touch. His body hard and straining against mine. My legs open, yearning for him to be inside of me.

I took a deep breath.

"Partner, that's the opposite of relaxing."

"Sorry."

He increased the pressure, pushing down. "Right here. Good. Bend forward, hands to your toes."

The backs of my legs screamed in pain. I had to bend my knees to reach.

"Your hamstrings are tight. Did you stop dancing?"

I started to stand, surprised he'd remembered I had dance training. But his hand on the small of my back held me in place, forcing me into a deeper stretch. "I've been busy," I grunted. "No dance classes in prison."

"Right. Deep breath." His palm remained firm on my back before he suddenly pulled back. "Now roll up, arms lifted. Good."

By this point, most of the novice and apprentice soturi had lined up around the track in the arena, daggers readily marking each soturion's starting point. Some were jumping in place while others were positioned in impressive lunges, their bodies rocking back and forth with energy.

"It's time," called the Ready. "Returning apprentices and novices know the rules. Newly sworn novices and transfers, remember this. Akadim don't stop. Akadim don't tire. And neither will you. If you stop, if you decide to take a break from the run, if you fail to follow the orders of your Arkturion, even now, expect to return tonight and do this again. Also remember, that runs are not the time for fights. You fight on this track, you'll be lashed on this track."

I swallowed, my eyes falling on the tall black whipping pole off to the side. Haleika had warned me at breakfast that

Turion Dairen and Aemon always picked one soturion to be whipped the first day of training—to set an example and get everyone in line.

"Don't look at that," Rhyan said. "Don't think about it. That's not for you. Eyes on the track, mind on your next step. That's your only thought. Look ahead, take the next step. See yourself in the place you want to be."

The ashvan soared into the sky, and tendrils of topaz light spiraled from their galloping hooves.

Sweat dripped behind my neck. My fear fell over me, gripping and twisting my limbs, already tight and uncomfortable. The soturi surrounding me were strong and deadly, their bodies covered in muscles. Their auras shimmered with power, and danger. I could sense their magic pulsing in their veins, feel the force of their unnatural strength. I'd seen what a handful of untrained soturi were capable of doing last night. Now I was with hundreds, far more skilled. Running alongside them now seemed stupid and dangerous.

"Don't look at them, they don't matter." Rhyan crouched into a beautiful lunge, the muscles so clearly defined in his arms and legs. "Get into position, just like this."

My hands gripped the dirt as it settled beneath my fingernails. My heart raced.

"Listen carefully." Rhyan's voice was low. "You're going to be the worst one out there."

"Screw you."

"I'm trying to help."

"I think we have very different definitions of the word, 'help,'" I said through gritted teeth.

"While I'd love to debate semantics with you, this is important. You *will* be the worst one out there. It's a fact. The sooner you accept it, the better. Because then you can let it go. This isn't a race. No one wins. Remember that. There are no winners. When you see the other's speed, you'll want to catch up. Don't. Don't try to race them, don't try to outrun them. You'll only hurt yourself pushing too hard or get sucked into the crowd. This is about stamina, not speed. You have to survive the hour, and you will."

Swallowing, my throat already dry, I nodded. But my stomach was still twisting, and the more soturi I spotted, the smaller I felt, like a kitten growling at fully grown lions.

"You'll grow stronger." His voice softened. "You'll get faster. But they are not your competition right now. You are."

I have two arms, two legs. My feet can run, my muscles will build stamina. My hands can learn to hold a sword, and my arms will strengthen to withstand its weight.

The ashvan descended in a rainbow of jewel tones, and the timekeeper rang the bells.

Rhyan was off before I could blink, running impossibly fast, vanishing through the others on the track. And at a much much slower speed, I ran. In a rush of sound, sweat, and flesh, my classmates passed me, and I was left to run alone for a blissful moment—until the fastest soturi completed their first loop and came upon me again. I turned around just before a herd of runners raced by. Some sped faster when they neared, others slowed to mutter curses under their breath. The message was clear: I wasn't welcome here.

I nearly tripped to avoid bumping into Naria, who had clearly run too close to me. A rush of older novice soturi raced together, and I stumbled, the force of them like a gale-force wind. I ran off the track, disoriented, but quickly jumped back on, narrowly avoiding tripping over a row of daggers at my feet. The damned things had to be jumped over constantly.

I took a deep breath. It wasn't a race. I just had to survive, no matter how humiliating the run was. Once I'd grown comfortable with my pace, I started to feel all right, almost energized. But when we hit the twenty-minute mark, shooting pain seized my stomach, and I doubled over with cramps.

Haleika and Galen ran beside me, quickly offering solutions. They flanked me, running interference from those attempting to herd slower runners off the track as I breathed into my cramps, massaging my stomach. But this only angered everyone running around us. It seemed like the longer we ran, the more violent they became, attempting to bump into me, or running right on my heels.

"You're not here to help your friend," Turion Dairen yelled. "You think akadim slow their chase for friends? They'll thank you for the easy kill. And destroy you. Now move! Faster!"

Haleika's face fell, her bottom lip jutting out in protest.

Leander ran by, red with exertion. "Grey, go!" He leapt over a series of dagger hilts, dust exploding from his heels as he landed.

"Hal, we've got to." Galen's voice turned apologetic. "Keep going, Lyr."

Haleika sped up, and Galen joined her.

My feet dragged through the dirt. Dust clouds rose behind me. My body simply slowed down. I was faint, weak, and so so tired.

"Speed up!" shouted Aemon. "Final five minutes. Anyone who doesn't increase their speed runs again tonight!"

My stomach twisted as somehow everyone on the track ran faster. My skin itched from the heat and sweat mixed with dust that had pasted onto my skin. Tears ran down my face as I forced myself to run harder. Shadows loomed as the ashvan took flight, and the warning bells of the approaching hour rang. I was so close to finishing, if I could just keep going.

The horses galloped their descent, leaving blue streaks of light in swirling patterns across the sky. The bells rang. I slowed my pace, nearly sobbing in relief.

"Soturion Lyriana," shouted the Ready. "Dagger! Now!"

The Godsdamned dagger! I'd just run past it. I'd been so focused on the hour's end and going faster I'd completely forgotten to place myself properly. Now I was nearly half a mile from the finish line.

Shit! My arms pumped desperately, but I was barely at my starting speed. The few stragglers on the track sped up. Lady Pavi was just behind me. Someone from the sidelines called me slow. Asherah. Disgrace to soturi. Another voice shouted that I wasn't a true Lumerian.

My legs burned, and my cramps returned with a vengeance. I was twenty feet away. My face was on fire. Fifteen feet. There was a storm thundering in my belly. Ten feet. I stumbled, running off to the side. Something struck me from behind. I hit the ground.

My cheek smashed against the dirt as dust exploded in my mouth and tears spilled.

Pavi stomped on my hand. "MOVE!" she screamed.

Wincing and coughing, I sat upright, trying to wipe my face with my injured hand. Dirt was plastered to my face, sticking to my sweat. My sides ached so much I couldn't stand. My hand was too weak to support my weight.

There was a ringing in my ears, but distantly I heard the Ready scream my name.

I hoisted myself up, chest heaving, breath short, and ran the last few feet to my blade. I grabbed my dagger and collapsed to my knees.

My guts twisted with pain burrowing deep inside my belly. My hands pressed to the ground, my fingers digging into the dirt as pain wrenched through me.

Someone sat behind me, pulling my hair back, a steadying hand rubbing up and down my spine, soothing me.

"I've got you." Rhyan.

His deft fingers smoothed back the loose strands of my hair just as I leaned forward and threw up my entire breakfast. I coughed, gagging on the vile taste, and vomited again.

My stomach seized. Throat burning, I retched, releasing bile.

"You're all right." Rhyan held my braid out of the way, his strong hand moving soothingly up and down my back. "Is there more?" he asked quietly. "Let it out. You'll feel better."

I coughed until I swallowed, grimacing at the aftertaste. My stomach felt raw but empty. I wiped my mouth, barely registering my embarrassment. I'd never thrown up in front of anyone outside of my family before, much less an audience. "I'm done."

"Easy now," he said, helping me sit. Hand still steady on my back, he draped a cold towel over my shoulders. "Keep this on your neck. Deep breaths. I'll get you some water."

Rhyan had been gone for only a second when someone grabbed me from behind and hauled me to my feet.

"Wait!" Rhyan yelled at my assailant. "She needs rest!"

Someone dragged me toward the other end of the arena as I tried to dig my heels into the dirt, but I only stumbled forward.

"Pole." Turion Dairen released me at last, staring down at me.

"What?" My stomach twisted, and a dizzy spell washed over me. I coughed and felt the bile burn through my throat again. The brutal stand now hovered above me. Ropes fell from the apex, blowing in the breeze, casting dancing shadows on the ground that made me dizzy.

"Three lashes at the pole," he said.

"Lashes! For what?"

"Fighting during the run."

Fresh tears filled my eyes. "Fighting! Pavi ran into me."

"Five lashes."

My whole body was shaking, my vision blurred, but I affected my best heir voice to keep the panic from bursting out of me. He couldn't be serious, he couldn't actually think this was a good idea. "Turion Dairen, do you think my father, your Arkasva—"

"Your father!" Turion Dairen spat. "Your father gave you to us to become a soturion. Lords and ladies train amongst those without titles. Heirs to the Arkasva don't get special privilege here. Did not Lord Viktor Kormac's father also send him?"

"But…." To my humiliation, my voice broke. "I don't have the same…." I gestured at my classmates. I didn't want to have to say out loud that I was powerless.

"Seven lashes!"

"So there's no punishment for Pavi?"

"Ten!"

"Turion," said Aemon, striding toward us. He was dragging Lady Pavi behind him, his fingers curled around the shoulder of her tunic. "I meant to bring Soturion Lyriana over to the pole to watch as Soturion Pavi receives punishment for starting the fight."

"Arkturion, she—"

"I know, Turion. I know what happened, and that's why Soturion Pavi will be whipped and Soturion Lyriana will watch."

Turion Dairen's jaw twitched, but he nodded. I'd always known he was a prick, but I'd never realized the full extent of it. Something told me he took a certain pleasure in carrying out the punishments.

Aemon addressed our rapt audience, his voice full of menace and threat. "You know what happens when you disobey direct orders. Let this be a lesson to you all to remember yourselves."

A chill washed over me. I'd never seen a whipping before, and I didn't want to. The whips at the Academy were infused with magic, designed to cut open a soturion's back, inflict immense pain, and create wounds that didn't easily heal. One lashing was supposed to be as painful as it was humiliating for a soturion to endure. The entire practice was barbaric, like a bound five. So much effort was put into weeding out the weakest soturi.

And I was not even a true soturion. Without magic...I didn't even want to think about what a whipping could do to me.

Rhyan's jaw tensed as he stood to the side with Pavi's apprentice, who looked furious.

"This is ridiculous," Pavi said. She spoke frantically, a kind of desperation in her voice. "Her grace ran in my way. I didn't do anything on purpose. She fell, it wasn't a fight."

"Then three lashes should ensure you do everything on purpose from now on to watch where you're going," Aemon said.

"Is this how it's going to be, Arkturion?" Viktor Kormac stepped forward, his black eyes narrowed on me. "My father feared allowing a non-magical soturion into the Academy would lower its standards. Soturion Pavi did exactly as you asked. But now she's to be punished because someone who shouldn't be here stumbled into her way? Are we all to be punished for her grace's failings? I thought she'd be held to the same rules as the rest of us."

Aemon's eyes darkened, his expression like that of a death God's. He was the Ready—vicious, dangerous. His aura pulsed with violence. Brutal shadows emanated from him, crackling through the air. Viktor stepped back, and the rest of the novices waiting on the edge of the field visibly shuddered. Pavi paled.

"Any soturion who attacks another without warning will be punished," he said, his voice rippling with power. "There is no special treatment for anyone, including you, Soturion Viktor—a fact your father is well aware of. One more question, and you're next. We do not tolerate petty, childish attacks, which is exactly what this was. An act of cowardice and spite. Soturion Pavi, for the offense of interfering with another soturion's training, you will receive three lashes." The Ready jerked his chin.

Turion Dairen grabbed Pavi's arms, violently thrusting them above her head. She whimpered as he tied the rope around her wrists, pulling and tightening them until she elicited a grunt of pain.

He moved behind her, pulling on the laces on the back of her tunic. It fell open, exposing her back and shoulders. My breath hitched with understanding for the odd design of the garment, meant to come apart easily for punishment. Though I wasn't the one being tied up and publicly undressed, I felt the humiliation of it, felt how close I had been to this fate. Pavi was a lady of a noble Ka, niece to the Bamarian Senator, best friends with Naria...it was unlikely she'd ever expected to be in this position.

I stood behind her, beside Rhyan, and Aemon. Pavi twisted and strained to set her eyes on me, black and filled with fire. She got in one look before Dairen took hold of the whip and yelled, "One."

He swung his arm back, muscles flexing. The whip hummed as it snapped through the air, ending in a horrid thwacking sound against Pavi's bared flesh. She cried out. An echoing gasp escaped my lips.

"Two."

I swayed on the spot as another lashing tore through Pavi. She screamed, the sound so full of pain it was almost animalistic.

Rhyan stared at the ground, looking sick himself. He was bent over, hands splayed across his thighs in what might have been a bored, casual stance. But his expression gave him away.

A roar erupted from Pavi on the third hit. This was the one that cut her back open. Fresh blood fell as the whip hit her skin. Turion Dairen released her arms from the rope, and we were dismissed—but not before Pavi stomped toward me, her opened tunic flying out on either side of her torso, blood running down her legs.

"You'll get yours, Batavia." Pavi spit at my feet then stomped off, leaving me frozen on the field.

"Now bathe. You smell like shit," Dairen yelled. Every novice and apprentice in the arena stood, gathering their belongings and heading for the doors.

Aemon pulled me back.

"Your grace," he said quietly. "I will always punish those who deserve it. But next time...if you're involved, I'll have no choice. Don't let it happen again. The wolves are watching, reporting our every move. One misstep, one favor revealed to his highness, and your bargain dies."

My knees weakened as I pictured my arms over my head, my own back splayed open for all to see. I trudged across the field, grabbed my bag, and headed for the door. The Katurium was flooded with soturi, crowded together, all pushing their way toward the baths.

"Watch out for Batavia, or you'll be whipped next."

I wasn't sure who'd said it, but it was like a dam had been unleashed. Everyone in the hall turned, focusing their attention and anger on me. I could feel the mixture of auras pulsing. They were full of contempt, distrust, and fury.

"The Ready's in her father's pocket," came a sneer. "Teach her a lesson."

My heart stopped as soturi from Ka Kormac turned around, their wolfish grins spreading across their faces with cruel, wicked hate. They stalked toward me. I backed up into another soturion, and another.

They wouldn't. I was an Heir to the Arkasva. I was a lady. But I was supposed to be one of them now. And they seemed only too happy to remind me.

There was a yell, and Rhyan appeared, shoving his way through the crowd before he wrapped his arms around me, rushing us away from everyone. Instinctively, I tightened my arms around him as he positioned us away from my would-be attackers, our backs against the wall. Every soturion in the hall glared. My body was shaking uncontrollably. Rhyan's hand slid behind me and clamped down on my lower back.

"Stand straight," he muttered under his breath. "Close your mouth. Stare back." His hand pressed into me again, pushing me forward, steadying me. His fingers curled in my tunic, knuckles pushing against me. "Look at them. Right at them! Head up. Remember who you are."

I sucked in the air around me, desperate for breath, and then a lifetime of having been raised at court and taught to make an impression and remind everyone of our Ka's strength kicked in. I stood taller, glaring down at everyone.

A door down the hall opened, and Turion Dairen cursed, yelling at everyone to get into the bath.

The crowd dispersed, and Rhyan released his hold on me.

A jerk of his chin was all he gave, asking if I was all right.

I nodded, and then I headed for the baths.

CHAPTER EIGHTEEN

THE GIRLS' BATHING room housed endless pools full of steaming water, white marble benches, and, in that moment, hundreds of naked bodies. Most proudly displayed their assets while others were casually draped in white towels. I stared as I entered, automatically comparing myself to everyone around me.

I'd always liked my body. Knowing Tristan appreciated it, I'd never given its size, shape, or curves much thought. Concealing cuts and bruises was my main concern. But now there was no way I could avoid facing how inadequate my body was for the task at hand. I had curves where my classmates all had the sinuous lines of warriors. I faced bodies made entirely of strength and muscle, muscle I'd never imagined on myself. Some of the novices who'd just sworn their oaths had defined abdominals and thickened thighs that had not been there even a week ago. I remembered watching Naria run from the ocean this summer to her towel on the beach. Her legs had been so skinny, like a young girl's. But now they were sinewy and thick. Strong.

I could train. I could replace fat with muscle. But no matter how hard I pushed myself, I'd never have a body like theirs.

Not without magic running through me.

The door slammed behind me, echoing with a thud that alerted the entire room to my presence. I'd been so busy staring, I'd released the handle. Girls stopped drying their hair, and those splashing in the pools stilled. Only the running waters, tinkling through the room, could be heard as I became the center of attention.

Haleika, who'd waited for me, urged me forward, but I couldn't move. I couldn't undress in front of them. Not when I was about to reveal nothing but softness and weakness—as if my run and that scene in the hall hadn't been humiliating enough—and certainly not when I had to protect my back, as I was still healing from the cuts and bruises Meera had inflicted on me during her last vision. I had to bathe without anyone growing any wiser that I had previous injuries. I anxiously looked down at the golden cuffs adorning my arms, all specifically placed.

"By the Gods," shouted Haleika. She splashed water in the nearest pool, catching several girls in the face. "She's just taking a bath!"

Cursing under their breath, they busied themselves, rinsing their hair, toweling off, and stepping into fresh clothes. A few nearby had the decency to look ashamed. But there were plenty who continued staring, looking with a heightened boldness, eyeing me head to toe, their expressions predatory.

"She should have been lashed," said Tani, edging closer to Pavi, her nose turned up.

"Shut it, Tani." Haleika eased me to the edge of a pool and untied my sandals. She glared until the girls bathing nearby turned away. I dipped my toes in, feeling heat rise up my legs. The soles of my feet tensed, but as the water rippled over my skin, the soreness eased.

Haleika slipped off her clothes and slid into the water. A surge of jealousy struck me as she revealed her abdomen. Her stomach had always been flat—lean bodies ran in the Grey family. But now her stomach was lined with muscled definition. Mine curved out, like it always had. It had never bothered me before—bellies did that—but now....

I reached for the shoulder of my tunic, wincing, and paused. I still had a captive audience. There was no way to undress gracefully without revealing the pain I was in or showing more skin than I'd intended. I'd stood before nearly all of Bamaria half-naked in the Oath Ceremony, but that had been a ritual. The exposure was considered sacred, and we had been hidden in shadows. This, this was something else entirely. Had I taken my clothes off with the others, it would have been nothing. Alone, I was a spectacle.

"Do you need help undressing?" Haleika asked quietly. She swam to the edge of the pool, looking up at me with concern. "We can wait until the baths empties a little."

I glared at the other bathers, whispering and sneaking sidelong glances. Naria kept her gaze boldly on me. Her expression showed disgust—as if she found my body revolting. Pavi was close to her. Tani and a team of other girls were applying sunleaves to her back and shooting me death glares. Most were simply watching me, daring an Heir to the Arkasva to strip naked, prove I was one of them.

Look at them. Right at them! Head up. Remember who you are. Remembering Rhyan's words, right then and there I made my choice.

Themselves to Moriel! All of them! I wouldn't be intimidated by them. Not in a bathing room built by my ancestors, not when their blood ran through my veins.

Every inch of me was in pain. My stomach still burned, and my feet throbbed as I removed them from the pool, but I stood tall. Cold air coated my damp calves, and white spots appeared in my vision. I took a steadying breath, and the spots cleared, allowing me to stare right at the girls watching —all of them. I lifted my tunic over my head, swallowing a cry of pain, and glared right into Naria's eyes as I unbound my breasts. Her cheeks reddened, and she turned away, reaching for a sponge. I paused, standing half-naked, breasts exposed, and settled my gaze on Pavi, who'd returned to glaring at me. I smiled at her as I pushed down my shorts and undergarments. She too was forced to suddenly busy herself with her hair.

Anyone else who dared look at me caught my eye and immediately looked away with reddened faces, diving into some other task. I unbound my hair, fluffing it out to fall down my back and cover Meera's handiwork. And then I fluffed it some more, just to drive the point home. I would not be shamed, not here.

I slid into the pool, my front to the audience, back to the wall, beside Haleika, giggling helplessly into her hands. "You always knew how to make an entrance." When her laughter died down, she said, "You can't show fear here. I can't explain it, but since the Oath, I can sense—almost smell it. If the others catch wind, they'll prey on you."

I pursed my lips together, willing myself to swallow despite my throat burning.

Haleika grinned, an almost conspiratorial twinkle in her eyes. "I think you just secured us this corner of the pool for the rest of the year."

I nodded, feeling the warmth of the waters wash over my skin.

Cleaned and dressed, I followed the first-year novices to class. In a long lecture hall, we received our first lesson on combat theory with an overview of Lumerian anatomy. There was a short recess, then a similar lesson on the basic anatomy of akadim. The following forty-five minutes focused on weapons, specifically starfire, mined in Ka Kormac's realm, Korteria. Having control over the mines had made them wealthy and powerful...too powerful. But we still relied on trade with the Afeya to forge the raw material. Following that, I attended class on the history of the soturi and healing.

By lunch, I was drained and still feeling queasy from the morning. I didn't have the energy to go back to my apartment for lunch, or find a restaurant in Urtavia, which meant I was trapped in the dining hall. My taste buds and my upset stomach barely allowed me to swallow the stew being served. Haleika insisted I not only eat something to keep up my strength, but that it was the most effective cure for an upset stomach. I doubted there was a cure for the way it tasted, but I managed a few small spoonfuls. To Haleika's credit, a little bit of my energy returned—which was good. I was about to start combat training with Rhyan.

He sat alone on the other end of the hall, his eyes sharp and roving the room as he chewed on a chunk of bread. A fresh tunic adorned him, tucked beneath black leathered armor and his belt. There was an arrogance in the way he sat: reclined, elbows comfortably on the table. It was the posture of a High Lord. He seemed so reluctant to embrace that side of himself, always trying to lean into and own his status as a forsworn. But he'd been raised to rule…and something in the way he sat showed it.

I wasn't the only one to notice. Viktor Kormac stalked past his table, the silver claws pinned to the shoulders of his tunic gleaming with the afternoon's sun. I stiffened, catching the predatory way Viktor sized him up and down. As the son of the Imperator and great-nephew to the Emperor, Viktor outranked Rhyan. But here, he was only a novice. Rhyan was an apprentice with kills under his belt—including an akadim. There'd be no contest in a fight.

As if he realized this too, Viktor stepped back, and with a nod, sent five of his wolves forward to circle Rhyan's table. All five were apprentices, including Viktor's, Brockton Kormac. He was a brute of a soturion with the beady, watery eyes of the Bastardmaker.

Brockton moved behind Rhyan, bracing against the table on either side of him, caging Rhyan between his arms. His muscles bulged.

Haleika and Galen stiffened beside me, as the insult was sensed across the dining hall.

"Five," Haleika whispered.

"Morons," said Galen. "Hart's killed akadim and survived a bound five."

A sensation of ice-cold power seeped through my bones. Rhyan's aura expanded as another wolf stalked by.

"You don't belong here, forsworn." Brockton leaned forward, his cheek against Rhyan's.

Rhyan stiffened. Several more Kormac wolves herded together, their beady eyes hungry for a fight, their stances and auras saying they were ready to pounce.

"Where don't I belong?" Rhyan asked casually. He shifted his weight, pulling his cheek away from Brockton's. "At this table? In this room?"

"In this country!" Brockton sneered.

"That's patriotic of you," Rhyan said. "I thought only Bamarians took offense at foreigners here. Are you not from Korteria?"

"You know damn well where I'm from."

"And you're offended I'm in this country? Is there something I should know? Has Korteria joined with Bamaria then?"

All around the room, novices and apprentices bristled. I felt my own breath catch.

"No, gryphon-shit," Viktor said.

"Funny, because the other day, I met armed soturi bearing the sigils of Ka Kormac."

"We're protecting everyone," Viktor said. "Donating our resources to keep things safe."

Rhyan scrunched up his nose in response. "In that case, maybe you should send some actual soldiers next time. It took one kick to knock your pups on their asses."

"You shit-eating mother-killer," Brockton snarled. He turned his head suddenly, his mouth against Rhyan's cheek, teeth bared, lips pulled back.

One second, Brockton was over Rhyan, and the next, he'd flown into the wall, his back smacking against the stone. A small hurricane blasted through the hall, cold as ice, with a burning fire underneath. It swept through the room, pushing everyone down into their chairs. All the Kormac wolves, including Viktor, were now on their asses.

"Like I said," Rhyan stood, seething, "actual soldiers next time." His green eyes burned as he stared down the room. He settled his gaze on me.

"Auriel's bane," Haleika said.

Galen rubbed his arm, lips pursed.

Before I could react, an aura swirled through the room—powerful, predatory. The soturi of Ka Kormac stilled, their muscles tensed, their focus on a single point. Viktor was the only one who seemed unaffected as a sneering smile spread across his face.

I was slow to look; I already knew the face of the man who'd entered the Dining Hall. I knew the deafening pulse of his lupine aura. It was the man I most feared.

The Imperator.

CHAPTER NINETEEN

"I SHOULD GO." I grabbed my things, and rushed through the doors, praying the Imperator wasn't there to see me. Rhyan was already down the hall, turning the corner, before he entered what would be our private training room. I caught up and closed the door behind me.

Rhyan stalked through the space like an angry cat, surveying the equipment. The armory was full of mostly dull weapons, stacks of mats, punching bags, gloves, wooden blocks, and a very tiny first aid kit. He hauled a giant mat leaning against the wall to the ground. Then another. He looked like he was trying to line them up evenly, but in his anger and frustration, he only half accomplished the goal before storming toward a window to open it.

I bent forward to fix the mats, groaning a little from the movement.

He spun on his heels, golden afternoon light streaming in through the window behind him. His dark brown hair had taken on a golden halo, and as his emerald eyes fixed on me, the hard edges of his mouth softened.

"How's your stomach?" he asked.

My cheeks reddened. "I'm keeping my lunch down."

"Good sign." He stepped onto the mat. "We're going to focus on basic training. First thing we need to do is increase your strength and stamina."

My hands twitched, still sore from Pavi. "My stamina didn't do so well today."

Anger burst across his expression, his nostrils flaring. "That was not your fault. Pavi was completely out of line. So was Turion Dairen. Prick."

I joined him on the mat.

He stepped closer, assessing me. "But, considering where you're at and that you seem to have a target on your back, we need to increase it."

"Where I'm at? The worst in my class...in all the classes in the history of the Academy."

One eyebrow narrowed. "I didn't say that, and I will make you do a second run if I hear any more nonsense. You're just untrained."

I could feel my cheeks burn. "Same difference."

"Lyriana." Rhyan laced his pronunciation of my name with his northern lilt, almost like there was an extra syllable in the middle but not quite. It was more of a heartbeat. I lifted my eyes to meet his. "If there was a battle of wits in the arena, those soturi would be dead before they took their first breath."

"You think I'm that smart?"

"Come on, partner, we both know you are." He stalked toward me. "Now let's use that brilliant brain of yours to become a strong soturion. And your stamina was impressive. But we can do better. Stand straight." He reached for me, ready to make an adjustment to my posture. Our door opened before he could touch me. Aemon walked tersely into the training room, followed by the Imperator.

All the air left my body.

Rhyan dropped his arms. "Your highness. Arkturion." He bowed low in respect.

Pulse pounding, I bowed as well.

"The Imperator is here to report to Emperor Theotis on your progress," Aemon said.

"What progress?" Rhyan glared at the Imperator. "It's her first day."

"Yes, well, if I don't see where she begins, how will I know how far she's come?" The Imperator swept his black and golden cloak behind him. "I've already received report of your performance this morning."

"She started where we expected," Rhyan said. "Why don't you stop wasting my time and see where she is come spring when the Emperor arrives?"

"You'll do well to remember that you are also here with privilege," the Imperator bristled. "Circumstances that can be reversed on my pleasure. If you truly mean to prove your devotion to Bamaria, I'd stop offering insult to my Ka. They're sacrificing their lives to protect this school." His wolfish eyes slid over me. "Now our greatest wish is to see Lady Lyriana, forgive me, Soturion Lyriana, fulfill her end of the bargain." He waved in dismissal. "Proceed."

"Only a few minutes," Aemon said sharply, quickly adding a "your highness," before he left us alone with the Imperator.

I swallowed, desperately wanting to crawl out of my body. I waited for Rhyan to finish his adjustment, but he only stood before me, arms crossed.

"What is the first rule of being a soturion?" Rhyan practically growled the question. There was a kiss of his icy fury in the room as his aura swirled.

I blinked, trying to remember if that had been covered in the morning lectures I'd attended, but it hadn't. Or I'd missed it with my exhaustion. My eyes swept from the Imperator back to Rhyan. Fuck. I'd certainly studied the basics of soturion training years ago. But I couldn't pull the facts I needed from the recesses of my mind I knew they were hiding in. "I don't know."

"You don't know?" drawled the Imperator. "What ignorance."

My hands curled into fists, but I willed them flat against my legs, my chest tightening.

Rhyan's expression darkened, but he remained still. "Try again, novice."

Had Aemon recently mentioned it in passing? I was wracking my brain for any scrap of memory, any lesson, or scroll. I knew the names of several important arkturi, and theorists on battle strategy. But I could feel the Imperator's eyes on me and couldn't think straight, couldn't remember more than just a few names. Sweat ran down my neck. My heart thudded, remembering the Bastardmaker's hands on me...on Jules.

"I don't know the first rule," I snapped. "That's my answer."

The Imperator made a sound of disapproval.

Rhyan turned. "Well?" He spread his arms wide. "Do you need to see anything else?"

"I need to see her answer the question."

"She has answered. She doesn't know. Can we entertain you some other way?"

The Imperator's lips curled. "This falls on you, boy. If she doesn't know the answer, you make her know it. If not, Ka Batavia will reevaluate why you're here." He nodded, dismissing us. "When I return, I expect her grace to know something. Her ignorance is embarrassing."

Rhyan ran his fingers through his hair. He tried to curl some over his scar, but since his trim, it wasn't long enough. "She will," he muttered as the door closed.

My hands tightened into fists, fingernails cutting into my palms. "My ignorance. MY ignorance. How dare he! Ignorant fucking brute. I know everything there is to know about becoming a mage and the history of our people. I've read rare scrolls he's never even heard of and can translate High Lumerian in my sleep."

"So can I," Rhyan shouted. He ran his hands down his neck, hands clasping behind him as he threw his head back. "It doesn't matter!"

I stepped back, surprised at his outburst.

He exhaled sharply, the energy from his aura retreating. His hands fell to his sides. "I'm sorry." He drew closer, shaking his head. "You know I think you're brilliant, I do, but we're in a new arena. The old rules don't apply here." His jaw tensed, nostrils flaring as his hands flexed at his sides. "He's going to make it harder for both of us, isn't he?"

Harder for both of us…. Gods. Rhyan must be miserable being paired with me. If I failed…he'd fail. He'd lose his new home and return to being forsworn. "I'm sorry you were matched with me. I'm putting you in danger with how terrible I'm performing."

Rhyan folded his arms across his chest. "You're performing fine for day one. Let me worry about my place here. You focus on yours."

I stared, feeling the weight of both our places on my shoulders despite what he'd said.

"That's an order." His expression hardened. "You need to worry about you. I've been taking care of myself a long time. I'll be fine. Agreed?"

I exhaled sharply. "Agreed."

"Good."

"Great," I said. "And since it's bound to come up again, what is the first rule of being a soturion?"

He looked thoughtful, tapping a finger against his chin. "I can tell you the answer, but you'll learn better if you figure it out on your own." He shrugged. "Take a guess."

I swallowed, desperate to give the right answer. To ease his fears that I would not be his doom. To ease my own. But my mind was blank, and I could only call upon my small experiences so far. Which, beyond my morning lessons on anatomy and weapons, came down to the run and the Oath Ceremony.

"Is it...is it that we aren't to have any sort of—that novices and apprentices aren't allowed to fall in love?"

His expression darkened. "Why was that your first guess?"

"I...I don't know." My mouth went dry. "Well, is it?"

"No. That's the oath we swore, not the first rule. But you're on the right track. The first rule is our guiding principle in a fight. It's the reason we swear the oath in the first place."

I bit my lip, confused and no closer to an answer than before.

He stepped forward. "We swear at the Oath Ceremony to form our kashonim. To join in a lineage, in friendship, but not to fall in love. And yet, there isn't a more intimate relationship than the one that develops between an apprentice and novice. But we're never to fully acknowledge or act on it. Why?"

My heart pounded as my head swam with visions of Rhyan in my dream. Naked and burning, his skin red, his body pressed against mine in the most intimate way.

"I-I don't know," I said, flustered, still hearing him say "intimate" in my mind. I felt like an idiot. How many scrolls had I read in the library and I couldn't answer this basic question? "I'm sorry."

"Don't apologize," he said, sounding sincere. "You never needed to know before. But you'll get it. Tell me this, what are the words of the oath?"

Conjuring my memory, I said, "I am a soturion. I pledge my heart and soul to the fight against evil, to the protection of the innocent, to the promise of a better world. And in my pledge, I will forsake everything and everyone that should come between me and my fight?"

Rhyan gave an encouraging nod. "Yes, but it's not a question. You need to say it like you mean it. Go on."

Steadying my voice, I repeated, "And in my pledge I will forsake everything and everyone that should come between me and my fight."

"Better. Keep going."

I swallowed, a lump forming in my throat. "I shall fight beside my fellow soturi, I shall honor my Ka and all my vows. And I shall fight with my lineage...my lineage," I said again, trying to sound confident, "always working to end all evil. And if I shall be forsworn, if I should put others before my duties—"

"Stop. That there. That's the answer. 'If I should put others before my duties.' Being a soturion means doing whatever it takes to stop evil. It means you never let an akadim escape."

I frowned. "The first rule of being a soturion is never let an akadim escape?"

"Here's how I learned it. Say you came upon an akadim attacking someone you loved. What would you do?"

My mind flashed to Meera and Morgana. "I would fight the akadim off of them."

Rhyan shrugged. "All right—you manage to separate them, and you see the person is injured and needs help, they're likely close to dying. The akadim was mid-feed, but now it no longer has easy prey and runs away. What do you do?"

"If my loved one is dying? I'd get them help. Bring them to safety and—"

"Wrong. You never let an akadim escape. You go after it."

"What? No. But then...my loved one could die."

Rhyan smiled grimly. "While you're saving this person, what does the akadim do?"

"It runs away?"

"It escapes," he said, voice rising.

"So what? It's gone then, and I saved a life. Isn't that what we do? Save people?"

Rhyan didn't acknowledge the question. "You just deprived the akadim of a soul to eat. It's hungry, it was feeding until you came. So what's its first instinct?"

I shrugged, out of answers. "Tell me."

"You haven't eaten all day, and you're starving. I place a bowl of pomegranate seeds in front of you...the most delicious, ripest, juiciest, sweetest seeds you've ever smelled. Your stomach is rumbling. You're ravenous, you reach for a handful." He gestured, mimicking picking seeds and bringing them to his mouth. "They're just about to touch your lips. You open your mouth, it's watering, your belly's burning with hunger."

My mouth did water at his words.

"And I smack them from your hand and take them for myself," he said sharply.

I laughed nervously at the sudden turn. "You take my pomegranate seeds?"

"I take your pomegranate seeds. What do you do? Fight me for it? Or go for easier pickings, reach for more, just as ripe and sweet, from the bowl in front of you?"

I sighed. This had to be a trick question. "I'd reach for the bowl."

Rhyan's good eyebrow lifted. "Exactly. That's what an akadim would do, too. Reach for more, reach for whatever's easiest. What you have to remember is that for them, the world is their bowl, and the supply is endless. If you stop to care for someone and let the akadim run, if you let it go, it will find someone else. It will kill someone else. Or worse. And after it kills—or Gods forbid, has made them forsaken, turning them into an akadim—where are you? Still with your loved one, safe for now. But what can the akadim do after it's eaten? It can go find another victim. And another. And make more forsaken who become more akadim. So, what did you do? Who did you save?"

"The person I love."

"And in doing so, you condemned countless others to death. And maybe even your loved one, should that akadim or one of its creations come your way again."

I shook my head. "That's a ridiculous expectation to put on us. What if someone else kills the akadim?"

Rhyan shook his head. "What if they don't? That is our way of life. I know you don't see it that way. You weren't taught or prepared. You were training to be a mage. I get it. But this is the first rule of being a soturion. Our oath says, 'if I should love those whom I've sworn not to.'" His gaze was so intense I blinked. "We swear not to love or care for our fellow soturi beyond the link that keeps us at peace, or offers strength, in order to be prepared. If you see a fellow soturion taken down—even if it was your best friend, your kashonim —you don't hesitate. You go after the akadim. You kill the akadim. And you save the life of every person it would kill or turn. If you come upon one, no matter what's happening or who's affected, it's your duty to bring its end."

"That seems…like such a ridiculous burden to put on a person."

Rhyan sighed. "It is. But to be a soturion, you have to shoulder the burden. The first rule is this: you stop the threat."

"I stop the threat," I repeated dully.

"And how do you stop the threat?"

My head hurt, trying to process the logic and fear of what this life meant. I threw my hands up. "I fight him?"

"The first rule is to stop the threat," he said. "The second, akadim are weapons. Their bodies are designed to kill. But you must reach for your sword. It puts you at a disadvantage."

I rolled my eyes. "Of course, it does."

"No, it puts every soturion at a disadvantage. This is why you train your body to be a weapon. All right? We're going to increase your strength and your stamina. Now reach your arms overhead. We'll begin with the One Hundred and Eight Postures of the Valya."

For a moment I stared, dumbfounded. One hundred and eight?

"Rule number three," he said. "You follow orders. Every single time. It keeps you safe."

"Fine."

"You stop the threat," Rhyan said. "Rule number one. Rule number two, the akadim are a living weapon. None but the soturi stand a chance against it. And to be prepared, rule number three, you always follow the chain of command. Arkturion, turion, soturion, apprentice," he pointed to himself, and then to me, "novice. Now reach overhead."

I did.

Rhyan instructed me to stretch and bend forward, again and again until I could touch my toes. He told me to jump, run in place, and hold myself up in a plank when I failed to do a single push up. For hours he gave orders, pushing me through each of the 108 Postures of Valya.

Rhyan was relentless, pushing me, correcting my form, practicing every posture and position perfectly beside me. The final hour rang through the Katurium, and through the window, I could see the ashvan taking flight, blue streaks trailing behind them. The Academy's first official day was over. The halls filled with the sound of students talking excitedly and doors opening and closing. But Rhyan didn't seem remotely close to dismissing me.

I collapsed in a sweaty heap on the mats.

He gracefully sat beside me before he lowered himself to his back, crossing his legs and pulling them in toward his chest. He'd done every single thing I had today...more, because the apprentices trained with each other in the morning while the novices were in lecture. He'd barely broken a sweat.

"I can't move," I said.

"Take a break."

I glared at him from the corner of my eye, my muscles jelly, arms flopping out on either side of me. "I was hoping you'd say take the rest of the day off." I wasn't sure I was going to be able to get up. Forget my apartment, I lived here now. On this mat. This was my new home.

"Just some easy stretching, I promise," he said. "You don't have to stand anymore...but you do have to sit up."

"Easy stretching?" I raised an eyebrow. "I'm really starting to doubt your understanding of the word."

He released his legs, rolled onto his side to face me, and propped himself up on his elbow, resting his head in his hand. "Are you going to challenge me on the connotation of every word I use?" he asked, lips quirked.

I gave a sideways glance. "I thought you were looking forward to our debates."

He chuckled. "To be fair, I didn't think I'd constantly be forced to defend my own personal usage."

"Your own personal usage is my best weapon against you. How else am I going to challenge you?" I asked, weakly gesturing at my exhausted body.

"Your brain is by far your most dangerous weapon, your grace. But I'm sure you can find other ways," he said, looking at me through thick eyelashes. They stood out now that his eyelids were slightly hooded. "Which word would you like me to define? Easy or stretching?"

I turned on my side, too, resting my head in my hand, a perfect mirror of his posture.

"Easy," I said.

"Easy." His eyes were sparkling, and in a flash, they dipped down the length of my body, resting on the curve of my hip, before rising to meet mine again. His own lips curled into a full smile. "The opposite of hard."

Heat pooled in my belly, as if his gaze had burned me. "You truly are a master of stating the obvious," I said, my voice breathy.

"When you're forsworn, you've got to be master of something."

"I bet you're master of lots of things," I said, my temperature rising.

Then Tristan burst through our door.

CHAPTER TWENTY

I SPRUNG TO my feet, turning away. What in Lumeria was I doing? Lying on the floor with Rhyan—flirting.

Rhyan who was my apprentice. Rhyan whose blood ran through my veins and in my armor, cementing a deadly blood oath that meant we were forbidden to each other. Rhyan whose oath was the last thing I should be thinking of because I wanted to marry Tristan. Rhyan who'd kissed me so sweetly beneath a tree on the summer solstice years ago and was now haunting my dreams and senses.

"Maybe you can't tell time, Hart, but training hours are over." Tristan's blue mage robes had been swept behind his shoulders, and his silver belt was low on his hips, making his scabbard prominent. He rested a hand on the hilt of his stave. The stave that had bound me.

"Then it's good to know I can rely on you to be her grace's personal clocktower." Rhyan rolled onto his back and with a swift kick of his feet, jumped to a stand. He swiped two towels off a rack, wrapping one over his shoulders. He flung the other one at me. "We soturi," he said jovially, "no brains in our heads…. Oh, wait, that includes her grace now. Sorry, were you trying to insult me for being a soturion, for being forsworn, or is this personal?"

Tristan's hand closed around the stave. "Just wondering why you're keeping her late. I let my novice leave an hour ago."

"You may be shocked to learn this, Lord Grey, but she's a bit behind."

I glared at Rhyan, who only shrugged as if to say, *Well, it's true.*

"She's done now." Tristan cocked his head to the side, brown eyes darkening. "I trust you won't interfere with my taking her away this time?"

"I see no bars," Rhyan said, a small growl in his voice.

Tristan strode across the room to me. "My grandmother wants to have dinner tonight."

My heart leapt. "To give us her blessing?"

"I think so. She seemed desperate to see you."

That was promising. If I could get her blessing, we could be engaged. I'd be Ka Grey...I'd have another powerful Ka to back me if the Imperator tried to send me away.

"I'll be there," I said.

"You should go home now to bathe and change. I'll meet you. It might help if she spends a little time with you alone."

"She can't go," Rhyan said.

Tristan narrowed his eyebrows. "I believe we've established that training hours are over. Her grace is not your prisoner this time. She's going with me now."

"Her grace was never my prisoner. Nor have I ever arrested her," Rhyan snarled.

Tristan's hand curled into a fist around his stave.

"She has combat clinic tonight," Rhyan said. "Academy rules. You see, a soturion's day lasts a bit longer than the day of a mage."

"Needing all the hours you can get just to find your way to the door?" Tristan asked.

"Again, should I be taking these insults personally? I'm assuming you don't mean all soturi…which now includes the youngest Batavia."

"Her grace," Tristan said.

Rhyan stomped forward. "If you want her grace to survive this training, you will never burst into my personal training room again, my lord."

"Enough!" I shouted. "Both of you!" Myself to Moriel, these two could never be left alone together.

They both took a step back, silent, watching me.

I'd forgotten about combat clinic. I wracked my brain for all I knew about it, trying to decide if there was a way I could do both the combat clinic and the dinner. The clinic for novices lasted anywhere from two to three hours and involved watching and participating in fives, then observing fighting maneuvers demonstrated by the soturion running the training. Apprentices attended their own clinics twice a week —otherwise they were expected to shadow soturi on patrol. The apprentice and novice clinics were separate aside from one night a month when we observed each other.

I inched closer to Tristan. "Can we risk asking her to reschedule?"

Tristan frowned. "You know she won't."

Fuck. I couldn't afford to miss combat clinic—not the first day, not with the Imperator still in town. But I couldn't afford to offend Lady Romula either. Missing the clinic tonight was playing with fire, but if I didn't attend to Lady Romula's dinner in my current position, I risked not being invited again. Even with my full status in hand.

I turned to find Rhyan. His back was to us as he rolled up our mats and piled them in a corner. Exhaling, I made my decision. I had to play the long game to ensure my safety. I had to secure my engagement.

"Tristan, I have to go to the clinic. Your grandmother will be fine eating dinner a little later than usual," I announced. I gave Tristan a look, one that clearly let him know I was lying. He nodded in understanding.

"Of course," Tristan said, voice stiff. "We can delay the dinner."

"Perfect. See you tomorrow, Rhyan."

Tristan spotted my bag on the ground and hauled it over his shoulder before taking my hand. "I'll walk you back to your apartment."

Rhyan turned when we reached the door. He reached into his bag then tossed a small pouch my way. "Take a hot bath, add these salts. Good for sore muscles. And stretch before bed. Don't stay at the dinner too long."

I nodded and followed Tristan into the hall.

"Your apartment only has a shower, right?" he asked.

"Right," I said. "We have baths here, though. Or I could go to Cresthaven."

Tristan shook his head. "That'll take too long. Bathe here. I'll wait in the hall."

Sitting in the heated waters alone without the prying, judgmental eyes of my classmates seemed like Heaven. "You'll guard the door?" I asked.

"With my life." Tristan squeezed my hand.

A few minutes later, I sank into one of the smaller private pools, dumping the entire contents of Rhyan's pouch in the water. Steam rose from the bath, scented with lavender and sun tree oils. I let the hot water rush over my body, leaning my head against the pool's edge, and closed my eyes.

Ice cold water smashed against my face. I sputtered, unable to breathe or see. My head plunged under. Water shot up my nose and into my mouth. I barely had the sense or strength to lunge out of the pool, but as I rose to the surface, strong hands forced me back under. I was drowning, my arms flailing and legs kicking.

And then the hands were gone. I shot to the surface, slamming onto the marble floors as I gasped for air, coughing and spitting up. Goosebumps prickled over me; I was freezing in the cold air that bit my naked body. Ice water littered the pool's edge. Shivering, I scrubbed the excess water from my eyes, frantically searching for my attacker. A small bucket had been left by the side of my pool, and on the other end of the room, I could just make out a single figure heading for the back exit—tall with silky black hair, and an opened tunic with a back full of bandages. Pavi.

The front door creaked open. "Lyr?" Tristan asked.

I slid back into my pool, splashing water everywhere and hissing in pain as my bare skin scraped against the bath's edge. "Fuck!"

"Are you all right?"

"I'll be out in a minute," I called.

Tristan closed the door, and I jumped out of the pool, grabbing a towel. Pavi wasn't going to forgive me for her lashing. I'd made a powerful enemy today. I'd have all of Ka Elys after me now, both the Bamarian and Elyrian branches.

CHAPTER TWENTY-ONE

AN HOUR LATER, I left for dinner and ran right into Haleika and several other novice soturi wearing fresh practice tunics. I completely stood out in my silver gown, especially with my hair pinned back and curled to showcase my diadem, glittering over the center of my forehead. Lady Romula needed to be reminded of my station. But to everyone who saw me, it was very clear that I was most definitely not on my way to combat clinic.

"Your grace." Haleika sidled closer. "What about clinic?"

"Your grandmother called on me," I said quietly.

Understanding flashed in her eyes. One did not turn down invitations from Lady Romula. Her grandchildren knew that best.

"Can you cover for me?" I asked. "Sign me in? I'll be at the next one, but tonight...."

Haleika bit her lip. "Forging your signature...I don't know."

"It's fine, I grant you permission. Please?" Forging signatures of the ruling Ka was illegal, but she'd be fine. And I'd be at the next one, hopefully with an engagement ring.

Haleika twirled a loose brown curl around her finger then nodded. "Of course." She squeezed my hand. "Good luck, Lyr. I hope it goes well. You and Tristan deserve to be happy."

I gave her a tight-lipped smile. "Maybe we'll be cousins after tonight."

"I'd love that," she said.

I hung back as Haleika engaged the other girls in a conversation, steering them away from me, and managed to get out of the apartment building unseen by anyone else before I flew into the countryside of Vertavia. Ka Grey resided in large individual homes all surrounding the Grey Villa, their most prized possession. Glittering waterways flowed out from the Villa, only two stories high. Where it lacked height, it more than made up for in width, and it was sculpted out of pristine gray stone. Of course.

Two mages wearing bright blue robes with gray sashes stood guard at the Villa's entrance. Pinned boldly over their chests was the Grey sigil, the silver seraphim wings and silver moon. Ka Grey had always relied on magic instead of soturi for protection. It had worked to my benefit that day in the city, but now that I was a soturion, it would not further my case with Tristan's grandmother. Reaching the front entrance, I was escorted inside and officially announced.

"How wonderful to see you, your grace." Lady Romula stood at the top of the staircase. Her hand, weighed down in silver rings, held the banister tightly as she ever so slowly descended the steps. She was an old woman with old legs. But Lady Romula enjoyed making others wait. Taking someone's time was as pleasurable to her as taking money.

"And you, Lady Romula. Thank you for having me tonight."

"Thank you for honoring us with your presence at the Villa."

CHAPTER TWENTY-ONE   265

A minute passed since she'd greeted me. The Villa was only two stories and the steps not that high, but she was only a third of the way down. I folded my hands before my waist, the portrait of noble piety and patience.

Lady Romula touched the bottom step and paused, pointedly checking her hair, which was swept up in a series of braids on top of her head. I was used to waiting for her, but this crossed the line to insulting. She'd gained the upper hand, having already taken something from me without permission—my time.

"What a beautiful dress," I said as she stepped onto the foyer. Old age had not touched Lady Romula's skin the way it had others of her years. Gold and silver seemed to have a way around that—as did a life of ease. Her lips, however, were always dried and cracked and painted a dark red. She leaned forward to kiss me on each cheek. I tried not to cringe as her mouth brushed roughly across my skin.

"Oh, this?" She gestured grandly at her gown. "From last summer." Her formal dress was of course silver, a mix of satin and silk cloth gathered at the waist behind a belt of hundreds of delicate pearls and diamonds. She looked ready to attend a great ball, not spend an evening at home. "Lady Arianna has also called on me tonight with your cousin, the Lady Naria."

I swallowed, attempting to relax my hands at my side. It didn't mean anything. Aunt Arianna called on members of the Council all the time. There were a hundred reasons why the Master of Education needed to call on the Master of Finance for dinner. But knowing Naria was coming left my blood boiling. She was the last person I wanted here as I attempted to gain Lady Romula's blessing. At least I wasn't the only one missing combat clinic.

"Come, darling, let us retire." She took my arm, leading me swiftly around the corner—her knees suddenly working just fine. Two stories high and full of open windows, plants, and chandeliers made of diamonds and gold, the sitting room was meant to impress upon guests the immense wealth of Ka Grey. Oil paintings of their ancestral lords and ladies covered the walls from floor to ceiling. Lady Romula reclined on a couch, resting on silver velvet pillows, and snapped.

Two goblets brimming with wine floated through the doorway. The glass stems landed between our fingers. Lady Romula took hers with ease while I clumsily balanced mine and retreated to the couch on the opposite side of the room. A circular pool full of heated water stood between us, and I attempted to lie as casually on my cushions as she did.

Lady Romula's lips smacked together in admonishment. "I always forget how meager your father has you living." She took a long sip of wine. "Three young ladies on the verge of ruling society with no servants, no luxury. Bamaria used to be the leading edge of culture. In my day the parties, the fashion…." She shook her head. "Things are so austere now. How are you to function when your father deprives you so?"

I coughed. We used to have luxury, parties, and public appearances, but with the riots and the assassination attempt on my father, plus Meera and Morgana's vorakh, Bamarian culture had been put on hold. I conjured my sweetest smile and lifted my cup. "We try to set an example for all, including those less fortunate. Knowing the plight of the common Lumerian will make Meera a better leader. But I confess," I said with a wink, "it's why I so enjoy coming here."

She laughed wholeheartedly, raising her glass. The wine was the same color as her lips.

"We must remind you of what you're missing. Perhaps you can convince the Arkasva to bring luxury back to Cresthaven."

"One may hope," I said. "Bringing more Ka Grey into Cresthaven will only improve it."

Lady Romula grinned. "This certainly must be a pleasant contrast to the Shadow Stronghold, hmmmm?"

I nearly choked on my wine. My fingers tightened around the stem of my glass. "Contrast is not the word I'd use," I said carefully. I took another sip. A long one.

She winked, waving her goblet about. "It's a shame. My daughter's ring, lost to the Shadows who would never know what to do with it. Do you think we'll ever see it again?"

My entire body tensed. I could hear the accusation in her voice. As if I'd told Tristan to throw his mother's ring—my engagement ring—away. She was still pissed and saw the loss as my fault.

"I can only hope. Perhaps Lady Sila may be interested in a trade at the next Council Meeting."

Lady Romula pursed her lips as if this idea were ridiculous. "How are you faring, my dear? I must say, your father has made some rather unusual choices lately."

"One might say we've had unusual circumstances lately."

"Of course. We've had unusual circumstances for nearly twenty years. You've known nothing else. Life must seem normal to you, but it was and remains to this day quite a scandal that a man rules in Bamaria after a thousand years of rule by the women of Ka Batavia."

"Does it bother you that a man serves as Arkasva?" I asked carefully.

Lady Romula rolled her eyes. "I am Master of Finance on Bamaria's Council. What do I care what lies between the legs of our ruler so long as I maintain my position and wealth? But many would disagree. And in light of your condition," she said with a sniff, "a belief is spreading among the common folk that your father's rule is tainted. That you're suffering as a result."

I straightened, thinking of the mob that had formed on Auriel's Feast Day and all the shouts claiming he was false. I'd just heard similar comments today amongst my classmates. How widespread was the belief that my father shouldn't be ruling? It must have fully permeated Lumerian society if Lady Romula was mentioning it.

"Good evening, Grandmother." Tristan entered the sitting room wearing a bright blue tunic. A silver scarf draped over his shoulder. He gave me an encouraging look, but I could only manage a tight-lipped smile. Nothing in our conversation hinted at her softening or giving the blessing we both desperately needed. Marrying Tristan was one thing, but doing so without Lady Romula's support and protection was pointless.

She snapped her fingers, and another goblet glided over the threshold, attempting to make its way into Tristan's hand, but he waved it off, and the goblet floated away. He was already rushing to my side and taking my hand.

"Grandmother," he said, "I'm so glad you called for this dinner. We have something important we want to discuss with you. You know how much I love Lady Lyriana."

"Of course, darling, but first we must greet our guests."

For right at that moment, Arianna and Naria were announced.

Aunt Arianna, looking beautiful in a one-shouldered gown of blue, entered first. She wore her golden seraphim wings on her shoulder and showed off a new golden cuff on her bicep. It was similar in style to mine with golden seraphim feathers covering nearly half her arm above the elbow. She happily gave me a hug, asking how my first day of soturion training went, while Naria skulked behind, looking furious at my presence. She had also worn blue, but rather than wrapping the fabric over one shoulder, she'd crossed the material over her breasts, baring her stomach and leaving her cleavage on full display.

"Don't you have combat clinic tonight?" she asked.

"Don't you?"

"I was excused by my apprentice, but something tells me you weren't. You're not supposed to receive special favors."

My stomach twisted. Would she report this to Rhyan? Or worse...to Viktor Kormac?

Naria's eyes wandered to Tristan, as they had so many times over the years. He looked away embarrassed, eyes downcast...almost in shame. He was flushed, clearly thrown off by Naria for some reason. I stepped in front of him, glaring at Naria.

"Something tells me you should keep your nose out of this," I said, taking Tristan's arm.

More drinks floated in, and Lord Trajan, Tristan's grandfather, arrived. I accepted a goblet before dragging Tristan into the corner.

"What was that look?" I asked.

"What look?" He still wouldn't meet my eyes. What in Lumeria?

"Since Naria arrived, you won't look at me."

"I'm looking at you." His brown eyes lifted.

I narrowed my gaze. "You looked embarrassed back there. Why? Since when does a look from Naria affect you?"

Tristan chewed his bottom lip. "We shouldn't talk about this here."

My hands flew to my hips. "So, there is something to talk about?"

He pulled me away from the rest of the guests into a small hall, alone.

"Lyr, you have to promise you won't overreact."

"I'll promise after I decide if what you're about to tell me deserves an overreaction."

"Lyr."

"Gods, Tristan. Just tell me already."

Shrugging his shoulders, he said, "Last week, Naria came to me, and...she offered herself."

"She what!" I turned to storm back into the room and punch her—magical soturion strength or no.

"No, wait!" He grabbed my arm. Wine sloshed onto my hand. "I told her no, of course not."

"She offered herself! To you! When I was in a prison cell!"

"Lyr."

"The week I was locked up and supposed to be engaged to you!"

"I refused her! She thought...she thought Ka Grey wanted an alliance with Ka Batavia...just not with you."

The truth of that burned through me. "And she actually thought she had a chance with you?"

"Well...." He looked down again.

"Tristan! What in Lumeria are you not telling me?"

"Nothing," he said. "Nothing. Just...." He sighed. "Nothing happened between us. Nothing at all. Not last week."

My eyes widened, and my chest rose and fell with a violent exhale. "Explain."

"Do you remember the summer solstice three years ago? The forsworn bastard was visiting."

The night I'd danced with Rhyan. The night we'd kissed.

"What about it?" I asked carefully.

"I was dancing with Naria, and...."

"You slept with her!" I yelled.

His hand was on my mouth a second later. "Shhh. Lyr. No! But...close."

I threw my hand against the wall, needing to find my balance. I'd known Naria carried a torch for Tristan, and that he'd had...well, he'd had quite a few affairs before me. He'd always kept quiet to avoid Lady Romula's wrath and had taken every measure possible to avoid pregnancy. I was the first girl he'd ever openly courted. But put in context against my imprisonment and what had almost happened between us the other night…knowing Naria had gone to him…had once kissed him, touched him….

"I'm going to kill her," I seethed.

"No, you're not," he said gently. "You're going to calm down because it meant nothing. Remember why we're here." He took my hand to his lips and kissed it.

I barely had time to react, to remember to soften my hand under his touch. To submit, to be in love. But I was furious. This was unbelievable. My own cousin had tried to undo my engagement and stuck her little lackey Pavi to attack me today. I could still feel the cold ice water running down my back. And now to learn she'd kissed him, touched him…it made me sick.

But Tristan, as furious with him as I was in that moment, was right. I took a deep breath. I had to be calm. I needed my boyfriend's Godsdamned grandmother to bless our engagement in order to protect myself from exile. My nostrils flared, and I could feel my chest heaving despite the deep breaths.

"Fine," I snapped.

"You don't look fine. You're two seconds away from smashing that glass with your grip." Tristan took the goblet from my hand and floated it into the other room. He wrapped his arms around me, pulling me close. "I'm sorry. She meant and means nothing to me. You know that. The others who came before you…that's all they were. Before. I've only ever loved you."

He kissed my cheek, softly, sweetly. Like he meant it. But if he knew about Meera and Morgana, knew the secrets inside my golden arm cuff and beneath my tattoos, he'd call for their deaths like he'd called for Jules's. His love for me… it wasn't enough. It would never be enough.

I would never be enough.

I blinked back tears. "You're right. I'm overreacting."

After another kiss, I let him take my hand and lead me back to the party just as everyone retired to the dining room.

The first topics of conversation were stilted and silly enough, full of weather and gossip amongst the nobility in Bamaria—who was speaking to whom and who was not, and which Ka was currently in favor. I was already exhausted and sore from training, and the inane dinner discussions made me want to scream. If only Arianna and Naria weren't here, I could focus the conversation where I needed it—on my engagement to Tristan. I'd also be less focused on how much I wanted to rip Naria's head off.

"I do find it odd now that Arkasva Batavia has allowed the presence of a forsworn," said Lord Trajan.

Tristan snorted. "I've had several run-ins with him. He's the worst kind of criminal."

I straightened, not liking where this was going.

Lady Romula grimaced. "It's a sign that things are making a turn for the worse. But, your grace, isn't he the apprentice assigned to you?" She smacked her dry lips in further disapproval. "You should have been attached to the most noble apprentice available. It's only proper for one of your station. One must wonder what your father intends."

"His grace is doing all he can for the good of Bamaria," Arianna said quickly. "And I have seen the young man fight. You wouldn't call him forsworn if you saw his bound five."

"I was not aware the opposite of criminal was warrior," Lady Romula said. "So he's good in a brawl. Bravo! How does that make him less forsworn? You know what they say. He killed an innocent boy in training with his bare hands. Killed his own mother in one of his rages. He's unstable, I hear, completely unable to control his aura or temper. His father is Imperator—second in power to the Emperor in all of the North. If there was a shred of innocence in that boy, he would not be hiding on the other end of the Empire. Either

Imperator Hart could not legally absolve him, or he could not pay for it—both suggest serious wrong-doing. I don't like it."

"I can't speak to his accusations, but he was vouched for. And the boy did kill an akadim," Arianna said. "Plus, the Ready is keeping an eye on him. And Lyr." She smiled and gave me a wink.

"That shouldn't be on Lyr to do," Tristan said.

"Of course not. The entire situation is beneath her station." Lady Romula sniffed. "Blood ties with a criminal. His filthy blood now runs through your veins. And you're now cursed to pass it onto any future children you might have."

Tristan's children, she meant. Her great-grandchildren. She already saw them as tainted.

"Tristan," I said, desperate for a new conversation, "tell us about the Mage Academy."

Naria's eyes lit up, and she leaned forward, exposing a rather large amount of cleavage considering the setting and resting her breasts on the table. Was she serious? With me there? And Lady Romula? "How was your first day of classes? For me, my apprentice started with the toughest training protocol there is, but I was able to move through it with ease. How's your novice, Tristan?"

"It was fine," Tristan said, looking away. His eyes found mine.

Naria turned her gaze pointedly at me, realizing I was the cause of his silence. "Your grace," she said, her voice too loud for the dinner table, "it was lucky you avoided being whipped today. Isn't it?"

"Whipped!" yelled Lady Romula. Her eyes widened in horror, her mouth hanging open.

Silverware clattered to the table as everyone turned to stare at me.

Tristan's knuckles whitened. "Did they touch you?"

"No!" I shouted.

"Animals are whipped," Lady Romula said gravely, covering her eyes. "The soturi have always been so barbaric!"

"Mages aren't much better," Tristan snapped. "We use our staves to punish, inflicting burn marks for misuse of magic."

"And how many mages were burned today?" Lady Romula asked. "None, I suspect. While soturi beat each other on the daily."

Aunt Arianna turned on Naria, grabbing her arm, her fingers pressing into her skin. "This is not appropriate dinner conversation, my dear."

Naria shrugged out of her mother's grip. "I was just asking because I was concerned."

"I was not whipped," I said, wanting the subject dropped. I tried to wear the calm, powerful expression of an Heir to the Arkasva. "We can't say the same for Lady Pavi Elys."

"Senator Janvi's niece!" Lady Romula said.

"Yes, and Naria's best friend. Isn't that right, cousin?"

Naria's eyebrows narrowed. I took Tristan's hand on the table, entwining our fingers.

Lady Romula clapped. "Forget such unpleasant things. Let us retire for dessert and wine in the sitting room."

I put my fork down. I'd barely touched my food, not that there was much to begin with. Despite Lady Romula's exorbitant tastes in luxury and wine, she was cheap when it came to meals, serving bird food at dinners.

Naria sat with her mother, engaged in conversation with Lord Trajan. The smoke of moonleaves wafted from his long pipe as he reclined on a velvet couch. His feet lay over an oversized pillow, and the laces of his sandals came further undone with each exhale. Tristan and I had cornered Lady Romula on the other side of the room.

"I know how wonderful it is. I paid for it." Lady Romula cut off my compliments on the newest painting in the sitting room.

I smiled. "Of course."

She waved me off. "You'll need to brush up on your skills, my dear. Flattery, while effective, is too obvious for someone of your status. I'm older than I look, so let's get to it. You want my blessing."

I sat up straighter, ignoring the aches in my legs and back, and affected my most genuine expression. "Lady Romula, I believed we'd always had it. I came to reassure you that despite any changes in my life, one thing remains constant. My love for Tristan." Something twisted inside of me. Rhyan's green eyes flashed in my mind. Emerald, sparkling, roving up and down my body, settling on my hips and then higher to my eyes, seeing into me.

"Unfortunately, it is those changes in your life which have left me without assurance."

Tristan bit his lip. "Grandmother, I love her. More than anything." He squeezed my hand.

"Lucky when need and desire marry," Lady Romula said. "I've known Lady Lyriana since she was in the Arkasva's belly. But sometimes love is not enough to keep a person safe." She smiled sweetly. "Tristan, my love, the silver snaps bloomed last night. Lady Arianna has a liking for them. Would you show her and Naria to the garden?"

My heart sank. She was not going to give her blessing. Not tonight. This entire dinner was an exhausting waste of time, time I should have spent recovering from training or going to combat clinic like I'd promised Rhyan. Guilt at missing it and lying to him gnawed at my insides. And there was no doubt Naria would use it against me.

I began to stand and take Tristan's arm, but Lady Romula pulled me back onto the couch. "We shall talk some more, you and I."

"I would like that," I said sweetly, watching warily as Tristan walked over to Arianna and Naria. I didn't like the idea of him going anywhere with her, now that I knew what a true backstabber she was.

The moment they left the room, Lady Romula drew closer. "Listen here, your grace. You are too sheltered to know, but I spoke true earlier. There is unrest in Bamaria. I know you love your father, but a man ruling Ka Batavia has broken one thousand years of tradition. I was not there when her grace, High Lady Marianna, her soul freed, wrote her will."

"*Ha Ka Mokan*," I said.

"Who am I to judge what she wished. Perhaps it was her best option, maybe she had some reason to choose her husband over sister despite tradition. Maybe the sickness went to her mind. But now we have a viable, legal, and traditional alternative to rule in place of your father, an Heir Apparent who has been of age for two years, a woman, and the direct descendent of Marianna."

"*Ha Ka Mo—*" I started, but Lady Romula waved me off.

"Yes, yes, her soul freed. No one doubts your piety, my dear. You should know at the time of your mother's death that many believed your aunt Arianna would take the seat or be regent to the Lady Meera. Many thought your father should have stepped down for her to take over and restore order, especially after her grace's nineteenth birthday, but he has not, and two years later he seemingly has no plans to do so."

I clasped my hands in my lap to keep them from shaking. This was everything I'd feared. Meera was the Heir Apparent, but she would never become Arkasva, not with her vorakh. The moment her visions had come, any possibility of my father stepping down had died. How many others were thinking this? How long before they realized why she couldn't rule? Or why Morgana couldn't?

"What's more, Lady Lyriana, we're coming close to two decades of allowing a foreign soturi inside our borders. Do you understand how insulting it is to know Ka Kormac's soldiers are stationed in Bamaria? To hear that there's been even a seed of doubt regarding our ability to protect our borders or to protect from within when Ka Grey has been removing vorakh filth for years? And now you have no power." Her expression darkened, and she lowered her voice. "You must be careful now. Your father's Shadows won't want me speaking, but I will since you concern my grandson, and what affects you, unfortunately affects him. A threat is brewing in the pits of Bamaria, one that will come to pass soon. Your life is in danger."

CHAPTER TWENTY-TWO

THE OLD WOMAN'S eyes were cunning as she watched me. Whatever she thought threatened me, it made her nervous, too. "The Emartis's calls for a female Arkasva only grow louder," she said.

"The Emartis?" I asked. "Who are they?"

Lady Romula's eyes narrowed. "Does the black seraphim mean anything to you?"

My whole body turned cold. Meera's vision.

Lady Romula snapped her bony fingers. A small scroll floated through the door, gliding into her outstretched hand before she gave it to me, a note of disgust on her face. She pulled out a handkerchief to clean her hands.

I unrolled the parchment. Painted into the center was the altered sigil of Ka Batavia I'd seen that day at the festival, both in the crowd and on the pin that vendor had tried to sell to me. It hadn't been a coincidence, that pin hadn't been a mistake. Beneath the odd sigil of the black seraphim beneath a silver moon, someone had written:

Shekar arkasva! Time for the false arkasva to be removed and for our true Arkasva Batavia to take her place. Join us in truth. It comes either way.

Me Arkasva, Me Emar.
My Arkasva, my truth.
Ani Dhara Me Sha El Lyrotz
The Emartis.

My mouth went dry. They'd sworn their oath in blood, making it an oath they had to uphold lest the old magic claim what was owed.

Lady Romula pursed her red painted lips together. The wine she drank had dried them into tiny cracks.

"These were sent to all the ruling Kavim in Bamaria. They've been silent, biding their time for seventeen years since your father took the Seat, and in that time, they have organized. They believe the Laurel may only pass to a female. A lady of Ka Batavia."

"No, that was just an angry mob led by my uncle Tarek." My throat tightened, and just like that, everything fell into place.

Lady Romula watched me closely. "Your uncle Tarek was killed. But the Emartis survived. You think a disorganized, angry mob could kill the Arkasva of Bamaria? There were spies who slipped past the Shadows, double agents, and traitors willing to sell secrets for coin. There were plans in place. Plans that were not lost. Plans that are still in existence from the look of this letter. And by my count, they've only gotten bigger and more fanatical."

I was going to be sick. I clutched the couch, leaning forward. The Emartis had caused the riot all those years ago. They'd attacked my father and caused enough instability to open the door for Ka Kormac to enter Bamaria. Aunt Arianna had been arrested for treason because of them. And with the Emartis rising again, Ka Batavia looked poised to fall as swiftly as Ka Azria. My breath shortened, and the walls felt like they were closing in as my body started to seize with panic and cold.

Take my hand.

Small details. Stay present.

I felt the smoothness of my dress beneath my fingers, tasted the remnants of wine on my tongue, inhaled the scent of Lady Romula's floral perfume, applied too heavily. I felt the itchiness of my shift against my breasts, the dull ache spreading across my back, the soreness behind my calves and in the arches of my feet, the tightness in my hands. I was at the Grey Villa. I was safe. Nothing was going to hurt me here, not today. We were surrounded by mages, sworn to protect us.

I was safe. I was safe. I was safe.

I willed the walls to stay in place, the ceiling to remain firm.

"The current line of succession is a lie in their eyes," Lady Romula continued. "And now with your situation, they believe your Ka cursed. They want a woman. And if we are to learn anything from history, they are willing to take severe actions to make it happen. They tried to kill your father once, my dear. They will try again, and if they come in contact with you—they won't hesitate. You're tainted in their eyes."

A numbing sensation crept through me.

Lady Romula's eyes moved behind me and brightened. Her cracked lips stretched into a grin. "Ah, is there anything more beautiful than freshly bloomed silver snaps? Only happens right when fall is around the corner."

Arianna and Naria returned, both wearing the silvery flowers in their hair. Tristan walked behind them, a glowing bouquet in his hands that he brought to me.

I was vaguely aware of Naria's death glare as I accepted the snaps. I inhaled the sharp scent of the flowers, needing something else to anchor me, to keep me from fainting, from drowning in panic.

"Have you two come to an agreement, Grandmother?" Tristan asked.

Lady Romula shook her head. "There is much unrest in Bamaria now. And I don't like unrest. The economy suffers, and the future becomes unpredictable, unsafe. Before I give my blessing to your union, I need some guarantees that Tristan's birthright is secured. That Ka Grey is protected. And as long as the Emartis are about, I do not trust Ka Batavia or their Arkasva with my most prized investment. We've already lost one priceless heirloom to this mess." She glared at Tristan, her eyes flicking to his bare hands.

"What might allow for such a guarantee?" I asked through clenched teeth.

"Stop the threat," she said.

How very soturion of you. It took all I had not to yell at her, first for being so impossible, and then for comparing Tristan's worth to a Godsdamned ring.

She leaned forward, taking my hand, her skin papery thin. "I have always supported your father. And I know you care for my grandson. But after my son and daughter-in-law were murdered by that vorakh monster...." She dropped my hand, making a noise of disgust, and took Tristan's hand in hers. "He's all I have left, the future of Ka Grey. We get comfortable sitting in our villas and fortresses, announcing our titles before our names. But even Ka Azria was comfortable, and look where they are now."

I stared at my knees, terrified my face had turned red. Was she simply warning me of how quickly a Ka could fall? Or was she hinting that she knew about Meera and Morgana? She could end things between me and Tristan. She *would* end things.

But she hadn't. I took a deep breath.

She didn't know. Just a shrewd old lady determined to play her cards right.

"You understand, my dear," Lady Romula said. "I will not bargain with Ka Batavia as long as these threats loom."

And as long as these threats loomed, I desperately needed her bargain.

I crushed the flowers to my chest. Tristan cocked his head, his aura surging with anger.

"And what if I say myself to Moriel and marry her anyway?" Tristan asked, his hand reaching for mine. "Will you disown me as an heir to Ka Grey, force me out of the Villa?"

I gawked, almost touched. In another life I would have loved the romanticism of it. Yet as much as I'd pushed against the political nature of our union...Tristan's love was worthless to me without it.

Lady Romula looked between us. "Love is sweet, my dears. But it does not replace security. Good night, your grace." She extended her hand to Tristan. "Help me up the stairs."

I sat on the couch alone, fuming and scared, the message from the Emartis held tight in my hands beneath my flowers. I'd come here for assurances, and now those assurances were on me to deliver, but I had no idea how to offer them.

Arianna extricated herself from her conversation to recline onto my couch, propping her feet on a floor pillow. "You look troubled. What horrid thing did Lady Romula say now?"

I held the scroll tightly, concealing its contents. A silver snap petal fell into my lap.

"Arianna, would you answer a question truthfully?" My stomach turned. I'd never questioned her before. There'd never been a reason to, but now.... "Did you agree with my mother's decision to name my father Arkasva?"

She blinked. "I admired your mother in every way. She was wise and always careful with her choices."

"You never thought you should have been named to the Seat?"

Aunt Arianna laughed so hard she snorted. "My dear, I was third in line." She shook her head. "That was never the plan, never in my thoughts. I spent my life preparing to be on the sidelines. To support my sisters. You understand."

Guilt over my own desires to rule twisted inside of me. I, too, was third from the Seat. But I was not content to play a supporting role forever.

She shook her head in confusion. "Where is this coming from?"

I handed her the Emartis scroll. "This is being sent to the nobility."

She unrolled the parchment, her eyes widening as she took in the image of the black seraphim and read their decree.

"Did you know they were still active?" I asked. "After all these years?"

"I didn't even know they existed when I was arrested." She tore the parchment in half. "They're scum. Weak, pathetic babies crying in the streets because they did not get their way. We are Ka Batavia," Aunt Arianna said fiercely. "And we have ruled for a thousand years. Whatever is the will of the Arkasva is the will of us all." She reached an arm around me, and I flinched. Something pinched my back. "The Ready stopped them before, he will stop them again."

If only Lady Romula were so confident.

"My dear, go get some rest. You have training tomorrow."

She pulled her arm away. Her golden cuff had pinched me.

"Without magic," she said, gently patting my back, "these seven months won't be easy. And we all need you to survive training. Promise me you're taking care of yourself."

As our seraphim soared over Vertavia, I rested my head on Tristan's shoulder.

"She'll give in, Lyr. She knows how much this means to me. To us."

"What about Naria?" I asked.

He groaned. "She has nothing to do with this."

"You almost slept with her and didn't tell me. She still wants you. Why else would she come tonight? What if you get tired of waiting for me? And your grandmother prefers her."

"She doesn't. And I won't," he said fiercely, pulling me against him. "I'll wait for you. As long as it takes." He rested a hand on my thigh. His sigil ring caught the blue light of an ashvan's hooves. I couldn't allow him to offer me this sigil without Lady Romula's blessing, and she wouldn't act until I'd stopped the threat of the Emartis.

Tristan and I parted at the seraphim port in Urtavia, walking in opposite directions, him toward the Mage Academy, and me toward the soturion apartments. An escort of Ka Grey walked silently behind me, casting a silver dome of light around me.

When I reached the main entrance to my apartment building, I found another message from the Emartis, their black seraphim staring up at me in mockery of my Ka's sigil.

Another scroll.

CHAPTER TWENTY-THREE

I TURNED TO see if Tristan's escort had noticed. He kept a respectable distance behind me, too far to see the scroll with any manner of detail.

Trying to keep my voice steady, I croaked out, "I'm fine here. Good night." My throat had gone completely dry.

"Your grace." The escort bowed low, extinguishing the dome of light surrounding me. The tip of his stave glowed blue as he walked off into the night.

I tore the scroll into pieces, heart hammering as I opened the doors to the lounge. Parchment crunched beneath my feet. Scroll after scroll after scroll lay strewn across the floor, all bearing the mark of the black seraphim.

Had they done this to every apartment in Urtavia? Myself to Moriel. I needed to destroy every last letter before anyone woke up and noticed. There was an apprentice soturion on call for emergencies, but I didn't want to bring anyone else into this. Not unless I knew I could trust them. I needed Aemon.

Quickly, I set to work, collecting each and every scroll until I'd made a giant pile in the center of the room. I lit the fireplace, feeding all of the traitorous letters inside. Except one. I tucked it into my belt and ventured back outside.

Aemon had a home inside the fortress of Cresthaven, but during the Academy's school year, he resided in his townhouse not far from the Katurium.

I scooped up the hem of my dress, walking briskly over the waterway. Soturi stood on duty, still and alert in the shadows. Flashes of steel swords and golden armor glowed in the moonlight. No sign of silver. Ka Batavia was protecting the city tonight—a relief. A few of the soturi seemed startled to see me at first, but easily recognizing me, they bowed their heads in respect.

Aemon's townhouse was far more peaceful looking than I'd have expected of the warlord, serene with perfectly trimmed moontrees canopying a wall of black obsidian that surrounded the property. Sentries in the golden armor of Ka Batavia walked the perimeter. Only one stood still before the wall's entrance, his dark eyes narrowing.

"State your business," he ordered.

"Lady Lyriana Batavia," I said, stepping into the light. "Let Arkturion Aemon know I'm here."

The sentry's eyes widened. He looked me up and down, doing a double-take on my face and diadem, before bowing. "Apologies. We were not expecting you, your grace. Open the gates!"

The black obsidian doors glowed in the moonlight as they creaked open. I was greeted by another soturion before the townhouse doors. He gestured for me to enter, calling my name out as I did.

I'd never been inside Aemon's townhouse before. I expected weapons everywhere, perhaps more obsidian or black-painted walls—something that marked him as the Ready, as Bamaria's personal God of Death. But the décor was tranquil, peaceful. The walls had been painted a deep stone gray, and the rest of the room was full of dark, muted, calming colors. It was all very similar in tone to Morgana's room. Torch-lamps protruded from the walls to offer light, but only half had been lit—perhaps because of the late hour.

I stepped into the center of the foyer. There was a rush of footsteps, sandals slapping against the marble floor, and then the red cloak of the Arkturion flashed before my eyes.

But it wasn't Aemon who stood before me. It was the warlord of Ka Kormac. The Bastardmaker.

His black, beady eyes roamed over my body, his tongue flicking out to wet his lips.

I took a step back, nearly falling out the door. Where was Aemon?

Pushing my hand against my hip so hard I was sure it would bruise, I took a deep breath. I had to do anything to keep myself grounded and here in the present, to keep myself from panicking at the sight of him.

"Lady Asherah," he said. "Rather late to be visiting your Arkturion." His eyes flicked behind me. "Alone without an escort. And in such revealing fashion."

"Soturi-in-training do not require escorts." My heart pounded. "What are you doing in his home at this hour?" I demanded.

The Imperator stepped into the foyer, the golden border of his black robes shining under the firelight, showing off his power in my country, over my own father, and now, apparently, permission to be in our warlord's home after hours. "Quite late for her grace to be out on her own dressed as such."

The Bastardmaker grinned. "Wouldn't want any rumors to start now."

I barely remembered to dip my chin, making the smallest of curtsies, before I stood tall, daring myself to make eye contact. "I have business here."

The Imperator's eyes narrowed to thin slits as he clucked his tongue. "Lady Lyriana might have business here at such an hour, but *Soturion* Lyriana, who didn't know the first rule of being a soldier, ought to be in bed, not demanding audiences with men who outrank her. You look very well for someone who just entered their first combat clinic."

My heart pounded. "Thank you," I said.

He stepped forward. Gods. Did he know I'd skipped?

"Waryn will escort you back. I know soturi-in-training don't require escorts," he snarled, "but novices don't come banging on their Arkturion's doors at midnight either."

I froze, unsure how to respond, because he was right. And I didn't know what role I was playing anymore. I was either Lady Lyriana—a role that I'd been nearly forced to forfeit— pulling rank and demanding to see a member of my father's Council. Or I was breaking the third rule of being a soturion, which was following orders. At the least...he seemed unaware I'd already broken my promise.

The Imperator broke into a wolfish grin. "Shall you accept my generous offer of a personal escort home now?"

But the Ready entered the room in a dark shadow. "Lady Lyriana, we shall meet. Good night, Imperator. Arkturion. Thank you for your visit."

The Imperator swept past me for the door. "Come, Waryn, let's retire. We'll leave her grace to her very important business." He pushed aside Aemon's sentry, leaving the soturion scowling at the foreign warlord. The Bastardmaker stepped outside, but the Imperator turned to me suddenly. "By the way, your grace, did you ever learn the first rule of being a soturion?"

My mouth opened...it was there on the tip of my tongue, but I couldn't speak. I couldn't will myself to submit to his game, even just to prove that I knew it.

The Imperator's lips curled as he crossed the threshold. "They told me she was smart."

Aemon gestured me to his side. "Your grace, it's late. You shouldn't be here now—nor should you be outside at this hour."

"I had reason." I fished for the scroll in my belt, stepping into his shadows. Aemon took it without question. "All the noble Kavim received this message, and I found over a hundred of these in my apartment building tonight."

"Fucking Emartis," Aemon said as his eyes reached the bottom of the scroll. His aura pulsed, dark, thundering, weighing heavily on me. I'd never want to be on Aemon's bad side.

I cleared my throat. "I thought someone should check the Mage Academy for these. They could very well be in every apartment and home in Urtavia."

Aemon withdrew his energy, and the dark thundering cloud evaporated. He shook his head, looking disgusted. "Every last one will be destroyed by dawn. You did well to come to me, but you've done enough. This is for me to worry about. You know what your job is right now. I'll have one of my guards escort you home."

"Aemon," I swallowed, throat dry. "Lady Romula said my life is in danger. Am I a target for the Emartis?"

"Yes," he said, voice dark. "But you're an Heir to the Arkasva. You've had more targets on your back since the day you were born than you'll ever know or should be aware of."

I shuddered. I'd grown up constantly shadowed by soturi...always thinking them a nuisance. It hadn't occurred to me—since I'd never known otherwise—that they were keeping me safe. If anything, I'd felt the opposite about them after Jules.

"And now?" I asked. "How many targets are aimed at me?"

"Enough that you have round-the-clock protection circling your perimeter—but not within your classes at the Katurium," he snarled, as if he'd wanted it to be otherwise. "You have to learn to protect yourself there. I can't protect you from your classmates. But every time you step outside the university borders, I have shadows on you."

"Markan?" I asked.

Aemon pursed his lips together. "Your grace, you have to stop making obscene gestures every time you see him."

I glared.

Aemon rolled his eyes. "Fine." His expression softened to one of concern. "Don't fear the Emartis. They can't touch you now. But the Imperator...."

"What was the Imperator doing here?" I asked angrily.

"You have other concerns to worry about. Like getting enough sleep for training tomorrow. I know what time you came home last night. Tonight's hardly different. You can't keep doing this. You have a full day of training, classes, and clinic—there isn't time for you to do anything else. But since I know your tendency to stick your nose where it doesn't belong...the Emperor just approved an additional five units of Ka Kormac's soturi to guard Urtavia."

"Five?" My heart stopped. "Are they to come all at once?"

Aemon nodded. "And now I need to station those fuckers in places where they won't cause more trouble."

Each unit was known in High Lumerian as an eshayim. One hundred. Five eshayim meant five hundred Korterians were marching on Urtavia right now, and when they got here and joined the already full camp of soturi, we'd have two thousand foreign soldiers. A legion. An armed legion in our country.

"Soturion Tarum," Aemon called. "Escort the Lady Lyriana to her apartment."

A sentry rounded the corner into the foyer and saluted Aemon. "At once, Arkturion."

"You're not to breathe a word of this to anyone," Aemon said. "And, your grace, be ready. With a legion of Ka Kormac watching us, I will not be able to save you from Academy punishment again. Whether you deserve it or not."

My stomach knotted, my mind flashing to Pavi's back being torn open, her arms tied helplessly to the pole. I followed his sentry into the darkness.

CHAPTER TWENTY-FOUR

MORNING CAME TOO quickly. I spent the night tossing and turning, my dreams full of the Emartis, Lady Romula, and legions upon legions of Ka Kormac soturi marching through Bamaria, their sandals kicking dirt everywhere until the waterways were covered in filth. It was enough to make me sick as I sat up in bed. To top it all off, my body was sorer than it had ever been thanks to Rhyan's training. It had hurt just to roll over. Standing up nearly knocked the breath out of me, and I had to lie on my back just to lace up my sandals because bending over was too much.

I joined Haleika and Galen for breakfast in the Katurium's dining hall, but the thought of eating made me feel nauseated. My vomiting display on the track still haunted me; not just had it been utterly humiliating, but throwing up in that way had been painful.

In the end, Haleika assured me it was better to eat now instead of later just to keep up my strength. I wasn't sure I believed her, but I acquiesced and made a small plate of flat bread, hummus, and fruit before downing the largest mug of coffee I could find. As I drank, she caught me up on what I'd missed the night before. Viktor had been selected to be in the center for the first fight along with other soturi from Ka Kormac.

"No one wanted to attack his grace," Galen said, stretching his arms overhead.

Haleika rolled her eyes. "Very convenient for him."

Galen shrugged. "At least we get tonight off. No clinic until tomorrow."

"That's right!" Haleika perked up. "Maybe we can eat dinner at that little corner restaurant we found. You know the one with the waitlist at the festival?"

"Dinner?" Galen's lips quirked.

I turned away, allowing them privacy to make their date, or whatever it was, for the evening. I watched the other soturi in the hall. I scanned each and every single one, looking for parchment in their bags, discarded scrolls from the Emartis, signs of black wings, a false sigil, anything. But every classmate was clean—at least as far as I could see. No one seemed to be acting nervous or strange, no more than I was used to observing.

I turned back to my plate, pushing a piece of flatbread around the hummus.

"Sound good, Lyr?" asked Haleika.

I dropped my bread. "What?"

"If you and Tristan join us for dinner?"

"Oh." I thought of all the homework I already had and how I'd gone a whole day without checking on my sisters. Plus, a rebel group, the one responsible for crippling my father, was on the loose, and I was one of their prime targets.

"Shekar…." The word sounded in the air, rising above the conversations all around me.

The hair on the back of my neck prickled, and I turned, making eye contact with a group of girls who wore the orange of Ka Elys. They all stopped talking at once and turned away from me, staring down at their plates with an unnatural level of concentration. They barely seemed to breathe, engaging in the sort of forced silence that came from being caught by the very person you were talking about.

A pit formed in my stomach. Were they simply talking about me the way people always talked about me? Or had they uttered the word shekar?

I twisted in my seat to find Naria's table. She sat with Viktor and Pavi. All three openly glared at me. Pavi turned toward Tani. She folded her arms across her chest, one leg smoothly crossing over the other.

"Lyr?" Haleika asked. "Dinner?"

"Sure," I said. "Tristan and I can come to dinner."

Haleika grinned. "Come on, let's get our spots on the track."

I cleared my tray, still full of untouched food. I was already dreading the idea of being out in public, being seen and scrutinized, and going out like everything was normal, like the city wasn't being occupied by Ka Kormac. But I wanted to get a feel for the energy in Urtavia now, and, despite Aemon's warnings, I wanted to search for more evidence of the Emartis. My engagement to Tristan depended on it.

Out in the arena, the morning sun beat down on the field, giving the white stadium seats and the inner field grass a golden glow. I yawned and braided my hair just as Rhyan motioned me to join him on the track.

Carefully, I walked over, fully aware of his eyes on me, the steady, intense gaze that watched my every step. I stretched out beside him, my dagger in the ground next to his, handles gleaming with gold. I was already warm.

"So, partner, are congratulations in order?" he asked, leaning forward into a lunge.

"Congratulations?" I asked nervously.

His good eyebrow lifted, but he continued staring ahead as he spoke. "You know? Felicitations. Best wishes. *Tovayah maischa.*"

"Good luck? For what?" I asked.

He turned toward me, and his green eyes flashed pointedly to my left hand. "Did Lord Grey finally propose?" His jaw tensed.

"Oh." Right, I'd gone to Lady Romula's to get her blessing for our engagement after I'd allegedly gone to my first combat clinic. I groaned, eyeing my ringless finger, and sank deeper into my lunge, trying to get my leg to bend at the same angle as Rhyan's. "He didn't."

Rhyan frowned, his jaw flexing as he repeated his lunge on the other leg. He returned his gaze ahead. "How was your first combat clinic?"

I sucked in a breath. "Viktor's wolves are going easy on him," I lied carefully.

He nodded, lips pursed together. "This run will be like yesterday. But worse."

I narrowed my eyes. "Have I told you how much I enjoy these pep talks of yours?" Pushing my hips back, I went into a half-split, feeling the stretch behind my sore calves and thighs. By the Gods...my legs hurt. "They're about as good as this stretch."

Rhyan grunted, sinking deeper into his pose, the muscles in his arms popping. "You're sore from yesterday. Plus, you're tired. Your body isn't used to re-energizing so quickly after what it's been through, so factor that in. You can't run on fumes."

My pulse spiked at his warning. He was right. I stared at the pole, imagining Pavi tied to it, helpless, furious, her back sliced open, and the cries of pain she couldn't help but release. I sucked in a breath.

"What do I do?" I asked.

"Same as yesterday," Rhyan said. "One foot in front of the other, eyes ahead. Go slower today—by all counts, your body will force you to. Listen to it. It's nearly as smart as you are. And, remember, it's not a race."

"No winners," I grumbled, watching half a dozen soturi take their place beside us. "I know."

"Did the bath salts help last night?" He shucked off his tunic, revealing the stretch of his shoulders and the gryphon tattoo across his back. My breath hitched at the sight of his muscles rippling as he tossed his tunic onto the grass. He tightened the leather belt holding the half-tunic around his waist and turned to face me.

"Yes, thank you," I said, pulling my eyes away.

"I'll get you more." He paused, his gaze roaming up and down my body. "You eat?"

"A little."

He eyed me carefully, like he didn't believe me, but nodded. "Good."

Aemon walked onto the field, his Arkturion cloak, golden crimson beneath the sun, billowing behind him as he called us to order. My fingers dug into the dirt. My throat dried. Rhyan took a deep breath beside me. The bells sounded. We ran. It was awful. But somehow, I made it through the run without incident. Desperate to avoid a repeat of the previous day, I focused on pacing myself toward the end and grabbed my dagger just as the bells rang. But the victory was short-lived. I threw up again. This time, Haleika was there beside me—ready with a cool towel and water—while Rhyan watched from the sidelines, arms neatly folded across his chest.

He gave me a curt nod as I shakily made my way to my feet and headed off to the baths.

I sat through my classes in silence, taking as many notes as I could, but each lecture was harder to focus on, and I found my concentration waning with each passing hour. I ate lunch slowly, still feeling off, only managing about half my plate. As the day went on, my body had grown sorer and sorer. I was dreading training with Rhyan even as a small part of me couldn't wait to see him, to be alone with him. This was dangerous territory to be in—and one I regretted about five minutes into our session.

He didn't take it easy on me at all, and he was a lot less talkative than the day before, donning a constant frown on his face. Gone was the friendly Rhyan, the one who liked to banter and debate words with me or help me find the answer. Gone was the Rhyan who seemed to soften with me, just a little, like he had the night we'd danced, and kissed.... This version of him was all ice and surliness, cold and blunt with his words. He barked order after order, barely looking at me unless he had to.

"Am I...?" I swallowed, shifting deeper into a squat. My legs shook, and sweat poured down my back. The mat was slippery with perspiration. I was about to fall over but determined to stay upright. "Am I doing this wrong?" I asked.

His frown only deepened as his eyes scanned my body. With a noncommittal grunt, he announced the next position.

I fell out of the pose, my muscles shaking like jelly. He said nothing, only began the next demonstration.

I could see his frustration with my performance all over his face. I was failing at this, and he knew it. The thought made me want to cry.

Stopping the Emartis and every other threat coming my way felt impossible, and rightly so. But this felt equally as hard. I hated it because everyone else here was succeeding without problem, and if I failed, Rhyan failed, and so did my sisters. I remembered Rhyan's words, that I wasn't to worry about him, but something inexplicable inside of me did worry, and nothing I said or thought seemed to be able to stop it.

I was sore as fuck when I left, my muscles wobbly and useless. It took me four times as long as it should have to make it back to my apartment building and up the stairs. I sank onto the floor of my shower and let the water warm to the hottest temperature it could. Then I stayed there, letting it pound against my back as the bathroom steamed until I had the strength and concentration to stand again.

I barely had any energy to do my hair for dinner and opted for a simple blue dress that didn't require a shift and tied at the shoulders. The only jewelry I wore was what I had on: my golden arm cuff, its seraphim wings concealing Meera's vision logs, and two thick golden bracelets around both hands. I left my diadem in its box. Even if I hadn't minded announcing my station to every guest at the restaurant, I didn't have the strength to hold my arms up long enough to set the golden circlet against my forehead and tie it through my hair.

Tristan met me at the front entrance of my apartment building, flanked by his two most loyal mage escorts. Behind him, a litter already floating above the shoulders of four Ka Grey mages was ready for me to enter. I nearly sighed in relief. I couldn't walk one more step today.

I snuggled against Tristan's chest, inhaling the mint and salt scent that clung to him, my eyes half open as I watched the city pass slowly through the gauzy silver curtains of the litter's windows. We slowed as we approached the restaurant, and the litter shifted side to side as the mages lowered us to the ground. Tristan exited first, holding out a hand to help me stand and step out onto the street. Urtavia was full with Lumerians from all over the Empire walking in every direction, talking excitedly, taking advantage of the final days of summer to enjoy their night in the city. Many were heading to dinner themselves, dressed in their finest dresses and robes. Freshly cut leather sandals laced up their calves, and sparkling jewelry gleamed off their skin.

We walked up to the restaurant where Haleika and Galen were waiting, standing very close together beneath a red awning above the entrance. It was the first time in days I'd seen them in their normal clothes. Galen donned a white cape held together by a golden scroll pin at his left shoulder. He looked every bit a member of Ka Scholar. Haleika had settled on a silver dress that flowed out at the waist—typical Ka Grey wear, though far less ornate than what her grandmother had chosen the previous night. She'd kept her green soturion cloak over her shoulder, styling it like a cape to match Galen. The overall effect made her look like a princess.

"Our table will be ready in fifteen minutes," Haleika announced cheerfully. "I heard the food is amazing!" She rubbed her belly and did a little hop-step on silver sandals that sparkled with every swish of her dress.

Tristan frowned. "Fifteen?"

"No!" Galen said. "Fifteen minutes is really good for a place like this. Come on, Tristan. Be cool."

Tristan scoffed and nodded at one of his escorts. "Speed that up, please." He tossed the mage a silver coin purse.

"Tristan," Haleika groaned. "Stop. You make us look like snobs whenever you do that."

"I make us look like we want our food." He pulled me close, his arm around my waist.

"You're going to get our food spat in," Haleika said with a pout.

"Nonsense. They're going to make it with care, seeing as how I'm willing to pay."

Haleika scrunched up her nose. "Ugh, we didn't have a reputation here. That was half the appeal." She shook her head. "Now we will."

"Ka Grey and Ka Batavia have reputations everywhere. Anyway, it's for a good cause," Tristan said. "Look at Lyr, she's going to faint if we don't feed her soon."

"I'm not going to faint!"

Galen gave me the side-eye. "Well…."

"Fine," Haleika said. "But if you insist on being a complete and total snob—don't give me that look! You know what you are! At least have the decency to go inside and bribe them yourself. Don't send your escort."

"Whose side are you on, Galen?" Tristan asked.

Haleika slid beside him, a seductive grin on her lips as she stared up at him beneath thick, blackened lashes.

Galen held up his hands. "As a representative of Ka Scholar, who does not, by the way, have a reputation here—"

"Because your Ka never takes their noses out of their scrolls," Haleika said with a sly grin.

Galen smirked, shaking his head. "Not getting in the middle of this. But on the stance of the possibility of having my food spat in, I'm very, very against."

"Lyr?" Tristan grinned, squeezing my waist.

I rolled my eyes. "Everyone knows you bribe by your own hand when you don't want to look like a snob. They teach you that in Introduction to Lumerian Nobility."

Tristan laughed. "I think I failed that class." He pressed a kiss to my cheek and released me. "I'll go in myself. Just remember, I'm doing this for all of your benefit. Not mine. Lyr's going to faint. Haleika won't stop rubbing her belly. And, Galen, you're eyeing me like I'm a meal."

"Dream on!" Galen laughed heartily.

"Now I'm going to go in there, on your behalf, and plead, on your behalf, because you're tired, hungry soturi in desperate need of sustenance."

"Whatever helps you sleep at night, cousin," Haleika said. "Go. Live your life as a snob. Enjoy your spit-food!"

The escort tossed the purse back to Tristan but followed closely behind as his lord vanished inside the restaurant's front door. Galen turned toward Haleika, who was still standing close to him, and ran his hand down her arm.

I tried to remember the bet Tristan and I had made about them, but that seemed like ages ago. Surely, one of us had won. As Galen gave Haleika a quick kiss on the cheek, I directed my attention back to the city behind me.

A group of mages walked down the waterway, talking animatedly. I looked up, accidentally making eye contact with a short man with reddened cheeks and a long black mustache that curled at the ends. He stopped walking so suddenly that the mage in his party who walked behind him crashed into his back and cursed. The short man continued to stare at me. All at once, I saw the flash of recognition in his eyes, the way his mustache jumped and his lip quivered as he watched me watching him.

It was the vendor from the festival, the one who'd had the Emartis pins with the black seraphim wings on the sigil for Ka Batavia.

Just as quickly as he recognized me, he averted his gaze, looking pointedly at another mage in his group and laughing loudly as they ambled past us. The vendor looked away, then back to me. He was attempting to appear relaxed and nonchalant, but I saw the extra skip in his step and his attempt to speed up and get away from me.

More parties of mages and soturi swarmed the streets, ambling past shops, stopping in front of restaurants to inquire about dinner reservations. But I had my mark, and kept my eye on the vendor.

"Haleika," I said without thinking, "can I borrow your cloak?"

"Are you cold?" she asked, already unpinning the green material and handing it to me. "It's still warm out."

"I...um...." I caught sight of Tristan in the window, laughing with the restaurant owner inside. His silver purse passed easily into the other man's hand. The owner shook his head, looking embarrassed, then broke into a shy grin. Tristan, despite being a snob, did have a way of charming almost everyone he talked to.

I shook my head at Haleika. "I'm buying Tristan an early birthday present. Now's a good time for me to sneak over to this store I think he'd like without him knowing. And, you know, I'd rather not be recognized while shopping. It's just for five minutes."

"Do you want company?" Galen asked. "It's getting pretty crowded out there."

"No," I said, staring down the street. The vendor's group was almost out of my line of sight. I'd have to hurry. "My escorts are my shadows. I won't be long. Tell Tristan I, um, needed to stretch my legs."

I pulled the edge of Haleika's cloak over my hair, red in the setting sun, and felt a burst of energy I hadn't thought possible minutes before. I quickly moved past the restaurant and the next building, sliding in and out of the Lumerians crowding the streets. There was an opening, and I managed to position myself right beside a long row of overgrown bushes. I pulled Haleika's cloak closer and I blended in instantly. Despite my sore legs and exhausted muscles, I began to jog then shifted into a full-out run until I was racing down the street. I caught sight of the vendor again. He separated from his party and turned a corner I recognized, down a street full of jewelry shops. Ramia sold in this quarter.

I turned after him, running faster to keep up, my sandals sliding against the waterway and my legs appearing and vanishing, going in and out of focus.

He slowed as if sensing me and turned around, glancing anxiously behind his shoulder.

I held my breath, tugging the cloak over my face, stilling my body, allowing the fabric's magic to fully camouflage me. The vendor smoothed the ends of his mustache and turned, continuing at a quicker pace.

I quickened my pace, too, veering off the waterway to a small park running alongside the street. I slipped behind a line of trees, lifting the skirt of my dress so I could avoid the fallen branches of moon trees littering the way.

The bells clanged, shouting the hour, and blue lights lit up the red-and-orange-streaked sky as the sun began to set. The distraction had been just enough for me to lose sight of the vendor. There were rows of shops along the street opposite the park—all nearly identical in appearance.

I cursed, rubbing my hands up and down my arms. What was I hoping to accomplish anyway? Tristan would come looking for me in another moment, and now I was out in the park running like an idiot, alone and vulnerable. I walked a few steps farther, trying to catch sight of the vendor, but the entire mission had been futile and a waste of my nearly depleted energy. With a sigh, I turned around, stepping on a tree branch. The stick snapped in half, and I froze just as I heard another snap right in front of me.

A silver blade pointed right at my throat; tiny flames danced on its edge.

"Don't scream."

CHAPTER TWENTY-FIVE

MY STOMACH DROPPED as I looked up and found myself face to face with the vendor. His hand shook, and flames ignited on the steel pointed toward me. The blade had been forged in starfire. It was expensive. And deadly.

I stopped breathing, unsure I could muster a scream even if I wanted to. Then his eyes widened, focusing on my face. "Y-Your grace," he said. He lowered his blade immediately, and his arm hung limply at his side. He bowed low. "I did not see you. I have never been invited to the fortress so I didn't know your face before. I'm sorry...I didn't know it was you when we met. Or that you followed me just now."

I eyed his blade. His fingers were uncomfortably strained around the hilt, not allowing for maximum movement or control. I didn't know much about weapons and fighting—not yet—but I'd seen soturi demonstrate proper weapon holding, and this wasn't it. The blade was pointed down. It was sharp, but wielded by this vendor, it wasn't necessarily a great threat. I straightened, straining to see him as the sky darkened. "You seem to have a great deal of trouble recognizing me," I said. "You admit you saw me back on the waterway. And you knew just now who I was. If you didn't think I was following you, who were you expecting?"

He shook his head, his cheeks flushed. "No one," he said.

My hand went to my belt, fingers sliding over the hilt of my dagger. I had no idea how to use it—but the man before me seemed just as clueless. And yet, I didn't think this man was truly dangerous to me. At least, not in that moment.

"Then you won't mind sheathing your blade?" I asked. "It's a crime to threaten an Heir to the Arkasva whether you recognize them or not."

He nodded quickly, clumsily replacing the dagger in its hilt. "Apologies, your g-grace. Please. I swear to Auriel, I didn't see you, didn't know it was you. I can bow to you and make amends."

"I'm not interested in you bending a knee, nor am I so easily offended."

He shook his head, nodding so vigorously his mustache bounced. "W-What can I do for you?"

"That pin you had the day we met," I said. I was done with small talk and running out of time. I needed answers, and I needed to return to Tristan before he discovered I wasn't shopping.

The vendor frowned. "N-No. Those were a mistake like I told you. A bad batch. Very costly to throw away. But I did. I threw out every last one in your honor."

"Batch?" I asked, heart hammering. "So there was more than one pin with black wings?"

He stepped back, still shaking his head. "I'm not a believer," he said. "I just…I just wanted money to…to send to my family. Someone asked, I delivered. It meant nothing to me, just money."

I stepped closer. "Who asked?" I slid my hand across my belt, moving from the dagger to my coin purse. I had gold in there. Maybe I could also engage in some bribery tonight.

But the vendor reached for his belt and lifted his dagger again, his hand shaking.

I jumped back. Even if he was an unskilled fighter, the blade was sharp. Its starfire core made it deadly. "You're crossing a line, vendor. You need money? I have gold." I produced the coin, holding my hand out to him, palm up. "I can pay. Pay more than whoever approached you."

His eyes lit up as they focused on the coin in my hand. His lips quivered.

"Tell me," I said, heart pounding. "What do you know about the Emartis? Who requested the pins?"

The vendor turned bright red, and a panicked look crossed his face as he stared at something behind me.

"I'll pay double what they offered," I said, praying I had enough. I didn't know how big or well-funded the Emartis were.

He seemed to consider. That was good. That meant he could be bought. At the very least, he was an opportunist.

"Do we have a deal?" I asked.

"I'll…I'll need that first payment."

"You can have all the payments you want if you tell me what you know."

He started to nod. A bird screeched behind me, the sound seeming to snap him to attention. He stared past me again, and something changed in his expression. There was a note of finality in his eyes. "I-I can't. I'm sorry," he said. "*Shekar Arkasva!*" He lunged for me, blade tip aimed at my belly.

"Stop!"

Everything seemed to happen in slow-motion. The silver blade rushing toward me. My feet stumbling back. The wild, scared, and violent look in the vendor's eyes. The broad starfire sword gleaming with flames as it pierced through his belly.

His mouth fell open, blood dripping down his chin. A sandaled foot kicked at his groin, and the vendor slid backwards off the blade that had impaled him. His body hit the ground, his arms landing at an awkward angle. His eyes were wide open as he lay beneath the trees, blood seeping into the black earth beneath him. Beside him, his starfire blade lay, useless.

I whirled and found myself face to face with Markan.

"What did you do?" I snarled. I'd had him! I'd had him in the palm of my hand! I'd had a source, someone close to the Emartis. He'd only changed his mind when he'd thought he'd been caught—when Markan had appeared. He'd been terrified and alone. He'd clearly needed money for something or was being blackmailed. I ran my fingers through my hair, breathing in and out through my mouth. Fuck!

"I saved your life, your grace," Markan said with a grunt. He swiped the dead man's dagger and pocketed it in his belt. "Nice piece." Then with a shrug, he approached a nearby stream, dipping his blade in the waters. The fires went out, and the sky darkened. Red blood swirled through the water and dissolved. "What is this? Now you're a soturion, you're actively attempting to put your life in danger? Like I don't have enough to do." He sneered. "Get back to your party. Your other escort will take you."

I hugged Haleika's cloak tighter around myself. My body was going cold. Markan had just killed a man. Right in front of me. The water from the stream made light tinkling sounds. The sky was darkening rapidly, the clouds turning indigo, and the scent of pine was everywhere, mixing for me with a light and floral scent coming from Haleika's cloak. And at my feet, a man lay dead.

I exhaled sharply. "What other escort?" I asked.

Markan dried his blade with his cloak and jerked his chin behind me. I turned and found one of Tristan's mages. He was a tall, spindly man, the one who usually went after me when I wandered off or walked me to my door after I said goodbye to Tristan. I'd never really paid attention to him before. He'd been the one to clear the path for me when I went after Rhyan in the streets.

Markan rolled his eyes. "Did you really think your father was letting you sneak off on your own? Or that you were that clever? And you!" Markan turned his wrath on the escort. "Thought you were on top of it. I'd have killed him sooner."

The mage pursed his lips. "I've been by her side the entire time. I do not have the same license to kill for her grace as you do."

"So that wasn't just mage weakness?"

"I perceived no true threat in his aura until you showed yourself."

Markan's eyes narrowed. "You're saying it's my fault he pulled a knife on her grace? Can you escort the lady back to her little dinner party without incident while I clean this mess, or do you not have license for that either?"

"We're going," I said. I wanted to get away from the body. Away from this place. Away from Markan. I strode forward past the mage and cursed.

"I'm sorry, your grace," the mage spoke quietly. "I should have acted sooner. This was not something for you to see."

I closed my eyes. I'd seen worse. I'd watched Jules being ripped away before my eyes while everyone sat still and did nothing. Though this…this was close. Tears burned my eyes, and I blinked them back, attempting to compose myself. I had my own clean up to do now.

"Tristan ordered you to follow me?" I asked. "Or did the order come from my own guard?"

"An agreement was made on both ends. My lord is fully aware of my watching over you. He encourages it."

My hands balled into fists at my sides. I felt so stupid. And betrayed. It was one thing when I saw his escorts…but to know they were following me in secret? I knew to look for soturi—I hadn't thought to keep my eye out for Ka Grey mages.

I stared back at him, knowing he'd walked by my side or behind me countless times. In another few seconds, I had his name. "Bellamy," I said. "Your name is Bellamy?"

"Yes, your grace." He lowered his chin.

I placed the gold coin, still in my hand, into his. I'd held onto it so tightly there was a light indentation in my palm.

"For your silence," I said. "Please." I outranked Tristan. I could overrule his orders, even to his own mages and escorts. But they still worked for Ka Grey and were expected to report anything they saw.

If Tristan knew about this, he'd overreact. He'd never let me out of his sight again. I could not allow him to get any closer to me than he was, especially not when I now had limited time with my sisters.

"Your grace," Bellamy said simply. With a small nod, he pocketed the coin and held up his stave, releasing a white dome of light around me. "Are you all right?"

My heart pounded, and I hugged my arms around my chest. I'd accomplished nothing tonight. I'd learned nothing, and that had cost a man his life.

"I...just want to get back to Lord Tristan." And order a very large glass of wine.

"Right away, your grace."

A few moments later, we were back at the restaurant, and I slid into the empty seat by Tristan's side. Flatbreads and bowls of various dips and salads peppered the table.

I unpinned Haleika's cloak, carefully scanning it for any rips or stains.

Tristan gave me a careful look before handing me a menu. "Everything all right?" he asked. The question wasn't for me; it was for Bellamy.

"Just fine," I said. I held my breath as Bellamy resumed his position across the room, watching Tristan. He gave his lord a small nod that Tristan returned, looking satisfied. I exhaled, sure Bellamy would keep his word if he wanted to keep the extra coin flowing.

I tried to relax, to sink back into my chair, but I couldn't. The whole thing grew more terrifying the more I thought about it. The vendor had had no malicious intent toward me. When he'd said he wasn't a believer, he'd sounded sincere. He was simply an opportunist.

The look in his eyes…. I blinked the image away. I couldn't think about it. Aemon had been right. I'd had threats against me my entire life, and I always would, as long as I retained my birthright. But the vendor…he'd been scared. And I had sought him out, it hadn't been the other way around. I squeezed my eyes shut. What in Lumeria had I been thinking? That following him would lead me into the heart of the Emartis's lair, and I'd just tell them to stop and then go back to Lady Romula and announce it was done so I could marry her grandson? And then what?

Gods.

I felt sick. I wanted to go home and crawl into bed, but if I didn't eat, Tristan would know something was wrong. I did what I had to. I straightened my back. I fixed my face, donning the mask of Lady Lyriana, Heir to the Arkasva. Tristan didn't question it—we were out in public. Even he wore some version of his public mask. I slid down the golden circlet holding the menu together and unrolled the parchment, scanning the available options. We ordered sample plates of every dish and wine, and I pretended to care about what my friends said, and not fume over the fact that Tristan's own escort had been secretly on my detail. And he'd known.

I barely spoke the rest of the night and picked at my food. It was tasteless to me anyway. I couldn't stop seeing the vendor's lifeless eyes, and I couldn't stop searching outside for signs of the Emartis, signs of the black-winged seraphim, or shouts of *Shekar Arkasva*. All I did see was Markan circling the perimeter, his hateful eyes on me through the restaurant's window, and several rough-looking, silver-armored soturi from Ka Kormac taking position as the hour changed again.

Returning to my apartment, I left Tristan at the door with a quick kiss, retreated upstairs to my room, and fell immediately into a wine-induced, dreamless sleep.

The following day passed by in a blur: throwing up after the run, suffering through endless hours of lecture, and Rhyan's nearly impossible training routine.

"Are you ready for clinic tonight?" he asked when the session ended.

I looked up in surprise from the pile of exhaustion my body had made on the floor. I'd curled my knees against my chest, and my cheek had been pressed helplessly against the floor as I caught my breath. Gently, I pushed myself up into a seat, a questioning look on my face. Aside from ordering me around, he'd barely said two words to me all day. He hadn't even called me "partner." In fact, that had been his longest sentence in hours.

"Sure," I said. What was there to be ready for anyway? I just had to show up, watch the fight, and pretend I understood what I was looking at. "I'll be fine."

"Really?" he asked, his good eyebrow lifted.

"Don't worry," I said, shifting on the mat. I'd left a sweat stain in the shape of my body. "I promise to be the worst one out there as usual."

"That's not what I...," he began to say, but I was already scrambling to my feet and gathering my things.

"See you tomorrow," I said and pushed myself out the door.

I thought I could feel him staring after me, but I didn't care. He couldn't push me around all day, not speak to me, and make me feel awful about myself, then somehow expect me to wait around and chat, not when his behavior ran so hot and cold. I was already tired of predicting which version of Rhyan I was about to interact with.

Hours later, as the sky blackened into night, torches lit the open circle of the arena walls. It was a warm night, too early in the year for a chill, but I felt an icy numbness creep through me as I stepped through the doors.

There were three silver circles across the field, hovering off the ground. Bindings. Circles meant to trap each of the fighters in the clinic and limit their space. The silver color indicated they weren't the same magic as the bindings used on Lumerians for arrests, the kind that could cut someone off from their source of power, the kind that had been used in Jules's arrest, the kind Tristan had used on me.

Even so, my skin felt irritated at just the thought. My fingers opened and closed in anger at my sides. I couldn't bear being trapped inside one of those things or feeling it burn against my skin. Not again.

I joined a line of soturi and signed in, noting the place from the previous night where Haleika had forged my signature. The line continued up into the seats surrounding the arena, though I spotted a few soturi heading back out to the silver circles.

"Lyriana, wait!" shouted a voice with a northern lilt.

I froze and turned slowly to face Rhyan.

I shook my head. Apprentices weren't scheduled to watch our clinic for weeks. "What are you doing here?"

"I...I was worried about you," he admitted. "So I came."

"Worried I'd make you look bad?" I asked.

"Lyr," he said gravely. "No."

Something in the seriousness of his words and expression cut through me, and dread began roiling inside me. There was some fact I'd forgotten to check.

His nostrils flared, and he pulled me aside, down an abandoned hallway, into a darkened corner. I was backed against its stone wall, away from everyone else's prying eyes and ears. His arm shot forward, his hand pressed against the stone beside me, essentially trapping me.

"You skipped the first night, didn't you?" he practically snarled as he spoke, his breath hot against my ear.

"Yes."

"You lied to me!"

"Yes," I admitted. "But so what? It's one night. I'm here now! I—"

"I knew it!" He threw his head back and groaned. "Godsdamn it, Lyr! If you'd gone Monday, you'd have seen the schedule for the week."

"Why would I need to see the...." My heart raced. The truth of what I'd been realizing for the last minute was starting to come into the light. Shit.

"Aemon wanted to put you in the middle of a five the first week."

A five? Me? No. I couldn't breathe. I was—I was going to be in the center of a five? Tonight? Trapped inside one of those Godsdamned silver bindings while five soturi attacked me?

"No! Why? I'm not ready. I can't.... He knows I'm not strong enough yet!" I shook my head. "Why would he do this to me?"

"He's trying to help you. It's week one. The novices you're up against have the least training right now that they'll ever have. They're also not as strong as they're going to be. It's your best chance to come out of the fight unscathed."

"Because even if I train, I still don't stand a chance?"

Rhyan shook his head, his eyes narrowed. "No one has said that. Aemon had to throw a bone to the Imperator. He's noting every clinic you're not active in. And you not showing up Monday...it should be no big deal, but it won't be to him. Aemon's doing this to protect you."

"Fuck." The ceiling filled with the sound of stomping feet as the rest of the soturi raced to find seats for the clinic.

"When you said you were fine today, I knew.... I should have checked and made sure you were ready. Myself to Moriel. I knew it. Knew you still didn't respect the chain of command. And I was busy trying to—fuck. It doesn't matter now." He shook his head, his eyes blazing, the muscles in his arm straining. "Don't lie to me again."

"I had my reasons."

He leaned forward, his forehead inches from mine, his musky scent enveloping me in the heat. "You think the Emperor gives a damn about your reasons? The Imperator?"

I held my stance, refusing to back down, refusing to let Rhyan throw me any more off balance than I was. "I'm doing what I have to do!"

He shook his head in disgust. "You told me you were going to take this seriously."

"I am!"

"Showing up when you're supposed to is taking this seriously! Not fucking lying to me on day one."

"Sorry," I snapped. "Did I hurt your pride?"

"You think that's what I care about?"

My gaze fell on the three silver circles, and fear gripped me. "Rhyan, stop, I'm sorry," I said sincerely, and reached forward, gripping his tunic. His hand closed over mine. There was something instinctual in the movement, natural. Like when we'd held hands in the prison long after my panic attack had subsided.

"It's all right," he said. And then as if he'd just noticed the contact between us, he let go of me. My hand dropped to my side.

"I didn't mean to lie.... I just thought I had to.... It's done. I'm here now. Tell me. What do I do?"

His jaw flexed as he glanced between the arena and me, but his gaze softened, the fury and fire in his emerald eyes fading as they locked with mine. "I know. And, Lyr, I'm... I'm on your side." He exhaled sharply, stepping back.

"They'll be clumsy," he said. "Not sure yet how to work as a team. Trying to show off and one-up each other. Not yet focused on proving themselves in a fight. You won't be in there long. You don't need to fight them. Just survive. Avoid, duck, and retreat as much as possible. No one has combat moves yet—not on day three."

I bit my lip, trying not to cry.

"We'll work on this. How to get through a five. You have strength, Lyr. It's just different than theirs right now, but you can still use it against them. Just stay focused. It will be quick." Rhyan gave me a slow nod, then took another step back, arms folded neatly across his chest, allowing me the space to leave our corner. Two of the circles were already full of soturi, preparing to fight.

The third, the one in the very center, had five soutri I didn't recognize—the five who would be fighting me. Four were female. One was male. Ka Kormac. Shit.

The silver rings hummed with magic, buzzing and sparking with glittering lights.

I wrapped my arms around myself. "Rhyan, how…how hot are the circles?"

"The bindings?" Rhyan's green eyes raced back and forth as he shook his head. "Not hot. Cold. Ice cold."

I swallowed and stepped forward, closing my eyes. I was back in the temple. Tristan looked pained as he held up his stave, and the fiery ropes came out. I shrugged my shoulders, feeling them against me, the memory still too strong.

"It won't be like before when…." Rhyan said. "They aren't wrapped around your body."

I stared up at him. "How did you know?"

He reached for me, his hand brushing against my arm, before he pulled back, flexing his hand at his side. "Just focus on what you need to do now. All right? Can you do that? Stay in the present?"

I nodded, biting my lip.

"I'll be here after," he said. "Don't worry. Aemon wouldn't let this go too far. No one is supposed to...." He closed his eyes slowly. "In Bamaria, the rules of conduct are stricter to —to minimize injury. The goal isn't to interrupt training or purge soturi who are...." He shook his head. "You're going to be all right. I'll find you as soon as it's over."

Blue lights flashed across the night sky as the bells rang, louder than they ever had before. The sound echoed and vibrated inside of me, banging against my every bone and muscle. Beads of sweat rolled down the nape of my neck, the leather laces of my sandals cut into my calves, and a roaring from the crowd pounded against the brewing breeze as I stepped onto the field.

CHAPTER TWENTY-SIX

MY FEET TOUCHED the grass, stepping, stepping, stepping until I reached the silver circle. My hands opened and closed into sweaty fists. The bells came to a halt, and the silence seemed to ring louder through me than any other sound in the arena. The binding circle glowed and sparkled, the silver almost appearing like starfire as small flames licked the conjured magic. But those were merely the reflections of the torches lighting the stadium from above.

Beyond the silver binding, five sets of eyes watched me with disdain. I could feel their impatience with me and sense their itchiness to start the fight, to release the violence and energy their magic was building up inside of them. Still holding my breath, I stepped forward, feeling the ice of the binding's magic sweep out to kiss my skin. Then I was through, the freezing magic nipping at the backs of my arms and legs.

It didn't hurt. The magic wanted to let you in, but it would not let you out—not until the spell was recanted. While Rhyan had been right and the magic wasn't tied around my body, it still jolted me into feeling just as trapped, just as helpless as I had been the night Tristan had used it on me.

Blackness bled into the indigo sky. The stars were dulled out by the fires circling above. I positioned myself in the center of the circle, my attention now on the cheers erupting all around me. Every fighter was in place. I took in a deep breath, eyeing my opponents. The one male from Ka Kormac was already sneering at me. His hair was dark, unlike Viktor's, but he had the Bastardmaker's beady eyes.

The other four female soturi, I watched closely. Tani was there, already gleaming with sweat. She sneered as I got closer, baring her teeth. Though she was from Ka Elys in Elyria, loyal to the Ka who'd replaced Ka Azria, she was always by Pavi's side and had been sneering at me since Pavi's lashing. Two more of the soturi I faced were also Ka Elys with ashvan horses adorning their armor. They shared a look with Tani that left my throat dry. They blamed me for what had happened to Pavi and were now in an arena with free reign to make me pay.

The last girl I didn't recognize. She had the whitish blonde hair that was common in Damara, and her armor showed a cresting wave. Ka Daquataine, like Haleika's apprentice Leander. Maybe not my enemy, but Damara always produced soturi with natural strength.

Turion Dairen stepped onto the field, his cloak flying behind his shoulders as he stepped onto the center dais. Fuck. He was in charge tonight. I wasn't going to be given any slack. My opponents knew this, too. Their eyes gleamed watching him.

I tensed and tried to listen to Dairen's instructions, but his voice was drowned out by the ringing in my ears. Each circle had fifteen minutes to fight. All blows were to be below the neck. When it was our turn, we were to go until he called time at exactly fifteen minutes. There'd be a discussion after, a critique of each warrior—what went well and what went wrong—and then the next circle would fight.

My stomach twisted. We were in the center circle, which I guessed meant we'd go second. I started to exhale, knowing I'd have at least fifteen more minutes without pain.

But without warning, Dairen called on the center circle to begin.

A bell rang, and immediately I was surrounded, everyone shifting into fighting stances, rocking their weight back and forth on their heels.

I held up my arms, forcing my hands into fists. I remembered to put my thumb over my fingers, but that was all I had. I swallowed hard, my stomach twisting, sweat rolling down the back of my neck and beading across my forehead.

Rhyan had said I had strength, my own kind of strength, but I didn't know what that meant. More importantly, I didn't know how to use it.

There was a shout from the stands: "Batavia!" It was condescending. A call to attack, not in support.

I looked up to see who'd yelled and immediately regretted my decision. The call was answered by several wolves howling.

"Silence," yelled Dairen, but the very little amount of concentration I had was already gone.

Someone hit me from behind. I collapsed on the ground, my body completely giving out. I barely had a chance to get myself up before I was surrounded with no space to breathe. I couldn't even distinguish who stood where, they were so close, their sandals all right in front of my face in a sea of marching leather.

I started to stand, but another blow to my back forced me down, followed by a hand on my head, pressing my cheek into the dirt.

A horn blew. "Below the neck only!" Dairen shouted.

I swiped at the set of legs in front of me, scratching with my nails across their skin.

Whoever it was cursed and jumped back. It was just enough of a window for me to roll back onto my feet and duck beneath the arm of the soturion from Ka Kormac. I raced to the edge of the circle, but the bastard was faster and on top of me in seconds. I sped up, heart pounding, and stopped just a few feet from the binding, ducking low. He ran ahead, his entire body slamming into silver light.

The magic hummed as it connected to him, its sparks erupting into fireworks.

"Fuck!" he screamed. "Fuck!" He turned around, blowing on his hands. The magic of the binding was cold—Rhyan had said *ice cold*, but he'd left out the part about it being so cold it burned if you ran into it.

Fury lit in the soturion's black, beady eyes. He rushed at me.

Spinning on my heels, I ran straight for Tani, Viktor's soturion breathing down the back of my neck. I was already out of breath, and a cramp was forming in my side. I couldn't keep this up. I wasn't going to last long in here, not when facing five. Tani held her arms out for me.

I dodged and ran. Viktor's soturion slammed into the binding again, roaring in pain and frustration. Tani leapt away from the silver, worry in her expression. Maybe that was the strength Rhyan thought I had. Observation.

I could always spot soturi in the city and countryside in their camouflage. I always sensed where people were, when they were watching. The warrior from Ka Kormac had no finesse or skills, just brute strength. He was too focused on getting a hit on me that he'd already run into the binding twice. Now Tani appeared afraid of it. I could use that to my advantage—I could stay close to the inner wall and let the ice kiss my skin, knowing the others were now determined to avoid it.

So I ran, my body all but hugging the humming silver ring. This worked for about a minute, but despite her horrible taste in nobility, Tani figured out my ploy. She backed up, waiting for me to reach her. I could either crash into her, face the wrath and pain of the binding, or move back into the center.

I had no choice. I turned, just barely dodging past the Kormac soturion, and doubling back.

I ran right into the blonde girl from Damara. I spun around, but I was losing energy and starting to get dizzy. She grabbed me from behind, her arms impossibly strong, locking around my belly.

"Let go!" I yelled.

"Make me," she whispered in my ear. "Asherah."

Before I could react, she grabbed my cloak and pulled, covering my head with its excess length. I couldn't see. I could barely breathe.

My body was too hot and all at once too cold. Panic set in.

My breath came short; I was shoved to the ground. I stopped trying to fight back in order to protect myself.

Then the kicks came.

The first kick to my hip knocked the breath out of me. I wheezed, my limbs splaying across the floor. Then more came, each followed by an insult.

"Asherah." Kick.

"False heir." Kick.

"Fake Lumerian!" Kick.

"You're nothing here."

I clutched my belly, the pain unbearable. I was coughing and retching, and fresh tears welled in my eyes with every hit. I couldn't breathe. I couldn't think. I grasped at the armor over my chest, sucking any air I could get, wheezing for them to stop, but my words barely came as a whisper, and the cloth was tightening around my face. My attackers were closing in. The walls were closing in, the Katurium was going to fall, Jules was being taken, the panic was taking over me....

I was hauled to my feet, my ears roaring. My cloak fell back over my shoulders. The arena blearily came into focus.

Two of my opponents grabbed my arms, holding them out wide, pushing my armor up, and leaving my belly exposed.

The Ka Kormac soturion stepped in front of me, rubbing his hands together, a hungry look in his eyes I'd seen before from the other wolves. He was pure predator, and I was the prey.

Bells were ringing, and my vision blurred. He formed a fist, blowing on his knuckles, and swung his arm back.

Gods! He wasn't the best strategist, but one punch from his fist was going to destroy me.

The ringing grew louder, and there were shouts pounding through my ears. I struggled against the soturi holding me, writhing desperately to be free. I had to escape, to get away. I tried to yell. There was a roaring sound now.

The soturion laughed, taking off at a run. Tani watched, vengeance dancing in her dark eyes.

"STOP!"

The words I'd been trying to scream, to shout at the top of my lungs, came at last. But not from me.

Rhyan.

"It's time!"

The soturion's fist headed for my stomach. My vision blurred, but the hit never came. Rhyan shot forward, leaping into the circle. He intercepted the punch and pulled the soturion away.

"It's time!" he yelled again. "Turion! Call it off! Now!"

"Get out of there, Hart," Dairen yelled. "Apprentices don't go into novice circles."

Rhyan's arms were around the soturion from Ka Kormac. He lifted him up, turned away from me, and tossed him forward. His aura exploded, a storm of ice and freezing cold.

Dairen's hair blew back from the force, but he only sneered in response, stalking toward us. "Can't you hear the bells, or do you all need your ears checked?"

"You didn't call time," said the soturion from Damara, looking uncomfortably between Dairen and Rhyan.

The two soturi holding my arms immediately dropped them. Tani was glaring, her arms across her chest. She pouted and kicked at the grass beneath her feet.

I stumbled backward, my legs folding in half. I started to sink to the ground, my injuries beginning to catch up to me. Gods. Everything hurt. Everything.

Rhyan moved forward, heading for me. Then he stopped suddenly, turning his attention back to Dairen. All at once, he seemed to release the energy from his aura. The cold vanished, the wind stopped. His power was so suddenly turned off, I'd wondered if I'd imagined the whole thing.

"You going to let me out of here?" Rhyan asked. He sounded bored, and impatient. But there was a distinct edge to his voice—one that reminded me he was raised to be high lord.

"Do I look like a mage?" Dairen asked. "The hell is wrong with you, Hart? Jumping in after her? Did you think we did things here like your father? Did you think we were going to let her die?"

Rhyan's jaw clenched, and I realized that was exactly what he'd thought. Or that I was so weak and powerless I was doomed anyway. Neither possibility felt comforting in that moment.

"No," Dairen said. "You want to jump in here like an idiot, you can wait in here like one until we recant the spell. Have a Godsdammed seat if you want. Or stand. But you'll wait in there like a novice if you want to act like one."

The Ka Kormac soturion snickered at this while the others glanced back at me, sneers and looks of derision all over their faces.

My knees buckled. I wanted to sit down desperately. And cry.

When Dairen turned away, returning to the center of the field to address the other novices, Rhyan made his way to my side.

All eyes were on me. And him.

"You all right?" he whispered.

I stumbled forward, dizzy and in pain. I clutched my stomach. Gods. No. I couldn't be sick. Not again, not with such a focused audience. Not after my first true test as a soturion.

"Lyr," he said, a hand shooting out to my back to steady me. His palm pressed flat against my tunic, grabbing the material and pulling back. The subtle pull pushed my shoulders back and forced me to stand straighter. As I stumbled back, I pushed against his hand. It remained steady, literally holding me up. How was he that strong?

"Deep breaths, partner," he said quietly. "I'll get you out of here as soon as I can."

My eyes closed. The pain throbbing through every single muscle was the only thing keeping me from falling over.

I couldn't hear a word of the discussion or critique. I only knew I'd been humiliated. I looked weak and pathetic, and every second I stood there, I felt worse.

Finally, a mage ambled up to the circle, her stave pointed at the silvery ropes binding us inside. She swept the stave in a circle and uttered an incantation beneath her breath. Blue light sparked forward, swallowing the rope whole.

I felt the air warm instantly around me, and something that had been pinching my chest relaxed.

The other five soturi began to exit the field, all heading for the bathing room.

The only bright spot in the night—we weren't forced to wait around until the end after the fight. We had the option to leave.

Rhyan walked silently beside me, leading me down winding halls until we came to a familiar door—our training room.

Only after Rhyan closed the door to our room did I sink onto the mat, tears already spilling. He was before me in an instant. His hand was on my chin tilting my head up. His thumb ran against my jaw. His nostrils flared, and then he was gone, rummaging through his bag and pulling out bandages and ointment.

"I'll get you cleaned up," he said.

But my anger and fear and frustration had bubbled to the surface, bypassing my pain.

"What the fuck!" I yelled. "Even putting me in at the start, I still had the shit kicked out of me. And they weren't just…." I pushed the tears back and swallowed bile. "This wasn't just some exercise, or clinic. It was personal. They were after me. And it's not going to stop just because Dairen calls time or the night ends. They're going to come for me any chance they get."

Rhyan set down his first aid kit and moved to crouch in front of me. "They might."

"Everyone out there has one goal in mind—making sure I fail. Gods. It's only day three. How am I going to make it through seven months?"

"You'll make it. You're not going to fail." He squeezed my arm. "You're going to get stronger."

"How?" I asked. "I have no magic, no real strength that can fight against the muscles they carry." I buried my face in my hands. "I can't do this. I'm not strong enough. I'm not cut out for this. And everyone out there fucking knew it. They're going to delight in my failure."

"So what? Fuck them and their opinions." He squeezed my arm again. "You do have what it takes. It's not up to them how you face this. It's up to you if you fail or not. Forget them. Their opinion means nothing. All that matters now is what you think. Nothing else."

"Right, my opinion and the Imperator's." I laughed, the sound harsh and bordering on hysterical as I looked up at him, his face inches from mine. More tears fell. "You've never lost to the Imperator before."

His nostrils flared. "I've lost plenty. And I did so as the son of an Imperator. Trust me, the closer you are to one, the bigger the losses. That doesn't mean I'm giving up."

"It's not the same. You have the chance to succeed here. You have power. You're one of the best soturi in the world."

"No, I'm—"

"Please. You've killed an akadim. You took on a bound five without a scratch." I pulled my arm from his touch.

"I didn't start with that. I worked my way up to it. Lyr, just because your power didn't show up the way you expected at the Revelation Ceremony doesn't mean you don't have any. Listen to me, you do! You're more powerful than you realize."

"Right, I'm powerful," I said sarcastically. "So powerful I can just stand against the ruling dynasty of the Lumerian Empire. So powerful I can tell the Emperor to give me another chance when he sees how weak I am. Don't deny it. I saw how frustrated you were when the Imperator observed. And tonight, Rhyan, you lost it with me, because you think I'll fail, too."

"I don't."

"Gryphon-shit!" I jumped to my feet, and all at once, I lost my balance. I stumbled forward, and my vision blurred. Rhyan was right there, his arms wrapping around me.

"Hey." He pulled me against him, settling us on the floor. "You need to sit down."

I pushed him away, untangling myself from his arms. "You think I don't know. You think I don't see the look in your eyes or understand the weight I carry for both of us. If I fail, you fail."

"That is not true. And I told you, don't worry about me."

"Really? Because all I hear is you telling me I'm the worst one. How I need to accept how horrible I'm going to be at all of this. Like accepting it makes it any easier."

"That's not what I meant, Lyr," he said gently. Once more, his hand reached forward, fingers flexing before resting on his knee. "I'm not trying to insult you. I know I sound harsh, but I'm trying to help. You have to trust me."

I shook my head, wiping away tears. "Right. Help."

"Please," he groaned. "Can we not argue about semantics now?"

I shifted, and my tunic rubbed against my back. I hissed, crying out in pain, suddenly so dizzy. Every part of my body was aching.

Rhyan stiffened. "You're hurt. Let's take care of that first, and then we'll—"

"I'm fine," I said, automatically shifting my back away.

"You're not fine." He moved closer to me, his eyes roaming all over my body. Without warning, he leapt to his feet and circled around me.

I jumped, too, nearly falling over and turning to hide my back every time he moved. My sides were aching. My stomach was nauseated, and his circling was making me dizzy. "Stop it. Stop! I can take care of it myself."

One eyebrow lifted in confusion. "Lyr, you just got the shit kicked out of you. Sit down and let me help."

I was in pain. So much pain. But I couldn't let him help me. I couldn't let him see. What if he found my scars? My healing cuts? My faded bruises? What if he started to put two and two together?

As if I wasn't suffering enough, fire raged through my wrist. The pain boiling inside my veins was a warning, a reminder of my oath and the consequences I faced if I ever, ever allowed the secrets of my family to be revealed.

Remember, remember, the scars seemed to speak in my mind in a strange, echoing voice.

I squeezed my wrist trying to numb the pain. I was about to be sick.

I give you my oath in blood. We four keep this secret. We four die by this secret.

"Just sit down. I'll be gentle. Let me just see if you need any bandages anywhere. Then we'll get you some ice."

"Great," I said. "And then you can run me ragged in training tomorrow and reopen every wound, deepen every bruise. I don't think so."

"There's more to being a soturion than just magic strength. I want to show you. But...it also means taking care of your body. Especially when it's injured."

Everything inside of me was shaking, burning, raging with the secrets I carried, the secrets I was risking everything to protect. "Right," I said. "But myself to Moriel, I sure as hell don't need you to help me." The fire felt like it was bursting through my arm, consuming me. If I didn't get away from him soon, I was worried I might pass out from the pain. Fuck.

"Lyr, come on."

So I said it—the one thing I knew would hurt him, would make him leave me alone.

"I don't need your fucking help. Forsworn."

His jaw clenched and nostrils flared. "Fine. Your grace." He offered a mock bow and stormed out of the room, slamming the door behind him.

I sank onto the ground. The fire in my wrist stopped, the pain receding all at once. I was left with the guilt of what I'd said, how I'd treated Rhyan, and all the other injuries I'd suffered sprang to life.

A minute later, the door burst open. Rhyan dropped a bucket of ice on the floor. His eyes met mine, blazing with fury and something I couldn't name.

I thought for a second he'd changed his mind—that he had read past my bluff and anger and embarrassment—but he only slammed the door a second time and disappeared.

I spent the rest of the night putting myself back together and making it back to my apartment.

CHAPTER TWENTY-SEVEN

RHYAN WAS COLD to me the next day. Or, rather, colder than usual. He didn't invite me to stretch beside him before the morning run. And after my usual post-run vomiting, he didn't wait around to see how I was doing. He just strolled back inside to the baths.

During our training session, he was practically barking orders, demanding I stretch, run, and jump on command. Again and again, he worked me through the training protocol, not asking if I was all right, if I needed a break. And unless he needed to check me for posture or body alignment, he refused to look in my direction. Any semblance of the rapport and friendship we'd developed was gone. He looked and acted every bit the cold high lord accused of murder.

I'd had my reasons, and I'd been half mad with pain from the clinic and my blood oaths acting up. But I knew I'd broken something between us, and perhaps there was no way to repair it.

The moment the final bells of the day rang, he stepped off the mat, grabbed his bag, and walked out the door, not even bothering to close it behind him.

I dragged myself back to my apartment where I collapsed on my bed. I couldn't sleep, but I couldn't move either, so I lay there staring at the ceiling as the lights began to fade.

I came to when the bells shouted the new hour. If I got myself up now, I could bathe, eat dinner, and then read through the multiple chapters of homework I'd been assigned in lecture on weapons. But it had been days since I'd seen my sisters.

It had been two weeks since Meera's last vision, so we still had another two or three weeks before the next one was likely. But Morgana was most likely in need of my oils and brews. Plus, we needed to discuss the threat of the Emartis and what it meant that Markan had killed the vendor.

Aemon had gotten me alone in the hall earlier, giving me a long, hard look.

"You survived clinic," he said.

I could only nod. Rhyan's explanation for why I'd been thrown to the wolves so early in the year had made sense, and I knew Aemon would do all he could to protect me. But I was still furious. Aemon had known I'd skipped the first clinic, and he'd neglected to warn me when I was at his house.

It was his own form of punishment. He was sending me a message: I couldn't mess up again, not if I wanted to keep my bargain.

"No more veering off course during city outings," he said. "Your escorts already have their hands full."

"Who was he?" I asked. I could still see the vendor's lifeless face in my mind. "Who was he connected to?"

"A threat we stopped."

"He could have been more than that. If Markan hadn't—"

"Markan has done his job exactly as he is supposed to ever since he came into your father's service. Now do well to remember as a novice soturion, you're under mine. No more looking into this, no more rogue hunting trips or going after the very same rebels who want to kill you. Your job is to survive training. Not walk straight to your death. Go."

Aemon had dried up as an information source, but I still had Morgana.

"Gods, Lyr," Morgana said when I stumbled through the doors of Cresthaven. Euston and Rhodes eyed me carefully. "You look like shit."

"Hello to you, too," I said.

"Upstairs," she said, already dragging me along. "Meera's waiting."

I spent the evening filling them in on everything that had happened that week and everything I'd learned. Neither of them had any more information or insight though. We eventually made our way to the kitchens, devouring a cake we found and brewing extra moon oil. Morgana convinced me to take my own supply for pain relief after training. When I got back to my room, I mixed it with some sweetened wine and drank it all in one sip.

Tristan arrived for a late-night visit, but I was so far gone, he simply put me to bed. I woke up alone, my vision blurry and my body still aching. I had completed my first week of soturion training. I was alive. I supposed that was its own type of victory.

But it wasn't enough.

Before I knew it, the days began to blur together. I'd wake up at dawn, slog through a small breakfast and coffee, run for an hour, sit through five hours of lessons, eat lunch, and train with a sour Rhyan who, since our fight after the clinic, refused to say one single word to me beyond his teaching and training instructions. I'd leave the Katurium, watching an ever-darkening sky promise the shorter days of fall and winter, and somehow make my way back to my apartment to shower and find dinner. By the time I finished eating, it was time for combat clinic or to force myself to focus on texts and homework assignments.

Most nights ended with me writhing against Tristan late at night, hoping to keep him happy, though since the dinner at his grandmother's, there'd been no further talk of our engagement. And if I wasn't with Tristan, I was sleeping on flights back and forth from Cresthaven.

A month of training had officially passed, which meant over a month had passed since Meera's last vision. There was never any rhyme or reason to when she had them. Sometimes three months passed with nothing. Sometimes we only made it four weeks. In the two years she'd had the visions, I'd learned that four weeks was the only amount of time we could count on to be safe—after that, a vision could come any day.

Being so far from her and from Cresthaven left me uneasy, and Morgana was little help. Her own vorakh was worsening, and she was using more and more of the moon oil I brewed, drinking more wine, and smoking more moonleaves than I'd ever seen. I wanted to be able to get to her and Meera if needed, especially now that we were in Meera's danger zone.

At least the Emartis seemed to have gone silent—for the moment. Either the killing of the vendor had left them spooked and they had less support than they'd anticipated, or if Lady Romula was right, they were biding their time, growing more powerful, and setting more plans into action. The last option seemed the most likely and left my stomach turning every time I considered it.

Another week passed, and I stumbled into the Katurium. Rhyan had included a particularly brutal training session the Friday before full of squats and weights. Even though it was Monday, I was still completely sore and wrecked. I had managed to land a kick to his chest and finally mastered the punch he'd been teaching me since my stay in the Shadow Stronghold, but knowing that I'd be going up against soturi who'd mastered that punch weeks ago was quickly dimming my victory.

Plus, today marked six weeks since Meera's last vision. I was going to be on edge until it happened.

Haleika gave me an odd look at breakfast as I sleep-drank my coffee. "Lyr, the circles under your eyes have circles. Were you up really late last night?"

"Unfortunately," I said. I was drinking it black, and though it tasted like shit, I kept drinking. It was the only thing keeping me semi-conscious.

Galen laughed. "That's no way to talk about your extra-curricular activities with Tristan." He shimmied his shoulders.

"Galen, gross!" Haleika stuck out her tongue. "He's my cousin."

"You're right. How about we discuss your extra-curricular activities?" Galen's eyes sparkled with mischief.

"Only if you want to talk about yours!" Haleika smacked his arm.

I crossed my eyes in my half-awake haze. Were they actually together now? Or was this just more teasing? I'd started to lose track weeks before, and neither of them ever confirmed or denied anything.

Haleika turned toward me and lowered her voice. "Are you ready for tonight?"

I shrugged. "I can throw a punch now. But so can everyone else. Rhyan showed me some more avoiding tactics for the five and how to use the silver ring against my opponents."

On a rare day when he'd seemed more talkative, he'd admitted that I had been holding my own during the first part of my clinic, and that it had been brilliant to use the Ka Kormac soturion's strength against him. He had me practice evading, standing still, and letting him run at me until he gained full momentum and jumping away at the last second. It had been a nice moment between us. But then I'd missed my cue, and instead of leaping out of the way, Rhyan had leapt on me.

We'd crashed onto the mat, his body pressing mine down, both of us breathing heavily, our eyes meeting. Then he'd rolled off to the side and announced we were back to our regular training protocol. His ice shield back up.

"Lyr, you know it's not just regular clinic tonight. It's a habibellum. Everyone is fighting in the arena, and the apprentices are observing." Haleika's brown eyes flicked across the room to land on Leander.

I swallowed. "Habibellum? So we're all...all of us?" I gestured around the room.

Galen looked excited. "The Katurium mage sets up like a dozen silver rings, and some of us go in, and others are out. Then the mage will release and create new rings as they see fit. But if you're out of a ring, any soturion is game for a fight."

Shit. It was bad enough that I had to participate in the clinic and that Rhyan would be there, but this...fuck.

I took a very long sip of coffee, my gaze landing on Rhyan. He looked up like he'd immediately sensed me, then returned to the scroll he'd unraveled at his table and continued to read alone but with that air of power and purpose. Everything in his body language still said he was a future high lord. Though the wolves of Ka Kormac still watched him, they never did more than circle him—not since that first day.

We shuffled onto the field for the morning run. My sandals sank into the grass, and within seconds my feet were soaked. It had rained all night long, and fog blanketed the entire city of Urtavia, leaving no sign of the sun. Mist swirled through the arena, leaving the air damp. Another storm was coming and would probably be here by the end of the night.

Despite not speaking to each other, I'd been running beside Rhyan lately. As I was wiping the mud off my sandals and stepping onto the track, he signaled for me to join him. I threw my head back, almost dizzy with exhaustion, and managed to place my dagger into the ground beside his.

I was supposed to begin the stretching protocol he'd had me memorize the week before, but I simply stood there, yawning, hunched over with my hands on my knees.

"Lyr," Rhyan hissed. "Hey!" He snapped his fingers in my face. "Wake up!"

I rubbed at my eyes, realizing I'd fallen asleep standing up. Myself to Moriel. I should have downed another cup of coffee. My head was pounding. "I am awake."

"Not enough," he muttered. "Fuck. Lyr, open your eyes."

I did, but barely. Rainy, foggy days always made me want to curl up in bed for the day and either sleep or read a scroll. My current exhaustion levels weren't helping.

He shook his head. "Just keep your eyes open. No more sleeping on the track."

I glared but took position, only wobbling slightly before the bells rang. Aemon appeared in the field, sweeping his arms overhead. The bells sounded louder and louder, and in the sky, the ashvan horses raced over clouds on their patrol. Blue lights glowed faintly behind the fog in the sky.

It was time for the run to start, but Aemon didn't call it.

A strong gust of wind blew across the arena, powerful enough to push me back. I stumbled into Rhyan's arms. His hold on me tightened instantly. There was a rumbling sound in the sky—not quite thunder but similar. The wind picked up strength, and the fog seemed to grow thicker.

I expected to feel raindrops falling, but instead it looked like the fog was moving, almost like clouds. There was another crack of that thunderous sound, and a shadow appeared in the fog, pushing against it. The shadow blackened, the color deepening until little lights sparkled through.

A black seraphim, glittering, majestic, and so completely wrong emerged from the haze.

The Emartis.

"Get the mage!" Aemon screamed. His vadati stone glowed blue at his ear as he began barking orders too low for me to hear. Turion Dairen's eyes widened, and with his hand on the hilt of his sword and a nod to his arkturion, he raced through the nearest entrance.

There was a crack, and the seraphim disintegrated, falling into thousands of fiery pieces that vanished into the fog just like fireworks.

My heart pounded. Was this just a dramatic way to send a message? Or was it something worse? I caught sight of Naria holding hands with Viktor. They looked elated, staring up at the sky as if this was some wonderful performance.

A horn blew, and a seraphim filled the sky—a real one this time. My mouth went dry. This was all wrong. The seraphim was a baby with its wings still white, not the gold of maturation. It was too young to carry a load on its back, too young for a flight like this. It had no carriage on its back, just a single rider in black mage robes. It was flying lower and lower toward the arena.

The Katurium mage entered the arena, her blue robes swirling at her sandals as she ran across the muddy field with her gold and silver stave pointed at the sky.

"Bring him down!" Aemon yelled. "Bring him down, now!"

"Arkturion, the seraphim!" called the mage. There was anguish in her voice. Bamarians disagreed on many things, but seraphim, especially baby seraphim, were sacred.

"Do it!" Aemon roared, and light burst from the mage's stave, shooting into the mist and fog, heading right for the seraphim and her rider.

"*SHEKAR ARKASVA!*" screamed the rider. With his shout came a blast of power, a wind so forceful it pushed me off my feet.

I stumbled back, only then becoming aware of the fact that I was still being held by Rhyan.

"The Katurium's a no-fly zone," I said calmly. Too calmly. Numbness crept up my fingers. "And it's illegal in Bamaria to fly seraphim whose wings are still white. They're flying too low…," I continued, as if by narrating what was happening without feeling, it would somehow make it all right and keep me from losing control and giving into fear.

"All right, partner," Rhyan said. He sounded strained, worried.

I only looked up at him in response.

"Lyr," he said, squeezing me against him. "Lyriana." There was fear in his voice and urgency, a quiet desperation that I registered too slowly. He was trying to pull me away, to get me out of the arena.

Only then did I realize the panic around me. The wind conjured by the rider had knocked most of the soturi onto the ground or pressed them against the walls of the stadium. My hair was blowing in every direction. Somehow, Rhyan had kept us both standing. "We have to go!"

"Hart!" screamed Aemon. "Get her out of here. NOW!"

Shouts of "Protect the Heir!" sounded in the distance, a call for my escort to cover me.

"EMARTIS!" the rider yelled. "The false Arkasva will pay! And so will his heirs!"

The Katurium mage retaliated with blue sparks that cut through the mist and fog, lighting the arena like we were under the ocean. The rider flew into black smoke.

More black seraphim emerged from the fog, their wings taking shape, their beaks sprouting from their heads. Blue lights cut through the creatures, and they shattered into a thousand pieces. These weren't made of smoke or fading flames; when these seraphim shattered, shards of black glass sliced through the wind as they fell.

"Lyr!" Rhyan screamed. His hand found mine, and our fingers entwined as we ran for cover with the other soturi. Every door to the Katurium was bursting open. Novice and apprentice soturi ran inside as Bamaria's soturi entered the arena in formation, preparing for battle.

"Lyriana!" Turion Brenna shouted. "Hart, let's go." Brenna reached us, grabbed my other hand, and immediately turned, running at full speed until my feet were practically dragging. "Can you carry her?" Brenna asked, her grasp on my hand loosening.

Without replying, Rhyan pulled me against him, his hand sweeping beneath my knees as he scooped me into his arms and continued to run. We were inside the Katurium, following Brenna who wound through the hallways and back outside. Another mage was waiting for us, a silvery white dome of protection already conjured.

"In!" Brenna shouted. "Hart, back to her apartment. Stay with her until further notice. Backup is already there and stationed along the way."

More black seraphim swirled the sky, and in the distance, I could see Aditi, Aemon's warhorse, tearing through the fog with Aemon on her back and his sword out as they chased the rider.

Everywhere I looked, black glitter, smoke, and glass fell from the sky. Something else was falling, too: scrolls.

Scrolls upon scrolls rolled across the ground, getting stomped and stepped on by everyone running for cover.

I wanted to reach for one. I wanted to read it, to know what was inside, but we were joined by Markan and two other soturi from my father's guard.

"She's not cleared for flight," Markan barked at Rhyan. "We're staying at her apartment until the threat is stopped."

"I can't go to Cresthaven?" I asked, tightening my grip around Rhyan's neck.

"Not when there's a rider in the sky trying to kill you!"

Rhyan tightened his grip on me in response. My building was coming into view.

"They attacked over the Katurium, not Cresthaven," Markan continued, his tone derisive. "What's that tell you, your grace? You're the target."

I squeezed my eyes shut, filing the information away. This hadn't just been an Emartis demonstration or attack but a message to me in particular.

Did they know I'd gotten the vendor killed?

Or was this more superstition about my lack of power?

"No attack on Cresthaven?" I asked.

"No." Markan held open my apartment building door, and Rhyan rushed me inside.

I swallowed. I wanted proof my sisters were well, but Markan's words eased some of the worry aching inside me.

Our mage kept our protection dome up as we climbed the stairs. On every level we passed, I spotted another soturion of Ka Batavia in the shadows.

Markan unlocked my apartment door. Bastard! I didn't care if he'd been my personal escort since birth, he didn't get to have a key to my apartment. He stood outside, allowing me and Rhyan in.

Over the threshold, Rhyan gently set me on my feet. The moment my feet touched the floor, it was like a torch had been lit inside of me.

"I can't stay here," I said, already putting my hand back on the doorknob.

"It won't be that long," Rhyan said.

Now the true panic was setting in—not just the shock and numbness I had been feeling earlier. I was locked in again, helpless again, away from my sisters, and unable to protect them when they needed me.

I turned the knob, but it was locked. I'd been locked in from the outside. Fucking Markan! Why was the man in charge of protecting me always in my Godsdamned way!

"I'm locked in," I snarled. "Fucking bastard!"

"Lyr!" Rhyan put a hand on my shoulder. I snapped around to face him. He breathed deeply, concern all over his face. But there was something else flickering behind his eyes. Relief. As if he was relieved I'd finally gotten upset.

I shook my head, realizing just how calm I'd been, how odd I must have seemed to him in shock. But that numbness was gone, and my emotions were overwhelming me.

"I can't...I can't do this again! Be locked away like this."

"You're not locked away," he said gently. "You're free. Hey, Lyr, you're free. This is temporary. Everyone here just wants to protect you."

I shook my head, knowing he was right, knowing everything he said and the protocol being followed made sense, but I still felt helpless and panicked like a caged gryphon away from its young. "I just can't keep being helpless, forced to sit still while my family is—"

"Your family is safe. Cresthaven was not a target, and it's been secured by your father's guard. Lyr, hey, you are anything but helpless. And you don't have to sit if you don't want to." His good eyebrow lifted. A joke, he was attempting to make a joke. Now. "Or keep standing, your choice. But you're not a prisoner, and you're not weak. The moment the threat is over, that door opens. It will be soon. I have it on good authority. Now in all seriousness, why don't you sit down? I'll get you some water. I know you're exhausted. You can use this time to rest."

I scoffed. "Yet, here we are again, and you're still my jailer." But water did sound good. So did sitting. I made my way to the couch.

Rhyan offered me a small smile. "I'll get your water."

He returned a moment later with a cold glass and pressed it into my hands. His lips quirked. "And for the record, still not your jailer. Maybe your waiter. But mostly, I'm just a neutral party."

"Not anymore, you're not. You're partly wearing the symbols and colors of Bamaria now. You have Ka Batavia in your veins."

Rhyan stilled. "Then that makes you partly Ka Hart."

I know you.

And suddenly, that connection, that thread between us that I thought I'd broken, it was back in full force and being pulled taut. I didn't know how, but I could feel it, and I knew he could too from the way he'd frozen. He shifted in his seat, looking like he wanted desperately to leave. So why wasn't he?

"Rhyan? What are you doing here? Why are you protecting me?"

"Well, I was with you when the attack happened."

I shook my head. "Right, but you...you don't have to be here now. You've barely said a word to me in the last month, which I get after what I said to you, but...with all my escorts at the door...why wasn't I handed off to them?"

Rhyan cleared his throat. "I...."

"You just...you look like you want to go. So..."

He glanced away and sucked in a breath. "There's something you should know. I wasn't simply allowed to be here because I slayed an akadim. I know you've heard the rumors, the reasons why I'm forsworn. And one akadim kill in my belt wasn't enough to absolve me, even with my Uncle Sean vouching for me. Especially since I declined to swear my loyalty to the Arkasva. In exchange for sanctuary here, I had to agree to additional services on your father's behalf."

I narrowed my eyes. "What additional services?"

"Protecting you. It wasn't an accident when we were bound together as apprentice and novice." He shook his head. "I knew it was coming the moment you told me you were going to be a soturion. Because I swore to your father that I would protect you with my life. The reason I didn't hand you off to your escorts is because you were never not in their hands. I've been part of your personal detail team since I stepped foot inside Bamaria."

CHAPTER TWENTY-EIGHT

"YOU...WHAT! YOU'RE part of my escort, and you never told me? You've been spying on me!" How many secret escorts did I have?

"No, Lyr. Not spying. Just...keeping an extra eye on you. I don't follow you. I don't report on anything you do. It's nothing like that. I just...I'm required to take a few shifts each week in the evening. Mostly, I've been circling the perimeter of your apartment building. I've trailed you in the city a handful of times."

"Did you trail me on my birthday? When I found you in the streets?"

He bit his lip, nodding.

I couldn't believe this! So this was why he sometimes acted so protective of me. This was why he'd sworn I'd be safe that night in the Shadow Stronghold. Not because... because of any connection between us, but because...because he'd been ordered to.

"So that's the real reason you were mad I lied about clinic before. Were you supposed to be trailing me? Did my going off course get you in trouble?"

"No. I wasn't mad. I...I was worried about you."

I put my glass of water on the small table beside my couch. "Just…don't talk to me anymore. Luckily, you've already gotten that part down."

"Lyr, I…." He groaned. "I've had my own reasons for how I've acted."

Before I could reply, my gaze moved from the glass of water to another item on the table—one that hadn't been there when I'd left the apartment earlier.

A small scroll lay on the table, identical to the ones that had just been falling from the sky.

"What is that?" Rhyan asked, his voice immediately going cautious. His eyes were alert, now scanning the room for any threats or signs of entry. He moved his body closer to mine, immediately going into protective mode.

Just like he had been trained. Just like Markan would have.

I took the scroll in my hands, gently breaking the seal—the sigil of Ka Batavia, seraphim wings beneath a full moon. But the wings weren't gold, and the moon wasn't silver. The seal had been forged in black glittering wax.

Dearest False Heir,

You do not need to go looking for us. We have decided to come to you. Know this is for the highest good of the country you insist you love. Your father is false. He lets in a forsworn soturion, he allows akadim to swarm our lands, and he gives away the protection of our borders to a foreign ruler. Soon he will give up his Laurel and his Seat as well.

A coward he is. Like you. Like your sisters. Remember Ka Azria… It won't be long now.

Me Arkasva, Me Emar.

The Emartis will prevail.

Soon.

I tossed the scroll onto the table with a yelp, like it had burned me.

"It's from them?" Rhyan asked. He reached for the scroll on the table. "May I?"

I nodded and watched his eyes move rapidly across the page, all the way to the bottom. Then his eyes shot up as he read the words again. He rerolled the parchment.

"I need to show this to Markan. Aemon will need to know, too, Lyr, and—"

"Your grace," I said. "Since you answer to Markan and Aemon, since you work for my father, you can call me 'your grace.' Not Lyr," I seethed. "Not partner."

He squeezed his eyes shut and nodded. "As you wish."

I didn't wait for him to finish opening the front door—he had a key as well. Who didn't have access to my apartment? Apparently, the Emartis did, too! I shivered, covered myself with my arms, and retreated to my room, slamming the door shut. When Rhyan knocked a few minutes later, I didn't answer.

An hour passed, and my front door opened. I could hear footsteps followed by a sharp rap on my bedroom door. "Lady Lyriana, your grace, it's Eathan."

My father's Second. Finally, a report on what was happening at Cresthaven.

I joined Eathan in the living room, noting Rhyan had taken position like a sentry in the corner, standing alert. Eathan sat down beside me. His hair was pushed back and as gray as his robes—the twin to my father's, announcing his station to everyone who met him.

"Lockdown has ended. The threat is over, but your classes have been canceled for the day while we sweep through Bamaria. Apprentice soturi are being asked to join the search. Instruction will resume tonight with your habibellum."

"What happened?" I asked. "Was anyone hurt?"

"All is well. Your father and sisters are in Cresthaven, safe."

"Thank the Gods," I said. "And the rider? Has he been captured?"

Eathan's expression was grim. "It doesn't matter."

"Doesn't matter? If they caught him, we can learn the Emartis's identity. Their plans! Eathan, this is their second spectacle this year."

"I know," Eathan said. "And I wish I had better news. I wish I could say we could learn something more about them, but that only would have been if we'd captured the rider alive. Or whole." His expression turned grim. "Aemon had him in his grasp until...." He shook his head, a haunted look in his eyes. "I don't know what magic it was, but he was gone instantly, your grace. He fell to the ground in pieces."

My stomach twisted and knotted. Something was crawling up my throat—I was going to be sick. Not over the method of his death—terrible as that was—but over his willingness to do something like that. If the Emartis were willing to die for their cause, die horribly at that, then there was nothing that would deter their next course of action. Fear began to bubble through me, and my hands shook.

"The vendor," I said.

Eathan's brow furrowed. "You think they are connected?"

I had told Eathan what happened that day in the city park with Markan even though I knew he'd received a full report. Still, I felt it was important. I'd wanted him to know the connections I was making, the possibilities we needed to consider to track them down.

Eathan had listened patiently but had only said opportunists exist everywhere, and that most men were cowards—regarding the vendor's behavior toward me. I'd left out the fact that I had also bribed Tristan's escort afterward.

"I just...." I tried to make sense of it all, of the clues they'd left, and what they might mean. "The fear they experience, is that normal? The vendor was terrified when he thought he'd been caught talking to me. And this rider, willing to...to die like that." I still had to process what Eathan had said. *In pieces.* "Does that...does that tell us anything about who might be controlling them? At the heart of the mission?"

"Someone powerful," Eathan said. "Someone who was able to bribe or use magic to get into your apartment." He held up the incriminating scroll.

"The Imperator?" I asked.

Eathan's eyes darkened. "Your grace, I've never liked that man either. But you'd do well not to speak disparagingly about him. It's not good for Ka Batavia and especially not good for your position now. Especially this week. Because the attack happened over school grounds, Arianna had to notify him. He's on his way."

"He's coming to Bamaria? Again? He was just here!"

"I know," Eathan said.

"But it wasn't an attack on the school! It was an attack on me."

"And you're a student at the school which his soturi protect."

"Gryphon-shit. Eathan, you know that! This is a Bamarian matter and a Bamarian matter alone. He shouldn't be coming here!"

Eathan sighed. "The Imperator has his arrangements with Ka Batavia's Council. I am sorry, but I am not the one negotiating here. I'm merely the messenger."

I bit my lip. The Imperator coming here was bad. Always. But especially after another incident in Bamaria—it was going to give him all the leverage he needed to add more legions.

"And is his highness coming alone? Or is he bringing Ka Kormac legions with him?"

"He said he'd come as quickly as possible. Legions tend to slow travel down, so my guess is no."

My stomach was in knots. "Even one soturion of Ka Kormac remaining armed in Bamaria is too many." I shifted in my seat. I'd lost my posture hearing the news. Sitting up straighter, I asked, "What now? What do we do?"

"We do not do anything, your grace. Attend the habibellum tonight, that's your job. That's all you can do. The Shadows are on this. Aemon's sent his best soturi to investigate. We'll get them. In the meantime, of course your security detail will increase."

"It's increased a lot lately." My eyes flicked to Rhyan. He remained still and stoic in his corner.

"I know." Eathan sighed, reaching for my arm. "We will also be adding in some wards and additional spells to your apartment. Mages are on their way now to increase your protection." He bowed his chin. "Your grace. Get some rest." He stood and headed for the door, nodding at Rhyan. "Soturion."

"My lord," he said quietly.

Eathan closed the door behind him.

I blinked. One second, Rhyan was several feet away, standing guard in a corner of my living room. The next, he was right in front of me, his hands flexing at his sides.

"You never told me you were there for the death of that man. The jewelry seller?"

I narrowed my gaze. "Oh, did your security team not let you in on that detail?"

"Lyr! Do you realize how dangerous that was? To follow someone you don't know into a dark place? The park has so many hiding spots, it's perfect for an ambush."

There was another knock on my apartment door, but before I could say anything, Tristan strolled in with his two usual mage escorts—including Bellamy.

My throat tightened, and I looked at Rhyan carefully, pleading with him not to say anything in front of Tristan about the vendor's death or what Eathan had just revealed.

The moment Tristan laid eyes on me, he was across the room. "Are you all right?" he asked, scooping me into his arms.

"I'm not hurt," I said. "Are you?"

He answered with a kiss, his hands gripping my waist, pulling me in close. "Better," he whispered in my ear. "Now I'm with you." His mouth was on mine again.

"Tristan," I said, breathlessly. "We're not alone."

He rolled his eyes. "I know." He caught sight of Rhyan standing back against the wall.

"Now don't stop on my account. You seemed like you were enjoying having an audience."

"What's he doing here?" Tristan asked.

"He...he helped me get to safety during the lockdown," I said. "So did Markan and the rest of the Bamarian legion sleeping outside my door."

"Well, the lockdown's over, Hart. We'll be going now. Maybe you can lock up."

"She can't go," he snarled. "Not until her new security detail is established. So you'll just have to perform your little show to us audience of three. Me, your two...oh, I remember you!" Rhyan sauntered toward Bellamy. "We met in the Shadow Stronghold. You tried to push a stave against my throat." Rhyan pointed to his neck and growled, mocking Bellamy's attack.

"Then you can go. We've got it from here," Tristan said. "She has me, two world-class mages, and as Lyr said, a Bamarian legion outside her door."

I waited to see if Rhyan would protest and insist on some excuse to stay because he was on duty. But he simply nodded and walked toward the door. "See you at the habibellum, your grace." His aura spread across the room, frosty, distant, and dark, like an endless forest buried beneath the snow.

Tristan sat down with me, rubbing my leg, asking hundreds of questions about the day I'd had. I couldn't focus on him. Instead, I found myself watching Bellamy, looking for any sign that he'd betrayed me to his lord. We made eye contact. His eyes closed slowly, and he lowered his chin.

I nodded in return. Then the exhaustion truly hit. I excused myself to my room. Tristan followed. I let him lay down beside me and gather me close so that my back pressed against his chest. Still feeling a gust of Rhyan's glacial aura, I tugged my blankets higher and went to sleep.

I opened my eyes in the dark. My entire room was pitch black. I was alone. I remembered Tristan getting up at some point because he had to leave and prepare for a test he was administering for novice mages.

I assumed that my magic wards were up if he was gone, and no doubt Markan, or even Rhyan, was stalking the building's perimeter.

For what seemed like the hundredth time that day, someone was knocking on my door. No, not knocking— pounding furiously. The door sounded like it was two seconds from splintering in half.

Groggily, I slid out of bed, still wearing my practice clothes and sandals, and shuffled across the room, tripping over sweaty tunics and a stack of scrolls.

"Thank the fucking Gods, Lyr!" Morgana spilled into my room. I slammed the door behind me as she fell to the floor, grabbing her head, her face screwed up in pain. With a wave of her stave, the torches tucked into each corner of my room flared to life.

"Emartis?" My heart raced as Morgana moaned, writhing on her hands and knees. How many hours had I been out? "What's happened?" I sank to the ground beside her, reaching for her hand. "Morgs! Talk to me."

"You have to come," she croaked. Her aura was icy, freezing, but not the crisp glacial feel of Rhyan's aura. This one was biting, bitter, and violent, with a darkness that pounded deep inside the ice. It was a feeling that only came when one thing was happening. Fuck.

"Vision?" I knew the answer to my own question. I'd fucking known this was coming. Meera was suffering, and I wasn't with her. But neither was Morgana. My stomach twisted. *Morgs! Where is she? Is she safe?*

"As much as she can be. I—" Morgana's body went taut, and she hissed in pain. Tears sprang to her eyes. "Fuck, Lyr. Let's go. NOW!"

I grabbed her arm, helping her to stand. She was so cold, and Meera wasn't even here. "Is she safe?" I asked again. "Morgs! Where is she?"

"Cresthaven," Morgana rasped. "I...I tied her to the bed. I couldn't do anything else. She only responds when you're there."

My eyes widened in shock. "You tied her to the bed? Myself to Moriel!" I threw my head back. Shit. If Morgana had been there when the vision started, tied her up, and flown here...how much time had passed? How much more time would pass before we got there? The longer she'd been having visions, the longer the visions lasted, and the more chances she had to hurt herself or someone else. But if she was left alone in her vision too long, if someone couldn't pull her out, we could lose her. The vision could claim her mind.

"Move it!" I pushed open the door, half-dragging Morgana into the hall and down the stairs. The halls were full of novices all dressed in their training tunics, walking purposely to the door.

What time is it?

"Almost six."

I have my habibellum in exactly one hour. Shit. All right, I'd go with Morgana to Cresthaven, make sure Meera came safely out of her vision, and fly right back to the Katurium. It was doable. Maybe I'd be fifteen minutes late. Rhyan would be pissed, but so what? At least I'd be there. And Meera....by the Gods...Meera would be safe.

Hurry, I urged Morgana. *How is she? Can you tell?*

"Still in the vision."

I tugged her arm forward, speeding up our walk. We were almost at the seraphim port. Just a quick ride, and we'd be at Cresthaven. I could do this. I could pull Meera out. Then I'd fly back. It would be fine. I would handle it.

The ashvan horses took off, streaking the night sky in bright, glowing shades of blue. The timekeeper began to call the hour.

My heart raced. I had exactly one hour.

"Lyr," Morgana froze.

I urged her into the carriage before us, its seraphim lying patiently on the ground.

"The Imperator's there," she said.

Cresthaven! Meera!

Morgana swallowed and shook her head. "No, he's...at the Katurium. He came to observe...." She closed her eyes tight, her mouth grimacing in pain.

"What? No. He can't be. Arianna only notified him of the attack today. He couldn't get here from Korteria that fast. Not in one day."

"He wasn't in Korteria," Morgana said darkly. "He was in Elyria. He was...waiting—waiting for an invitation because —fuck. Lyr, he'd planned to see you fight tonight. He's here to test you."

My hands shook at my side, and my stomach churned violently. He was here. Here already after not even a full day's notification of the Emartis attack. He had been waiting for a reason to visit. I thought of my earlier comments to Eathan, that someone powerful was behind the Emartis, someone everyone feared enough to die for. He'd brushed me off, but I was beginning to think I was right.

The Emartis caused chaos. Chaos caused danger at the school. That danger allowed the Imperator to bring in more of his soturi. Gods. What if the Imperator really was behind it? I had seen Viktor during the chaos. He'd looked calm, not even remotely worried—like he had prior knowledge. Like he was in on the plan.

I pushed away the thought. One thing at a time. First, I had to help Meera.

"Cresthaven!" I screamed at the seraphim.

I sat on the edge of my seat, knuckles turning white from clutching it while Morgana crouched in the corner, hands rubbing at her temples in pain.

"She's still in the vision," she said darkly as the carriage landed. The whole trip had taken over a quarter of an hour.

I squeezed my eyes shut and inhaled. I had to stay calm, I had to pull Meera back. But I'd never let her be in a vision this long. Never. I didn't know what it would do to her.

The carriage floor stilled, and I jumped up, leaping from the carriage before the seraphim fully lay down. I slid, landing awkwardly on my foot. "Fuck!" I yelled, but I kept running, ignoring the pinch forming in my ankle.

"Open the doors!" I screamed at Euston. He was alone in his post and looked startled to see me flying down the waterway. "Now!"

Euston obeyed, and the doors flung open just as I reached the promenade. I could feel the watching eyes of our sentries, hiding in their camouflaged cloaks. It didn't matter.

I entered Cresthaven and rushed up the stairs, racing two at a time, until I could fly down the hall into Meera's room.

Blood. That was the first thing I saw. Blood dripping down her face where she'd scratched her cheeks and at her wrists where she'd strained against the black bindings. They'd been spelled to tie her arms over her head. Identical bindings held her feet down.

Morgana had said she'd tied her to the bed, but those weren't ties. Those were bindings. The kind Tristan had used. The kind meant to cut you off from your power. Morgana had done a shitty job of it, only managing to tie down Meera's body and cause minor burns and cuts. It hadn't stopped Meera's vision, only slowed it down, prolonged it.

MORGANA! She had to get up here now and remove the bindings before they caused any more harm than they already had.

I threw myself on the bed, attempting to untie them, but they were so hot, I could barely hold onto them. If I held her down, would I hurt her more?

I straddled her hips, forcing her bowed body back against the bed, and grabbed hold of her face.

"MEERA!" I pushed her ashen hair behind her ears, across her temples, trying to find the face of my sister, the true face of Lady Meera Batavia. But all I saw was a monster. Her hazel eyes had rolled back, and all that remained was empty white.

She roared at me, her teeth gnashing and her hands straining to claw at me. Every move she made put her in contact with the bindings, and she hissed, screeching in fear and pain.

MORGANA!

"Shhh, Meera, it's all right. Stop struggling. Meera, please. It's me. Don't hurt yourself."

My words only made her double down on her fight; she perceived my presence as another threat.

I pressed my forehead against hers. I called her name. I cried out to her. It had always worked before. She came back when she heard my voice, when she saw my face. But she was screeching so loudly she couldn't hear a word I was saying, and I wasn't sure she could see anything.

"Meera! Meera, it's me! It's Lyr. Please! Please come back to me."

She stopped struggling. Her body went rigid, and her eyes rolled back down their sockets.

Relief began to tear through me, but it came too soon. Before me appeared not hazel eyes, but black ones. They were eyes I'd never seen before. They slowly slithered from side to side, observing and assessing the room before stopping and focusing right up at me.

A salacious grin spread across Meera's mouth, and blood dripped down her nose.

"Asherah," she said. It wasn't her voice. It was a sound I'd never heard come from her mouth before. Dark and gravelly, it was like ten voices, both male and female, had been fused into one. "ASHERAH! We will have you yet!"

Fear gripped me, and I lost my hold on Meera. She bucked hard enough to throw me off her body, off the bed. My back smacked against the floor.

Morgana burst into the room, one hand over her face, her fingers clawing at her hair in agony. She moaned and held up her stave, aiming wildly at Meera and the bed while I rolled away on the floor.

Blue light exploded, lighting up the room, and smoke rose from Meera's wrists and ankles. The bindings were gone.

But the vision hadn't ended yet.

Meera screamed and flew off the bed. She landed on top of me, and a swift punch to my face blinded my vision. I saw only white, glowing white light, twinkling like stars. Then the pain caught up with me, and tears formed.

Meera went rigid again as she was flung off my body. Morgana gave me a small nod before her own eyes rolled back, and she collapsed, her hand no longer holding onto her stave. It rolled out of her palm across the floor, just like Jules's stave had.

I jumped on Meera, screaming as I held down her hands, and attempted to get her legs to still and stop kicking.

One second, I had her, the next she'd flipped me over again. The air whooshed out of me as my back smacked the floor. Then she was over me.

Her hands were everywhere, scratching, clawing, and hitting while I burrowed deep into my mind, pulling out the trainings Rhyan had run me through. I ducked away from her attack, blocking each hit and managing to slide out from under her. For a moment, my mind cleared, all of my training from the past month clicking into place. Meera progressed forward in slow motion as I anticipated her next attack. Her eyes met mine, and the terror I felt at seeing her like this, at what it meant and the fact that Morgana had passed out from the pain, rushed back to me.

Meera gained the upper hand. I raced for her bed, jumping onto it and grabbing her blanket, then leaping back to the floor with it. She ran around the opposite side of the bed to meet me, fingers out like claws. I ran for her, covering her body with the blanket and pinning her to the floor. She couldn't scratch at me anymore, but she could still hit and kick and scream.

"Meera!" I pulled the cover back. I had to see her face, make her see me. "Meera!"

And then she did. I checked the clocktower on her nightstand. Its white marbled base had been covered in paint. By my estimate of when it had started, she'd been in her vision for three quarters of an hour—more than double the longest of her previous visions.

I slid my golden cuff down my arm, pulling out the scroll I kept inside. A spare pen lay on Meera's dresser, amongst discarded paintbrushes, and before she could stir, I logged in the data.

"Lyr?" Meera's voice was scratchy and weak, but thank the Gods it was her own voice.

I hastily rolled and pushed the scroll back inside my cuff, my penmanship sloppy, and slid the golden bracelet back up my arm, trying not to wince. She'd scratched me all the way from my wrist to elbow.

"I'm right here," I said. "Are you all right?"

I wrapped my arms around myself, starting to shake with the cold.

"Fine," Meera said. In the corner, Morgana lay on the floor, still passed out. Her teeth began to chatter.

"Morgana?" I asked gently, crouching by her side. Another of Meera's blankets had fallen on the floor in the struggle, and I pulled it over Morgana's shoulders, carefully placing her stave on the night stand. I had only thirty minutes to return to the Katurium, and I'd only make it in time if I left that second.

I had to go. I had to leave. But I couldn't until I knew both of my sisters would be all right. I rushed over to Meera's sink, wetting a towel and handing it to her to wipe the blood from her face and arms. Then I crouched by Morgana.

Morgana? Morgana! Wake up!

She stirred beside me, moaning, her arm stretching forward, reaching for her stave.

"It's on the nightstand," I said.

"Give it to me," she hissed.

I did. Whimpering, she sat up, shooting jagged blue sparks across the room. She conjured a tiny blue fire in a glass bowl by the window. A towel floated from the top shelf of Meera's closet into the sink basin, which released steaming hot water. The towel came to Morgana, wrapping itself around her forehead.

"I burned your wrists," she said groggily, looking to Meera.

"You didn't mean to—"

"I'll fix it. I'm sorry."

"Help Lyr first. She...." Meera's eyes registered the time. "She has clinic."

"And the Imperator's here, waiting for me." I shook my head. "What can I do? What do you need?" I eyed my sisters. They looked like they'd been bound and beaten.

"Go," Meera said. "Lyr, I'm all right now. And Morgana is fine, too. Go! We'll take care of ourselves."

Shakily, I got to my feet. "Are you sure?"

"Get out," Morgana said, her voice cold. "Now. I'll come by later. We'll talk."

I was already at the doorway, feeling empty, off-centered, and terrified. Those voices that had come from Meera's mouth, those eyes—they hadn't been the effects of a normal vision. It was like something else had come through her, possessed her.

Was this it? Was it the madness, come for her already? The scrolls I read all said it eventually would, that anyone with visions would eventually be farther than Lethea, drowning deep in an endless pit of insanity. It was the same madness that drove one mage to butcher Tristan's parents right in front of him.

Morgana shook her head, reading my every thought. "You don't know that, and you're still standing here. Go!"

A lump had formed in my throat. I was barely holding on, barely keeping it together. I'd never seen my sisters like this before, and I'd never see them again—not if I didn't leave. But even as I turned, racing down the stairs, through the Great Hall, and outside the fortress, I couldn't shake a sinking feeling deep in my gut—that I was losing Meera. And I wasn't strong enough to stop it.

CHAPTER TWENTY-NINE

THE CARRIAGE DOOR shut behind me in Urtavia as my seraphim lay her beak down on the waterway, exhausted from her journey. I ran faster than I'd ever run before, my feet carrying me to the Katurium, through the winding halls, and out into the arena.

The hour had been called when I was still in flight, and I'd seen the ashvan running beside my seraphim, their hooves leaving behind blue sparks of light that faded into mist and fell like rain into the sky before evaporating.

No more than a quarter hour could have passed, making me fifteen minutes late. Usually, it took twenty minutes just for everyone to reach their seats, or to step out onto the field in their circles if they were in a five.

That hadn't been the case tonight. There was a deafening silence and stillness as I entered the packed arena. Endless pairs of eyes watched me until every hair on my arms stood on end. I'd always known the feeling of being watched, of being put on display to be observed and judged. But this was a far greater audience than I'd ever experienced before. And a far angrier one at that.

I knew it deep inside my bones. I wasn't just being tested tonight. I was on trial.

Torchlights lit up the night sky in fiery circles leading up the levels of the Katurium's stadium seating. A single ashvan galloped through the sky, his hooves racing just over the fires and leaving small blue sparks above the golden-red flames. That was new. I couldn't decide if the ashvan was solely there for my protection or as an added safety measure for the entire Katurium.

Also new was the fact that the arena's seats were full, fuller than I'd ever seen them. Each seat was occupied by a soturion with silver-pelted armor. I didn't have to count to know that five units of Korterian soturi, loyal to Ka Kormac, surrounded me. Five units. We were now occupied by a full legion.

Either the Imperator was behind the Emartis's attack or he'd stationed his soturi on the borders of Elyria for a month in an encampment for this very reason, just waiting for the moment to cross the borders back into the Empire and Bamarian lands. Bastard.

On the arena's ground, my classmates were spread across the field, each paired with their apprentices and being ordered through warm-up stretches. Soturi were everywhere, lunging, stretching, and tightening the laces on their sandals. A dozen silver circles glittered across the field, all being carefully avoided by the novices and their apprentices. Their magic hummed, calling out with a sinister force. The Katurium mage's stave was drawn as she inspected each of the bindings she'd cast. Aemon and Dairen stood in the center of the mayhem on a small raised platform. Tonight they were dressed in full battle regalia, their armor shining beneath the torchlight. Beside them was the Imperator and the Bastardmaker.

His highness's cold black eyes fell on me before he looked away, surveying his soldiers. I stiffened, my breath quick, uneven, and labored as the pinch in my ankle began to increase.

Still, I strode forward purposefully, crossing the arena's track to the inner field, ignoring the pain, ignoring the speculation even as I saw Viktor and his apprentice Brockton sneer. Haleika gave a small, almost sympathetic smile from Leander's side. I locked eyes with Aemon as I drew closer. The disappointment on his face was almost too much. But I was Lady Lyriana Batavia, Heir to the Arkasva, and I kept walking like I owned the arena, like I'd meant to be late, like I had a purpose. Because I did.

A cold breeze rustled through my hair. No, not a breeze— an aura. One far more familiar to me than I'd wanted to admit. A warm, calloused hand gripped my wrist from behind, tugging me back.

Rhyan's energy exploded around me on contact, a hurricane of fire and ice whipping through the air.

"You're late, and the Imperator's here! What were you thinking? You're scheduled to be in the center of a five and —" He froze. His green eyes widened and flashed with fury as they took in my appearance. They ran across my face, looking me up and down as his breath caught. "Gods. Lyr." His voice was barely above a whisper. I watched as his jaw tensed and he swallowed, some emotion I didn't recognize washing over him. "You're hurt." His hand ran down the length of my arm, scanning for injuries, and pulling me closer as his eyes moved slowly over my face again. "What the hell happened?"

"I…what…no." I shook my head. "Nothing, I'm…."

Rhyan went preternaturally still. "Who did this to you?"

I shook my head. "No….no one."

But he wasn't listening to me. Instead, he was pulling me back, away from the crowd, away from prying eyes. Rhyan's gaze flicked studiously to my ankle, noting the injury. He slowed, but kept us moving at a brisk pace. I tried to make up for it, to hide the pinch, but he shook his head and slowed even more.

"I'm fine," I protested.

"You're not fine." His hands had wrapped with impossible gentleness around both of my wrists, careful not to apply pressure and hurt me, but firm enough that I couldn't escape. He guided me to a private, shadowed corner. There was a marble statue there of Arkturion Athenaya. The warlordess defeated a small army of akadim terrorizing the human lands outside of Bamaria. She rode on an ashvan, depicted with his front legs kicking as Athenaya brandished her starfire blade. We moved behind her, deeper into the walled corner she kept hidden until we were completely alone, and even then, he didn't let go of me.

"Rhyan? Stop it! What are you—?"

"Lyr, tell me what happened." His aura cocooned me, no longer the bitter ice or raging hurricane but a calming cool darkness, more like a night sky full of stars. "Who was it? Who hurt you?"

Instantly, my pulse spiked, my wrist itching at his words. He'd spotted my injuries—injuries from Meera's vision. "I'm fine. I tripped on my way here. All right? Let's go. I need to get out there."

"Lyr...you...." He shook his head. "You can't even put weight on your right ankle without wincing. You're not fine. There's blood on your tunic, and," he cupped my cheek, his touch gentle, his face so close to mine as he examined me closer, "you have a cut under your eye. It's already swelling."

"Because I tripped!" I tried to shake him off, to keep him from looking too closely and observing any more than he already had. "What is this? You're so determined to prove yourself as my guard, you're looking for things that aren't there? Let me go!"

He released me and took a step back, but he still blocked my exit. His shoulders rose and fell with his breathing, a dark anger now pulsating through his aura. "This has nothing to do with that. Before I was your guard, I was your friend. And I protect my friends."

I felt the shift in his aura as he spoke the words. No longer full of worry and concern; it was now infused with an unsettlingly calm, violent determination.

"When I left your apartment earlier, you were fine. Now tell me. Who did this to you?" Red burned through his cheeks as he pushed his fingers through his hair with a violence I'd never seen from him before. Something in his eyes went dark and feral. "Where is Tristan?" His voice had gone so deep, his body so still, I knew if I offered any confirmation, he'd be on the hunt, racing to track Tristan down and hurt him even with the Imperator watching. I could feel it all over his aura. The need to fight, the need to protect me.

"No!" I shouted.

"Who else was with you between now and then? Who else could have done this? I left you alone with him and then you show up late, limping, looking like this!" He paused, his good eyebrow lifting. "Gods! That's why you didn't want to be rescued on your birthday? You were safer in prison?" His nostrils flared, his chest rising and falling as deep shadows crossed his eyes. He looked feral in that moment, like he was struggling for control, battling some primal desire to hunt down whoever had hurt me. I couldn't let him.

"Rhyan!" I shouted. The blood oaths in my wrists were on fire. He was too close to the truth. "No! Tristan never laid a hand on me. Not like...not like you're thinking. I swear on Auriel. He never—would never...." Unless I had a vorakh. Unless I stood in the way of him arresting my sisters for vorakh. I shook my head. "Rhyan, please. Just stop. You're completely off track, and I need to go out there for the habibellum."

"Lyr," he pleaded. His jaw remained tense, his eyes searching mine. Something lifted, his rage turning to concern.

"I'm not." His voice softened. "You've been hurt before. You think I wouldn't know? I see you. I see you hide your injuries."

"I don't!" My eyes searching his, desperate, pleading for him to let it go. To forget whatever he'd thought he'd seen. To stop asking questions.

His hands flexed at his sides, fingers curling into fists, then lengthening in frustration. "You wouldn't let me help you after the first clinic. Gods! I shouldn't have walked out, I should have known—"

"Rhyan! Stop it! Please! I can't...we can't do this right now. The Imperator is watching me! He came to watch me tonight! To test me! You know he's looking to hold my performance against me in any way he can, and he's going to use it against you, too! Remember?" Fresh hot tears burned behind my eyes.

He took my chin again, a finger brushing softly over my cheek. "I remember." He sucked in a breath. "But I'm finding it really hard to care about that when you're hurt."

"Well, you need to start caring," I said. "Because I have no choice. He won't allow a single excuse." I straightened my back, trying to summon whatever courage remained inside. "And I won't give him one." Not if it could trace back to my sisters. Not when the Emartis had threatened me with Ka Azria that very morning.

A raindrop fell behind Rhyan, landing with a soft plunk on the ground. It was followed by another. And another.

Rhyan's shoulders slumped. "I hate this," he said. "I know you...you're seeing me differently, now you know I'm your guard. But when I swore to you in the Shadow Stronghold that no harm would come to you, that I'd protect you whenever I could...Gods, Lyr, I meant it." And just as he had that first night, he pressed his fist against his heart, tapping it twice, then flattening his palm over his heart.

My eyes searched his. "You can't protect me from this."

He pressed his lips together, his eyes full of determination. "Yes, I can." Rhyan released my chin, leaning his entire body in toward mine until his breath brushed against my ear. "Do you know the words to call on kashonim?" he asked, voice low. I could feel his heart pounding through his aura, and my own pounded in response, dread drowning me with every pulse, every breath. I leaned back against the cold, damp wall behind me, needing a way to steady myself, to feel grounded.

Kashonim. Calling on the blood power of my lineage to lend me extra strength. To take all Rhyan had and use my body as a conduit for it to flow through.

I shook my head. "I don't know if it will work," I said, heart pounding even faster. "It's too dangerous. It tears through you." I recalled all the soturi passed out on the ground after the Oath Ceremony. They'd had a rush of power and then none. "I'll pass out from the force of it after a minute."

"No." Rhyan paused, stepping back as footsteps sounded behind him. Shadows filled our corner then vanished. Alone again, he continued, "It only tears through you when you use it all at once. It's usually meant for big pushes, life or death. But this is different, you only have me. Remember, my lineage was broken. So it's not that big, and I'm not fighting tonight. I don't need it. It's yours. All yours. I promise, it won't tear through you if you don't let it. You just have to ration the power. Use it carefully. You can do that. Think stamina, not speed."

It was the same advice he always gave me about running.

I balked, fear racing through me. I wanted the extra push, the extra power and strength. I needed it. I was tired and limping, and I'd already been beaten up tonight. Even though I was drawing power from only Rhyan and not an entire kashonim, the force of him was so considerable, so full of might and strength, I imagined it wouldn't be so different from calling on a full lineage. That force might knock me right out and put me in more danger. Not to mention, using kashonim on other students was illegal.

I shook my head. "It's too risky in front of the Imperator and Aemon."

"It's too risky not to do it," he hissed, the muscles in his jaw flexing. "Not with your injuries." Another raindrop fell, then another. "You didn't answer my question. Do you know the words?"

"Rhyan."

"Answer me."

"I…"

He held a hand up. "I'm ordering you, as your apprentice. Answer me. Do you know the words?"

"Yes, I know them. But—without magic of my own—."

"It's blood magic. My blood is your blood. It's in your veins, in your armor. I'm Ka Batavia now, you're Ka Hart. Remember? It'll work."

He was right. I knew he was right. The blood oaths mutilating my arm had proved it. I had no magic, but I was still touched by it, still bound by its manipulations.

"But what about all the maneuvers I haven't mastered?" I still wasn't great at sparring with just Rhyan. Now, I wasn't just going to be fighting one person, I was going to be in the center of a five and then released into a habibellum with all of the novices at the University intent on attacking—attacking me, in particular.

"Focus on getting away. Evading like before. Not fighting. You're not trying to impress the Imperator with your moves —you're trying to survive. And you're going to. Use the extra push from my strength to escape the first five. Then find your friends and stick close to them—they'll protect you."

"Apprentices," Aemon called, "to the sidelines. Novices, take your positions."

Rhyan gestured for me to follow him out of our corner until we emerged beyond the statue of Athenaya and her horse. Raindrops ran in rivulets down the statue, and a small puddle was forming at our feet.

The crowded field began to clear as apprentices exited toward their seats and novices took their positions. Those in the fives all braced themselves as they passed through the burning cold rings of silver. The movement caused the bindings to all spark with energy and life, buzzing with each body that passed through it, reforming and reinforcing its power each time, until one by one they were all trapped. I was next.

"You're in the seventh circle," Rhyan said.

I nodded. Of course. Front and center to entertain the Imperator and Bastardmaker, so they could prove to everyone the idea of me being a soturion was a complete and total joke. The weight of the night, the stakes of what was about to happen, started to hang heavy on me.

Rhyan squeezed my arm. "Call it. I'm ordering you to. Now, Lyr." He gave me one last glance, then he was off, vanishing into the crowd on the sidelines.

I took a step forward, willing my body to find its own energy and strength, something to keep it going when the kashonim ran out. But my knees shook, and I still felt that horrible aching exhaustion I'd had this morning, now coupled with my new injuries and what was probably a swollen ankle. Only pure adrenaline and fear kept me going.

More rain fell. The already damp ground was quickly becoming soaked. My sandals sank into it. A raindrop splattered across my nose, and I closed my eyes, chanting the words quickly and quietly.

"Ani petrova kashonim, me ka el lyrotz, dhame ra shukroya, aniam anam. Chayate me el ra shukroya. Ani petrova kashonim!"

Fire erupted in my wrist, right where Aemon had cut me, the opening where Rhyan's blood had crossed and mixed with mine. All at once I felt it, a rush of energy and power, ice cold strength shielding my body and a raging fire within breathing new life into my muscles. The soreness in my body was wiped away, the pinch in my ankle was stitched back into place, and even the swelling in my face went down. The fire and ice raging through me now were all Rhyan, and for a second, I felt him so closely, so intimately it was like we were joined and I couldn't recall where my body ended and his began. His voice was in my head as if I were reading his mind.

You can do this, Lyr. You're strong.

As quickly as the connection was bridged between our minds, the feel of him inside me was lost. The blood magic was complete. All of Rhyan's strength, all of his power and energy, was mine. I felt as if I'd slept for days and drank several cups of coffee.

The moment the power settled inside of me, I found Rhyan on the edge of the field. His skin went white, and his scar reddened, standing out, obvious even at a distance. His eyes found mine. Rhyan took a step, his gaze focused on me, and he stumbled, reaching for the nearest wall for support. His chest heaved with exertion.

"Welcome to the first novice habibellum of the year," Aemon called out. His voice echoed across the arena, his volume created by an amplification spell. "We've just completed a full month of training. Now it's time to show your work." Aemon's eyes found me again. His mouth hardened before his chin jerked ever so slightly to the Imperator by his side. "We are also honored tonight by his highness, Imperator Kormac, and Arkturion Kormac. Reassuring to see our allies here, especially after the unfortunate fireworks this morning." There was a collective bow from all the soturi in the arena. "Novices, prepare for battle."

I reached the circle assigned to me, standing right before the Imperator and Bastardmaker. Inhaling deeply, I entered the binding, feeling the cold snap at my skin, the silver of the ropes reflect against my armor. I moved to the center, standing feet apart, knees bent, hands in fists.

The entire arena lit up. Golden light illuminated the flaming torches circled over us, and for the first time, I could see my opponents clearly.

Viktor, Naria, Pavi, and two other brutes from Ka Kormac. All five sneered at me, hungry wolves ready to pounce on prey they'd desired for a long time.

Then the light vanished. Thunder clapped in the sky. The clouds had finally moved from scattering random raindrops to the full storm that had been brewing since this morning.

Even with Rhyan's power coursing through me, energizing me, heightening my awareness, I knew the truth. I was the lamb these wolves would rip to shreds.

I swallowed hard, the fires flickering above my head faded into a black night sky.

Naria took a step forward, her arms taut at her side, ready to fight. Raindrops pelted against my face.

Aemon lifted a torch into the night, his eyebrows drawn, and mouth tight. "Begin."

CHAPTER THIRTY

NO ONE MOVED. I held my fists before my face, an instinct I had from facing Meera. Slowly, I turned in a circle, seeing Viktor, Naria, Pavi, and the two Kormac brutes. No one attacked. My heart pounded harder. What was their plan? To kill me with anticipation?

Naria stepped forward, and I tensed before she stepped back. Pavi did the same, then Viktor did, all laughing hysterically as I prepared for each attack only to be left spinning on my heels alone.

"Like getting wet?" Viktor asked.

I dug my heels into the ground, hoping I'd have a moment like before when I was with Meera. I hoped my mind would clear, and I'd know what to do, how to fight back. But my mind felt fuzzy as a raindrop splashed across my nose and another landed on my cheek.

Pavi licked her lips. "Finally getting yours, bitch," she said.

I whipped toward her, my arms shaking with the force of keeping my hands fisted.

"Finally," I said, hoping I sounded braver than I felt. "Your little dog Tani wasn't well suited to the job."

I fell face forward. Wet, muddied dirt and grass exploded inside my mouth, and I coughed and wheezed, the wind knocked from me. Stars blinked in my eyes. I'd been kicked from behind by one of the Kormac brutes. His knee dug into my back, and my arms and legs splayed out around me. Someone grabbed my hands, and someone else took my legs as he climbed off. I was flipped onto my back and slammed into the ground, hard. I wheezed, seeing more stars pop in my vision and feeling raindrops smacking against my cheeks. Naria grabbed my head, pulling it up hard enough to snap my neck, and pushed it back down into the ground. I tasted blood in my mouth.

Viktor flung himself on top of me, his hands in a vice-like grip around my wrists as he held them over my head.

"Come on, Lady Asherah," he sneered, his mouth over my ear. "Fight back."

I growled, trying to buck him, but someone kicked me in the side, their toe going through my waist. I lost my breath, vision blurring. Another kick came from the other side into my ribs. My head rolled back. The pain reverberated inside of me. I could feel Rhyan's strength gathering inside me, desperate to explode and protect me.

I had to slow down…stamina, not speed. But everything already hurt so badly.

"Get up, you bitch," Pavi said. She stepped on my hands just like she had that first day. "That's for my back." She spat.

"You never belonged here," Naria said, leaning over me.

My heart pounded. Viktor's hips were hovering over mine, and as if we'd noticed at the same time, he slammed down on top of me, the move violently intimate. I gagged, both from the impact and the disgustingness of it.

"Maybe she's been staying because she cut a deal with the Ready," he said, grinding into me. "Are you giving it up for him? Alternating nights with Lord Grey?"

"Get. The. Fuck. Off," I spat. My legs kicked uselessly beneath him.

"Make me," he said, pushing down again. "Without power, without any strength…what else are you good for?"

I exploded. White hot fury like ice and fire pulsed through my veins, and I bucked, throwing him onto his back. Dizziness was like a cyclone spinning through me as I flipped onto my stomach. My head rolled to the side, but I somehow made it to a crouched position before I was slapped from behind and forced back onto all fours.

"How'd she do that?" one of the brutes asked.

I started crawling, but someone grabbed my legs and pulled them out from under me. My face slammed into the ground, and my chin scraped against it. More blood burst into my mouth. There was another kick to my ribs, and another, and someone was punching my back.

The rain fell freely now, and another round of lightning lit the sky, followed by thunder that doubled the rainfall.

Tears fell freely down my face as I was kicked. Again. And again. And again.

I wasn't going to last much longer. If Rhyan hadn't given me his power, I knew I'd already be unconscious. I was only awake because of it—but it wasn't enough. I had to get away.

I tried to roll free, to wrench my legs and hands out, but nothing was working. I had Rhyan's power running through my body, but it would burn through me soon.

Naria hauled me to my feet.

"Fight back, cousin," she snarled. "You're embarrassing us."

"It's your grace, you fucking traitor." I spat; blood landed on her cheek. There was a look of horror and disgust on her before she kneed me in the belly. I wheezed, doubling over. She slapped my back, then slapped it again as I desperately tried to breathe and recover from her hit.

I realized, even in my weakened state, she could have me. She could end me right here, but she wasn't. She was just slapping my back. Naria wasn't attacking me the way the others were, as if some unspoken familial bond was keeping her from doing her worst. If I could keep her angry, keep her distracted, I had a better chance of getting through this than if I faced the others.

"You're not going to survive here, you powerless wretch," she yelled. "Just give it up. Or you, too, will end up in Lethea. Just like—"

"Don't you dare speak her name, you daughter of a traitor! You'll never have what I have. And Tristan," I snarled. "I know what you tried with him. And you failed. He never fucking wanted you. I will always outrank you in every way —power or not."

Her face twisted into a grimace of hurt and anger. I'd hit too deep, but I'd meant to. How dare she bring up Jules now, in a habibellum?

"Fuck you," she said and handed me off to Viktor. "Do whatever you want to her."

He gripped my arms so tightly I knew I'd have bruises on them for weeks. He lifted me up, my toes just scraping the floor. My stomach twisted. I was going to be sick.

His eyes were black, soulless, his expression feral, so much like his father's, and the Bastardmaker's. "Tell me, Lady Asherah." He leaned in. "Ever thought about me when you're beneath Tristan?"

I kneed him in the groin. Viktor's eyes widened before he yowled in pain, his face turning red as he stumbled backwards, gripping me.

I landed on top of him, flipped over onto my back beside him, and got to my feet, running for the border of the five. If I could get to the silver circle, I could threaten them with its pain. But Pavi was already on top of me.

"You think your little trick will work on me?" The punches came lightning fast with the kicks, but suddenly, I was able to see clearly. Like before, I knew what to do. I knew when to duck, how to block. Rhyan had said fighting was half being aware of your surroundings and half choreography. I had both skills, and with his power backing me up, I was suddenly holding my own, keeping my ground, and sending my attackers back in a way I'd never thought possible before.

A minute passed, and then another. I could feel my power waning, the surge of Rhyan's energy and strength starting to burn through me. Still, I was defending myself, my space, my right to be here.

"Shekar Arkasva."

The words echoed through me. I stumbled, my foot sliding in the mud, my ankle—already injured from earlier—twisting further. I collapsed on the ground, mud caking the backs of my sandals and legs. Though my attackers were closing in on me, I searched the habibellum. Who had yelled it? Who had dared?

The move cost me. I was caught by Viktor's soturi and handed over to Pavi.

She grabbed my arms, wrenching them behind me as one of the brutes surged forward, arm swinging.

This was it. I was going to be knocked out.

I knew I had to use the full force of Rhyan's power. It was that or pass out.

With a primal scream, I broke free from Pavi and raced at the brute, staying along the circle's interior until I was behind him. I leapt onto his back, punching and kicking everything I could touch.

A horn blew, and lightning flashed.

The silver circles vanished across the field, one by one. I didn't wait, didn't hesitate.

As ours began to dissolve, I jumped from his back and ran, arms covering my face as insults were hurled behind me. I stumbled through one fight and then another. A hurricane churned inside me—ice and fire and rage and strength and Rhyan. It was all too much. Between the fighting and Ka Kormac and the Emartis…I was going to burn out. My flame was nearly extinguished.

"Hal! Haleika! Galen!" I screamed. "Hal!"

"Lyr!"

Haleika was across the field, running for me, brown curls flattened with rain to her head, mud splattered across her legs and shoes. Galen ran on her heels, holding his arm at his side like he'd been injured. Thunder clapped, and rain fell so heavily I couldn't see. Blue domes of light began to pop up around the field, each one catching the rain that fell, offering a reprieve to anyone fighting beneath it.

The small distraction cost me, and a Ka Kormac brute found me first, his teeth gnashing as his pudgy rain-soaked hands reached for me.

I was running out of strength, slipping in the muddying grass, my energy burning out. Haleika was racing toward me, but she wouldn't get to me in time. In one final push, I used the power inside of me to throw him off, crouching down and kicking his legs out from under him.

My vision went black. The pain of every hit, kick, punch, and scratch reverberated through me. Blearily, I saw Rhyan on the edge of the arena, his hand gripping the wall to hold himself up. His eyes were fixed on me, and he was yelling, roaring my name, but there was so much noise in my head I could barely hear him. He seemed suddenly so far away. Everyone did.

Haleika was screaming. Someone else shouted, "Emartis!"

Lyr! Rhyan's cry sounded in my head, our minds connected once more, just as the kashonim closed and our link severed. Silence filled my ears.

My world went black.

CHAPTER THIRTY-ONE

I SPUTTERED. WATER was in my mouth, rolling down my throat, splashing in my eyes, and rushing up my nose. Coughing and spitting, I rolled onto my side. Had the rain gotten that bad? I opened my eyes. The thunderstorm had ended; it'd stopped when I'd been passed out. Turion Dairen stood over me, an empty bucket swinging in his hand. Bastard.

"Missed part of the fight," he said.

"I…what?" I tried to look to the side, still coughing. My neck creaked. That was when the pain really hit me. With the kashomin out of my system, by the Gods, it was the worst feeling I'd ever had. I coughed again, nearly gagging, realizing mud—and blood—was in my mouth.

Blinding white light filled my vision, and I felt another cough but suppressed it. I couldn't take it, couldn't bear to move my ribs. My vision went in and out of focus. A sob wracked through my body. Pain unlike anything I'd felt before—worse than the nahashim burning their way through my body—pounded everywhere. Every muscle ached and stung. Tears fell down my cheeks freely. It hurt to breathe. Gods. It hurt so bad.

"Soturion Lyriana," Aemon said. "Stand."

Panic fluttered inside me. How? How could I stand when my body had been broken?

"Stand," he ordered. "Now," he said under his breath.

We were being watched. The Imperator was near. I had to obey.

Crying with every shift, every movement, every bit of pressure, I rolled fully onto my side, into a seat, and then somehow onto shaky legs—legs that nearly gave out beneath me. I stood and nearly fainted on the spot.

"Arkturion," I said, wiping at the disgusting taste in my mouth.

"Soturion," he said, "you missed the habibellum."

"Sorry, I was incapacitated."

"Yes," Turion Dairen said. "You passed out rather completely. Strange, when we don't allow for any contact to the head."

My eyes found Rhyan's across the arena. Did Dairen suspect us? Know what we'd done?

"I thought I lasted pretty long," I countered.

Dairen scoffed.

"I told you, Aemon," the Imperator said. "This is a waste of valuable resources. She missed the habibellum with her weakness, and I didn't see a single properly executed maneuver to escape the five or fight back. Her grace is just as powerless now as the girl she was weeks ago. What has she been doing for the past month?"

"She's been training. She's on the mat with me every single day and has never missed a class," Rhyan yelled. He was pale. The scar running through his left eye was red against his skin. I'd never seen him look so weak, like he was struggling just to stand. Sweat perspired around his forehead, and his hair curled at the ends. "She's doing her best."

"Her best?" asked the Imperator. "Considering what's at stake for her grace, I'd imagine she wouldn't be picking and choosing which parts of training she deigns to do."

"She's not," Rhyan shouted.

"By my reports, she knew nothing her first day—had not studied, had not prepared. She skipped her very first combat clinic. And tonight she was late. That does not sound to me like someone taking her training seriously. Nor does it sound like someone who's going to improve. We follow the chain of command here. And Lady Lyriana Batavia has not been following. She has disobeyed her Arkturion several times, a crime which demands punishment."

A hush of astonishment made a wave through the crowd— a watery mixture of fear and vindication. Storming over the wave was a whirl of energy, a hurricane of dark power emanating from Aemon as his face changed, his expression no longer angry but furious.

"End it now," the Imperator said. "She's not doing her part. Clearly."

"She will," Aemon snarled, "when she realizes what it means to truly be a soturion. Turion," he called to Dairen, "bring Soturion Lyriana to the pole."

Everything hollowed out inside of me. "No!" I shouted, my ears ringing. "No!"

"Arkturion!" Rhyan yelled. "You can't. She's injured."

"I can't? Would you like to be next, Soturion?"

"Sir," he said. "That's not what I meant."

"We follow the hierarchy of command," Aemon said. "Something you'd do well to remember. The Imperator is right. Soturion Lyriana missed her first combat clinic. She chose to disobey the command. She chose to arrive late tonight. And now she will suffer the consequences."

Dairen grabbed me around my waist, hauling my body across the field.

The shouts coming from the stadium seats—the howls of Kormac's wolves—rang in my ears, mixing with the jeers of my classmates. It all became one unbearable blur of noise.

I tried to push my sandals into the ground and stop Dairen from dragging me forward, but all my strength was gone, replaced by battered muscles and bones. Struggling against him hurt. He was holding me too tightly, his fingers pressing into sensitive bruises as he brought me before the pole.

It was impossibly tall and black, stretching into the night above me, promising punishment and pain.

Dairen pulled me forward. I felt the exhaustion consuming me, my consciousness fading as my body attempted to manage my injuries. He pressed me against the pole, which was shockingly hot and dry, having absorbed heat from the fires of the arena. He lifted my arms just like he had Pavi's, securing the rope around my wrists, then pulled them up so high I stumbled forward, my chest smashing into the rounded metal as I tried to find balance on my toes.

"POLE! POLE! POLE!" The shouts grew louder, and with them, so did my panic.

My body started to shake. Every part of me hurt. I was having trouble breathing, tied up like I was, like an animal, with over five hundred wolves from Korteria howling at me.

"Aemon!" Tears fell freely down my face. I'd seen what this had done to Pavi, and she had magic in her body. "Aemon, please!"

He was already by my side, eyebrows drawn tightly together. "I'm sorry," he said quietly. "If there was any other way, I'd take it. But there isn't. They came here for this. They were waiting. Lyr, you sealed your fate being late and with that one skip. They knew. I have no choice. You have to be punished."

"Aemon," I sobbed. "Please. I'm sorry. I'm so sorry. I'll never do it again."

"No," he said, his voice deadly calm. "You won't. Not after this."

"Aemon! Don't!"

"If I don't do this, he will end the deal," he hissed. "Do you understand?" Loudly, he announced to the arena, "Soturion Lyriana has been sentenced to three lashes for disobeying orders."

He turned from me as tears fell down my cheeks. The soturi in the stands cheered.

"Arkturion," Rhyan called out. He was slowly moving towards us, his face still red, his body slick with sweat and rain. "She's barely standing. I understand she deserves punishment. Not like this. Wait. Let her recover." Rhyan stood back, something aloof and cold in his expression.

"She'd be standing if she'd completed her training like everyone else," the Imperator said. "You'd do well to make sure she does so." He gave Rhyan an appraising look, a snarl curling his lips. "Were you in a fight yourself, forsworn? You look…quite depleted."

I stilled.

Rhyan rolled his eyes, folding his arms over his chest. His head rolled back just for a second, but then he straightened, looking like the consummately cruel and bored high lord everybody believed he had been destined to be before turning forsworn. I wasn't fooled. He was ready to fall over, clinging to the dregs of energy inside of him.

"No fights tonight, your highness," he said, voice laced with cocky confidence. He turned back to Aemon. "As for her grace, I know the rules. But I, for one, would rather not train a corpse tomorrow." He sounded bored and was making an effort to appear dismissive, but there was an unmistakable edge to his voice, his northern lilt like an undercurrent of anger.

The Ready glared. "You will train her in any condition she appears in. Question me again? You'll be up here. You were already lax in making sure she attended clinic."

The Bastardmaker snarled. "Looks like her grace will finally earn her stripes today."

Rhyan stood behind the pole, positioning his face directly in front of mine. His green eyes were wide, his nostrils flared, and jaw clenched as his hands balled into fists, a silent fury coursing through him. The fear I'd seen in his eyes had returned. Something like a soft kiss of wind blew toward me, mere remnants of what remained of Rhyan's power.

Turion Dairen moved behind me. My heart pounded. He reached for the ties on the back of my tunic as convulsions wracked through my body.

"No, Turion," Aemon cut in.

For the barest moment, I let hope return. I wouldn't be lashed. I started to exhale.

Aemon stepped in front of me, the whip in his hand. "I'll do it."

I looked up, barely believing what I was hearing. The Ready's eyes darkened, and Rhyan's mouth fell open, one eyebrow raised in shock. Aemon never did the lashings. That was a Second's job. The idea of Aemon doing that to me... he'd practically raised me in Cresthaven, he'd been like a second father.

No, no, no, no.

My forehead fell against the pole. I squeezed my eyes shut. It was like Tristan pointing his stave at me all over again. Aemon had even said the exact same words: *I'll do it.*

He stood behind me, his anger pulsing violently like a storm cloud. I was barely hanging onto consciousness, barely able to breathe, as he reached for the pull of my tunic.

I tensed. There was a loud rip, and at the same instant an icy breeze brushed against my bared back. The sides of my tunic hung loosely on either side of me.

The crowd roared; their voices full of bloodlust.

I swallowed hard despite a dry throat, aware that I was openly crying, that my entire body was shaking like a wild animal's. I was suddenly so cold, shivering uncontrollably.

Humiliation and fear swam through my blood. The indignity and exposure—it was insufferable.

"Three lashes," Aemon called again.

I sucked in my breath, tremors exploding up and down my arms. My fear was growing, and I was freezing under its force.

Shock. I was going into shock.

Some small part of my brain remembered the same thing had happened after we'd gotten the news that Jules had died. My body had frozen, and I'd just...stopped. I hadn't moved again for three days. Only Meera's screams had pulled me out. It had happened again just this morning, on this very field.

"Deep breath, Lyr," Rhyan said. He teetered on his feet, looking ready to fall over, and yet, his hands were balling into fists, shaking at his sides. "It'll be fast. Over before you know it."

The Imperator gave him a sharp look. The ropes dug into my wrists, and my arms, already battered and bruised, felt a fresh, stabbing pain from being tied up too tightly.

"I'm right here," Rhyan said, his voice low. "Don't look at him, don't look at anything else. Look right here. Eyes on me."

"ONE!" Aemon yelled.

My eyes squeezed shut. I could hear the vibration of the whip as its echoing lash pierced the wind to strike me. On contact, I gasped, making some unintelligible, animal-like sound, a noise that shouldn't have been able to come from my mouth. A feeling like a thousand daggers slicing through me exploded over my skin, each one burning like fire. I'd been punched and kicked where the whip hit, and now the fire and pain and torment of it all tore through me. Distantly, the crowd whooped and cheered. Howls called and responded across the arena as wind blew through the hundreds of torchlights above my head.

Sweat and dirt rushed down my forehead and into my eyes faster than my tears could clear them. I screwed them shut. Something was wet on my back, sliding down to my waist.

Blood. I was bleeding. Aemon had torn me open on the first try.

"TWO!"

The second lash came faster, and I coughed up blood as fire blazed across my back. I screamed, not recognizing my own voice, unable to control myself.

My knees buckled, unable to withstand further pain. My body hadn't been designed for this. My back had been torn open and torched with what felt like flames. I was going to faint. The sides of my tunic, what remained of it, were dampened with sweat, and fresh blood dripped in thick rivulets down my spine, creating a river that pooled in the small of my back. Several drops fell and splattered between my feet.

"Last one, Lyr," Rhyan said. His voice was low, his northern lilt even more pronounced. "One more. Just one more."

Tears ran down my cheeks. Humiliation and terror and pain all became one hideous monster that dug its razor-sharp claws into my body and devoured me. I shook, knowing the third lash was coming, knowing this was the one that might break me, might rip me in two. Before I could prepare, Aemon shouted, "THREE!"

I screamed, blood spurting from my back, landing in fat droplets down my legs, and pooling between my feet. I was going to be sick. I was going to faint.

"Release her," Rhyan demanded.

Aemon snarled in response to being given an order, but he was already reaching for my arms when the Imperator stepped forward.

"Aemon," he drawled, a finger pressed against his chin in thought. "I do not see sorrow or repentance on her face. She will disobey if not properly punished. I think a fourth lash is in order."

"No!" Rhyan released an anguished cry.

"Aemon," I sobbed. "I...I can't...p-please. I am sorry. I am...." I wanted to say repentant, but even that was too much for me.

Aemon was breathing heavily, his eyes wild with rage. He spit onto the ground, right at the Imperator's feet, then stepped back and adjusted the whip in his hand. His aura swirled, dark and heavy, mixing with the cunning victory of the Imperator. There was a collective inhale of breath around me in anticipation.

"No. Aemon."

Humming filled the air again—the sound of a whip flying.

The Imperator's black eyes burned into me as the Bastardmaker licked his lips.

The humming grew in volume, in intensity. It ended in a spine-cracking snap.

CHAPTER THIRTY-TWO

THERE WAS A roaring in my head, and my vision sparked with white lights. Blood rushed down my arms as they slammed into my sides like deadweights. I stumbled forward, crashed into the burning hot pole, and pushed myself away, stumbling to the side to collapse on all fours. A scream of pain wracked through me, the sound blaring in my ears. I couldn't tell if the sound was solely in my head or if it had left my mouth as well.

I was in so much pain, I'd gone beyond caring. A storm was thrashing inside of me, and my arms gave out as blood slid down them, mixing with the dirt, the mud, and the rain. I fell forward, my nose crunching against the ground. I barely turned my head in time to puke some horrid mixture of blood and bile and whatever the fuck I'd eaten for breakfast half a lifetime ago. I was screaming again, tears burning down my cheeks. My stomach was on fire, twisting, pinching, and pulling until I threw up again, my bruised ribcage screaming in protest.

A hand pressed against the nape of my neck, strong fingers pushing into the tops of my shoulders, soothing me.

Rhyan.

I retched as his other hand reached for my forehead, pulling back the loose strands of hair. His palm remained there, flat and cool against my skin, a calming presence. What remained of his power he cast toward me from his aura, a cool breeze against my burning hot skin. Still, I screamed and cried and threw up more bile even as he held me, and continued sending soft cooling winds against my hair and face.

"I've got you," he said. "It's all right. It's over now."

"Can you stand?" Aemon asked, his voice lowered to a whisper. "Lyriana. Lyr! You must stand." He jerked his chin at Rhyan. "Get her up."

There was a burst of Rhyan's aura, burning ice. Rage, and fury carried on a wind so powerful, Aemon braced himself. And then just as quickly as it began, the ice stopped. Aemon glared at Rhyan, his lips pulled back into a sneer. Rhyan's nostrils flared, but he nodded back to his Arkturion in submission.

Strong arms wrapped around me, firm but gentle, and I was lifted to my feet. Rhyan's hands were firm on my waist, avoiding my back. Rhyan bore my weight with his arms, carrying me even as my feet touched the ground. How was he doing that? How after he had no remaining strength of his own. And part of my guard or not, I didn't understand why he was still here with me. Every second he stood before the Imperator and Aemon, pale and weakened, he risked getting himself in trouble again.

Rhyan started to move back, but I wasn't ready to stand on my own, I was too weak, too hurt. He pressed his hands to me again, palms against my hips. My head rolled back, but something in Aemon's voice, a concern and a command, had me standing straighter, my feet flattened, pins pinching the soles as my legs grudgingly accepted weight.

"Stand, your grace. Leave her," Aemon ordered Rhyan. "She will do this. She must do this."

Rhyan stepped away, but his hand, large and steady, pressed against my lower back. I leaned into him, desperate for the support, needing something, someone, to hold me up. Slowly, he pulled his palm back until only his fingers supported me, allowing me to find my balance.

Aemon nodded. He jerked his chin again, pointing at Rhyan. The message was clear.

I needed to do this on my own. Like a soturion.

"Satisfied?" the Ready asked, snarling at the Imperator. His expression was that of a Death God's. One wrong move, and he'd kill.

"Her grace has proven nothing but her utter disdain for our rules and our ways," the Imperator said, sweeping his black cloak over his shoulder. The golden threads glowed under the firelight. "I'm not willing to allow this experiment to languish one second longer than is necessary. The Emperor is to visit Bamaria this winter for Valyati. Her grace will be tested then. She'd better make her remaining time count."

Valyati. Winter Solstice. Less than three months away. Three months! He'd just cut my remaining time in half—time I needed to prepare and find answers. It was gone, just like that, because he could take it. He'd never intended to honor his side of the deal.

I was vaguely aware of the commotion around me—my classmates yelling and jeering, satisfied I'd gotten my due. Pavi looked exceptionally pleased, as did Naria.

There was a cold breeze in the air, a sudden dampness that chilled my bones. It would rain again soon.

I knew Aemon had ended the clinic and dismissed everyone from the arena, but I remained by the pole, barely standing, barely conscious of my surroundings.

"Get her out of here," Aemon barked at Rhyan. "Clean her up."

"Yes, Arkturion."

"Your grace," Aemon said, voice lowered, concern clouding his eyes. He grimaced but looked more like the Aemon I'd known as a girl, the one who'd always watched over me—an extra uncle at Cresthaven. "You're never to end up here again."

I either nodded, or my head was bobbing. Aemon turned in dismissal. I felt a hand on the nape of my neck again, guiding me, directing me forward. It moved softly, gently, to the small of my back—the one place I wasn't injured.

"I've got you, Lyr, I'm going to take care of you. You'll be all right," Rhyan said.

My classmates filed out the arena doors, watching me as I walked. After what seemed like an eternity, my body screaming with every step I took, we reached the edge of the arena's field, and Rhyan opened a door, directing me inside the Katurium. The halls were lit with torchlight, too bright for my eyes. I wavered, my stomach twisting again, my head light and heavy all at once. I wasn't going to make it back to my apartment. I was barely going to make it to the end of this hall. Rhyan turned suddenly, leading me down an abandoned hallway.

"Where...?" I started to ask, my voice croaking, before he guided me to a small table.

"Put your hands here," he said, placing them on the tabletop for me. He ran his hands down my arms, squeezing my wrists before stepping away. "I need to cover your back."

Right, my back was exposed, my tunic hanging off my shoulders—no, my back, the actual skin of my back was opened...bloodied.... Drops of blood on the floor trailed down the hall. I swayed at the sight.

"Hold on to the table," he said. "Just for a minute while I grab supplies. I'll be fast."

I squeezed my eyes shut and burst into tears all over again. Rhyan was there one second, then he was gone. I was losing track of my surroundings, losing track of time. He seemed to instantly reappear down the hall with a large bag slung over his shoulder.

"Got them," he said. "Just stand a minute longer. All right? I'll clean you up more when we get home. But I need to take your tunic off, Lyr. Is that all right?"

I made some barely intelligible sound in response, but it was enough.

Rhyan's hands were on my shoulders, sliding off the remains of the fabric that covered my arms. He pulled the tunic down past my waist, letting it pool around my feet on the floor. Behind me, I could sense him bending to his knees, slowly lifting my feet, one at a time, to step out of my clothing, while supporting me with his body weight. Then he rose and reached in front of me, hands sliding between my arms with the ends of a large white cloth that he tied in a knot beneath my breasts. He'd covered the wounds on my back. The cloth wasn't tight, not attempting to staunch the wounds...that wasn't possible, not when they were the result of a magically infused soturion whip. But the cloth would keep me from bleeding all over myself and getting an infection.

I swayed a little. My vision went out of focus again.

"I've got you." A strong arm reached across my shoulders, and another swept under my knees as he lifted me into his arms. My head fell against his chest. His heart beat next to my ear, the thrum loud and steady. His scent enveloped me— musky, woodsy. I pressed my face against his chest. "Hey, partner...stay with me." His arms tightened around me. "Lyr? Lyr, stay awake for me. Just a little longer."

My eyes closed.

When I opened them, I was lying on my belly on a bed. But it was not mine.

"Where am I?"

"My place," Rhyan said, looking uneasy.

"How long—?"

"Not even fifteen minutes." His jaw tensed. "I'm going to get you cleaned up. Just relax."

I let my head fall down on his pillow. It smelled like him, that unique scent of musk and trees. I felt dizzy lying there and looked down at his sheets. I was getting blood everywhere. I tried to push myself up onto my elbows, but Rhyan was immediately by my side.

"Don't move," he said.

"Your sheets," I said weakly.

Rhyan shrugged. "Just blood. It'll wash out. Try not to move until I get you patched up." He sat beside me. "First, I need to remove the bandage on your back."

"The what?" I asked.

"The bandage. The one I tied around you in the hallway," he said.

My mind raced. Gods. He'd removed my tunic...tied a bandage around me to protect my back...because it had been splayed open.

I inhaled sharply, fear suddenly overwhelming me. The scars, the bruises, the hurts I carried from two years of Meera's visions....

No. Every scar on my back, every bruise, could be explained from tonight, from the lashing. But still...still I felt the panic rise inside me. I felt the scar on my wrist flame with fire.

Remember your oath. Remember, or suffer the consequences.

He'd started to guess earlier. He'd seen the evidence of Meera's punch to my face and the limp I'd gotten running to her, and he'd blamed Tristan. I squeezed my eyes shut.

"Is that all right?" Rhyan asked. "Taking off the bandage?"

"Um," I said, my chest tightening.

"I'll be as gentle as I can. Promise. I've...had to treat these sorts of wounds before."

"Rhyan, I…." I trailed off, panicking. What was I going to say? Please don't treat my wounds. Let me do it myself. Also, forget what you saw earlier. He wouldn't. And I couldn't do this on my own. I could barely move. I was probably seconds away from passing out again.

"You're going to be all right," he said. "You're safe with me now. It's over." He slid off the bed, crouching next to it so his face was just inches from mine. "I'm sorry. So sorry I couldn't stop that from happening to you. I wish I could have." He shook his head, swallowing roughly. "I won't let anything or anyone else hurt you tonight. I swear."

I sniffled, terrified, my body shaking and convulsing uncontrollably. But I nodded.

His jaw clenched, and one hand reached forward. His fingers pushed my hair off my face, smoothing it behind my ear. "I have some moonleaf candles I can light. They might help."

I winced, a sharp pain running through my head. "Do you have the leaves?" I asked. "If you burn them, they work faster." I'd learned this trick to help soothe Morgana's headaches.

One eyebrow lifted in surprise, but he nodded and moved through the room, gathering the leaves and lighting them in a bowl. The scent immediately filled the air, and I relaxed. A little.

The mattress dipped beside me as Rhyan sat back down.

"Lyr," he said. "Tell me honestly. Should I get someone else here to be with you? Do you want Lord Tristan?"

"No," I whispered.

His expression tightened, his mind no doubt on his earlier accusation.

"I want you," I said.

He nodded, his jaw muscles working.

"It's not what you think. Not because he hurt me. I…I can't explain now…it all hurts."

"I know. I'm going to do something about that. I'm taking the bandage off now." His hands were light on my back, then slowly they slid underneath me to my belly.

I sucked in a breath as his fingers found the knot he'd made beneath my breasts. His knuckles brushed against them accidentally. He froze.

"Sorry," he said. "Can you lift yourself up? Just for a second."

I swallowed and propped myself up on my elbows, a pained moan escaping my lips.

"Perfect." He deftly untied the knot and pulled the bandage free. "Lie down."

My chest crashed back onto the bed; the energy it had taken to hold myself up for even a second was almost more than I had. Rhyan tossed the cloth bandage on the ground.

It was soaked in blood.

I screwed my eyes shut, burying my face in his pillows.

"Can I take this off?" he asked, his hands on the bindings for my breasts. It was already loose and falling off of me.

There was a flare of heat in my wrist. The half-shift holding my breasts was the final barrier between me and any old scars I carried from Meera, the evidence of the secret I kept. My body began to shake. Panic flared anew within me.

"It's all right," he said. "You're safe with me."

"Yes."

Gently, he undid the remaining ties and slid that off as well, and my entire back was bared to him.

"And this?" he asked. A hand with fingers full of calluses slid down my arm. He stopped right over the golden cuff I always wore. "Can I remove this?"

"No!" I said quickly. "That stays."

"I'll work around it," he said.

He pressed a cool wet cloth against my skin. Rhyan moved it slowly, gently, mopping up the blood across my back.

"You're all clean," he said. "But I need to prevent infection. This might sting a little."

"Are you on duty now?" I asked through gritted teeth. He ran the cleansing ointment over my back. He was wrong. It stung a lot, even with the scent of moonleaves smoking through the room. I buried my face in his pillow to keep from screaming.

"No. I'm here because I want to be." He added some more oil, and I made a sharp, pained sound. "Sorry." He leaned forward, his chest pressing against me from behind, and dropped something fluffy by my head. "Here's another pillow. Squeeze it when it hurts."

I did. And I bit down on the one beneath my head. "Fuck."

"That's the last of it," he said softly. "The sunleaves will soothe the stinging." Rhyan was quiet for a minute, switching to rubbing the paste onto my back. "Why does it matter if I'm here on duty or not?" he asked.

I turned my head, looking over my shoulder at him. "It matters."

Another moment passed as he chewed on the corner of his lip. "Why?"

I frowned. "Because...I thought we were friends. And then you stopped speaking to me."

One eyebrow furrowed. "I've never gone a day without speaking to you."

I groaned. "Talking that wasn't just you teaching me."

He shook his head. "Even on the brink of death, you're trying to have word debates. I'm going to set the bandages now," he said. "Are you a stomach sleeper?"

"What? Um...I guess so, sometimes...." I laid my head back down. I was too tired to try and hold it up.

"You need to sleep on your stomach tonight." His hands were on my back again, smoothing out the bandages. "Lyr," he said quietly. His hands ran up my back over my shoulders, paused, then pulled away. "I have been quiet with you. And I'm sorry. It's not...not that I didn't want to speak to you."

"You were mad?" I asked. "Because of what I said?"

"No, I forgave you. You were in pain that night. Talking to you...." He sighed. "Talking to you is my favorite thing about being in Bamaria. But...I had to stop. It was for the best. Please, believe me." Rhyan slid off the side of the bed and crouched down beside me, his face inches from mine again. He reached forward, pushing another loose wave behind my ear. "How do you feel?"

I sniffled. "Like I had the shit kicked out of me and got whipped." A solid tear escaped my eye.

"I know." He nodded. "You're staying here tonight so I can watch over you. Make sure you don't roll onto your back or spike a fever in your sleep."

My brain immediately threw a hundred thoughts at me. I couldn't spend the night in Rhyan's bedroom. I was half naked, in his bed.... Plus, I needed to check on Meera and Morgana. And I needed to be back in my own apartment in case anyone came looking for me, like Tristan.

But I was so tired. I couldn't bear the thought of moving, and Rhyan's bed was so comfortable and smelled so good....

"Before you close your eyes," he said, "drink this. It has moonleaf oil. It will help you sleep." He helped me sit up, leaning my body against his, just long enough for me to take a few sips from a silver flask. It was a similar brew to what I made Meera and Morgana but stronger. And spicier. The effect was almost immediate, the pain ebbing and my body relaxing. While I sat, leaning against him, he worked meticulously to remove the sheets I'd bled on from beneath me. Shifting me onto his lap, my head cradled against his neck, he placed a clean one on top of his mattress. I lay back down as he capped the flask and placed it on a small table.

"You only have one bed," I said, settling back onto my stomach. The sheets smelled clean, but still like Rhyan.

"Congratulations. Your math skills are well intact."

I rolled my eyes, or at least I thought I did. "Where will you sleep?" I asked drowsily.

The corner of his mouth lifted. "Same place I did when I watched over you in prison," he said. "On the floor. If you need anything, I'm right here."

Blearily, I reached out and took his hand. He was still sitting beside me. His fingers immediately entwined with mine.

"I'm sorry," I said. "I'm sorry I lied to you...and...."

"Shhhh." He squeezed my hand. "You don't need to apologize. Not tonight. Plus, I'm sorry, too." He loosely draped a blanket over me and tucked the ends beneath my arms. "I am...sorry I let...let things be the way they were the last month."

"You asked if you could kiss me," I said suddenly, the words slipping out of my mouth before I could think.

"What?"

"Under the stars...in the trees." I was already losing consciousness, but the way he'd asked for consent every step of the way tonight as he'd healed me, it reminded me, brought me back to that first kiss—the first time he'd asked for permission.

I want to kiss you. Can I?

"Summer Solstice?" he asked, his fingers tightening against mine.

"We danced," I said. "And you asked to kiss me."

He stared back at me, one eyebrow lifted. "I did," he said, a small smile spreading across his face. "And you said yes."

"I said yes." A small smile spread across my face.

He leaned forward, his face mere inches from mine, a conspiratorial spark in his eyes. "I did call you lover that day."

I sucked in a breath, my lips suddenly aching for his. He moved in, or maybe I moved, and then his lips hovered just above mine. I could feel it, feel the energy between us, feel his aura cocooning, caressing me. My lips were vibrating with it, tingling the way it had after we'd kissed those three years ago. I closed my eyes, his musk and pine scent intoxicating, his breathing heavy. His forehead pressed against mine, his skin warm and soothing. It wasn't a kiss. It was something else. My breathing was his breathing, and there was just the barest, gentlest brush of his lips against mine.

And then he pulled back. My eyes shot open, my lips almost in pain from the loss as he shifted away from me.

"Lyr." He shook his head, swallowing roughly. "We can't."

My stomach dropped. "Because you're my guard," I said, half-attempting to convince myself he was right.

"Yes."

"And because you're my apprentice."

His eyes darkened. "That we can never forget." His jaw muscle flexed. "And because you're not free to be with me. Because you deserve better than a forsworn."

"Rhyan...."

He released my hand. "Because three years later, I still feel the taste of your lips on mine. Because I can't forget you, the way your body felt against mine, the way your scent wrapped around me. Because I think about that kiss all the time. Because I dream about you at night. Because, if I kiss you now, if I get one more taste, you'll consume me."

He shook his head again. "That was why I stopped talking to you. Why I—it doesn't matter. Forget I said anything. It's not your problem. You just need to recover, to feel better."

And then his lips were on my forehead, pressing the softest kiss against my skin. "Sleep." He blew out the candles, his bedroom darkening with only the faint scent of smoke in the air.

CHAPTER THIRTY-THREE

RHYAN'S HAND WAS on my forehead, right where he'd kissed me, when I woke.

The sun wasn't up yet. Only a small candle on a corner table offered light. Embers flared from the remaining ashes of moonleaves smoking in a bowl.

"Hey there, partner," he said. "How do you feel?"

"Like death." I leaned into his hand. I had a raging headache, and the pressure was soothing.

"You were thrashing," he said. "And you spiked a fever, but I think it's already breaking. I've been giving you cold compresses, and...using my aura to keep you cool."

"I'm sweating," I said weakly, feeling the moisture on my forehead and the back of my neck. Even the pillow beneath my face felt damp.

"That's good."

I turned on my side, and for a second, a bout of nausea hit me. I sat up, the blanket slipping from my shoulders. Just as quickly, the sensation released, leaving me with the realization that my breasts were completely exposed right in front of Rhyan.

He pulled the covers back over me. "I didn't see anything."

"That's exactly what people say when they saw something," I moaned. I pressed my palm to my temple, my whole head pounding.

"Swear to Auriel." He pressed a hand to his heart but also pulled the blankets even higher over my shoulder, his jaw tight. "Listen, we need to get you back to your room before sunrise. Before we're seen."

"How much trouble will we be in for this?"

"We didn't do anything we shouldn't have," he said carefully.

No, we just talked about kissing, and almost…. My fingers brushed against my lips, still sensing the almost feel of his.

"It's expected for an apprentice to care for their wounded novice," he said. "But with us, well, there's been a lot of attention on you, and I think it's better if you don't have anyone see you quite so injured. Not yet."

"What time is it?" There was no light coming through his window.

"Almost five in the morning."

"You're right." Keeping the covers tight around me this time, I started to sit up again, moving gingerly. My head swam. "Gods."

"Lay back down, Lyr. You're in no condition to walk."

"So how exactly am I supposed to leave?" I turned back to my stomach, letting it sink into the mattress.

"Me. I'll carry you. I'll do all the work. You just keep resting."

"Because I need to be ready for training?" I closed my eyes, the idea of physical movement, of stepping foot back inside the Katurium, making me physically sick.

"Because you need to heal. Stay on your belly. I'll get you something to wear."

Within seconds, I fell asleep again. I woke to Rhyan pulling a tunic over my head. Gently, he lifted one arm, then the other, sliding them through the sleeves.

"How did you learn to dress unconscious people?" I asked into the pillow.

He let out a huff of amusement. "My best friend, Dario. Often finds himself with a great need to drink more than everyone else and remain unconscious when he should be getting up for training." He sat down beside me. "Ready?"

I reached up between the press of the bed against my torso for the hem of the tunic bunched around my collarbone and pulled it down my belly. "Ready."

"All right, partner, onto your side, up you go."

I turned over, and Rhyan scooped me into his arms. Weakly, I wrapped my arm around his neck, my head falling against his chest as he stood. The motion left me dizzy. And impressed. How did he still have strength left? He hadn't been hurt, but he'd torn through all his energy stores, giving them to me, and then he'd cared for me all night, even using what was left in his aura to freeze out my fever. He blew out the candles as he passed them. A tug of nausea pulled in my stomach, and I clenched my eyes shut, breathing deeply through my nose. I couldn't get sick again, not in his arms.

Rhyan headed for the door, and somewhere in the hall of his apartment building, I passed out again. I woke to my apartment door unlocking. There was a loud click, and we were inside. But we weren't alone.

The entire place had been lit up—there were candles and floating torches everywhere. Even floating amethysts had been spelled to light up the way they did in the Great Library.

"Aren't you two cozy?"

I startled, nearly falling out of Rhyan's hold.

Lounging on my couch, his feet propped up against the arm, was the Afeya, Mercurial. His blue skin had taken on a warmer hue than before, more of a midnight color against the flames.

"What are you doing here?" Rhyan asked, backing over the threshold.

"Ah, ah, ah," Mercurial scolded. He swept his silken black hair over his shoulder, gathering the gleaming locks into sections that he began to braid. "I wouldn't go out there into the hall, not with the sun so close to rising. Soturi waking from their beds, stumbling to use the bathing chambers, seeing our forsworn apprentice and his novice entangled in each other's arms after a night alone together. Most forbidden."

I could feel Rhyan tensing against me, standing straighter and holding his ground.

"Come back in here," Mercurial crooned. "You know I'm right. Plus, it's so warm."

As if on cue or perhaps some machinations of the Afeyan, a door opened down the hall, the sound of it followed by muffled, sleepy voices.

Rhyan stumbled forward, and my front door slammed shut behind us.

"Much better," Mercurial drawled. "Welcome to the party."

"Put me down," I said, heart pounding. I couldn't face Mercurial like this. Even weakened, I needed to be on my own two feet.

Rhyan released his hold on me at once, setting me down. I stumbled, dizzy and disoriented. It took me a moment to find my balance. The brew he'd given me was starting to wear off, and a fresh bout of pain, sharp and biting in my back, elicited a gasp.

"Her grace looks like she is in desperate need of her bed. I believe she was in desperate need of it all night. But, based on the fact that I see from it here it is empty—how scandalous." His lips formed an exaggerated "O" shape, and his eyes widened before he slapped his hand over his mouth. "I think we can safely assume that the Lady Lyriana Batavia did not see her own bed tonight."

"She's hurt," Rhyan snarled. "And you shouldn't be in here."

"Shouldn't I?" he asked. He wiggled his nose, and green vines formed within the braid he'd created, tying themselves off at the end. Red flowers bloomed across the vine, shining against his black hair. "It seems you both are in need. And I have a great ability to satisfy such...cravings."

"We'll alert Arkturion Aemon you've trespassed," Rhyan said. "It's one thing to approach us in temple. But this is her grace's private apartment. Get out. Now."

"So rude," Mercurial said, snaking his hips as he stood. He sauntered over to me, running his fingers over the arm of the tunic I wore—Rhyan's tunic, at least three sizes too big for me.

"What a fashion statement," Mercurial crooned. "Did this come from the private collection of Lord Rhyan Hart?"

"Still not a lord," Rhyan seethed.

"My mistake. Did this come from the private collection of his not-lord?" Mercurial stepped in front of Rhyan, close enough that their noses nearly touched. "Any in my size?"

Rhyan shook his head, rolling his shoulders back, but he held the Afeya's stare. "Arkturion Aemon will be hearing about this."

Mercurial burst into laughter, the sound just as hypnotic and bell-like as it had been that first time in the temple. "I expect he will. But I am here right now. Let us have a little chat. My dear, Lady Lyriana. What do you know of the Afeya?"

I swallowed. This was a trick. He was trying to lure me into asking him a question, into making a deal. Rhyan caught my eye, shaking his head ever so slightly.

My eyes met the Afeyan's. His were dark, hypnotic. I swayed a little on the spot, grabbing for a side table, blinking until my head was clear. "I know what I need to know," I said carefully.

A wide, feline-like smile spread across Mercurial's face. "Then you'll know that I am only here with great interest.

And great purpose."

"Or you think her grace is desperate enough to fall for this." Rhyan stepped forward, angling his body in front of mine.

"Been to the library lately?" Mercurial drawled. "I brought some of their lights here for you. In case you've missed them."

"Seems like you already know the answer to your own question. I found their selection not to my satisfaction on my previous visit." He had the scroll I wanted, Sianna's second scroll of writings, the only known recounting of a Lumerian without power. He had planted *The Fall of Asherah and Her Loss of Power* with Ramia just to toy with me, just to make me desperate enough to ask him a question, to strike a deal.

"Thank you for coming to see me," I said. "But I really must rest now. Please, let me know in advance before your next visit, so I can...unlock the front door."

"You've always had a quick wit. But I'd expect no less from you, from who you are, who you were, and who you might turn out to be."

I bit my lip, squeezing my hands into fists at my side.

"Oh, you want to know what I mean?" he asked, his voice dripping with sugary sweetness.

"She hasn't asked you a single question," Rhyan said.

Mercurial rolled his eyes, tapping his shoulders as he sauntered toward me. "But she wants to. I can smell it." The Afeyan's eyes sparkled. "Taste it. Luckily, I'm in a generous mood. This is for free." He waved his hand at me. The pinch in my ankle vanished.

I shook my head, my pulse spiking. He couldn't do magic on his own free will. And Afeya didn't offer freebies. They couldn't. Their magic only worked when commanded. Who was he working for? How had healing my ankle served them?

"Better?" he asked.

"Yes, thank you."

Mercurial shrugged. "We can't have you limping like that. Not when you are, who you are. And I know you won't ask...rules of conduct and all that, so I'll ask for you. What do I mean? What is Mercurial trying to say? Well, what if I told you, your grace, that you were the most powerful soturion in history?"

I shifted my weight uneasily between my feet. He really had healed me. But I wasn't going to play his game. "I have no interest in being the most powerful soturion in history."

A chuckle escaped his lips. "I didn't say I'd make you one. I said you were one."

"We're done here," Rhyan said. He still wore his armor from last night and had strapped his sword to his belt before carrying me out. Now his hand rested on its hilt, his reddened fingers closing around it.

Mercurial's eyes narrowed. "So, it's like that. Good morning, then, my not-lord. Your grace."

My door flung open, but Mercurial vanished into thin air. With him went the amethyst lights and the candles, each one burning out and disappearing until my apartment darkened, barely lit by the rising sun. A second later, the door slammed shut.

I clutched my chest, breathing heavily, then stumbled into my bedroom for the bed, falling face-first into it.

"Lyr," Rhyan was right beside me, smoothing back my hair, resting his palm on my forehead. "Myself to Moriel. I'm going right to Aemon about this. How could he get in here?"

I shook my head. "You got rid of him fast when he suggested I was the strongest soturion."

Rhyan smirked. "If you're the strongest soturion in history, what does that make me?" he asked.

"Second," I groaned. "Obviously."

He smiled. "Just remember, he's dangerous. Don't let him get in your head." He released his hold on my forehead, smoothing his palm back over my hair. "Not hot anymore," he said. "But you still need to rest."

"I'm supposed to be in the arena in two hours. Pavi didn't miss any training after she was lashed. The Imperator will probably cut my remaining time in half again if I miss or I'm late."

Rhyan sighed. "Just rest now as long as possible. You'll go to the run and do the best you can, sit through your classes, and then when you get to training…we'll take a break."

I didn't know if Mercurial had done more than heal the pinch in my ankle, but two hours later, I was back on the field, staring at the pole in the morning sun, alive and awake. I was still severely injured, and my back was still on fire, but merely hours before I hadn't been able to stand, so I was taking this as a major victory.

Nameless soturi passing by me called out, yelling to me about the lashings, the sounds I'd made…I ignored them all.

I shuffled my way around the track. I was slower than I had been the first day, but I was still here, and if I had three months left, I was going to make them count. I wouldn't let the Imperator find one more excuse to use against me.

By the time I reached our training room after lunch, I was ready to pass out.

Rhyan walked in slowly, closing the door behind him before he crouched down before me, settling his bag on the floor.

"How are you?"

I swallowed. "I feel like shit."

"Lyr," he said, going still as his eyes ran back and forth across my face. "What happened last night?"

I glared, unsure where he was going with this. Were we going to have this conversation now? About almost kissing? About his confession to me? About the way I wanted to confess my feelings to him? "After the arena?" I asked nervously.

"No," he said. "I mean…what happened before you arrived?" His hand reached for my face, his calloused fingers brushing gently against my cheek. "You have a black eye. And a cut on your cheek. And before Mercurial healed you, you were limping. Not from the habibellum. Not from being lashed. You had these injuries before you entered the Katurium"

I sucked in a breath.

"Lyr, you can tell me. Was it…did Tristan hurt you?"

My hand instinctively covered my wrist, squeezing against the scars. "I already told you."

He shook his head. "Please, just…I want to help. You can trust me."

"Let's just train," I said.

"Fine." He opened his bag and removed cured sunleaves, moon oil, and freshly cut pieces of white cloth. "I need to change your bandages."

My skin prickled, my wrist burned, and an itch ran from the blood oath scars on my wrist all the way up to my elbow.

"No," I said automatically. "Don't."

"It won't take long, and this is going to keep you from an infection."

"I just…." I sat back, trying to angle my body away from his, my stomach turning. "I can take care of myself."

"Even I can't bandage my own back—and that's when I'm not injured." He laid the cloth straps on his bag and sighed. "You fight me on this almost every single time." He shook his head. "And I can't…I can't think of a single reason why you would, except if you're…." He released a shaky breath. "I used to hide my scars, too."

I stared up, meeting Rhyan's green eyes. He reached forward, tentatively, nervously, and wiped the tears from my cheeks. I hadn't even realized I was crying.

"You don't have to tell me." His voice was impossibly gentle. "But you can. Whenever you're ready." He looked out the window, biting his lower lip. "I know what it's like to be hurt. What it's like to heal wounds without magic." He got down on his knees, sitting across from me, his green eyes focused on me and churning with raw emotion. "Can I...?" He swallowed, his expression shifting like he'd just made a tough decision. "Lyr, let me treat your back." He wouldn't force me. But this was no longer a question. It was a command.

I wrapped my hand around my wrist, over the scars of my blood oath, over the tattoos hiding them. But there was no burning, no warning like before. He knew I'd been hurt but had allowed me to keep my secret. He wouldn't press, wouldn't pry. And on some level, I did trust him. I more-than-trusted him.

A part of my heart had been Rhyan's since I was a girl. When we'd danced that night under the solstice stars, my feelings had shifted, become something more. When we'd kissed, they had grown again and bloomed into something deeper, something primal. But then he'd hardly paid me any attention the remainder of his visit, and he was gone. Years had passed. And it hadn't mattered. I'd kissed other boys. I'd fallen for Tristan. And still, that piece of my heart was there, living outside of me, waiting for him, beating for him, and then he was back. Back in Bamaria. And now, he was in front of me, kneeling before me, wanting to help.

He still wore his armor. He'd been wearing it this morning when he faced Mercurial. He'd worn it all last night. While I slept, getting sweat and blood all over his bed, he'd sat awake watching over me, dressed completely ready for battle.

I nodded. "All right."

"Good." He sounded relieved as he got up to lock the door. He sat down behind me. "Can I take this off?" he asked, tugging on my tunic.

"Yes."

Slowly, his fingers undid the laces down my back, careful to keep the material away from my skin and wounds. He slid the tunic forward on my arms, completely exposing my back to him. I hadn't bothered with a shift. Just the idea of anything tight over those wounds felt painful, so I'd gone without. Now all that remained between me and Rhyan were the bandages he'd placed there last night. I leaned forward, holding the front of my tunic over my chest.

He ran his hands down my spine, gently, poking and prodding along the way, tracing the lines that crossed my back with a towel, then healing ointment, and finally a fresh batch of sunleaves.

He was silent as he worked, and I began to relax under his touch until finally he sighed deeply, pulling his hands away. "I don't think you'll be scarred," he said.

Involuntarily, I made a sound, something between a sob and a laugh. It was so stupid. It shouldn't have mattered. But my body carried enough marks already, marks I would never be free from.

His fingers grazed across my back, and I sucked in my breath. "The sunleaves are already closing the cuts. Aemon was careful not to layer your lashings. I know they hurt, but your back will be good as new in a few weeks. You're actually healing really nicely."

I shook my head, attempting to steady my voice. "I doubt it. I know what those whips are meant to do, who they're meant to be used on, and it's not someone like me—someone weak, someone powerless."

"Lyr, you're not weak. You have power."

"You told me that before," I said. "But it wasn't true. I had no power in the first clinic. And I only barely survived last night because of your power. I know Mercurial's dangerous, but you were so quick to get rid of him after he mentioned my power. Rhyan, you know I'm weak." I buried my face in my hands. "Weak and helpless. I couldn't...I couldn't hold my end of the bargain up," I cried. "I couldn't find my strength." A harsh laugh escaped from me. "Of course, I couldn't. I wasn't even strong enough to…to…." Tears rolled down my cheeks.

Rhyan's hands were warm on my back, his palms soothing against my shoulder blades before stroking down, applying the last of the paste. He stuck a bandage over everything, making sure it was secured in place. His hand lingered on my back, gentle. "You weren't strong enough to what?" he asked.

My chest tightened, and the backs of my eyes burned, as on fire as my wrists had been. Then I said it, the truth I'd carried, the shame that had covered my heart in a shadow for two years, "I feel like it's my fault. That I'm to blame. Because I couldn't save Jules." A sob wracked through me, and I hugged my knees to my chest.

I felt Rhyan get up, shifting his body in front of mine and gathering me into his arms. "That's not true," he said. "Lyr. It was never your job to save her."

"But I feel like it was! She would have fought so hard for me. And I just sat there, helpless. I watched. Watched it happen. Watched as she was taken away right before my eyes. The Imperator had her bound, and I watched. And the Bastardmaker, he…he carried her away. In front of everyone. We sat there in our finest gowns, and we all watched and did nothing! And I…I…."

"Shhhh, Lyr. It's all right. It's all right." His hand rubbed up and down my back. "It wasn't your job to save her. You weren't even of age—you couldn't have gone against the Imperator. You know that."

"I do, but I still feel like I should have thought of something. Done something more. Tried harder, been faster. I tried…after it was over, I tried to go after her, but Markan…." The tears fell freely down my face. "Markan drugged me. He dragged me back home unconscious."

"Gods," he sounded anguished. "I am so sorry. Bastard," he swore. "But, Lyr, look. Even if you'd gone, you couldn't have stopped them. Think about it. What was your father doing? The Arkasva? Or your sisters? Or your aunt? Or any other member of the Bamarian Council? When an Imperator wants something…there's almost nothing we can do to stop it."

Like invading my country with a foreign legion.

"I know." I sniffled.

"I think," Rhyan continued, "I think you've been shouldering the burden of what happened to Jules for a long time and unable to admit it. Because of how she's seen now. But, Lyr, you are blameless, and I would bet you anything if Jules were here, she'd tell you the same. She'd tell you you're forgiven, that you're not to blame, that it's all right to keep living, to get stronger, to fight back. It's not your responsibility to save everyone. Just yourself."

The scars on my wrist said otherwise. So did the black eye forming on my face, and the countless cuts and bruises that had faded into my skin. My whole face heated as more tears fell.

"I just feel so powerless," I said, my voice a hushed whisper.

"I know. I think I have an idea how you feel."

I shook my head. "Nobody does."

"I do. And I'm not just saying so. Lyr, I've…I've watched an Imperator take away the person who mattered most to me. I had to watch too, completely helpless. And I…I was lashed. And not when I had magic in my body—it happened when I was weak, when I was powerless."

I turned to face him. "You said…you said you used to hide your scars."

He stared down, blinking, his hands rushing to his hair, attempting to muss the curls and pull them over his forehead, over his scar. It was still too short to cover the wound, so he settled for shrugging his shoulders before meeting my eyes with his own—bright and green, beautiful, shockingly beautiful, even with the scar running through his left eye. It might have ruined another face, but instead of troubling Rhyan's beauty it added another dimension to it.

"I was thirteen the first time."

I reached for his forearm. "I'm sorry."

He jerked his chin up, jaw tensed as his arm slid out from my touch. "I'd offer proof of my healing, but there's some other artwork on my back, and I don't want you to lose confidence in me." He winked, attempting to make a joke, but his voice shook.

"You mean your tattoo?" I asked. He'd trained wearing a half-tunic a handful of times, but I couldn't recall a single scar or mark save the large gryphon, its inked wings spanning across his shoulders and wrapping around his chest.

I stared down at my own stars and sigil for Ka Batavia—a mask for my blood oaths.

Rhyan slowly pushed my hair behind my ears, applying the remaining paste to my cheek. "Yes. Thanks to the tattoo and some handy spell work, quite a few nasty-looking scars were removed. But the lashings, those truly did heal on their own." Sitting in front of me, he smoothed the last of the paste across my cheek, across the cut Meera had given me when she'd punched me in her vision. He glanced down at the open tunic covering my chest. "We can get this back on now." He reached forward, sliding the sleeves back up my shoulders. "I can tie the lacings for you—if you just hold your hair aside."

He patted my back when he finished, and I twisted back toward him. "Thank you. For everything."

His good eyebrow narrowed, but I had the impression he'd meant to move both. His scar was more than cosmetic, though he refused to admit it. "We're going to get you stronger, call on your own strength, so you can stop giving a voice to the feeling of being powerless."

"You know how to do that?"

"I think I might. Even after my revelation, my father used to bind me." His voice was quiet.

"Gods." My stomach knotted as I remembered the feel of the ropes Tristan had conjured. The burning, the humiliation, the pain…having to train while bound sounded unbearable.

Rhyan folded his arms across his chest. "He'd send his mages to bind me before the morning run. I entered fives the same way." His eyes darkened. "I was just like you in the beginning. Last in the run, tripping and doubling over with cramps. I was trampled and bullied. My father personally whipped me until I was sick all over myself. I threw up every day that first week after the run, making myself ill trying to catch up."

I reached out and rested my hand on his arm again. I'd been so angry at Rhyan and frustrated and scared the last month that I'd overlooked the fact that he was actually a really good teacher for me. All of his advice…it seemed like the advice he'd needed to hear himself.

He flinched, tensing, but this time he relaxed beneath my touch.

"It took a while, a long while. But I caught up, outrunning them, beating them at fives even with my hands tied."

"How?" I asked.

A shy look suddenly spread across his features. "Have you ever seen a gryphon before? A real one?"

"No," I said. "I've never been far enough North."

"I grew up with gryphons," Rhyan said. "Literally. Even used to help our Master of the Horse train them. In Glemaria, they do the patrol instead of ashvan, riding in circles every hour around the border. And we also use them for transport instead of seraphim." He paused, the edges of his lips quirking up. "They're…amazing. Beautiful and powerful. So strong and…just giant. Much larger than your seraphim. Tougher, too. I loved them as a boy." He smiled shyly. "I wanted to be one in a way. They seemed so free. Able to escape...or they looked like they could. Well. I'd mostly wanted one as a pet. My father, of course, said no. A gryphon would quickly grow too enormous to fit in my room, so...."

Something in my chest warmed, imagining a small Rhyan with wild, curly, dark hair and overly large green eyes just wanting to cuddle with a gryphon at night. He admired them because they looked free, but I could also sense what he'd left unsaid. He'd been lonely. Someone who acted as cold as he did, someone whose aura could freeze was alone. He hadn't just wanted a pet. He'd needed a friend.

"What would you have named him?" I asked. "If you did get a pet gryphon?"

He closed his eyes, smiling wide. "Aidan. He was my favorite hero in one of my mom's stories. Luckily, when I started school, I met one of my best friends. Also named Aidan. So don't feel too sorry for me never having gotten Aidan the gryphon. Aidan the human's a fine runner-up and kind of looks like a gryphon, actually." He chuckled. "Huge muscles, big beaky nose."

I laughed, too, and shifted closer to him.

"So little me was fascinated by gryphons and awed by their strength. To give you an idea, an akadim has the strength of five soturi, the gryphon has the strength of around twenty. And keep in mind, these are sky creatures—they just want to fly. But to keep them from flying off to the mountains, we tie a rope around their legs, somewhat thin so their movements aren't restricted, long enough for them to fly around but not escape.

"As a boy, I thought the ropes were magic, bound with some powerful spell. But when I asked my father's Second, he told me it was just plain old rope."

"Plain rope can keep a gryphon from escaping?"

He nodded. "See, when the gryphons are babies, they're so small and helpless, they have no strength at all. And when we tie them down, they kick and struggle to break free, but they can't escape. Because the rope is too strong—for a baby. Eventually, they stop trying. Then they grow up to be massive, powerful beasts. But no one ever tells the gryphons they've grown stronger than the rope. They learned the rope was stronger. So they don't even try, even though they could break free without any effort at all." Rhyan swallowed, staring intently at me.

His meaning began to sink in.

"One day," he continued, "I was watching the gryphons just allowing themselves to be tied down by such a puny piece of rope, all because they had no idea they'd outgrown it, no idea they'd changed and were stronger. Had no sense of the power inside of them. And I thought…why not me? What if I'm stronger now? Stronger than my father, stronger than everything he had used to try to hold me down, to take away my power." He gave a small smile. "Turned out I was right. I grew up terrified of my father. The day I decided to fight back, I found out very quickly that I was stronger, that I could defeat him. In a physical fight at least." He closed his mouth abruptly, a distant look clouding his eyes before he refocused on me. "You have power inside of you. Maybe not the power you were expecting, but it is a force you can wield, and when you stop feeling guilty for everything you couldn't do, stop blaming yourself for the past, you can tap into it. I decided this when I couldn't touch mine. I decided I had power inside of me that my father couldn't take, couldn't bind, couldn't strip away."

Rhyan's green eyes were blazing now. "You choose. You can let what the others think about you be right, you can let your guilt and shame hold you down, or you can decide your fate, assert the strength you do have, become stronger than ever before. But you have to claim it. And when you do, you can be freer than a seraphim. Stronger than a gryphon. No ropes can hold you. No cage can trap you."

I sucked in a breath, letting his words sink in. I was starting to believe him, believe he was right, believe I really could do this, and see that maybe I had been letting my guilt over Jules hold me back. Maybe in the two years since I'd lost her, I'd been too ready to help my sisters as if that would make things up to Jules. Maybe I'd been sacrificing myself to them since Jules had been sacrificed. And maybe, just maybe, I was punishing myself with Tristan, torturing myself for that perfect image I'd cultivated—the one I'd mastered when I'd watched her being taken away. The way I'd let him speak ill of her and hold me and kiss my hand.

Something in my heart untwisted. It was sore and raw. But I knew Rhyan had opened something inside of me, healed some part of me without even knowing it.

Swallowing, I asked, "Is that why you have the torn rope in your tattoo?"

He nodded. "If a gryphon just tried to tear that rope, they'd be free in seconds, but they don't do it because they don't know this. I wanted to remind myself. Every time I thought I couldn't do something, a task felt too big, an enemy too scary, I imagined they were nothing more than a thin, puny rope. And no rope can hold me. Every time you think you can't do something, imagine a rope in your mind. And tear that rope apart."

"So it is really possible to train without magic," I said, breathlessly.

He nodded. "That's why Aemon's pushing for you to stay, why I've always said you could do this and meant it. And you have been doing it. You've trained for over a month. You're stronger than when you first stepped foot in here. Last night, you were tired and injured. But the fighting you did— it wasn't all me. It was you. Lyr, true strength has nothing to do with magic. Any soturion who relies on magic alone will always lose in the end. The ones you see out there tearing up the track—most of them are relying on magic stores, not pulling it from deep within. There's a very big difference between a soturion who gains muscle at the Revelation and one who builds it themselves. The strongest, they find their power inside."

"Show me," I said. "I want to learn. I want to find that strength, that power." And surprisingly, I knew I meant it. Not just as a means to an end, as a way to protect my sisters, as a way to secure my status, or engagement to Tristan. I wanted to be strong—just for me.

He swallowed hard, his jaw clenched. "It's not that simple, what you'll need, what I have to show you. I'm obligated to continue training you according to the Academy's program. But outside of training hours…."

I could see him mentally sketching out the terms of what he was proposing.

"It would require more time. More effort. Starting before the run in the mornings. Staying later. Training on the weekends." He paused, his eyes intense. "It won't be easy. You'd have to commit. Spend less time with your family, friends, going to parties, sleeping…."

I bristled. "I can commit. But what about you?"

"I quit partying when I became forsworn, and I never sleep."

I searched his expression. Though attempting to make a joke, he was making a serious offer, sacrificing his time and energy. For me. But more than that, he was taking a risk. If anyone saw us and suspected our relationship was anything more than novice and apprentice, being expelled from the university or even banished from Bamaria would be a mercy.

A powerful, deep feeling rose up inside me. A desire and yearning. I wanted to say yes because I wanted the training. I was finally ready to give this my all. And I wanted to be around him more often. And that…that was so much more dangerous than whatever the Emperor was preparing for me come winter.

"If you ask me to train you, I'll say yes."

I started to open my mouth, but he cut me off.

"I want you to rest today. Think about it. If you commit to this extra training, you have to mean it. I won't make it easy."

"I know."

"And...what I said to you last night...what...almost happened between us. I won't say it again. And that will never, ever, happen again. Not if we're going to stay safe."

A pit formed in my stomach. He hadn't kissed me because he said I'd consume him if he did. But his lips had brushed against mine. And that had been all I'd needed to feel like I was on fire for him.

"You're right," I said.

"Then go take the rest of the day off. Think on it, and tell me your answer tomorrow."

CHAPTER THIRTY-FOUR

THE AIR FELT cool outside as I walked back to my apartment. Fall was finally coming, and I was ready. Ready for a change. Ready to release the past and to build up my strength with Rhyan.

For a rare moment, I felt oddly hopeful, like by some miracle of the Gods I'd have a handle on everything. I felt like possibility was suddenly in my life again, like I'd succeed.

I entered my apartment building and headed down a hall. A soturion stalked the shadows of the hallway, her cloak blending into the dark. This soturion wore a mask over her face, a mask of black feathers—a black seraphim.

Emartis.

She didn't see me at first. I stalked after her, already aware of who she was. I could always spot soturi—especially when I knew them, and I knew her. I knew the cut of that chin. I knew the characteristic dark, silky hair and golden-brown skin of the members of Ka Elys.

Tani Elwen, Ka Elys. Lady Pavi's lap dog and the soturion even more determined than Naria to make my life hell and make me pay for what had happened to Pavi.

I was done paying.

"Tani!" I said without thinking. Deep brown eyes glared at me through slits in the feathered mask. "It was you—you left that note, you broke into my apartment. I'm going to report you."

"Report me," she said with a laugh, stepping out of the shadows, pulling the mask off her face, and tossing it in her bag. "I'll report you," she snapped.

"Report me for what?" I asked.

"For using kashonim to cheat during the habibellum." She held up her hand to silence my protests. "You think I don't know what it looks like when it's being used, when someone weak, powerless, and pathetic suddenly has strength to spare? I've been watching you. I know what you're like in a fight— last month I fought you myself. No way could you have fought back or survived the way you did without taking all Rhyan had to give."

I glared even as my heart pounded. I couldn't reveal emotion, couldn't show I was upset by her truth.

A gryphon does not shed tears when it's called a seraphim. It knows what it is. Only a seraphim in the mask of a gryphon would be upset—for their truth has been revealed. Never show offense, or you reveal your truth to your enemies. Control what they see, and you control what they think.

Aunt Arianna's lesson was still fresh in my mind. I could use it and my own ability to play my role perfectly.

I stalked forward. "Even if you did say something, you have no proof. But I do...I've seen you and your mask."

"He was very concerned about you," Tani said, batting her eyelashes. "Very invested. I'm not the first, you know, to suspect there's something between you."

I could feel Rhyan's lips against mine, feel the fire coursing through my veins, the way even the memory of that barest, and lightest of touches had consumed me.

"I assume you're bored enough with your life to make up stories about me."

"You were always arrogant. But not for much longer. You lost three months of your precious deal with the Imperator for being late...you had your back splayed open for being a terrible soldier. What will the Imperator do when I report to him that you cheated in the arena? That there's more to your relationship with Lord Rhyan than just apprentice and novice?"

"He will do nothing, because there's no truth to your words. I'm going to marry Lord Tristan, and what you saw in the arena was a month's worth of training."

One moment she was several feet in front of me, and the next her face was inches from mine, her fist in my belly.

I flew backwards, my back slamming into a wall.

The pain that erupted on contact tore through me. But unlike the pain I'd always felt before—the kind that could break me or slow me down—this one left a fire raging inside of me. It was not a fire that would consume me, but one that was lighting me up from the inside.

I was on my feet in seconds, my thumb in position, my fist ready as I charged and paid Tani the same courtesy she'd afforded me.

Upon contact, her eyes widened, and she wheezed, doubling over. I kicked and pushed and slapped and knocked her down to her knees.

"Am I using kashonim now? Am I!"

She retreated from my attack, but I was faster, punching her shoulder into the wall.

"I will report you," I said. "And I'll find the others, too."

A drop of blood pooled in the corner of her mouth and ran down her chin. Her eyes widened in delight, and a smile spread across her face. She laughed, joyful glee ringing with every sound she made. "Report me?" she asked, laughing harder. "Report me? Do you know how powerful the Emartis are? How high up they go? How much protection we have? How much support?" She spit at me, the spittle coated in blood.

I stepped back, unsure if I believed her but terrified that I did.

It wasn't so much her words that had me on edge, but the brazenness, the absolutely fearless way she resumed her attack, kicking me and knocking me off my feet.

I was fair game to attack in a clinic or habibellum or even in between training and classes in the Katurium. But here, in my apartment building, when I was Lady Lyriana, she'd gone too far.

I outranked her in every way. My word would always be upheld against hers.

And yet, she was fighting back, claiming she had support, confirming that others were suspicious of what lay between me and Rhyan, that others might have seen the change in my strength, the lack of his, and suspected the exchange of power between us. No one had ever dared attack me so outright. No one but Naria, Pavi, and Viktor, the most powerful, noble soturi-in-training in Bamaria besides me.

That fact scared me more than anything. I'd guessed that the Emartis had support in high places. I'd guessed the Imperator was behind them. But hearing Tani confirm my suspicions, seeing her bold action back up her claims...it began to make my theory about the Imperator all too real.

Tani wasn't the Emartis, but she was as close to them as I was getting, and I was going to make them pay. Starting with her.

My strength surged, that moment of calm clarity settling like mist over me as I rolled on top of her, pinning her arms down, and punching her in the jaw. Rhyan was right—I had grown stronger in the past month, I'd just refused to see it. I'd been so hellbent on comparing myself to others, I hadn't compared myself to who I used to be.

I grabbed the neck of Tani's tunic and pulled. She bucked away from me, stumbling backward. Her bag fell over, the Emartis mask slipping out. I pulled my arm back.

"Lyr!" Aunt Arianna stood before us. "Lyr, what are you...?"

I immediately released my hold, rising to meet Arianna. She pulled me into a hug, then leaned back, examining my face. "Gods," she said. "Are you all right?"

Tani laughed behind me. "Oh, you have no idea what you're doing, your grace!" She laughed louder, facing Arianna. "Just a little in-between class session."

She was unhinged; she was farther than Lethea.

My aunt was on her in seconds. "And this symbol you carry? You get yourself up to your apartment right now and wait for me there. I know the rules of conduct for students better than anyone—I wrote several myself. And you are in gross violation."

Tani bowed her head, still allowing the blood to drip freely down her chin, grabbed her bag holding the Emartis mask, and headed for the stairs.

"Arianna, she—"

"I know," she said. "I know what she is, and trust me—she will not get away with this."

I nodded. "What are you doing here? You didn't come to see me—I'm usually in training now."

"I was hoping to catch you after. I came to inspect your apartment door and lock. I heard there were two recent break-ins. I'm going to ensure that never, ever happens to you again. Come on," she said. "Come upstairs with me. Catch me up on your life, and I'll inspect your apartment for any breaches in security. The new wards should be at full strength by now"

It was comforting to have Arianna there and just what I'd needed. I'd barely seen her in weeks.

After she left, I cleaned myself up and sent word to Tristan to come over later that night when it was dark. I wanted him to see as little of my injuries as possible. I'd be able to excuse them now without problem, but the more he looked at how hurt I was, the more he would look. And I couldn't have him doing that.

But first I flew to Cresthaven, checking on Meera and Morgana, both still exhausted and knocked out from Meera's last vision. There was little I could do except sit and talk with them until they both felt like calling it a night and climbing into bed.

Hours later, Tristan joined me in mine.

The following morning, I was ready. Rhyan had told me to think about the idea of agreeing to extra training with him, giving up my mornings, sacrificing my weekends, and finally, finally learning to tap into the depths of my own inner strength and power to use it...and I was going to say yes.

My heart pounded. I couldn't wait to tell him. Even though I was still sore, still hurt, and my back still felt like it was on fire when I put pressure on it or when it touched a wall, I wanted to get to the Katurium as soon as possible.

Tristan helped me lace up my sandals, playfully kissing the backs of my knees as he knotted the leather straps into place.

"Let's run," I said. "To the Katurium."

"All right, now who are you, and what have you done with my Lyriana?"

"I'm still your Lyriana." My heart pounded as I spoke, thrumming with the guilt of having lied.

He stood, pressing a kiss to the side of my neck and shoulder and squeezing my waist from behind, gently to keep his chest away from my back. "My Lyriana hates running, and she's injured."

"Afraid you can't keep up?" I asked. I grabbed a gold coin from my dresser, squeezed it into the palm of my hand, and taunted him at the door. He took the bait, following me down the stairs and out the front door where Bellamy waited for us. We weren't running, just walking, but I still felt an extra skip in my step over my decision.

As we passed Bellamy, I slipped him the coin. He nodded —my involvement with the death of the vendor was still between us and only us. Exactly as I wanted.

I kissed Tristan outside and wound my way through the halls straight to the arena. Tristan had had breakfast delivered, so I skipped the dining hall.

Immediately, I felt a change in energy in the stadium surrounding me. It signified an unwelcome presence that had been growing and growing.

"More wolves, indeed," drawled Mercurial, sidling up to me.

I froze. "What are you...? I mean, it's good to see you, Mercurial, First Messenger."

He dipped his chin in a bow. "More wolves," he said again, gesturing to the stadium seating. Indeed, the seats were full of soturi in silver, wolf-pelted armor. I thought they were meant to be occupying the city, not sitting here to watch training.

Gods. To watch *me*. But would the Imperator really...? Yes. Yes, he would. He would do whatever it took to unhinge me, to hurt me, to remove my father and our Ka from our Seat of Power.

"Silver wolves watch you," Mercurial said. "And black seraphim, too."

The question was on the tip of my tongue—he could sense it, could probably taste it. He'd said as much the other morning—he could smell it. His eyes lit up with an excitement so intense, it almost scared me.

"And blue Afeya," I said.

Mercurial grinned. "Your grace, what if I told you that you were the most powerful Lumerian in all of history?"

"So now I have advanced from strongest soturion to most powerful Lumerian overall." I shook my head. "I'm not interested. You're mistaken if you believe I'd make a deal with you over that. I don't desire that level of power." Just enough to protect my Ka, my country…and Rhyan.

Mercurial's eyes narrowed. "Now you've tried my patience by again refusing to hear what I am saying. I did not ask if this was something you wanted. I said what if you were? As deeply as I desire to have my Valalumir penetrate your heart…," he held his hand before him, palm up, and the star he had teased me with in the temple reappeared, shining, shimmering, and transforming into every color as he rolled it around his hand, "I am an Afeya with morals. I do not make deals to give people what they already are. I know you don't see it yet, but you will. And the day you realize it, the day you claim it, I will come to claim a favor that only you in all your power can grant."

I shook my head. "That day will never come. Me holding that much power or," my heart pounded, "me helping you."

"Both are inevitable," he said in a whisper. "Both will come to pass. Just you wait. They told you you were powerless. But they were wrong for even they cannot see."

I glared.

A wicked smile spread across his lips. "Did you truly believe that mere nahashim could scent what you truly are? Could find the well of your power? No. For they've never encountered your kind before."

My heart pounded, but I kept my lips closed, fearful I'd ask a question, fearful I'd give myself away. What did that mean? What couldn't the nahashim see? What was I?

"Wait and see." Mercurial watched me like a cat. "Wait and see."

He vanished again, reappearing in the stands. The diamonds on his arms and legs, centered in gold and silver whorls, caught the light and sparkled.

By now, the arena's field was filling with soturi, including Haleika and Galen, who fussed over me, wanting to make sure I was still recovering and would take it easy.

I joined Rhyan, dropping into a lunge beside him, my fingers digging into the dirt, my breathing even. He didn't look at me, only continued with his sequence of stretches.

At last, he turned to me, his gaze blazing as he met mine. "Did you think about it?" he asked, voice low.

I nodded. "Yes. And yes. I want to train with you. I want to learn what you know."

His eyes moved back and forth slowly, taking me in. There was something unspoken there—an agreement, and acknowledgment of our other arrangement. That if we did this, if we trained in secret—that would be all it was. Nothing more. We could be friends. We could only ever be friends. Both of our lives depended on it.

I tilted my head, and he visibly relaxed.

"Not this week," he said. "Let your back heal first." The clouds in the sky began to shift, a breeze pushing them out, revealing the morning sun. "At the week's end. We begin."

"At the week's end."

The bells rang, the hour was called, and I took off, feeling stronger than I had in a long time. I was surrounded by my enemies, by silver wolves, black seraphim, and blue Afeya.

Mercurial's words replayed in my head. He wanted something from me, saw something inside of me—some potential I wasn't aware existed. I didn't know if I believed him, that I was something else, something more than those snakes could see. But even if he was lying...he wanted something from me.

I pumped my arms at my sides, the knowledge that there may be power inside of me spurring me on. And for the first time ever, I passed a soturion on the track. I pumped my arms even harder, thinking of Valyati, the coming winter holiday, and the Emperor's visit and my test.

I would train. I would be ready. And I would survive whatever he threw at me.

I imagined a rope in my mind, and as my feet hit the ground and I rounded a curve in the track I saw in my mind's eye my hands gripping the rope, tearing in half.

I was going to find my own strength. I was going to put a stop to the Emartis, to the occupation of Ka Kormac in Bamaria.

I was going to reclaim my power.

I shifted in my lane, getting ready to pass another soturion.

I will come to claim a favor that only you in all your power can grant. Mercurial's voice echoed in my mind. He appeared, running beside me, his lean blue limbs quickly gaining speed. The diamonds on his bared arms and legs blinding me with their light. And then he vanished.

Rhyan's form replaced him on the track. Our eyes met, and for a moment, the coolness of his aura calmed me, his energy wiping out the unsettling feeling of Mercurial's presence.

But a dark laugh still echoed in my mind.

You're the fire.

GUARDIAN OF THE DROWNED EMPIRE

THE STORY CONTINUES IN THE DROWNED EMPIRE SERIES, BOOK 2

THE EMPIRE OF LUMERIA

There are twelve countries united under the Lumerian Empire. The 12 Ruling Kavim of Lumeria Nutavia.

Each country is ruled by an Arkasva, the High Lord or Lady of the ruling Ka.

All twelve countries submit to the rule and law of the Emperor. Each Arkasva also answers to an Imperator, one Arkasva with jurisdiction over each country in either the Northern or Southern hemispheres of the Empire.

In addition to the Emperor's rule, twelve senators, one from each country (may not be a member of the ruling Ka) fill the twelve seats of the Senate. The roles of Imperator and Emperor are lifelong appointments. They may not be passed onto family members. Imperators and Emperors must be elected by the ruling Kavim. Kavim may not submit a candidate for either role if the previous Imperator or Emperor belonged to their Ka.

Imperators may keep their ties to their Ka and rule in their country. An Emperor will lose their Ka upon anointing and must be like a father or mother to all Lumerians.

Empiric
Chain of Command

Country	Ruling Ka	Country	Ruling Ka
Glemaria	Ka Hart	Bamaria	Ka Batavia
Payunmar	Ka Valyan	Korteria	Ka Kormac
Hartavia	Ka Taria	Elyria	Ka Elys (*Ka Azria)
Ereztia	Ka Sephiron	Dumara	Ka Daquataine
Aravia	Ka Lumerin	Lethea	Ka Maras
Sindhuvine	Ka Kether	Cretanya	Ka Zarine

The Immortal Afeyan Courts*

The Sun Court: El Zandria, ruled by King RaKanam

The Moon Court: Khemet, ruled by Queen Ma'Nia

The Star Court: Night Lands, ruled by Queen Ishtara

Afeyan Courts are not considered part of the Lumerian Empire, nor do they submit to the Emperor, however, history, prior treaties, and trade agreements have kept the courts at peace, and working together. They are the only two groups to have shared life on the continent of Lumeria Matavia.

THE BAMARIAN COUNCIL

Each of the twelve countries in the Lumerian Empire includes a 12-member council comprised of members of the nobility to assist the Arkasva in ruling and decision-making.

The Bamarian Council includes the following:

Role, Name

Arkasva , Harren Batavia

Master of the Horse, Eathan Ezara

Arkturion, Aemon Melvik

Turion, Dairen Melvik

Arkmage, Kolaya Scholar

Master of Education, Arianna Batavia

Master of Spies, Sila Shavo

Master of Finance, Romula Grey

Master of Law, Kiera Ezara

Naturion, Dagana Scholar

Senator, Janvi Elys

Master of Peace, Brenna Corra

LUMERIAN RITES OF PASSAGE

Revelation Ceremony: All Lumerians are given a Birth Bind in their first year of life, a spell that will keep them from accessing their magic power whenever it develops. All Lumerians develop their magic along with puberty. **The Birth Bind** may only be removed after the Lumerian has turned nineteen, the age of adulthood. Any Lumerian who is nineteen may participate in the Revelation Ceremony that year, celebrated on Auriel's Feast Day. At this time, their binding is removed by an Arkmage, and they may choose whether they will become a mage and be offered a stave, or a soturion and receive a dagger. The Arkmage will cut each participant to begin an oath that completes itself in the Oath Ceremony. Participants traditionally wear white robes which are discarded after their choice is made. A cut is made to the left wrist for a soturion, and their oath is made by dripping their blood into fire. A cut is made to the right wrist for a mage, and their oath is made by dripping their blood into water.

Oath Ceremony: Following the decision to become a mage or soturion, every Lumerian will become part of a Kashonim, or lineage. This allows them greater access to power in times of need, as well as continues to establish bonds across the Kavim and keep the Empire united. During the Oath Ceremony, every mage and soturion becomes a novice, and is bound to an apprentice. Once the oath is sworn, the novice has access to the powers of the apprentice's entire living lineage. The apprentice is also duty-bound to teach the novice all they know. Romantic relationships are strongly discouraged between mage apprentice and novices.

Romantic relationships are strictly forbidden between apprentice and novice soturi as this can cause interruptions to their duties to fight and protect. Participants traditionally wear black robes which are burned before their apprentice dresses them in their new attire.

Anointing: After an apprentice completes their training, they will be anointed, and become a full-fledged member of Lumerian society. An anointed mage or soturion is one who has completed their training. Anointing ceremonies will also be performed anytime a Lumerian rises in rank, for example an Heir becoming Arkasva, or an Arkasva becoming Imperator or Emperor. Anointings signify a life-long role.

GLOSSARY AND PRONUNCIATION GUIDE

Names:

Lyriana Batavia (Leer-ree-ana Ba-tah-via): Third in line to the Seat of Power in Bamaria

Morgana Batavia (Mor-ga-na Ba-tah-via): Second in line to the Seat of Power in Bamaria

Meera Batavia (Mee-ra Ba-tah-via): First in line to the Seat of Power in Bamaria (Heir Apparent)

Naria Batavia (Nar-ria Ba-tah-via): Niece to the Arkasva, not in line to the Seat

Arianna Batavia (Ar-ree-ana Ba-tah-via): Sister-in-law to the Arkasva, previously third in line to Seat, Master of Education on the Council of Bamaria

Aemon Melvik (Ae-mon Mel-vik): Warlord of Bamaria, Arkturion on the Council of Bamaria

Rhyan Hart (Ry-an Hart): Forsworn and exiled from Glemaria. Previously was in first in line to the Seat of Power (Heir Apparent)

Auriel (Or-ree-el): Original Guardian of the Valalumir in Heaven, stole the light to bring to Earth where it turned into a crystal before shattering at the time of the Drowning

Asherah (A-sher-ah): Original Guardian of the Valalumir in Heaven. She was banished to Earth as a mortal after her affair with Auriel was discovered.

Moriel (Mor-ree-el): Original Guardian of the Valalumir in Heaven. He reported Auriel and Asherah's affair to the Council of 44 leading to Asherah's banishment, Auriel's theft of the light, and its subsequent destruction. He was banished to Earth where he allied with the akadim in the war that led to the Drowning.

Theotis (Thee-otis): Current Emperor of Lumeria Nutavia. Theotis was previously from Korteria, and a noble of Ka Kormac. His nephew, Avery Kormac, is the current Imperator to the Southern hemisphere of the Empire, and Arkasva to Korteria.

Avery Kormac (Ae-very Core-mac): Nephew to the Emperor, as Imperator, he rules over the six southern countries of the Empire, as well as ruling Korteria as the Arkasva.

Places:

Lumeria (Lu-mair-ria): The name of continent where Gods and Goddesses first incarnated until it sank into the Lumerian Ocean in the Drowning.

Matavia (Ma-tah-via): Motherland. When used with Lumeria, it refers to the continent that sank.

Nutavia (New-tah-via): New land. When used with Lumeria, it refers to the Empire forged after the Drowning by those who survived and made it to Bamaria—previously Dobra.

Bamaria (Ba-mar-ria): Southernmost country of the Lumerian Empire, home of the South's most prestigious University and the Great Library. Ruled by Ka Batavia.

Korteria (Kor-ter-ria): Westernmost country in the Empire. Magic is least effective in their mountains, but

Korteria does have access to Starfire for Lumerian weapons. Ruled by Ka Kormac.

Elyria (El-leer-ria): Historically ruled by Ka Azria, rulership has now passed to Ka Elys, originally nobility from Bamaria.

Lethea (Lee-thee-a): The only part of the Empire located in the Lumerian Ocean. Ruled by Ka Maras, this is the country where criminals stripped of powers, or accused of vorakh are sent for imprisonment. The expression "Farther than Lethea" comes from the fact that there is nothing but ocean beyond the island. Due to the Drowning, the idea of going past the island is akin to losing one's mind.

Damara (Da-mar-ra): A Southern country known for strong warriors, ruled by Ka Daquataine.

Glemaria (Gleh-mar-ria): Northernmost country of the Empire, ruled by Ka Hart. Imperator Devon Hart is the Arkasva and Imperator to the North. Rhyan Hart was previously first in line to the Seat.

Prominent Creatures of the Old World Known to Have Survived the Drowning:

Seraphim (Ser-a-feem): Birds with wings of gold, they resemble a cross between an eagle and a dove. Seraphim are peaceful creatures, sacred in Bamaria, and most often used for transport across the Lumerian Empire. Though delicate in appearance, they are extremely strong and can carry loads of up ten people over short distances. Seraphim all prefer warmer climates and are rarely found in the northernmost part of the Empire.

Ashvan: Flying horses. These are the only sky creatures that do not possess wings. Their flight comes from magic contained in their hooves. Once an ashvan picks up speed, their magic will create small temporary pathways to run upon. Technically, ashvan cannot fly, but are running on magic pathways that appear and vanish once stepped upon.

Residue of the magic is left behind, creating streaks behind them, but these fade within seconds.

Nahashim: Snakes with the ability to grow and shrink at will, able to fit into any size space for the purposes of seeking. Anything lost or desired can almost always be found by a nahashim. Their scales remain almost burning hot and they prefer to live near the water. Most nahashim are bred on Lethea, the country furthest out into the ocean, closest to the original location of Lumeria Matavia.

Gryphon (Grif-in): Sky creatures that are half eagle, half lion. Extremely large, these animals can be taken into battle, preferring mountains and colder climates. They replace seraphim and ashvan in the northernmost parts of the Lumerian Empire. They may carry far heavier loads than seraphim.

Akadim (A-ka-deem): The most feared of all creatures, literally bodies without souls. Akadim kill by eating the soul of their victims. The demonic creatures were previously Lumerians transformed. Akadim grow to be twice the size of a Lumerian and gain five times the strength of a soturion. Immortal as long as they continue to feed on souls, these creatures are impervious to Lumerian magic. Akadim are weakened by the sun and tend to live in the Northern Hemisphere.

Water Dragon: Dragons with blue scales that live deep in the Lumerian Ocean. Previously spending their time equally between land and water, all water dragons have taken to the Lumerian Ocean and are usually spotted closer to Lethea.

Agnavim (Ahg-naw-veem): Rarely sighted in Lumerian lands. These red birds with wings made of pure flame favor the lands occupied by the Afeyan Star Court. Lumerians have been unable to tame them since the Drowning.

Terms/Items:

Birth Bind/Binding: Unlike a traditional bind which includes a spell that ties a rope around a Lumerian to keep them from touching their power, or restricting their physical ability to move a Birth Bind leaves no mark. A Binding is temporary, and can have more or less strength and heat depending on the mage casting the spell. A Birth Bind is given to all Lumerians in their first year of life, a spell that will keep them from accessing their magic power whenever it develops. All Lumerians develop their magic along with puberty. The Birth Bind may only be removed after the Lumerian has turned nineteen, the age of adulthood.

Dagger: Ceremonial weapon given to soturi. The dagger has no special power on its own as the magic of a soturion is transmuted through their body.

Ka (Kah): Soul. A Ka is a soul tribe or family.

Kashonim (Ka-show-neem): Ancestral lineage and link of power. Calling on Kashonim allows you to absorb the power of your lineage, but depending on the situation, usage can be dangerous. For one, it can be an overwhelming amount of power that leaves you unconscious if you come from a long lineage, or a particularly powerful one. Two, it has the potential to weaken the mages or soturi the caller is drawing from. It is also illegal to use against fellow students.

Kavim (Ka-veem): Plural of Ka. A Ka can be likened to a soul tribe or family. When marriages occur, either member of the union may take on the name of their significant other's Ka. Typically, the Ka with more prestige or nobility will be used thus ensuring the most powerful Kavim continue to grow.

Laurel of the Arkasva (Lor-el of the Ar-kas-va): A golden circlet like a crown worn by the Arkasva. The Arkasva replaced the title of King and Queen in Lumeria Matavia, and the Laurel replaced the crown though they are held in the same high esteem.

Seat of Power: Akin to a throne. Thrones were replaced by Seats in Lumeria Nutavia, as many members of royalty were blamed by the citizens of Lumeria for the Drowning. Much as a monarch may have a throne room, the Arkasvim have a Seating Room. The Arkasva typically has a Seat of Power in their Seating Room in their Ka's fortress, and another in their temple.

Stave: Made of twisted moon and sun wood, the stave transmutes magic created by mages. A stave is not needed to perform magic, but greatly focuses and strengthens it. More magic being transmuted may require a larger stave.

Vadati (Va-dah-tee): Stones that allow Lumerians to hear and speak to each other over vast distances. Most of these stones were lost in the Drowning. The Empire now keeps a strict registry of each known stone.

Valalumir (Val-la-loo-meer): The sacred light of Heaven that began the Celestial War which began in Heaven and ended with the Drowning. The light was guarded by seven Gods and Goddesses until Asherah and Auriel's affair. Asherah was banished to become mortal, and Auriel fell to bring her the light. Part of the light went into Asherah before it crystalized. When the war ended, the Valalumir shattered in seven pieces—all lost in the Drowning.

Valya (Val-yah): The sacred text of recounting the history of the Lumerian people up until the Drowning. There are multiple valyas recorded, each with slight variations, but the Mar Valya is the standard. Another popular translation is the Tavia Valya which is believed to have been better preserved than the Mar Valya after the Drowning, but was never made into the standard for copying. Slight changes or possible effects of water damage offer different insights into Auriel's initial meeting with Asherah.

Vorakh (Vor-rock): Taboo, forbidden powers. Three magical abilities that faded after the Drowning are considered illegal: visions, mind-reading, and traveling by mind. Vorakh can be translated as "gift from the Gods" in High Lumerian, but is now translated as "curse from the Gods."

TITLES AND FORMS OF ADDRESS

Arkasva (Ark-kas-va): Ruler of the country, literally translates as the "will of the highest soul."

Arkasvim (Ark-kas-veem): Plural of Arkasva

Arkturion (Ark-tor-ree-an): Warlord for the country, general of their soturi/army.

Imperator: A miniature Emperor. The Empire always has two Imperators, one for the Northern Hemisphere, one for the South. The Imperator will also be the arkasva of their country, they have jurisdiction over their hemisphere but also act as a voice and direct messenger between each Arkasva and the Emperor.

Emperor: Ruler of all twelve countries in the Lumerian Empire. The Emperor is elected by the ruling arkasvim. They are appointed for life. Once an Emperor or Empress dies, the Kavim must elect a new ruler. The Emperor must renounce their Ka when anointed, but no Ka may produce an Emperor/Empress twice in a row.

Heir Apparent: Title given to the eldest child or heir of the Arkasva. The next in line to the Seat of Power or First from the Seat.

Soturion: Soldier, magically enhanced warrior. A Lumerian who can transmute magic through their body. May be used as a form of address for a non-noble.

Turion: Commander, may lead legions of soturi, must answer to their Arkturion.

Mage: A Lumerian who transmutes magic through spells. A stave is used to focus their magic. The more focus one has, the less a stave is needed, but the more magic one can use, the larger the stave may need to be. Arkmages (the high mages) tend to have staves as tall as them.

Novice: The term used to describe a soturion or mage who is in the beginning of their learning to become an anointed mage or soturion.

Apprentice: The term used to describe a soturion or mage who has passed their first three years of training. As an apprentice their time is divided between their own studies and teaching the novice they are bound to. This is done to strengthen the power of Kashonim, and because of the Bamarian philosophy that teaching a subject is the best way to learn and master a subject.

Lady: Formal address for a female, or female-identifying member of the nobility.

Lord: Formal address for a male, or male-identifying member of the nobility.

Your Grace: Formal address for any member of the ruling Ka. Anyone who is in line to the Seat of Power must be addressed so, including the Arkasva. A noble may only be addressed as "your grace" if they are in line to the Seat.

Your Highness: Reserved as formal address only for the member of Lumerian nobility serving as imperator. The term of address has also been adopted by the Afeyan Star Court.

Your Majesty: Used only for the Emperor or Empress. Previously used for the kings and queens of Lumeria Matavia. This can also be applied to the King and Queen of the Afeyan Sun and Moon Courts.

ACKNOWLEDGMENTS

There are so many people I need to thank for so many things. The journey to publishing Daughter of the Drowned Empire has been a long, and unexpected one. If you know me, you know that this all started as a dream my junior year of college, a dream that took hold of me. I was already playing around with the world of Lumeria, but it wasn't until that dream (which will be given to Meera as a vision) that I began to form Lyr's story. If you're part of my life, chances are you've had some influence on me and this story, and therefore deserve an acknowledgment. And I am so grateful for all of you. But here I will attempt to bring some small justice to the MVPs in this journey.

Atiya, this started with you and coffee at Barnes and Noble, and taking me seriously when I said I was going to be a published author. Also thank you for the lifetime of friendship! OkILoveYouDontDie!

Donna, my wifey. Words cannot express how thankful I am to have you in my life as one of my best friends and my critique partner. You are the harshest critic I know, and the best, and you have pushed, and believed, and supported me to get from the meh first draft I wrote in grad school to what it is now. Your friendship really has been everything to me, and I cannot wait to read more of your writing. Also seriously, thank you for the most epic emergency outline planning.

Sara, my fellow Pisces, seriously, being your friend has been such a highlight in my life. And being your critique partner has also been amazing. I love you, your family (especially when Google Photos thinks some of them belong to me), and of course our game nights (and all involved). I can't wait for more Sunday morning whiteboard/writing sessions, (and not getting arrested). Whenever you're ready, your book is going to blow mine out of the water.

Janine, walking into EN443 was one of those moments that changed everything because I met you (and Sara and Donna). Our long talks have been some of my favorites over the years, and we have both come so far. I think great things are coming for you and your heartwarming stories, and I just adore our friendship, and all of your insights into life, and into writing. I know we've been through it, but this is just the beginning.

Marcella, well, you made it onto the acknowledgements page, not the 'despite page'--I mean, where else was I going to put you, mini-me. You did break the book, and then you broke it again. But if you hadn't...then I don't think I'd be writing this right now while you sit on my couch (what's mine is yours). I'm so glad you decided we were going to be friends that day, and I cannot thank you enough for your encouragement and insights and the hours of non-stop talking, zoom-staring, writing retreats and road-trips. Y'all twins? Mother daughter? Give me that Dunkin!

Chris, mi amico supero. Thank you for just being one of my best friends, for believing in me, and for being willing to read basically every single shitty draft I ever wrote. Te amo.

Akosua, Evan, Dillon, you're always going to be some of my favorite people on the planet, and the fact that you all volunteered to be the earliest readers, and cheerleaders--thank you!

Julia, forever my roommate and soulmate, thank you for literally holding the space for me to believe I could do this.

Mom, thank you! Just thank you. Thank you for always supporting me while I followed this dream.

Eva, Michael, Elissa, Julie, it is an honor to be a part of the House of Mallis. I love you all so much, and I like all of you, too. I can't possibly find the right words for you, or what you mean to me, or your support, or the fact that we're not just siblings but friends who always have each other's backs, no matter what.

Dylan and Blake, and Hannah and Dani for giving me every reason to keep going.

Aunt Simone, all your support over the years, all the yoga classes, and always being there when I needed you.

Stef, for the amazing, unbelievable cover design! I love it more every time I look at it.

Danielle, for seriously kick-butt editing! Also, Christine, thank you for connecting us (and for 12-hour walk-and-talks about life).

Jordan, for catching everything I missed.

Steve, for being the genius behind my website, and for being my business advisor, and friend. Thanks for sharing Donna with me.

And you, yes you, for reading. Thank you. Thank you. Thank you!

Love,

Frankie

ABOUT THE AUTHOR

Frankie Diane Mallis lives outside of Philadelphia where she is an award-winning university professor. When not writing or teaching, she practices yoga and belly dance and can usually be found baking gluten free desserts. Daughter of the Drowned Empire is her debut novel in the highly anticipated fantasy romance Drowned Empire Series. Visit www.frankiedianemallis.com to learn more, and join the newsletter. Follow Frankie on Instagram @frankiediane, and on TikTok @frankiedianebooks.

Made in the USA
Middletown, DE
13 September 2022

10371815R00269